SHADOW WEAVER

CLAIRE MERLE

For Sean, West, and Lana.

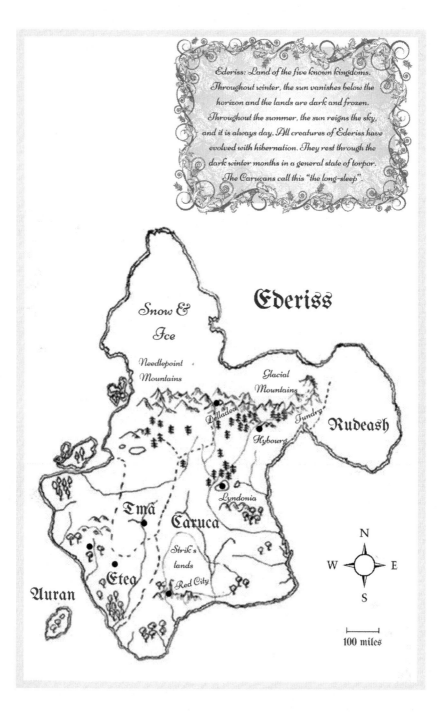

*Ederiss: Land of the five known kingdoms.
Throughout winter, the sun vanishes below the
horizon and the lands are dark and frozen.
Throughout the summer, the sun reigns the sky,
and it is always day. All creatures of Ederiss have
evolved with hibernation. They rest through the
dark winter months in a general state of torpor.
The Carucans call this "the long-sleep".*

Ederiss

Snow &
Ice

Needlepoint
Mountains

Glacial
Mountains

Delladea

Tundra

Rudeash

Hybourg

Lyndonia

Tmá

Caruca

Strik's
lands

Etea

Red City

Auran

N

W   E

S

100 miles

ONE

I splay across a rock, semi-frozen. The finger-deep layer of snow against my back softens the lumpy stone. My eyelids soak up the sun's amber rays. After three months of winter's endless darkness, I am making the most of this serene breath of sunlight.

'Mirra, get down here!' my little brother Kel shouts.

'I'm coming,' I say. But I don't move. Steal a few more seconds, longing for the all-night sun when it will be warm enough to lose our heavy parkas and furs and jump in the cool flowing river.

A thin layer of ice cracks as my brother leaps to my side of the stream. His boots crunch and scrape against the snow. I smile at his impatience, haul to my feet and slide down the rock, tiny white avalanches falling with me. Near the bottom, I hook onto a pine branch to stop my descent. Flakes clasp the needles. Ice necklaces hang in little trails between the branches, and a grey-backed spider's web dangles by my gloved fingers. The spider rocks in its diamond woven centre. Dead. But not for long. Like the fish and the beetles and the worms, it freezes when winter sweeps in, and reanimates in the spring.

'So what have you got?' I ask Kel.

My brother lifts his sharpened stick. He grins at the stiff pug-faced fish skewered on the end. He has excavated it from the bottom ice where the fish struggle for refuge as the top waters freeze during the onset of winter. No master spearing techniques.

'A Grump!' he says. 'Now you have to say it: Long live Kelson the great hunter!' Blonde tangled hair flops over his brow. His fur trousers and parka hang off him. He fattened up before we hibernated for the deep winter long-sleep, but now he's skinny again. The golden flecks in his blue irises glitter and swirl. He'll be six in a few weeks, so the shimmer in his eyes may not fade for another year or two.

'Excellent find, Kel. Well done.'

'No you have to say, "Long live Kelson, the great hunter!"'

'Long live Kelson, the great hunter!' I ruffle his hair. He ducks and I stride across the stream to fetch my pack, bow and fire bundle. We haven't long before the sun begins its rapid descent. Better to leave now and trace our snowy tracks back to camp, before dusk comes down over Blackfoot forest.

Kel's lined up the fish I scooped from the riverbed ice earlier. He's placed them two by two, like a ladder. Rainbow Sparkles, nose to nose; Suntrouts, nose to nose; Mudwaters, nose to nose.

'Did you do that?' I ask. A rhetorical question because there's no one out here for at least a four-day walk in any direction. Because other than Ma, Pa and Kel, I haven't seen another living person since Kel was a baby.

My brother nods, dropping the spear and picking up his wooden beetle farm. He inspects a frozen bug, turning the shell so it glistens. I gaze at the neat lines of his fish display. I'm wondering what he was thinking, when there comes a whisper on the horizon of my mind's eye. A flare of colour, so faint, I'm uncertain whether I'm imagining it.

Kel arranges the beetle in his wooden box and ties on the lid. He doesn't seem to have noticed. Prickles of heat flood my cheeks. We can perceive the shadowy memories drawn up by another person in the present if that person is close enough—within screaming distance on a windless day.

I stretch my attention through the forest. A memory drifts in the mind-world like mist through a valley. Growing clearer, closer.

Ruffled blankets. Wreaths of curly brown hair. Twilight glowing on wooden tumble-down walls.

Kel's head shoots up. He saw that. You couldn't miss it!

'Is Pa looking for us?' he asks. My heart skips up a beat as I scoop up the fish carcases, wrap them in deerskin and dump them in my bag. He must sense it's not Pa as well as I do.

'Put your pack on,' I say, forcing my voice to sound calm. With the churned up snow around the stream, and the broken ice, any attempt to conceal our presence will be useless. I strap on my rucksack and pick up my bow and quiver. Kel stands stiffly as I shove his beetle farm into his bag and hook the strap around his shoulders. His glittering eyes blaze with shock.

'Let's go,' I say. Hand in hand, we leap over the stream and half-jogging, half-running move east, away from the falling sun. Our boot prints guide us through skiffs of snow and crowded, prickly pines. If we manage to keep up the pace, we will be with our parents in fifteen minutes.

'Who are they?' Kel asks. Panic and our unrelenting speed make his voice breathy.

'I don't know.'

'Are they looking for us?'

How could they be? No one knows we're here. 'No. No, they're not looking for us.' Not yet.

'Did they find the magic door?'

Irritation flickers through me. Not at Kel. It's not his fault our mother decided the best way to deal with his nightmares was not to deal with them at all. So he believes when he was a baby we found a magic door into a forgotten land where the bad men couldn't follow. I think they should have told him the truth a long time ago. I was four when I understood that nowhere in the three western Kingdoms of Ederiss, nowhere this side of hundreds of miles of impassable mountains and frozen tundra, would I be safe until I was seven or eight and the golden sparkle in my eyes faded.

I squeeze my brother's hand. 'It's OK, everything's fine. We just have to get back to Ma and Pa.'

The smooth white surface is unpredictable. Our feet slam into gnarled roots, jarring our bodies. Sudden hollows leave us panting with the extra effort of extracting boots from deep snow. My fire bundle, wooden sun-clock and the fish thump around in my backpack. Kel wheezes, breath hissing in and out of his small chest. Far off, the wind moans through the jagged mountain range that blocks the north. An eagle screeches high in the empty vault of sky above our sheltered forest, searching the land for prey.

We have been jogging for ten minutes, when beyond the squeak and crunch of our boots and the clunk of our packs, I hear a dog bark.

'What was that?'

'Run!' I drag my brother behind me, clasping his gloved hand. 'Faster, Kel.'

We plummet down a drift, weaving between tightly clustered trees. The low sun glimmers and dances on the swathes of untouched snow.

Kel breathes in gasping snatches, his facing turning bright red. My calf muscles ache, pain shooting through them at regular intervals. It is too soon after the long-sleep for such exertion. Kel claws his fist against his chest and I know we can't keep this up.

'I got a stitch,' he wheezes.

'Just a bit longer.'

'It hurts.'

'All right,' I say, slowing a little. 'You're doing really well.'

He looks at me with such trust in his eyes, I feel sick. A sense of panic churns my empty stomach. He has seen stuff like this in my memories. And worse. Before he was born, before my one and only friend Asmine was taken, we lived in the Sea of Trees beyond Black Ridge Mountain, where hundreds of Uru Ana families hide their glitter-eyed children. Out-running bounty hunters and poachers was regular enough.

I've tried not to think of Asmine for the last few years, but even if my little brother has heeded Ma's warnings never to enter our minds, we all have memories that rise unbidden from the darkness. He knows what will happen if men find him, even if he doesn't understand how they came here.

Kel's hand snaps from mine. I reach to grab him but I'm not quick enough. He falls hard on a tangle of surface roots. I drop my pack and pick him up. His face looms before me before I swing him onto my back. There is a red welt on his bony cheek where he is cut, and snow and dirt on his forehead. He is holding back tears. His attempt at bravery makes my chest squeeze tighter and my own unwanted tears push up my throat. I swallow them down, and hook my hands together behind me to secure his legs. He buries his head deep in my fur hood, snivelling.

I hesitate for a moment, unwilling to abandon the fish, and my bow and fire tools. I throw Kel's bag up into a tree to hide it, then strap my own to my front.

'You have to carry my bow and quiver.'

'OK.' He bunches them under his arm and they press into my shoulder. I push forward, jogging again. We cannot be far now. Icy snow cracks beneath my boots. Our earlier prints have softened in the sun at the edges and now grow crusty and hard. This is tracking snow.

I think of setting out with the sunrise two hours ago. Desperate to get away. The week it takes for us to regain our strength after the long-sleep always drives me crazy. Hunkering around a spitting fire while strangling hours of darkness, unable to escape one another. I couldn't wait to be far from Ma's smothering memories. Now I search for her mind to guide us home. Oh the irony.

The dog barks again.

Much closer.

There are two men following it, but I find it difficult to gauge how far they lag behind the dog. One mind is as hard and impenetrable as a fort. The other feels like wrestling in mud.

I scan the trees and spot a pine with several stunted branches at the trunk. I drop my pack and slide Kel off my back.

'OK, Bud,' I say. 'Climb up as far as you can.' He stares at me, cheeks stained with tear lines. 'I'm going to get rid of the dog,' I explain. He wipes his nose with his sleeve and nods.

'You climb up and don't make a sound. Now. Quickly.' I lift him onto the first branch. Pine needles shake and snow flutters from the branches as he begins ascending.

I pull off my right glove, hesitating between knife and bow. Knife-throwing is my strength. I've been handling and throwing them since I was five, practising until my shoulders ached and my arms were strong. But a bow and arrow is the hunter's weapon and far easier with a moving target.

I unwrap the fish, cut off one of the Suntrout's heads and drop it away from Kel's hideout. Then I jog back twenty paces. Standing absolutely still, I wait.

High in the trees, wind rustles snow-tipped pine needles. Somewhere close by I hear tapping. A squirrel or perhaps a bird pecking its way out of a sealed tree hole. I sense hundreds of small animal minds, sleeping under the ground, in tree hollows and snow-dens. I flex the arrow in my bow, focus my thoughts.

The dog lets out a single bark. I concentrate on where I feel it bounding in our direction. Its shaggy white and grey coat emerges through the trees. Large yellow eyes. Tail pointing upwards. A beautiful wolf dog.

If I don't do this, it will keep coming. It will lead the hunters after us once we clear camp and vanish back over our maze of trails to hide our retreat.

The wolf dog slows, scenting the fish. I sight my eye down the arrow, tighten the flex on the bow. It looks up from my offerings, meeting my gaze. I release my fingers. The shaft spins through the air. There comes a loud yelp. The dog leaps forward and for a moment I don't understand. I think I've missed. But then the dog collapses on its hind legs, baring his teeth, ears flat back against his head, my arrow jutting out from its front leg. I grab my pack and return to Kel's tree.

'Hurry, Kel. Get down!' My brother scuffles and slips his way towards the ground. I reach out to help him from the last branch. His eyes flick over my shoulder. He sees something that makes him lose balance and cry out. I catch his arm to stop him falling, push him back into the tree. There is a small throwing knife in my waistband. I wind my hand around my back to retrieve it, and turn.

TWO

A lean silhouette leaps through the undergrowth with determination and speed. He is backlit by the setting sun, vanishing and reappearing between trees. I recognise my father's mind at once. Distracted by the men and the wolf dog, I hadn't sensed him approaching. He must have come looking for us because he heard the hound's bark. He must have followed our outbound prints, because unlike Kel and me, he cannot sense peoples' minds.

'Pa!' Kel shouts. My brother jumps from his hideout, not caring anymore about twisting his ankle or hurting himself. Not caring about anything but getting himself into our father's arms.

Pa scans the forest, blue eyes bright and keen in his rugged face. He takes in the injured dog, the cut on Kel's cheek, the state of me breathless from all the jogging and carrying and shooting. Then he hoists his bow onto his shoulder and lifts Kel into his arms, pulls him tight to his chest, one hand stroking the back of my brother's head.

Side by side, with their slim faces, and grey-blue eyes, it is easy to see they are father and son. Kel looks like Pa, and with all that blonde hair and warm yellowy-pink skin, he takes after my mother too.

We abandon the wolf dog and jog back to camp, Kel on Pa's back. My father says nothing as we move swiftly, the air growing chillier with the parting daylight. I can't tell if he's angry, worried or focused on what lies ahead. The next couple of hours—how quickly we can pack up and how far we can get without leaving obvious tracks—are crucial.

I wonder if we should have put the hound out of its misery, and what the men will do when they find it injured. My father did not take his knife to the creature and I couldn't bring myself to finish the job. My arrow had pierced its front leg. With proper care it will have a good chance of healing. That was what made me hesitate. And there wasn't time for such indecision, so I left it.

There is a break in the thicket, a downward slope where our camp nestles behind the high banks of snow we dug out yesterday. Smoke curls towards the sky, suspended in frosty air that preserves footprints, skinned pelts, and bone remnants, long after those who left them have gone.

As the wooden tent poles come into view, pictures shimmer in the mind-world.

Bare feet on warm stone floors. Hot water baths. She lathers oil that smells of summer and hope over her slim, sixteen-year-old calves.

It is the year before my mother met my father. Ma's reminiscing has this annoying way of echoing whatever age I am. Her thoughts break off as she hears our boot steps in the compacted snow. The smell of warm oats hits me and my stomach grumbles. Ma rises, cheeks red from sitting too close to the fire, wisps of blonde hair escaping the fur ruff of her hood. I am neither blonde like Ma, nor blue-eyed like Pa. My wide-set oval eyes and flat-bridged snub nose are typical of the Uru Ana. I resemble my mother's mother, who passed down the sight to Kel and me, even though it skipped Ma.

Pa puts Kel down. 'Get your clothes together,' he tells my brother. Kel crosses the clearing towards our sleeping tents. Ma intercepts him with a quick hug. Her eyes watch Pa and me anxiously, the lost gaze clearing. My father picks up a large copper pan, scoops snow and douses the fire. The flames suffocate with barely any smoke.

Once Kel has moved inside the skin tent where he and I sleep, Pa turns to me.

'How many?' he asks.

'Two.'

'Bounty hunters?'

'I don't know.' But if they set eyes on Kel it won't matter. They'll want him.

'How far behind the dog?'

'Ten minutes. Maybe less.'

'We leave here in five,' he says.

Pa and I dismantle the tents without another word, unknotting gut skins that secure poles to wooden beams, rolling up furs. Kel bundles his change of thermal underwear around his spinning top and collection of wood-carved monsters and soldiers. Ma pours her heavy bag of jewellery on a blanket, selects her most precious necklaces, bracelets and hairpins, then digs a deep hole to bury the rest.

Once we've finished with the sleep tents, father and I divide up the storage items. We tie fire drills, hatchets and cooking utensils along with the rolled furs to the wooden frames of our packs. Then I bind a roll of fur and half the fish to the carrying frame I made for Kel last year. Enough food to survive three days out here by himself in case we get split up. He would be without shelter, but once we're further north the snow is deep and he could burrow into a snow drift. It is a last resort precaution. One I don't want to think about too much because the nights are still long and freezing. Without the warmth of each other, it would be easy to fall asleep and not wake up.

Five minutes later, everything we can easily leave with is packed. Pa lays a hand on Ma's shoulder.

'Come on, Thyme' he says. 'We have to go now.' My mother nods. She straps on the pack Pa has cobbled together for her. Almost as empty as Kel's. Then she fetches her lute and cradles it against her chest.

I swallow down my annoyance, ignoring the lute as I tie the ropes of my rucksack to my belt and adjust the weight so it's evenly spread. Then I help Kel with his. He wipes streaks of mud and salty tears from his cheeks, gazing up at me, waiting for something.

'OK?' I ask.

He glances back to check Ma and Pa aren't listening. 'Will Pa kill them?' he whispers.

That night, twelve years ago, comes rushing back: Darkness and shadows. A man. Musty, sour breath. Fingers brushing soft fur. Fingers holding a blade. Asmine's father carrying Asmine. Running from the tent. Her arms clasping his neck. Holding on for dear life.

I wasn't there. But I saw it all. Over and over in my father's memories as we travelled east, leaving behind the Sea of Trees, leaving behind my friend and her family to find a deserted place where there were no other Uru Ana with glitter-eyed children, no poachers, no anyone.

'Sorry,' I say, pushing down the past. How much did my brother see? How much has he already seen because of me or Pa? Enough to give him nightmares when he was a baby. 'Try not to think about it.' I pull off Kel's glove, then my own. I entwine our fingers and nestle them into the pouch of my parka.

'No one will take you,' I say. 'Pa and I won't let them.'

'WE HIKE NORTH. The last rays of the day's sun seep through the spruce trees. It is not even the third hour after high-noon, but above us the sky turns a deep purply-blue and the first stars appear. Lucky for us, the moon is waxing and will not rise for many hours. It will be harder for the hunters to follow in the dark.

We are headed towards Jade Sword Mountain where we denned for the three-month winter long-sleep. The bitter winds and lack of vegetation make it the last place anyone would want to go. Pa's hoping the men won't track us into the desolate north. That they'll opt for one of our other trails leading east.

The forest thins. Spruce trees become scraggly and gaunt. My pack grows heavier and I'm starting to sweat. Snow blusters around us as the wind picks up. At first when the men stopped, once for the dog, then again at our camp, we increased our head start. But now they are gaining on us.

I am fairly certain they have not mercy killed the wolf dog. The only way to know for sure would be to enter one of their minds. But penetrating a mind is disorientating, I'm unpracticed, and it would slow us down. They're advancing so quickly, I wouldn't dare slacken our pace, even for a second. So I have to rely on them pulling up their own memories to the surface of the mind-world. And since they discovered the hound, they have been guarding their thoughts carefully. Which means they suspect we are not fugitives or hunters, but Uru Ana.

The one with the mind like a citadel is particularly impressive. I did not know it was possible for a man to conceal himself so well. The hunters who took Asmine had no such skill. They used the mist berry to dull their minds and hide themselves.

'Hey Kel,' I say, 'why don't you walk with Ma? It'll make her feel better.'

My brother's hood is pulled up so his face, apart from his scintillating eyes which gleam in the dark, is all shadow and grey. He gives a little nod, lets go of my hand and reaches across to clasp Ma's. Pa notices and I give him a pointed look. *We need to talk.*

'They're faster than us,' I tell my father once Kel and Ma are ahead. The light wind and crunch of snow dampens our words.

'It'll be dark soon.'

'I think they're proper trackers. They haven't paused once at any of the other trails to decide which way we've gone. The dog must be helping them.'

'They won't follow us into the mountains.'

'We're not going to make it to the mountains. They're right behind us.'

My father breaks the rhythm of his stride. 'What are you suggesting?'

'We should hide Ma and Kel and go after them.'

'We're not splitting up.'

I tighten my fingers around the straps of my pack and haul the whole thing higher on my shoulders. My back is hot and damp while my hands and feet tingle with the cold. The pack bears down as does my father's gaze. 'They're trying to hide their minds.'

'You've lost them?' His voice cuts the air sharply. He doesn't understand what it's like to sense another mind. And because the sight passed down from my grandmother, skipping my mother, Pa is dependent on my perceptions. It must be frustrating. He has to rely on me, yet he still wants to make all the decisions.

'No. They haven't taken the mist berries. But obviously they'll have figured out there are four of us. They'll know we're travelling with a child and that it is likely from the size of our bootprints that two of us are women. If they didn't suspect what Kel was, why would they be hiding themselves?'

'We can't leave your mother and brother alone.'

'Taking the hunters by surprise is our best chance.'

My father halts. His arm shoots out to catch my wrist.

Thrusting the knife. Blood spurting as it cuts soft skin. Blade jamming against cartilage.

His memory flashes, slamming against my mind's eye. I flinch and twist away. Father's gaze locks on me like the deadly tip of an arrow, but I'm more concerned about Kel. My brother's hand slips from Ma's as he cocks his head. He stops, focusing on the mind-world. As he glances back at us, I realise the images were too rapid to comprehend if you didn't already know what they were. If you hadn't already seen before and afterwards a thousand times. To him they will have registered as something ominous, something bad. I relax a little.

'We came here so that would never happen again,' my father says. 'I hope you never have to kill a man, Mirra. I hope your brother will never have to live with the burden of what you have lived with because of my actions.'

My cheeks sting with the cold and a mix of shame and defiance. I meet my father's gaze and the desire to fight drains from me. I am not thirsty for blood. I know what saving my childhood friend cost my father. The killings a dark secret he has withheld from my mother. But that is the difference between Ma and I. I understand there was no other way.

'Then we have to move faster,' I say.

THREE

We gave up jogging some time ago. We are all too exhausted now. Hunger gnaws at my stomach despite the bowl of oats I slurped down as we abandoned the camp. My head is heavy and woozy. Kel holds my hand inside my pouch again. He whimpers, but I'm too tired to console him. We are exposed to the eastern winds here and they mercilessly swirl up the snow and throw it against us. My mother has surprised me. She hasn't keeled over and she isn't complaining. She hasn't broken down and refused to go on. I guess we are driven by each other. No one wants to be the one who gives up.

Jade Sword Mountain rises ahead of us, its narrow peak like a sword saluting the stars. Black Ridge Mountain lies to the west, the Edelon mountain range and the vast tundra to the east. We have reached an open, sloping plateau. Land folds and undulates towards steep, jagged rocks. Only shrubs and stunted trees grow here. It is like walking through a wasteland of empty shadows. Except the snow. Snow everywhere, reflecting the shimmering light of the stars, enough light to stop the world from tumbling into pitch blackness.

Suddenly, like stars blinking—there, then not—I realise I cannot sense the men's minds. I spread out my awareness, grappling through the foggy emptiness. I cannot remember when I last reached for them. Two minutes ago? Five? Ten?

I lean over to Kel. 'Can you feel them?' I shout above the wind, breathing hard. His shimmering eyes meet mine, then cast sideways, concentrating. He shakes his head. Perhaps we're too tired. The pounding in my head muffles everything. And I am not used to the effort it takes to focus constantly, to stretch my attention across such distances. I stop, wiping tiny flakes from my top lip, the blustering snow replacing them moments later.

'What's the matter?' my father shouts.

A flutter of colour.

Something right behind us! I fumble with the knots of my shoulder straps. How did they get so close?

'Get ready!' My numb fingers free the rope and I shake off my pack. It falls with a thud. My shoulders are left feeling weightless.

'Go ahead with Kel!' Pa calls to my mother. 'Keep going!' He throws down his rucksack and prepares his bow. I slide off my fur mittens revealing furless deer-skin gloves which allow my fingers flexibility and strength without freezing up. Facing down the open hillside, I scan the horizon. Waves of wind-driven snow break over me, whipping the hood from my head, obscuring my vision. My hands tremble as I grasp an arrow from my quiver, pull it back in line with my cheek. The strain after the day I've had makes my arms shake, muscles barely holding up. Icy flakes burn my eyes like grit and a great haze of exhaustion muzzles the mind-world.

Pa is by my side, bow ready to fire, eyes scouring the plateau beyond as best he can. Every distant shrub looks like a man crouching, moving, sneaking towards us. I feel dizzy.

A blurred, muddy form appears on my inner eye. I aim for where I discern the image. Pull the arrow a notch tighter and release my fingers. The bone-tipped shaft spins into the night. Pa fires in the same direction. There comes a gruff cry. He's hit one of them. My thought is cut short by sharp pain. The top of my arm burns, liquid oozing across my skin. I drop my bow, and reach across my chest to extract the arrow. It's scraped the fleshy bit below my shoulder. Nothing fatal. Unless the arrow is poisoned.

I sense the bounty hunter before I see him. Rage. Blinding rage. His mind a jumble of fists and blood-fights. He hurtles towards us. Broad shouldered, tall. Pa doesn't even have time to reach for his sheath before he's stabbed. He stumbles. I scream his name, terrified. The only thing I can imagine which is as bad as Kel being taken, is my father dying. I pull the longer knife from my thigh strap, but my throwing arm is limp and useless.

'The boy's got the sight!' a gruff voice shouts. Not my father's attacker who is on top of him. The other one. Kel must have turned back when I screamed and in the darkness his sparkling eyes will have danced like fireflies. I clench my knife and dive towards the man running for my brother. *Keep going, Kel!* I think. It's the last thought I have. An instant later, a fist smashes the side of my face and my head rips back, crushing the nerves in my neck. A flash of white light. Everything is upside down and I'm falling.

THE NIGHT POACHERS snatched Asmine from the bed we shared, I had woken with bad dreams and gone to lie with my parents. Ma let me crawl in beside her and cuddled me back to sleep. Later, when she returned me to my bed she found Asmine missing. I couldn't help Pa and Asmine's father find the bounty hunters. The mist berries had cloaked their minds like rock and bush under winter's thick blanket. And they had forced Asmine to take the berries too. But now, as I lie in the darkness, pain pulsing in my skull, I realise this is different. The men who have Kel have no mist berries to hide behind. I know this because I saw the rage of the one who attacked Pa, the blinding flash of blood and fists on my inner-eye. I've never encountered a mind like it: crystal clear when it comes, yet so well protected.

Pa! I roll onto my side coughing up the snow I've been suffocating in. Colours sparkle at the edge of my vision. It's as though I'm seven again and my glitter-eyes are back, but I can actually see the dazzle in my own irises. I grow aware of the weight of the knife handle in my hand and close my fist around it.

'Pa?'

'Mirra!' My mother's voice is a soft, startled cry. I try to tilt my head, but it sends electric light shooting through my skull. Footsteps approach. My mother collapses beside me. 'Oh Mirra, you're alive!' she sobs. The neck of her lute dangles on her hip. Bits of wood and gut strings hang from the smashed concave body.

'Where's Kel?' I croak. 'Where's Pa?'

'Gone, both gone.'

I force myself to sit up. Ma is more of a hindrance than a help, picking and pulling at the fur of my parka. Blood trickles down my arm. I slide a hand down the neckline of my inner and outer parkas, beneath my cotton shirt, and press the injury. I am lucky. The arrow that hit me skimmed the skin's surface and the cold has constricted the bleeding. I reach for my father's presence, knowing he cannot have fallen far.

Timelessness, wildness, vastness. His mind is a harsh and beautiful winter land; it reminds me of a herd of giant deer skipping through a river, shaking themselves off on the other side, blooms of spray like diamonds raining down on Ederiss.

'Ma,' I say. She moans. 'Ma...' In the snow-reflected starlight, her hair glows pale gold as it whips out behind her. 'Pa's alive and I sense Kel. He's not far. We need to help Pa. Fetch my pack.' She raises her head. I can only make out the edges of her cheekbones, the curve of her high forehead. She tilts a little, revealing the glassy sheen of shock in her eyes. She nods, but it's as though she's not here. Up on her feet, she sways, searches about, returns with a heavy load.

'In the inside pocket, wrapped in skin, are the cotton pads.' I shout to be heard above the blow and howl of the wind.

'Cotton pads?' She rummages frantically. Every year since I was twelve and old enough to hunt, Pa has left us from anywhere between ten days to two weeks. He travels to the closest border settlements to trade the deer skin boots and coats Ma makes, in exchange for metal pans, medicine, grain and gifts for us all. Cotton pads are one of our staple commodities.

The seconds slip away, but I don't hurry her. She is shaken and panicked enough as it is. Finally, she waves the skin-wrapped wad in front of me.

'That's it.' I use my good arm to push to my feet, hold still for a moment, waiting for the spinning to settle. 'Follow me,' I say. We plough through snow and wind, exposed on this forlorn plateau, each step compounding the throbbing in my body. 'Don't let go of those!' I shout back at her, and notice by some miracle, she is also dragging my rucksack.

A pot, wooden spoons and a split bag of grain strew the ground. I shuffle past them, hoping she doesn't notice the blood glistening in the ruffled white terrain.

And then I reach Pa. He has fallen face-up, or rolled himself with the last of his strength. He must be breathing or I wouldn't sense his mind, but I kneel down and check his air passage anyway. Ma slumps beside me.

'My furs,' I say. She struggles with the gut string attaching the bedding to my pack. I reach over and cut the ties with my knife. 'Lift his head,' I instruct her. As she does so, I slip part of the fur roll under him. Then, with my knife, I rip through his outer parka, sheath the blade and remove my glove. 'Give me one of the pads, Ma. Be careful. Don't let any blow away.'

The skin wrap flutters in her shaky grasp. She removes a pad and pushes it into my hand. I slide my fingers beneath Pa's undershirt. Carefully, I tiptoe the pads of my fingertips up his chest to where I thought I sensed the knife go in. The shirt is soaked with blood. My fingers slip across his skin in the goop. The wound is higher than I imagined, severing the shoulder joint, not piercing his chest. I know when I've reached it by Pa's agonised cry. 'Hold on, Pa. Hold on.' I press the dressing against the gash. He moans. 'You're OK. I'm here. You're OK.'

'Is he OK?' Ma wails.

'He'll be OK. Get one of my undershirts, rip up two strips, long enough to tie around my arm.'

She does as I say while I concentrate on maintaining the pressure on Pa's wound. My knife-throwing arm burns. The inside of my cheek where I was hit aches. Every second Ma takes floundering to find a shirt, struggling to rip off strips, is like holding your breath under-water when all your body wants to do is come up for air.

'Have you done it?'

'I'm doing it.'

'Hurry, Ma.' I can't wait any longer. And Pa's cotton pad is sopping wet. I need to put another one on. She holds out the two strands. 'Good,' I say. 'Now I need another pad for Pa. I want you to hold him where my hand is. First hold him,' I say as she waves the pad at me. 'I can't move my bad arm.' She kneels on the other side of my father, pushes her palm against the skin of his inner parka. I take the pad and slide my arm under his shirt again placing the thick cotton on top of the first. 'Now while I've got him, put a pad over my wound and tie it down with the cloth strips.'

'OK, Mirra,' she says, teeth chattering, shoulders shaking.

It hurts to have her treating my arm while I'm taking care of my father, and it's awkward because she can't see what she's doing and has to work around my clothes. It seems an age has passed when the bandage is at last in place.

Here comes the hard bit—when she realises I'm leaving her. I cross Pa's other arm over his chest and tell him to keep up the pressure. While Ma covers him with bedding furs, I struggle to knot myself a sling. Then I throw together a light bag with a fur throw, my fire board and bow for making fire, a hatchet, my flask and my hunting bow.

'Mirra, what are you doing?' Ma asks, blinking up at me.

'Keep up the pressure on his wound. Once the bleeding stops, you'll have to build a shelter. Something low and small so the wind won't knock it down. Then you make a fire to keep Pa warm. As soon as you're sure the bleeding has stopped, boil up some water, let it cool and clean the wound. Make sure you keep him warm and don't try to move him. Pa will be able to instruct you after that.'

'You're going after Kel?' Fear and shock choke her voice. 'But you're injured, Mirra. Those men were huge. They'll kill you.'

It's at moments like this when I would give anything not to have the sight. Not to see what scuds the surface of my mother's thoughts: The man who'd run after Kel knocking her down. Kel screaming and kicking and Ma swatted off like an insignificant fly when she tried to stop him dragging my brother away.

Ma grew up in the wealthy town of Ebonaska. When she was eight years old, King Rex began rounding up the Uru Ana, drowning them or burning them. Her family hid their heritage, began the Carucan traditions of fasting and cleansing, avoided drawing attention to themselves and carried on, as neighbours, people they'd been friends with for years, were arrested and their glitter-eyed children taken. Her parents did not fight back. I try to remember that as contempt for my mother's weakness festers inside me.

I occupy myself with gathering the scant remains of our rations. Ice crystals have dampened the chickweed leaves. I take a handful, add a few stalks of the white root plant, two fish, and wrap them in skin. My parents will keep the cereal, tubers, most of the roots, and the leftover fish, enough to stave off hunger for four days.

Once I have the bare essentials I will be travelling with, I sling the hemp bag over my neck and adjust my sling. Ma stares at me until I meet her gaze. 'You know I'll never find Kel if they get too far. When he's in the Hybourg it'll be like looking for a needle in snow.'

'I know Mirra. But how can you do anything? You can't even hunt or build a shelter with that arm. You won't be able to make fire. How will you survive?'

'You worry about Pa. Clean the wound. Keep him warm.'

She nods. In the wispy light, tears stream her cheeks.

'We have to be stronger than ever Ma, you hear me?'

'Yes,' she says. 'Yes, Mirra. Just bring Kel back.'

'I will,' I say, fighting down tears. I bend down beside her and lean over my father. Awkwardly, I kiss his cheek, careful not to press anywhere that might hurt him. Ma throws her arms around me. Then we are hugging and she is kissing my face.

'I love you, Mirra.'

'I love you, too.' I am gentle as I break the grip of her arms around my waist. She doesn't stop me as I rise. I imagine her watching my silhouette slip across these vast forgotten lands. I don't wonder what she's thinking or how she'll manage with Pa. From this moment on, everything must be about what comes next. I can't afford to look back.

FOUR

The land cracks open. Giant boulders mark the murky descent into Blackfoot forest. My knotted hair, crusted with ice whips against my face. My legs tremble and my dry throat hurts when I swallow.

I crouch down, cut a piece of snow to melt in my flask, then check my position in relation to the Bright Star which resides faithfully over Jade Sword peak. From the direction the men have taken, my guess is they are returning to the river where they have set up camp. I shave off a second lump of snow and hold it to my swollen cheekbone and bruised temple. My arm throbs, but my head is worse. It pounds like I'm being struck over and over.

In my mind, I call up those last moments with Ma and Pa so that Kel knows Pa's alive and I'm coming. The mind-world ripples with his answer: running through the forest, hearing the startling bark of the wolf dog, peering down between snow-tipped pine needles while I racked my bow to shoot. I feel a small glimmer of relief. He is conscious and not wrapped so tightly into himself that I cannot reach him.

I sheath my knife, telling myself I've gained enough on them now to carry on at a good walking pace. But the truth is I can't continue jogging. The adrenaline drained, fatigue has settled over me so that my muscles and bones ache.

Trees. Nothing but pine and spruce and fir. They grow taller, denser, blocking the starlight. I trip and stumble many times, unable to see the ground, and every time, it's harder to get up.

To fill the bleakness in my heart and the rolling blackness before my eyes, I consider whether Kel was trying to tell me something with his memories of the wolf dog. If the men have not given the hound night-shade to subdue its pain, nor killed it, my chances of cutting Kel free and the two of us escaping without waking the hunters are zero. And I cannot take on either of the men. Even uninjured it would be pure idiocy to try.

But if I cannot steal Kel from their camp, how long can I follow in the shadows? With my injured arm I cannot build shelter, or wield fire with my fire board. Besides, I could not risk them seeing the smoke.

I strain to make out the trees in the darkness. I am beginning to lose my sense of direction and time. The thick canopy of pine branches obliterates the sky, but even if the heavens could guide me, I wouldn't stop to look up - I would never get going again.

I reach for the soft, feathery shape of Kel's mind to orientate myself. Luminously bright and as gentle as dandelion seeds. I have always loved the feel of it. Light and airy and bright. So bright! My wandering thoughts snap to attention. So bright because he has stopped moving and I am not far from him. So bright, because the bounty hunters' minds are sunless and dull in comparison.

They have reached their camp. It takes every fragment of will I possess not to collapse to my knees and rest for a few minutes. Sit down and you will fall asleep and freeze to death. Even bundled in my one fur, if I sleep without shelter or fire, I will die from the cold.

I slump against a tree, pack pressing into the muscle knots that riddle my shoulders. I am exhausted and I can't focus. My mind feels like dirty sludge. After a brief pause, I force my eyes open, shake off my pack carefully so as not to pull on my arm sling, and fumble inside for the skin with the chickweed and white root. I take a root and chew on it while thinking.

Staying outside all night, totally exposed is not an option. Nor is returning to Ma and Pa without Kel. Could I find my way back to our old camp? It must be less than an hour's walk from here. Yesterday we dug banks from the snowdrifts, which had formed in the clearing. I could burrow into one. But it would be too far to sense Kel's mind. And if the men woke and set off before me, I would lose them.

Have I passed a snowdrift recently? My mind seems foggy as I try to remember any slopes in the land where the wind might have blown in enough snow to dig out a man-sized hole. I mentally retrace my steps. Apart from dips and bumps the forest has been flat and dense for at least twenty minutes.

I crouch and sag forward, leaning my forehead against the pine trunk. Bark scratches my skin. I'm too tired to cry, but my distress at being so close to Kel, yet so far, is unbearable.

I wonder how he is holding up. It has been some time since he last attempted to communicate through the mind-world. Perhaps he is sleeping. Mentally, I reach for the luminous softness of his mind.

Entering a mind is not the same as seeing memories that echo in the now-time. It requires concentration and energy, and finding what you want is an art I am unpracticed in. There are minds that drag you under like the great surf of an ocean; minds that disorientate as though you're walking through woods but whatever direction you take, you end up back where you started. Kel's mind is as beautiful and light inside as out. I slip in easily, searching close to the edges for a recent memory.

He sits crouched near the fire, eyes closed, shivering. Smoke blows in his face and chokes his lungs but he's cold and probably too scared to move. He hunches inward as the crunch of footsteps encroaches.

'Please, please,' he whispers.

For a moment nothing happens, then the man standing beside him wraps a blanket over his shoulders. Still Kel's eyes remain shut. My chest clenches with sadness and anger. He must be beyond terrified!

'Come,' the man says. 'It is warmer in the tent.' He lifts my brother and carries him away from the heat of the fire. Stiff hide brushes Kel's face, then he is placed on a bed of furs. 'Did you eat enough?'

Kel nods. There is a rustle and a wet nose rubs against Kel's neck.

'Her name is Trix. She'll keep you company,' the man says. 'Now try to sleep. The worst is over. You will not be hurt.'

I return to my shivering body and the dark forest in a daze. It is four years since I last mind-travelled. There has never been any reason to enter my brother's mind, and I stopped foraging in Ma and Pa's memories when it began to feel like an invasion of their privacy. It made it harder to accept the everyday shortcomings of our meagre life in Blackfoot forest. I forgot how confusing it is, how you lose your sense of time and place.

I chew on another white root, perplexed by the hunter's behaviour. The man who showed my brother kindness did not have the gruff voice of the brute who snatched him. It must have been the one with the mind shaped like walls inside walls. The one whose physical and mental strength make him the clear leader of the two.

A plan forms in my head, a crazy plan, but now I am sure the dog is conscious, it is all I can think of to stay with Kel and not die in the process: become their captive too. An unidentifiable Uru Ana of my sixteen years, not yet enslaved in the tundra goldmines, would fetch a high price on the black market. The Carucans may despise our talents and believe our shadow powers doom us, but that hasn't stopped them from using my kind to fulfil their own greedy ends. The men will want me for the gold I can get them. And in the three or four days it will take to reach one of the towns, I will find a way for Kel and me to escape.

In the vast emptiness of the forest it is hard to believe there is anyone nearby until the smell of smoke drifts on the crisp air followed by a whiff of fish and garlic. My mouth waters and my stomach growls. A hundred footsteps from their camp, flames flicker between the trees, swelling out in an orange pool across the snow. I try to walk steadily and evenly, hood pulled over my head. The man who was kind to Kel is also the man who stabbed Pa. I hesitate. Perhaps my thoughts are too muddled.

Barking resounds across the clearing. They know I'm here. I steel myself, send up a desperate prayer to my mother's Gods that I will not be harmed, that this is not a mistake, and enter the glade. As their camp comes into view I see the men outside the large skin tent, gathering their weapons. They stretch arrows in their bows. I gulp, a frisson of terror like a sunburst explodes in my chest.

Both hunters are stripped down to their cotton shirts and deer skin trousers, despite the below-freezing temperature. The one with a sleeve rolled up and a dressing on his forearm has dark crisscross markings covering his bald head and face. At first I think some kind of hanging net casts strange shadows, but then I realise the marks are made with staining ink. His appearance is fearsome, but it's the other one I'm worried about.

Tall, broad, unflinching. The tattoos on his face make his lifeless eyes appear slanted and distort his crooked nose and thin mouth to resemble a beast of the forest: a bear or wolf. Shoulder length, wavy hair, folds into his furs to heighten the impression.

'What do you want, boy?' he asks. It is the voice of the man who carried Kel, though there is no softness in it now.

Stay strong, Mirra. You did not imagine the way he treated Kel. He is not as fierce as he appears to be.

I raise my good arm slowly, showing an empty hand. Then I pull back my hood. The beast-faced hunter does not react to my age or gender though I'm not sure I would recognise emotion in his strange face.

His companion stops scanning the shadows and turns. 'Is that a girl?' he growls, his low voice husky with lust. He steps forward, lips rising in a gruesome smile. A shudder slips down my spine and my whole body shakes.

Beast-face blocks his companion with his long bow, forbidding him from approaching me further. 'I said, what do you want?'

'I want to travel with you.' At the sound of my voice, the wolf dog starts barking again. I glance towards the skin tent, sides packed down with snow, Kel inside.

'She's alone,' the man with the fishnet head says, pushing away his companion's bow, sucking through his teeth. I avoid his disgusting mouth, study his arm instead, noting that his injury doesn't appear debilitating, nor would it stop him from effortlessly pinning me down.

'Come closer,' Beast-face orders. I edge towards the firelight, which dazzles after so much darkness. There is a tiny flexion of movement above his eyes where his eyebrows should be. He has recognised me. Rather he has recognised the bruising he left down the side of my cheek and temple. 'Forget you ever had a brother,' he warns.

Fishnet-head straightens, lust suddenly vanishing, replaced with suspicion. 'How did you follow us?'

'Your minds were clear enough.'

'She's a shadow weaver!' He reaches inside his shirt, pulls out a multi-faceted glass medallion and holds it up like it's a protection amulet. If I wasn't so exhausted and scared, I might have laughed at his stupidity.

'Enough, Brin,' says Beast-face. He looks at me now with a strange mixture of intent and regret, as though I've pushed him down a path he can't back out of, and won't, even though he wants to.

I swallow the lump in my throat, doubting my plan. 'You could get a good price for me,' I say quietly.

'And why would you want us to sell you?'

'You killed my father. I won't survive out here by myself.'

The moment he jabbed his knife into Pa flutters to the surface of his mind. There's something odd about the memory. It holds a precision and clarity that suggests he knows exactly where he struck Pa. As though he only meant to injure him.

'We left your mother alive,' he says.

'My mother is weak. I will not stay out here and starve to death with her.'

'And why would you starve? You shot my wolf dog well enough.' No emotion shows on his savage face or in his body, but the slight rise of his voice belies his affection for the creature. His anger.

'I'm injured,' I say.

He comes closer, sinewy muscles in his shoulders and forearms bulging as his body flexes. I recoil, almost tripping on a broken tree branch.

'Don't Tug!' says the companion he called Brin. 'Don't touch her.'

'You touched the boy,' he counters.

'The boy is too young to weave the shadows. But she—she is almost fully grown.' 'And worth a fortune,' Tug says.

The anxiety in Brin's voice makes my skin prickle, but hope also leaps inside me. His fear of my kind will stop him from trying to gratify any physical desires he has with me. Thank the Gods!

'She will have cursed us long before we reach the Hybourg,' Brin says.

The man named Tug does not share his companion's concerns. He moves so close that I almost retch at the stench of him. I'm not particularly small for my sixteen-years, as far as I know, but I'm like a child beside him.

'Prove it. Prove you have the sight.'

'The dog is called Trix. You told my brother the worst was over and you would not hurt him.' I hold his stare, despite the heat rising to my cheeks and the desperate need to look away. It is not his brute force that makes this man dangerous, it is his intelligence and the keen control he has over his own mind.

'And have you entered my mind?' he asks.

I shake my head. He lunges forward so that my heart skips a beat. I cry out in pain as he grabs the top of my wounded arm and drags me to the fire.

'Show me this injury.'

I fumble to take off my pack, arm flaring in agony. A movement by the tent catches my attention. Kel appears in the doorway flap.

'Mirra!' he shouts.

I gasp. There's something wrong with his eyes! White, shiny pus seals them shut. 'It's all right, Kel,' I hiss. 'I'm all right. Stay where you are!'

When I turn back, Beast-face is staring at me with an intensity that makes my flesh crawl. I remove my outer parka as quickly as I can, clenching my teeth against the pain. Unless he sees my useless arm, he will not risk taking me with them. The parka with the fur turned inwards is a tight fit and I have not removed it since the winter hibernation—it has not been warm enough. I can smell the snow den trapped in the deer fur, the perfumed oil we cover ourselves with to protect and insulate our skin, the sweat of the last eight days.

Tug inspects my wound through my ripped inner parka and undershirt. I tremble from the cold and from his touch, fighting the urge to throw up the white roots I have just eaten.

'You haven't cleaned it,' he says.

I scowl. 'I was in a hurry.'

Something sparks in his memories, so fast I can make nothing of it but a blur.

'We'll take her,' he says.

'No, we shouldn't. Let's tie her to a tree and leave her to the forest.'

Tug ignores his companion, pulling me towards him so that his nose is almost pressed to mine, his breath warm on my lips. 'You should know two things,' he says. 'You shot my dog.' He pauses, so that if I hadn't understood his affection for the creature, now there is no mistaking it. 'And I have no mercy for anyone who makes me regret a decision. Try anything and your brother will be the one who pays.'

I nod. He thrusts my two parkas into my stomach. I stifle a small cry, cling to the warmth of my fur, unable to tear my eyes from him.

'Clean the wound before you sleep. I wouldn't want to go to all this trouble just to have you die on me.'

FIVE

Kel's trembling and sniffling has given way to dreamless, exhausted sleep. I lie curled around him, my bandaged arm hooked across his waist. My eyes burn like they're on fire. After I'd dealt with my arm, Tug brushed my eyes with a warm, smelly paste. Now my eyes are sealed shut, which means Kel and I are as good as blind. It hurts so much I am afraid my sight will be permanently damaged. My hate and rage for our captors, is only subdued by the fear.

Outside, Tug and Brin move about, clearing up. The crescent moon will have risen by now, draping pale blue light across the forest. After a while, boots crunch across the compact snow, heading away from the camp. I push up on my elbow and reach through the mind-world to follow. I hesitate on the outskirts of Tug's mind, wondering when I push inside whether it will spin me into the high-walled labyrinth of dead-ends and secret passages. But it is surprisingly easy to remain near the outskirts where the memories form and slide back on a constant thread.

His senses are sharp and detailed as though I have moved inside his skin. I shudder at the bulk and strength of his body, the power in his legs and arms, the feel of his hands twice the size of my own. Embers and pine leaves prick my nostrils, the fresh, wet snow lies on my tongue and in my chest.

Brin leans against a spindly tree that rises tall into the soft night, his fish-net-head illuminated by moonlight. He chews on a piece of cinnamon stick, spitting bark from time to time. Tug folds his arms, drinking in his companion's animosity as though absorbing it through the pores of his bare chest.

'Keeping her is a mistake,' Brin says.

'You took the boy.'

Brin spits and wipes his mouth with his forearm. 'What's one thing got to do with the other?'

'Everything,' Tug answers, eyes straying to the forest darkness. I remember the wolf dog wrapped in his arms while I was cleaning my wound. Perhaps he has a weakness for underdogs and broken things.

'We should take her to the tundra camps.'

Tug snorts. 'Don't be ridiculous. A week to get there and a gold sovereign for our efforts. We sell her in the Hybourg, we'll get fifty times that.' He cracks his knuckles, then stretches his thick, naked fingers. I wonder how the cold does not reach his hands and his torso. 'Have you never seen one with their eyes settled?' Tug asks.

'Course not. And I'd rather it had stayed that way.'

'Listen, if you want to keep her out of your head, build a wall.'

'A wall?' Brin asks, confused.

'A wall in your mind.'

'A wall?'

'Forget it.' Tug straightens his broad shoulders and the muscles ripple and settle into place. 'We're keeping her,' he says. He turns from his companion, strolling back towards the camp where tent poles stand visible between long pine trunks.

'Well, we can't stand her up in the Pit and sell her along with the boy,' Brin calls after him. 'We'd end up dead.'

Tug keeps walking and Brin catches him up. 'We'll set out feelers,' Tug says. 'Find the right buyer. Someone discreet.'

'She's going to get us killed,' Brin mutters.

The flap of the tent whips up in the wind. I grow rigid as one of the men sets himself down beside me. An unpleasant scent of wet dog and fish wafts through the air so I know it is the Beast-face. His arm brushes my back. I gulp with rising panic, but he lies down and a moment later, Brin enters and lies down on the other side of him. There comes a faint whiff of smoke as the lantern is blown out.

Unable to relax, I listen to the low breathing of the men and Kel's snoring. I've never been so tired but sleep won't come. The wolf dog's breath blows against the back of my neck. Tug must have him in the fur throws beside him. I fight against my glued eyes, unable to open them. At first, I thought Tug blinded us out of superstition, because he believed our physical sight assisted our 'powers'. But he is not afraid of the glitter-eyes like Brin and most Carucans. For Tug, it is a matter of practicality: I can't see; I can't hunt. Only a fool would try to get Kel away from them now.

I reach for my lodestone necklace, press my finger into one end of the two-sided arrow. It is my compass and my guide through these wastelands, always pointing to the Bright Star when set on a floating leaf. Clinging to it, I eventually fall into a fitful sleep, still holding on.

THE NEXT THREE days we trek through an ever-shifting landscape, following the frozen river as it curls south-west through the Silvana hills, hills my father has pointed out many times from the glacial mountains. Tug binds our hands with thick rope every morning and we are dragged blindly along beside the sled, which scrapes across the narrow river as the two men pull their catch of deer, rabbit, and the injured wolf dog. Far easier the frozen river than hauling it across land.

Kel grows quieter and quieter. At first I draw memories around him, trying to offer comfort, but it does no good. He worries about our parents, and all hope he had of my being able to rescue him has vanished. Only at night does he pull close to me, wrap his arms around me and hold on as if I might disappear.

It is as I lie resting beside him, listening to his gentle breathing, and the men sit out by the fire, that I travel into their pasts, hoping to learn something that will show me a way out of this. Each night, I skim through their recent memories of the day's progress, matching my own interpretation of the shifting ground, the sounds of the forest, the change in the wind, with their mental images of the landscape. Through their eyes I see where we are headed. I memorise the angle of the sun and the peaks of the mountains, drawing a map in my mind of our progress. After I have done this, I search their lives for useful information.

Brin is an opportunist, born in the lands between Delladea and Rangrain, two northern forts on the tree line. Both forts are isolated from the rest of the Kingdom, and Brin's village lay outside the forts, outside the protection of any lord. It was often raided. Two of his younger brothers starved to death when they were children. He was thrown out by his father to make his own way in the world when he was twelve, struggled, thieved and served a vast array of cruel bene-factors.

Tug is infinitely more complex. Just when I think I have figured him out, some other passage from his past muddles it all up again. He has been both street-fighter and soldier, low-life drunk and strategist in noble circles. He has fought in campaigns that have gone far south to the Kingdom of Etea and far north, across the tundra, to the Kingdom of Rudeash. He guards many secrets, secrets he hides easily from my sight as though in some distant past he began purposefully concealing them from Uru Ana like me.

On the fourth day, we reach signs of civilisation and eat lunch, concealed from the river in an abandoned stone home. Brin and Tug do not build a fire. They move about silently, alert to signs of other hunters roaming the forest. From time to time a memory flashes in the mind-world, like lights on the horizon at the onset of winter. Ordinarily, our captors would have no trouble defending themselves against thieves and thugs; it is unlikely they would even be approached. But Kel and I, blinded and bound would arouse interest.

I'm sitting beside my brother, licking the tiny bones of a half-thawed mudfish when Tug approaches with his wet dog and sweat stink, liquid sloshing in a skin flask. Kel drinks first, swallowing and spluttering.

'Drink,' Tug orders. I hold my hands still. The rope presses into grooves where it has rubbed my wrists raw. What's going on? The flask is pushed to my lips and smells terrible. Liquid sets my throat on fire.

'This is going to hurt,' he says. The next thing I know, a toxic-smelling cloth smothers me. Tug rubs the damp fabric into my eyes. It sears like he's peeling the skin off my eyeballs. I panic. His hand claps over my mouth to stop me screaming. I fight, but Tug grips my wounded arm, which sets a new flare of lightning pain throughout my shoulder. I stop squirming so that he'll let go.

'Almost done,' he says. 'But if you scream again I'll knock your teeth out.' I nod, wanting this over with.

It finally ends. I scrabble to scrape up snow from the ground and pack it on my eyes. The agony ebbs, and I am left weeping pus. Dusky light weaves between my half-closed lashes, but they are no longer stuck together. I can see again. Sort of.

'Hold the boy,' Tug says.

'No, please, please,' I beg. 'Let me do it.' Kel's small fingers cling to my leg, and he whimpers. 'Please,' I say. Through a blurry haze, I see Tug nod at Brin, drop the wet cloth into my lap, and the two of them stroll away.

The idea of hurting Kel scorches a hole right through me. But I'd prefer he clings to me, that I am the one to talk him through the pain, than watch Brin hold him down while Tug dissolves the glue.

My tied hands make the job awkward. I dab Kel's eyes, let him rub his eyelids with snow, then repeat when he is ready. His body trembles and pus oozes between his lashes, but he does not yelp or cry out. Which is just as well. Tug wouldn't hesitate to come and shut him up.

As I work, I whisper to him that it's going to be all right. Though I know I'm a liar. It's not all right. I haven't stopped them doing this to him. And I'm starting to believe both of us will be sold into strange cities, slaved, and left to live miserable lives where the opportunities of ever seeing each other gain will dwindle to nothing. But I cannot ask him to keep hoping, if I give up. What chance does he have then? I will not live in the knowledge that my brother, not yet six-years-old, has been ruined, broken into a husk of his self, driven into apathy and hopelessness.

Pa once told me that a man who fights monsters must be careful he does not become one. Men risk turning into the very thing that nearly destroys them. Brin had his boyhood stolen and now he is the monster doing the stealing. I don't know what happened to Tug to rip his heart from his chest. But I must find out. Because he is the one I need to break if I am to save Kel.

SIX

Hooves thunder through the woods, the forest floor shudders with the approach of many men on horseback. Brin appears, running across the clearing. He hasn't even finished pulling up his trousers.

'Soldiers!' he shouts.

Tug kicks me where I sit cradling Kel's trembling body, my brother's eyes weeping pus, raw and itchy from the burning liquid. 'Get up,' he growls. He grabs Kel and drags him towards the stone shack. I follow as my brother edges into the dilapidated building, but hesitate on the threshold, fearing this is my chance, and I don't know how to grab it.

'You should leave our hands untied and not try to hide us,' I say. 'It would look better if it appeared as though we were all together.'

'We are all together.'

'Not captives,' I clarify. 'If Kel keeps his eyes down, no one would know we are not simply a family of hunters, returning to sell the deer and rabbit meat.' Tug grips the hood of my parka and pulls me onto the tips of my toes. The collar of my fur digs into my neck, choking me.

'If the soldiers find out you're a shadow weaver,' he says, 'they'll send you to the tundra camps. Or perhaps they'll decide you're too old and then they'd have to kill you in front of the little one.'

Camomile soap and summer grass invade my senses. Hair flutters about a pale neck.

Tug's incongruous memory is so unexpected, I grimace. Fortunately, he is too preoccupied to notice.

'There's no saving your brother once he's in the work camps,' he says. 'Most Uru Ana under those conditions don't survive long.'

'I'm not stupid,' I say through gritted teeth, because I can't breathe properly; because Beast-face understands me better than I understand him; he preempts my every move and thought.

'No one has ever escaped the camps,' he says softly. Some secret layer of meaning weaves between his words, reminding me of the way he has built his mind to hide many things from the probing sight of a shadow weaver. Has he worked at the tundra camps? Umbra, shadow weaver, glitter-eyes, these are the slighting names we are usually given, yet Tug uses the name our ancestors who came from Auran, island of the Rushing Winds, called themselves.

I slip through the cobbled doorway into the rotting remains of a broken home. Winter sun shines through the narrow windows and a hole in the roof. Thick shadows linger in dusty corners and it takes a moment before I find Kel crouched by a back wall. His head rests on his legs, arms wrapped over his tangled hair, as though to protect himself from an oncoming storm. I kneel in front of him and try to lift his bound hands in my own, but his arms are locked in a tight grip.

The land rumbles like a great beast waking. A distant voice calls orders. I close my eyes and reach towards the voice, encountering many minds. After thirteen, I stop counting. I don't try entering any of them. I don't want to lose my sense of time and risk the soldiers finding me in a half trance. My eyes flash open as a horse whinnies outside the front window, then blows through its nose.

'What are your names?' a man asks, his vowels rounded and musical.

'Tug Briggs,' Tug says.

'Brin Twinerben.'

'What is your business out here?'

'We were hunting.'

'You return while most are just setting out. How long have you been out here?'

'A week.'

'If you have been hunting, where is your sled?'

Hooves clop around the back of the stone building. I can no longer distinguish the voices enough to make out words. I concentrate on breathing steadily. The smooth light bay coat of a horse appears in the back window, a man's leg hanging off the side. The man jumps down and peers through the slim crack.

Kel looks up, the gold flecks in his blue irises shimmering in the darkness. I quickly cup my hand over his eyes.

'It is rare to see the King's soldiers so far north.' Tug's voice moves around the stone house. He speaks as though he wishes only to make conversation, but if I have learnt anything about him, it is that every gesture, every word is calculated.

A light scraping sound signals a presence in the sloping doorway. A tall man with dark hair and a dark green uniform. White bear fur drapes over his shoulders. He wears a fitted hat, also embroidered with the rare snowy fur. 'Anyone in here?' he asks.

'Perhaps you should tell us what you are looking for,' Tug says.

'Bring a torch,' the officer commands.

I squeeze my bound hands together, the blood in my veins turning to sludge. A second man approaches behind the officer, carrying a rag burning on a stick. 'Don't move,' I whisper to Kel. 'Whatever happens stay hidden.'

As the high-ranking officer enters, I slink to the centre of the room. He is suspicious of Tug and Brin with their half-empty sled, and expecting to find something. If he finds me, it should be enough to stop him checking further.

Flames lick the darkness. The officer steps beyond the shaft of daylight from the front window and stops. His eyes meet mine. He is younger than Tug and Brin, and far younger than my father. Shadows circle his brown eyes. Stubble darkens his pointy chin, except where stitches of a long scar dent the surface.

My arms dangle awkwardly in front of me. The officer lifts the sleeve of my parka and lowers the torch to my bound wrists. I follow his gaze. My hands aren't even shaking. Before I can stop myself, I have found the passage into his mind, and I am entering it.

Images ripple like concentric circles from a stone thrown into a still lake.

Summer. Handsome women in luxurious velvets. Exquisite gardens blooming with exotic flowers and fronds. Laughter. Sparring in a tournament. Dirt and sweat. A voice: 'The Prince will not make elite captain. Do you understand?' Hitting a hard, dirt ground. Stabbing a man in the leg. Running through dungeon passageways. Hooves clattering across a court-yard. A palace high on a hill fading into the distance. Scraping aside snow to reveal a frozen face, dead eyes, skin barely blemished by time. A soldier's uniform. 'The Prince's escort,' he whispers. 'All dead, but no Prince.' A letter with a royal seal. 'Find him.'

The memories seethe together and feel linked to each other, though I have the sense the rings are separated by weeks or even years.

Disorientated, I realise I have lost my balance. The officer grabs my shoulder. He steadies me with one arm, the torch held in his other arm flickers light across his face.

'Help me,' I mouth. He stares into my eyes, then releases his grip, turns, and strides from the shack. Beyond the doorway, he barks orders, and mounts his giant stallion. There come the sounds of the horses and their riders galloping into the forest.

I am standing frozen to the spot when Tug enters.

'What happened?' he asks. I shake my head. Apart from Tug and Brin, the officer's mind is the first I have entered for many years. It has left a strange sensation in my body, a feeling of being connected to something greater than myself. 'What did you say to him?'

'What do you think? He saw my bound wrists and decided I was not worth saving.'

'Where's the boy?'

Suddenly remembering Kel, I rush through the rubble, throw my arms around my brother, and lift him up. He wraps his legs about my waist. I haven't carried him like this for years, and it is awkward because neither of us can hold on properly with bound wrists and my injured arm. We clamber back out into the setting, afternoon sun.

'Must have had more important business to attend to,' Brin says.

'In all my years out here,' Tug muses, 'I've never seen the King's soldiers near the Hybourg. Something has happened.'

Something, indeed. I swallow and hoist Kel higher on my waist. I do not look at Tug as he scoops up the dog, shelters it in the top of his bag and straps on his rucksack. If I catch his eye, I'm afraid he will realise that I know what the soldiers are searching for. Though I have no idea how it might become useful, right now, it is the only advantage I have.

SEVEN

The valley shimmers with light, surrounded by snow covered hills, moonlit blue and eerie in comparison. But I would rather the cold hills any day because below us lies the most lawless destination in the Carucan Kingdom. The only place where Uru Ana are openly sold to the highest bidder. This is where the poachers would have brought my childhood friend, Asmine, if our fathers had failed to rescue her. This is where the vast majority of glitter-eyed children stolen from the *Sea of Trees* end up before they disappear forever: The Hybourg.

At the heart of a vast sprawl of stone buildings, campfires, skin-homes and winding streets looms the huge closed market, built from the black rock mined in these parts. The Pit, as I have heard Tug and Brin refer to it, rises above interlocking squares and lopsided taverns, a windowless monster. In the mind-world, it flashes and flickers with bright swirls of colour - memories surfacing and crashing against each other. The vast number of minds crammed together overwhelms me. In another sort of world perhaps the effect would be beautiful, but in a realm of thieves and criminals the chaotic clash resembles a battlefield of motion and pain.

'So,' Kel says. 'How exactly are you going to save us?' He scowls, jaw locked, mouth pursed. I meet his gaze, sadness heavier than water filling up my lungs. When I do not answer he pulls his hand from mine. It's like a slap in the face. I want to tell him I'm waiting for the right moment. That we have to stay positive, we have to believe that a window of opportunity will open for us. Timing is everything. But what if there are no opening doors, only doors closing behind us, and each time one closes we are shut further inside this dark, hellish world?

Tug unbound us after the incident with the King's soldiers. He suggested, as though the idea had just come to him, that it would draw less attention if it appeared we were a family hunting together. Kel would just have to keep his eyes down. When I said, for the sake of credibility, he should return my bow and knives, he confiscated my water ration. Brin proposed they skin the wildfowl, take only the furs and abandon the sled and carcasses.

Our captors are nervous, travelling light, ready for anything. Every time I've so much as twitched in the last three hours, Tug has been by my side, ready to stomp out mutiny. During our trek here, they speculated endlessly on the presence of the King's soldiers so far north, when it is (apparently) well known that the King is south, embroiled in war on the Etean border. For all their guesses, they never came close to the truth. The soldiers search for the King's son, Prince Jakut, who came north last summer and whose escort was found slaughtered not far from here before the long-sleep.

'You think the King's army is there?' Brin asks. The four of us stand on a ledge of the mountainside, gazing at the steep drop below. It is the first time since they unbound us that Tug has allowed Kel and I to stand so close together.

'No,' Tug says. 'They might send spies into the Hybourg, but there'd be a full-blown riot if the army tried to ride through it.'

In the moonlight, I take Kel's gloved hand. He wraps his little fingers around my knuckles and twists.

'They're going to sell me,' he hisses.

My muscles clench and my breath grows faster. If Tug and Brin take us straight to the Pit, in less than an hour, Kel may be bought by some rich lowlife, and I will never see him again. I eye the knife in Tug's belt.

The two men are staring down the mountain, absorbed by their reflections on what is going on in the Hybourg. My eyes flit to the wolf dog, head poking out from the top of Tug's rucksack.

Perhaps this is the window, and I need to give it a shove to get it open. Once we are in the town, we won't have two adversaries but thousands. Every man down there would maim, fight, perhaps even kill to get their hands on a prized glitter-eyed child.

You've run out of time, Mirra. It's now or never.

The tiredness in my limbs vanishes as adrenaline surges through my body.

'Tug,' I say. My voice sounds like a strangled squirrel. 'Tug,' I repeat. He turns, wariness already dancing in his eyes. I edge towards him. 'You don't need Kel. You could let my brother go, just sell me. I'm worth a fortune.'

He observes me coldly. 'Please,' I beg. 'Please, Tug.' I let the desperation I have kept mostly hidden slip into my voice. He turns back to the view of the Hybourg, as though the sight of me is too pitiful to behold.

That moment is all I need. I lunge for the wolf dog, seize her by the scruff of the neck and yank her from the bag. Tug spins, reaching for his knife but he has not anticipated the dog move.

I leap away, moving to the edge of the cliff. The dog is too large to dangle over the sheer drop, so I cradle her in my arms.

'Step back, Mirra.'

'Let Kel go before the mutt has another accident.' The wolf dog starts paddling her back legs. Carrying her with my injured arm is hard enough, without the extra struggle.

'You can't help your brother if you fall off the edge of a cliff.'

'Get going, Kel.' I glance around and catch the look of shock in my brother's golden-flecked eyes. 'Get going!'

He moves towards the slope, tentatively at first, then with more speed. In response, Brin crosses to intervene, but Tug holds out an arm to stop his associate.

I lock gazes with Tug, while dipping into Kel's mind. Through the blurry haze of panicked thoughts I see him scrambling up a rocky slope. *Run, Kel. Run!*

'You're sending him to his death,' Tug says. 'A cold, frightened, lonely death, if he is lucky. Ripped from limb to limb by savage, hungry beasts, if he is not. Now let the dog go before we have to scrape you both off the rocks below.'

Frustration and disappointment crush me. I have been patient. I have waited four days for Tug to make an error, to let his guard slip, to find a way through the fortress of his mind. And now I'm forced to desperate acts.

'You don't need, Kel. I'm worth a fortune.' I repeat the words over and over, but Tug is right. Kel won't get far by himself.

I hold out the wolf dog. Tug hooks her up, swings her over his shoulder, and drops her into the rucksack as though she were a kitten. I move away from the cliff edge as Brin swaggers towards me. I take a deep breath, trying not to be intimidated, but his fist rises and fires towards my face.

The next thing I'm aware of is the cold, and the pain. I blink at the night sky. Stars twinkle. For a moment I have no idea where I am. The world seems beautiful, quiet and frozen.

Kel's anguished cry shakes me back to reality. Everything beautiful vanishes.

Brin curses in the distance. 'Stop kicking or I'll knock you out.'

I struggle to sit up. My hand reaches for the enormous lump beneath my eye. A little way off, Brin twists Kel's arm, dragging him back down the hill. My brother shouts until a palm clamps over his mouth. Then he stops struggling.

Beast-face's only weakness is the stupid wolf dog. I should have thrown it from the cliff just to show him he doesn't control everything. Even now, he stands with his back to us looking at the Hybourg, as though our scrabble for freedom is so insignificant, it doesn't even bear watching through to the end.

I hug my arms around my chest and shiver. Snow has gotten into my hood, and a wet patch presses into my back. I clamber to my feet. I cannot bargain the information about the King's soldiers searching for the missing Prince of Caruca. I don't know if it is of any value to Tug, but if he suspected I knew something, he would simply beat it out of me, or hurt Kel until I revealed what I've hidden. A diversion to free

Kel is pointless. I need to escape with him, but with Tug pre-empting everything I do that's next to impossible. I have run out of time. The only option left is to offer cooperation during my own sale, in exchange for information concerning Kel's buyer. Tug doesn't care what happens to us after he has been paid—whether Kel and I escape our new masters is not his concern. But he will have difficulty raising a good price for me if he cannot prove I have the sight. And besides the dog, the only thing he cares about is coin.

I fight a sinking feeling, hold a chip of snow to my swollen cheek-bone, and hope Tug does not hold a grudge against me for threatening his precious wolf dog's life, for the second time.

EIGHT

We slink through backstreets of the Hybourg, Tug and Brin with their knives drawn, Kel and I wedged between them. My brother trembles and in the occasional flicker of firelight I catch sight of the new bruise on his face. I am terrified too. Behind these crowded walls, inside cramped homes built from the same black slabs as the giant market pit, there are more minds than fish in a river.

The relentless fragments of memory disorientate me. It is difficult to focus on the real danger; men who pass by hunched under the weight of giant hemp bags; the occasional group of gamblers gathered around dumpster fires, smoke twisting on the crisp air and cloaking their movements.

Beneath the smoke lingers an acrid, burning stink that sticks to my nostril hairs. Along with the animal dung and the dirty water coursing in drains, it is enough to make me clutch my stomach, and breathe through my mouth. We curve into a long street of tilted houses, and are met by the thunder of running boots echoing off the close walls.

Five boys appear from the shadows, tearing towards us. The oldest is about my age, the youngest smaller than Kel. Tug crushes Kel and I against a wall and Brin jumps to his side to conceal us. The boys fly past hollering and screeching before they whip into an alley and vanish, slapping boots and voices vanishing with them as though they have been swallowed into another world.

A ghostly silence hangs on the air, broken a second later by two men running up the street, shouting obscenities. They blunder past, knives glinting, fury in their eyes and their voices. My ears thrum with blood. I press Kel's head against me, feeling more naked here without my knives than in the forests and outlands.

I have not been near a town for nearly six years, since Kel was born. My yearning for a life beyond Blackfoot forest has grown with every passing long-sleep, but this is not the sort of place you can relax for one minute. This is not the sort of place anyone would desire to go.

Tug eventually allows Kel and me to breathe again by removing his crushing bulk. We hurry down the street, following Brin into an empty tavern with one torch burning in the arched doorway. If Tug intends to take Kel straight to the Pit and leave me with Brin, I have only moments to bargain. But before I can do anything, Brin pushes Kel towards a wooden stairway while Tug greets the innkeeper. Relief pools out from my stomach making my arms and legs limp. I want to hug Kel and cry. Instead, I reach for Kel's hand as he hovers before the first step.

'It's OK, Kel,' I say. 'They're just stairs.'

Brin bustles us up, then Tug arrives with the key to the room, and we all enter. One double bed, a fireplace, a bathroom. The bare essentials, but Kel has never been inside a room before and his face opens, fascinated and afraid. Tug checks the window and closes the wooden shutter. Both men unload their packs. Brin sets about tying Kel to the bed frame.

'You think anyone saw his eyes?' Brin asks.

'We'll soon know one way or another.'

'How are we going to get him to the Pit?' Brin finishes with Kel's hands and ties his feet, linking the rope so that Kel cannot stretch out. Tug picks up the dog and strokes its muzzle. Its tongue lolls, and it's panting though it's been riding in Tug's backpack.

'The same way we've made it here so far,' Tug says.

I keep my head lowered, trying to decipher if Beast-face is treating me differently after my stunt with the dog. If anything, he seems to pay less attention to me than before. He's seen what I've got and it doesn't stack up to much. But if I can get him to believe taking me to the Pit is in their interests, I could find valuable information about the man who buys Kel.

'I can warn you,' I say.

Tug's wolf-like eyes gleam at me. 'About what?'

'Anyone following us, lurking in side alleys, planning an ambush.'

Brin's gaze slides towards Tug and he shakes his head. Brin does not trust me. But it's more than that. He is still afraid of my talent, refusing even to bind me, though he has finished with Kel.

Tug puts the dog on the raised bed and ties my ropes himself. He jams my wrists together, fibre biting into my torn flesh. Then he stops, breath tickling my nostrils as he scrutinises me. Heat rises to my cheeks. His gaze seems to say he knows what I'm thinking—my reasons for going with them to the Pit. I might be the one that can trawl his mind, but he is the one that sees straight through me. Once I am bound, he picks up the dog and the men leave, locking the door behind them.

At least he didn't refuse to take me. Perhaps he's considering it.

'I'm thirsty,' Kel says.

'I know.' He must be hungry too. We have only eaten scraps for days. I scoot up beside him. There is not enough free rope to circle my arms around him. He leans against my side. I rest back against the bed frame and lie my head on his. The two of us, exhausted, half-starving, fall asleep almost at once.

I AM POKED and shaken towards consciousness. My body aches, my head pulses where Brin's fist met my face. It's like someone stuffed my cheek with small buds of snow cotton that push up into my eye. And the memories. The memories are draining. Even in sleep, the violence, blood and duplicity of the Hybourg has seeped into my dreams.

That shaking again.

'Mirra, wake up,' my brother whispers. I raise my eyebrows,

hoping my eyelids will move up with them. Prisms of light swim across my vision. It is day. How long have I been out of it? I scramble to sit from where I'm lying in a foetal position, feet and hands still tied to the bed frame.

'Hey, Bud,' I croak. The bruise on the side of his forehead where Brin struggled with him has turned a purply-blue. His skin is paler than ever, and moon shadows have formed under his bright blue and gold swirling irises. He stares at the floor near the door. There is a tray with two full bowls of white flaky slop. It has been purposefully left out of our bound-up reach.

Wood crackles in the adjoining washroom, the sound of a fire being lit with damp sticks.

'Which one?' I whisper.

'Tug,' Kel whispers back. Tug must be boiling water for the tub. I wonder how long he intends to leave us waiting. It is punishment for my defiance yesterday and Kel's attempted escape. Or it is simple logistics. He cannot unbind us to eat and wash at the same time. Perhaps our needs don't even enter the equation.

The tantalisation of food so close by, and not being able to reach it makes every passing moment torturous. Worse because we do not know how long we will sit here before Tug concedes to let us eat. Not wanting to give the Beast-face satisfaction in such torment, I turn my thoughts to Kel. Somehow, I will make Tug pay for the tattered hope and agony on my brother's small face. Somehow, Tug will regret the day he ever crossed us in Blackfoot forest. As the anger simmers, I remind myself that every second I have now with my brother, might one day be a second I would kill to get back. I push down the resentment and raise my bound hands to remove my lodestone.

'I want you to have this,' I say, twisting and fumbling to undo the thread. My trusted lodestone has been with me for five years. Rest it on a leaf in a river and it will always turn so one end faces north.

My brother's eyes flick up from the porridge. 'Why?'

'Because.'

'No point.' Despite his protests, I place the leather string over his neck, and hold it with my teeth to tie it. 'You're my north now,' I say, tucking it inside the fur of his parka. 'Wherever I go, I'll always be heading for you.'

Scowling, he turns his shoulder to me and fixes his gaze back on the food.

A sound of splashing water comes from the washroom. We both grow still. Tug exits amid a faint haze of lavender and mint. He kicks the tray towards us. The porridge slops down the sides of the wooden bowls. My brother stretches as far as his rope allows, grabs the bowl within reach and starts gulping. If I twist to the end of my ties, I could inch the tray close enough to take the second bowl. But Tug's eyes are glued to me. I have the impression I'm being tested for something I can't pass. I stare back, heart pounding in my chest. The wolf dog is no longer with us, I realise. And if it hasn't survived, I am to blame.

My body twitches as the hunger claws at me. I resist until Tug grunts, wanders across the wooden floor and closes the washroom door behind him. Manoeuvring myself as close to the porridge as I can get, I stretch out my fingertips and touch the tray. Easy now. I twist the wooden board across the ground. Finally, I can wrap my palms around the sides of the container. With shaking arms, I raise it to my mouth. The gruel is cold and tasteless but its like sunshine on my dry, cracked lips. I attempt to drink slowly. Kel grabs the tray and mops up where the mush spilt. He is licking and licking though there is nothing left, only wood splinters to prick his tongue.

'Here,' I say, giving him my half-drunk slop. He takes it without hesitation and I watch him guzzle it down, regretful to see it go. But after all these years of taking care of my baby brother, the gesture is instinctive and seeing him eat makes me feel better.

A faint shimmer of warmth oozes from the washroom, along with the smell of burning pine. The fire has taken. In the fort where my mother grew up, they had fires beneath the clay floors to heat the baths and the bedrooms. But I know from our cottage in the town we moved to when I was seven, after my glitter eyes had settled, and from my father's memories, in most places bath water is boiled, then poured into a tub.

A loud rap at the door makes Kel and me jump. A splash comes from the washroom, followed by the sound of wet feet slapping on the wood floor. Tug appears with a fold of material around his waist. His broad arms and hairy chest drip water. Wavy hair hangs around his tattooed, unshaven face. He walks to the door, knife handle curled in his fist.

'Who's there?'

'It's me,' Brin says. Tug's shoulders relax and he steps aside. Brin enters, emptying a large thread sack on the bed. I strain to see what he has brought. A grey dress, a pair of boy's trousers, a tunic, and a brassiere which is far too big for my flat chest. They mean to dress us up and sell us as prize objects to rich, scheming merchants. The idea sends invisible bugs crawling across my skin, but it will have its advantages. A wealthy man who believes I am a helpless, dainty shadow weaver, waiting to be bent to his will, will not pre-empt me the way Tug can.

'How are things looking?' Tug asks.

'They're being very cagey about who they're letting in and out. Rumours about the King's soldiers has got everyone on edge.'

'Not good for business.'

Brin glances at me before he speaks again. 'Maybe we should wait a couple of days.'

'No. Every day increases the risks.'

The tension in Brin's arms and fists relaxes. He is glad Tug has refused to wait. He wishes to be rid of me as soon as possible.

'Let's get the boy ready,' Tug says. Brin unknots the rope at Kel's feet, lifts him up and carries him to the washroom. Tug strides over to the window. It is high up in the wall and despite the cross slats angled to cut down the wind, a chill breeze leaks through when he opens the shutter. Droplets of water cool on his bare back, but he doesn't notice the cold.

'I've decided to take you with us to the Pit,' he says, watching the street below. 'You will be another set of eyes that can see what men wish to hide. Try anything again and I'll kill you. Or him,' he adds. 'Both of you. No matter how much coin it costs me.'

I nod even though he isn't looking. Thank the heavens! I dig my fingers into my palm and force my breathing to remain calm. I will see the low-life who buys Kel, travel through his mind and discover where he is from and what he intends with my brother's skill. And when Tug's purse is full from my own sale and he is thankful to see the back of me, I will escape and do what I am good at. I will track and hunt. Only not with beasts of the forest, but with the man who thinks he owns my brother.

NINE

By day the streets of the Hybourg are grim and depressing and seem only mildly less dangerous than the previous night. Watery sunlight struggles through the knitted roofs of houses built so close together, the residents have hung washing lines from windows on one side of the street to the other. Though it has not yet warmed above water freezing temperatures, the snow has long gone from the dirty walkways, pushed into enormous piles. The Pit looms in the distance, a black mountain with its head chopped off.

Tug holds tight to the top of my arm. His other hand rests over the knife sheath on his belt. Brin and Kel walk ahead, Kel dressed in deerskin trousers, a dark blue tunic and a cloak with the hood pulled well over his downturned head. So far, we have attracted no untoward attention.

We pass an open square where manacled men and women with bony, mud-streaked faces build a wall from a mountain of cut black rock. A covered water well stands in the middle of the square. A wooden pen holds a dozen wild fowl with red jowls and bright blue feathers. I have seen this bird in my mother's memories. They're popular for their eggs and meat, though they look too skinny to bother choking.

Apart from those chained, there are no women on the street. I go unnoticed because Tug did not make me change from my sturdy boots, trousers and parka. Still, I pull my hood further over my forehead and I'm grateful that our captors are not stupid enough to make me wear the dress in public.

We are now so close to the Pit I have to tilt back my head to the grey sky to see the top of it. From this distance, slit windows high in the framework have become visible, like small scars or pointy teeth. Unlike the Hybourg houses and inns cobbled from the black rock, the Pit walls are not decorated with broken coloured glass and reflective metals. The rock is smooth and appears seamless.

Before we turn the corner, I sense the storm up ahead. Hundreds of men choke up the mind-world. The scraps of memory create muddy, swirling layers upon layers. Inwardly, I shrink from the mayhem. Kel, who up until five days ago had never met a living soul other than our family, must be horrified.

A dark, arched tunnel where men swarm, distinguishes the Pit entrance. I count eight guards patrolling the crowds, marked by the strange metal bands laced up their bare arms, the black armour, the metal around their necks and their size. Each one of them is huge, as though they've crossed species with giants. Not the sort of men even Tug could scrap with and walk away from uninjured.

The crowd ebbs and sways with a tidal push as the swell grows on one side, then builds from the other. Even the men with slave women and children struggle to reach the guards and get inside. Men carry crystal and stone wares around their necks, crates of goods they wish to trade, animals in cages. Tug and I, tight against Brin and Kel, surf forwards on a wave of movement. Once we are deep in the throng there is a lull, and we are hemmed in with nowhere to go.

Brin elbows left and right, forcing tiny gaps. We weave one way, then the other, getting no closer to the tunnel. A pulse of energy in the mind-world hooks my attention. Not the Hybourg's usual, ominous violence, but something I sense is connected to Kel. Someone has taken an interest in him. Tug keeps elbowing left. I scan faces, searching for someone who doesn't fit the crowd. Small spaces open, drawing us towards a man who does not argue with his neighbour, who is not carrying goods, or pushing and shoving. And there is another like him further clockwise, waiting patiently. I shudder, realising we have been guided into a wide circle of men that do not observe one another, but their shaved heads and a square tattoo above the ear unites them.

Brin thrusts forward as a crack appears in the crowd, pulling us closer to the heart of the gang. I grasp his arm. He jerks, eyes flicking to me with repulsion. But he understands at once I have discerned something. Tug scrupulously studies the crowd.

'South-east,' I call to him over the rumble of men jeering, laughing, holding up their wares and shouting at the guards what they have to sell. Tug's gaze swoops over the gang. He nods at Brin and we retreat in the other direction towards a weak link in their circle.

There is a flurry of movement. Four men, like arrows from a multi-crossbow, shaft towards us, ploughing down anyone in their way. Brin yanks Kel behind him. Tug dives to his side. I draw my brother close and pull him to the ground. Realising I am not breathing, I force myself to suck in air.

Tug and Brin swivel their knives, taking up fighting stances. A slim man to my left with a long, whiskery beard holds a chinking crate. His occupied arms leave the knife on his belt clear for the taking. The blade is possibly frozen in the pouch because of the cold. The wooden knife handle looks battered and old. I glance at the two gang members Tug and Brin cannot see—the ones heading us off from behind. Neither pays me the slightest attention.

I grab the rusty knife. The whiskery man doesn't even notice as I take it from his belt. He is too busy trying to back away and save whatever he is carrying.

There is a loud shout. The four men in front besiege Tug and Brin. They begin fighting close quarters. One of the gang falls to his knees bleeding. Those nearby start pushing out, clearing a ring around the fight, but Kel and I are still penned in from behind. My stomach heaves, and no amount of deep breathing can calm the pounding in my chest.

Eyes glued to the fight, I automatically estimate the weight of the blade I have stolen. I may detest my captors, but naivety is not possible when you have the sight. There are worse fates than Beast-face and Fishnet-head. This gang is one of those.

Brin punches and parries the blows of a skilled adversary. The two others, recognising Tug's strength, prise him away from Brin's side. Knives slash at Tug's shoulders, thrust towards his legs. Tug's defence is unassailable, but he has no time to strike back.

On one side of the crowd, two more gang members close in. On the other, three guards, a head taller than everyone, plunge forwards. Men scatter around them. But they have a five metre wall to get through before they reach us, and while the crowd tries to keep their distance, excitement over the fight means people further behind are shoving forward for a better look.

I search for an opening, an escape. But if we tried tunnelling through the crowd, Kel would get crushed, possibly knocked to the floor. I am too small to hold the surging masses off him. And if anyone saw his eyes, we would be stampeded.

Shouts of encouragement fill the air. One man hollers numbers. I think he is taking bets on who will win or die. The nippiest of Tug's assailants retreats as the two newest comers join the fight. Tug seizes the opportunity to attack. But it's a mistake. A set-up. As he head-butts one man and elbows the other in the throat, the nippiest gang member uses the distraction, to leap in for a fatal strike.

Me. Gang man. Tug. If the gang takes Kel, it's over.

My mind empties. I breathe in, zoning out the shouts of the crowd. Exhaling, I flex my wrist and flip the knife. A gesture I've made a hundred thousand times. A gesture more natural to me than laughter.

The rusty blade spins once through the air. A fraction of a second before the man plunges his knife into Tug, my rusty blade catches his shoulder. He cries out, losing the force of his strike. As his blade jabs into Tug, Tug leaps back. The knife slashes Tug's furs, but gets no purchase between his ribs.

The man I've struck turns furiously, searching for the knife thrower. Tug executes the fastest punch I've ever seen, and his assailant falls to the ground unconscious.

As the guards reach us, the remaining gang members back away. I pull Kel beneath me. The one who has knocked down Brin, slithers into a sea of people. Three men sprawl at Tug's feet, winded and struggling for breath. I've lost sight of the other two.

'What's the reason for this?' a guard enquires. I am sheltering Kel with my arm, but I can't hide him altogether. The guard yanks him up. Kel raises his eyes, fear and shock in his blue and golden irises. People see. A whisper faster than the wind blows across the crowd. 'Better bring him through then. Before there are any more accidents.'

Tug helps Brin to his feet. The three guards surround us, one on each side, one behind. As we are wrangled forward, Tug raises the hem of his fur to inspect his side. There's a line of blood dripping like a claw scratch. As I raise my eyes from the wound, he looks at me. There is something new in his expression, but only the Gods know what he is thinking, because I don't understand Beast-face's emotions. Nor do I want to.

We enter a dank, putrid-smelling tunnel. It stinks of sweat, dirt and animal dung. It stinks of fear, depravity and the end.

TEN

High up in the enormous bazaar, daylight shards through slit windows, like swords vanishing into a pool of blackness. Low in the Pit, the only light comes from fire lamps embedded in the deep walls and men carrying torches. A cloudy gloom hangs across the indoor market. Men bargain and haggle over the goods they sell from portable stalls or from their own persons. But the real attraction is in the centre of the arena. Raised on great platforms as far back as the eye can see, sit rows of wooden cages.

I hold Kel's hand, both of us stunned. Tug and Brin press against us, one on either side. The escorting guards follow behind. The nearer cages contain wolves, wolverines, falcons, and eagles. As we progress further into the murk I see animals I don't recognise. Beasts with scaly skin, creatures that appear familiar, like deer, but their coats are striped and tinged blue.

A screeching cry pierces the arena. For the space of a single breath, the Pit falls silent to listen. Kel's hand becomes bone-cracking tight around my own. A flap of enormous wings beats in the sudden hush. Twenty feet away, a magnificent creature rises to the air. It shrieks again, wings pounding, cries echoing off the high black walls. It launches into the top of its huge prison, bashing the wooden bars. A heavy chain clangs around its webbed foot. Its mind comes to me in wild, enraged flashes of madness. It knows it cannot escape, yet it tries over and over, refusing to be tamed. Refusing to give up.

I have never seen a velaraptor, but my father told me stories of their existence in the glacial mountains. Almost impossible to catch. Carucans believe they are mystical creatures, with magical powers. Its wingspan is over six feet, the limbs featherless, muscular. Its enormous beak and wide lizard eyes give the impression of a bird crossed with a reptile.

Movement snaps my attention back to the remaining cages. The next forty feet of the Pit contain slave men, women, boys and girls. Lots of girls. Young, dishevelled, bruised figures, with dead eyes. The bargaining over them is ferocious and turnover quick, with two girls and one boy being paid for while we pass. Slaves are against the law in Caruca, but it is a law Pa says no one enforces. The vast majority of people wealthy enough to keep slaves have them.

Every part of my body screams to get Kel out of there. I should not have saved Tug from the knife of that gang member. A hard blade between the ribs would have resulted in a slow and painful death. A death Beast-face deserves. A death I fantasise about offering him myself.

Our group stops. For a second I'm confused. There are no more cages. The guards direct us down a dark passage leading into the Pit walls.

'Take the boy to the top of the stairs and wait,' one of them says. They hang back as we advance. Around the corner lies a flight of open metal stairs. Kel's legs knock together so Brin lifts him and carries him up. From the first stair, I turn to Tug. Blood seeps through his shirt, but he does not try to staunch it. Almost level with his eyes, I glare at him.

'One day,' I say, disgust, fear and outrage seeping through my trembling voice, 'far from now, I will make you suffer. You think it is no longer possible. But I will find a way.'

He stares at me without a single emotion. He knows I saved him with that peasant's rusty knife, but shows neither surprise nor gratitude. He understands it was an act of immediate necessity. 'Revenge is a fool's dish,' he says, a large hand clamping down on my arm, pushing me around, and up the stairs.

At the top of the stairwell, Brin and Kel wait in front of a cage door that gives access to a web of interlocking metal bridges, platforms and individual enclosures. Billows of drifting smoke rise from the Pit below, shrouding the cages in cloaks of grey. Fingers of daylight reach in from the high slit windows and bleed through the murk so it is just possible to fathom this horrific world. Most of the suspended cages are empty. But a handful of shadow children with sparkling eyes crouch in the darkness.

A guard accompanied by a small, shuffling man, clangs across the intricate weave of bridges. I kneel and pull Kel to me so I am blocking the door from his sight.

'Listen to me, Kel,' I say, holding tight to both his arms. My heart-beat thrums so hard my chest hurts. 'Whatever happens, don't give up. I will find you. I'm going to find you.'

A faint smell of urine tells me Kel has wet himself. His face is slack with shock. I'm not sure he can even hear my words, let alone believe them.

'Kel, promise me. Promise me you won't give up.' I cup my hands around his cheeks. His eyes lift to mine. 'That's it. You're strong, Kel. You are strong like Pa. You are Uru Ana and I will find you. No matter how long it takes. No matter how long it takes. You hear me?'

'How?' he whispers, his bottom lip trembling. 'How?'

'I don't know. But Ma and Pa are out there waiting for us to return. They will never stop waiting for you.'

'What if they take the mist berries and forget?'

'Pa's never taken the mist berries. He's never forgotten anything. He will never forget you. And neither will I.'

'Mirra, don't let them take me.' My brother's long wet lashes blink in panic. I'm afraid I will fall apart right there in front of him.

'I love you,' I say again and again. He hugs me so tight, I stop breathing. His little arms cling to my neck. His face pushes into my hair, the tip of his nose cold and wet against my skin. Tears spill from my eyes. I brush them aside.

Keys rattle in the barred door. I catch the guard's wary expression.

The small man's beady eyes watch me with interest. I imagine stolen glitter-eyed children don't hug their captors goodbye. Tug leans in close.

'That's enough.' There's warning in his voice. To all appearances, Kel and I do not look related, but if the guard or the clerk starts asking questions, Tug may force me to leave the Pit, and I will not see the man who buys Kel. Then how will I track him?

I prise off Kel's arms. 'Let go now,' I whisper to him. 'You have to let go.'

'Please don't leave me, Mirra. Please.'

'You have to let go.' I unclasp one little arm and at once, Tug has Kel in his grip and is lifting him and handing him over to the guard. I force myself to watch, in case my brother needs to see me standing strong. Not hopeless, not despairing. But as the huge guard carries him across fifteen-foot high metal platforms towards the cages, Kel doesn't look back. It cuts like a knife to my heart.

The scrawny man with the beady eyes produces a book of string bound pages. He scratches words with a feather nib, gets Tug and Brin to sign something and then produces a metal bracelet. Tug gestures that Brin will wear the bracelet. It is locked onto Brin's wrist with a key from around the man's neck. The man hands Brin a metal disc and then Tug is pushing me back down the stairs.

ELEVEN

My feet shuffle after Tug into a labyrinth of food stands behind
the regular slave cages. Men fry meat dishes in breadcrumbs
and brown powder. Sellers move around with nuts, teas, and berries. I
wander blindly, the spicy smells making me nauseous. I have abandoned him. He didn't turn around because he no longer counts on me.
He's stopped believing I can save him.

We climb steps and clang across a metal walkway. I glance at the
smoke roiling above us, glimpse the network of cages suspended overhead. Tug pushes me into a chair and sits down beside me.

A man arrives with a tray of mint tea, pine nuts and a long, cone-
shaped object. He places a cloth beside Brin. In red on the cream linen,
as though written in blood, is the number five. I stare at it. For a
second, I cannot rip through the emotional haze to grasp its meaning.

Tug's look brings me back from the numbness. I clench my teeth,
and take in where we are seated. The eating house is made of metal
barriers and arched walkways, reminiscent of a mammoth monster
skeleton. Bounty hunters with greedy faces and satisfied sneers guzzle
the offerings laid on their tables while they wait. Wealthy men in bear
furs press cone-shaped objects to their starward-gazing eyes.

I slide the cone-shaped eyeglass off the table, and hold one end to my eye and the other skywards. The glass magnifies the platforms above the food maze. Our position is ideal for viewing the caged children.

As I adjust to one-eyed vision, a girl with sparkling gold and green irises, wearing a frilly dress, comes into focus. Her hands clasp a shiny purse. She stares forward, motionless. She is terribly young, three or four years from her eyes changing. My airway closes making it harder to breathe, a sensation intensified by the cooking smoke.

The girl has been dressed like some rich person's pet toy. Perhaps for a spoilt daughter to play with, until she is six or seven and can be used for more treacherous tasks or be resold. I bite my inner cheek, anger flooding back. When I spot the number five painted across Kel's new blue tunic, the crush in my throat leaves me choking. Suddenly, the eyeglass is being ripped from my hands. It disappears inside the bulk of Tug's furs.

'Draw any more attention to yourself,' he says, 'and I'll lock you back in the room until this is over.'

I have attracted the gaze of a man sitting by a table three feet away. He appears neither old enough, nor wealthy enough to be a buyer, neither brute nor mercenary enough to be a bounty hunter. I catch his eye for less than a second, but it is long enough to worry he might have realised I am no boy. I twist away and grab a handful of nuts before Tug or Brin can stop me.

Making Tug suffer is not enough. He and Brin didn't snatch the three-year-old girl dressed like a doll. They aren't responsible for turning us into fugitives, for the hundreds of Uru Ana families hiding in the Sea of Trees, for the thousands more working in the tundra mines until they die of exhaustion. I will get my revenge on Tug, and I will kill the man that buys Kel if I have to, but every low-life scum who has sat in this dive, should know the fear of the children they trade here.

Pa's voice rings in my head. *Freedom consists not in doing what we like, but in having the courage to do what we ought.* His answer when I once asked why he didn't resent Kel and me, or more importantly our mother who never told him about her Uru Ana blood until I was born, for taking so much away from him.

Pa's answer had annoyed me and seemed evasive. But now his words seem apt. Someone ought to fight back, breed fear into the bounty hunters roaming the outland forests, attack the tundra mines. If the Uru Ana want freedom, they have to start thinking like they're free. Stop running and hiding.

Minutes pass, the attendant serving our table goes to and fro with folded pieces of cloth. From the conversations that ensue, it is apparent the two cloths Brin receives are offers for Kel. Tug is in no hurry to accept, but Brin is keen to do business and leave.

An image appears in the now-time, so clear it eclipses all the muddy snatches of memory swirling around the Pit and rouses me from my brooding.

A fire crackles in the hearth of a humble stone home. He crouches in front of it, furs wrapped around his linen shirt, warming himself. An old man sleeps on a thin mattress nearby. Beyond the window shutters, pale light skims the horizon. He opens his fist to examine two gold rings. One, a signet ring with letters and symbols around the ruby centre and symbols on the thick gold band, the other a hawk's head embedded in emeralds. He tosses them in his palm as though considering their significance.

I sit up straight and squint sideways to see the owner of the memory. Surprise shakes off all sullen exhaustion. It is the young man who noticed me earlier. Except now he holds the eyeglass to his face, which gives me a chance to take in his appearance. Bushy eyebrows, a whiskery growth of beard, greasy hair cut to his shoulders. He is not watching the Uru Ana cages, but directs the magnifying lens into the crowded Pit, tracking a guard.

As though sensing me, he lowers the viewing glass. I turn away at once. But in the mind-world I reach for him and am plunged into a desolate landscape much like a vast forest ravaged by pest or fire. I startle and retreat.

His mind reminds me of my mother's when, six weeks before Kel's second birthday, we woke to find she did not know who we were. The memory loss is an effect of the ancient Carucan ceremony of rebirth sometimes performed before the hibernation. If enough mist berries are consumed right before the long-sleep, it is said the soul travels through the spirit-world to return cleansed of all that ails it.

In my mother's case, she didn't forget her music or her dancing, her friends, the home she grew up in, the picnics and lakes and swimming. She didn't forget meeting and falling in love with Pa. She only forgot Kel and me.

But this man seems to remember almost nothing of the nineteen or twenty years he lived before waking a fortnight ago. I have never seen such total obliteration of memory brought on by the spiritual cleansing.

My heartbeat speeds up in anticipation. The odd whiskery beard and greasy hair resemble a disguise. The rings are those of a nobleman. I make sure no one is paying me any attention and slip back into his mind.

He stands in a washroom, examining a deep wound across his chest. It is a scar like a scimitar knife or a new moon.

'It is ready,' a voice says. An elderly man with clouded eyes and long silver hair stands reflected in the washroom mirror. The young man lifts the linen shirt back onto his bony shoulder, concealing the scar. The two gold rings now hang on a leather cord around his neck.

'Are you sure I gave you no other details of the attack on my escort?' he asks.

'I joined you,' the old man answers, 'only three weeks before the long-sleep, and we talked very little. You said the Kingdom believes you are dead in the attack, and it would be better if they continued to believe it. You spent most of your time with the Carucan priests in prayer, preparing for the ceremony of rebirth, and did not wish to speak of it further.'

Tug's pinching grip and his low growl bring me back to the Pit. 'Are you sick, boy?' he sneers. 'Do you need me to take you outside?'

I shake him off, feeling momentarily disorientated. My eyes dart to the young man. *Prince!* I remember how the King's officer had found the Prince's escort dead. The soldiers were searching for the missing Prince only three hours from here. Obviously, they did not imagine his royal highness could be in the Hybourg, mingling with the scum and maggots of the most depraved town in the kingdom. Which leads to the question, what is he looking for here?

A guard hands the Prince a sealed note. The Prince of Caruca opens it, his expression turning grim. Coin passes between the men. He folds the note and stands to leave.

'Yes, I'm sick,' I mutter. 'I need fresh air.' Tug scrutinises me. He knows I was desperate to come to the Pit and wouldn't leave Kel without an excellent reason.

'Fine,' he says, dragging me to my feet. Giant fingers press hard into my arm. He leans over and says something to Brin. Thrown by Tug's news we are leaving, Brin shifts on the metal seat and folds his arms. He is not happy. Mostly, I expect, because he does not like me being alone with Tug. He thinks I am casting spells over Tug's mind.

Tug thrusts me forward through the crowded food stalls and we make our way to the exit. In the mind-world I follow the Prince, trailing the distinctive shape of his blighted memories.

Brin will not accept an offer without Tug's approval, and the guards will remember us, so we should be able to get back into the Pit.

As we move through the dingy, fetid tunnel, I make a silent promise. I have never cared for the Gods, but if crossing my path with the Prince of Caruca is their doing, I vow to them I will not waste this surprising opportunity.

TWELVE

Outside, the stark midday light dazzles my vision. I pull the hood of my parka further over my head to shelter from the blistering wind and the eyes of hundreds of men. We slip around the crowds at the Pit entrance and stride across the square. Tug, with his knife in one hand and an arm around my waist, keeps pace. I move with purpose, afraid of losing the Prince's blighted mind among so many others. Once we enter quieter streets my task grows easier and I relax a little.

'I have found a buyer,' I say. Of course, I cannot be certain the Prince was in the Pit searching for an Uru Ana, but it seems a fair guess considering he has lost all his memories and will need someone to help him distinguish friend from enemy. Someone attacked and killed his escort, which means they probably tried to kill him too. If he wishes to return to his prior existence as the Prince of Caruca, he will need some assurance that his life is not in immediate danger from his closest friends and associates.

'We already have three offers.'

'Two,' I correct. 'And I did not mean for Kel.' Beast-face's gaze slides over me. 'What is your highest offer for my brother?'

Tug licks his lips and the balance of his shoulders alters as he walks. 'Ten Carucan gold,' he says. The faint memory of a cloth with the number seven written on it flutters in the mind-world.

'Seven,' I say. 'Disappointing.'

'More than I can earn in a year.'

'Another lie.'

He yanks me to a stop and leers in my face. 'You are not nearly as clever as you suppose.'

'And you are not nearly as stupid as you pretend,' I counter. My chin trembles, expecting a slap, but I do not look away.

'Who is this buyer?' he growls.

'The man the King's soldiers seek.'

His lip rises in an unamused half-smile. He is not happy I have managed to keep information from him.

'I can show you a man who will pay ten times for me what you will get for Kel. Even if the bidding reaches your precious ten Carucan gold. I will take you to this person and cooperate if you and Brin refuse all buyers for Kel and return him to our—', I cut myself off just before I say parents, '—mother,' I finish.

Tug raises his knife and brushes the blade along my neck. Two passersby arc around to avoid us. The freezing outdoor temperature seems to drop another ten degrees.

'You know you cannot trust me, Mirra. Why try to bargain?'

My eyes water with the harsh wind but my will steels and strengthens. Tug was once a man people trusted. He had values and principles. I have seen smoky echoes of an honourable soldier. I need to smash the barricade and pull the past into the present.

'There must be someone you have loved. Someone you would do anything to protect. I've seen the way you look at Kel. You don't have to do this to him. When you sell me you will get what you want. You will be a rich man.'

Something sharp pricks my neck. I gasp and feel warm blood trickling down my skin where he holds his knife.

'Never,' he snarls, 'make the mistake of thinking you can get inside my head.'

'Your life is pitiful and worthless! Why do you even bother?'

He draws the blade along, widening the cut. My heart hammers in my chest. I am terrified I have finally broken the stony facade of control and the consequence will be getting my throat slit. He pants hard as he stoops over me. I raise my watery eyes to his. I made a promise. To Kel, to myself, to the Gods. You will not overwhelm me, Beast-face.

Tug's gaze narrows, his breathing slows. He lowers the blade. 'Keep following the buyer,' he orders, handing me a dirty rag of cloth. I hold it to my neck, which bleeds far more than it stings.

We leave the imposing omnipresence of the Pit behind us and enter a shabby quarter with crooked houses. Streets no wider than a horse and cart. Cobbled back-to-back homes block out the day. Dusk gathers in nooks and doorways.

Overhead, washing flutters on metal sticks from first floor windows. Long strips of cord, tied with twisting mirrors and beads of glass, flap from door beams and shutters. Beggars sit in dark alcoves with missing limbs and burnt faces. I flinch when one unexpectedly rises from a pile of black rock, a strange necklace of forest green glass and scraps of metal rattling on his chest.

Tug stops, retrieves a piece of gut string from his pocket and uses it to fix the rag staunching my bleeding. It would be foolish to refuse his help, but I do not enjoy accepting it.

'Why are the houses decorated with mirrors and coloured glass?' I ask.

'Superstition is rife in the Hybourg and much of northern Caruca. The glass and mirrors are protection against your kind.'

I think of the night they snatched Kel. Brin wished to tie me to a tree and leave me behind, or sell me to the tundra camps. He tried to ward me off with a glass medallion. But not Tug. Tug told him to build a wall in his mind so I couldn't get into his head. Tug is intimately familiar with the Uru Ana. He is not afraid of us because he knows our capabilities and limits. He knows there is no magic to our extra sense, only the skill our own wit can conjure from what we discover about our adversary.

'There is Uru Ana blood in your family,' I guess.

A hood slides over his wolfish eyes. 'I have not the patience to walk in circles,' he answers, 'and with your brother about to be sold to our highest bidder, I'm surprised you think you have the time.'

'Brin will not sell Kel without you,' I say, doubt creeping into my voice.

'Why not?'

'You are the decision maker.'

'Well perhaps I'd already decided.'

He is lying. He must be. If I have sabotaged my only chance of discovering Kel's buyer I will never forgive myself.

'Brin cannot walk out of the Pit alone with a heavy purse of gold. Too many will observe the exchange. It is too risky.'

'Beneath the pit lie a score of underground chambers, a warren of tunnels with more exits leading into the Hybourg than you could count. The transaction will take place in a secured location and Brin will have no problem slipping back into the city unseen.'

No! I will not lose Kel like this! My hands grow hot in my gloves. Rage bubbles in my chest. I spin to face Tug.

'Did you tell Brin to accept an offer?'

'I told you when we first met, forget you ever had a brother.'

'You might as well tell me to tear out my heart and eat it,' I spit, jabbing my elbow up into his nose. There is a small, satisfying crack, followed by a prick of flesh above my hipbone—Tug's knife blade reaching through my furs.

A brittle laugh escapes my lips. 'You've just tried to slit my throat. Do you think I care about a little cut to the waist?'

He glares down at me, the bridge of his nose bleeding. A slight smile transforms his face. Not a sneer but a genuine smile, which grows as he sees my confusion.

'I only scratched your throat. Well, now you have vented your frustrations, tell me of your buyer. Who is the man the King's soldiers search for?'

Is this a game to him? Is it pain that brings Beast-face to life? I can no more manipulate him with words than a wolf or muskox. I thump down in the middle of the cobbled street, a dangerous and half-witted thing to do considering I am now wide open for a beating from his hard boots or passing thieves, but I don't care.

Tug kicks at me. 'Get up.' I stare forward, unresponsive. He grabs the scruff of my parka, lifting me off the ground as though I am a puppy. I hang heavily, fur pressing hard into my neck. 'Nothing a good dip in a well won't fix,' he mutters. He drops me and drags me across the cobbles. My teeth rattle in my skull. The bones in my back jerk and judder. I tense, and twist from his grip.

'Ah, alive, after all.' He sounds like he's enjoying himself.

'Without my cooperation, no one will believe I have the sight. You will get pittance for me. You might as well sell me with the other slave girls in the Pit.'

'Perhaps I will.'

'Then we should get my dress,' I challenge.

Tug barks in what could be a laugh that seldom sees the day. I bristle at his mockery.

'Pride is your downfall,' I hiss. 'You won't accept ten times the gold you could get yourself, because it isn't your idea. You want everything, but are prepared to give nothing. You'd rather lose and have it your way than swallow your pride.' The amusement in his eyes vanishes. He sinks his knife through my furs so it cuts my side. I yelp.

'I warned you of this, Mirra,' he says, thrusting me forwards. 'You try anything with me, it is your brother who will pay the price.'

An image flickers in the shadows of the mind-world, distant, as though trapped in a bell glass.

A girl, sixteen or seventeen, stands haloed by the sun. It shines in her chestnut hair, and sparkles on the sky-blue lake beyond. Her emerald robe rustles in the breeze. Her skin is as smooth as almond butter, her heart-shaped face defiant.

'I begged you not to go!' she shouts, raising her skirts and striding towards him. 'I begged you to let go of the wrongs done to us. You refused. You didn't even try. You were not fighting for me, Tye, you were fighting for your injured pride.' Bitterness flashes across her face. 'I am sorry you cannot rejoice in my happiness,' she says coldly. 'But I will marry him, whether you wish it, or not.'

The distorted memory segues into a fist fight. There is blood, shouting. Tug chases the memory down into the dungeons of his inner self. I glance at him. His eyes meet mine and despite everything, for a moment it's as though a veil lifts and we recognise something in each other.

There was his existence before this girl married another man. An existence where he was Tye, fighting for pride and justice. And there was who he became after. A man who gave himself a beast's face, who drank to forget, who turned to violence and pain to fill his blackened heart.

I was wrong. I can influence him. My words have unlocked what all my mental efforts to penetrate the fortress of his mind could not. I half-expect him to knock me out for the impertinent discovery.

Instead, he pulls me up, tips me towards the facade of a small inn and raises an eyebrow. It is the inn I sensed the Prince enter before I tried to break Tug's nose.

'How did you know?' I ask.

'We passed here two minutes ago and your step faltered then quickened.'

'We did not.'

'Through the alley,' he says, pointing his knife across the street. Beyond, lies a passage as narrow as a drain channel. It shafts onto a road running diagonal to where we stand—I had been taking Tug around a long way, intending to strike a deal before we reached our destination. I had not been aware of my own body giving me away.

THIRTEEN

A wall of heat and a babble of voices hit us as we enter the tavern. It is like stepping into a now-time representation of the mind-world. Incomprehensible noise and movement. Too many smells all crushed together—pies, drinking ale, sweat, meat. Tug expertly guides me through the raucous crowd to a dark passage with a wooden stairway. Either he has an excellent sixth sense, or he has been here before.

I check back to see no one has taken an interest in us and catch the expression on Tug's face. I'm learning to read the tattoo-distorted features. He doubts anyone capable of paying one hundred Carucan gold pieces would slum it here.

'He doesn't want to be found,' I say. But as I mutter the words, my insides contract with anxiety. Surely even a Prince in disguise would not live in such unimpressive quarters. Unless he has been stripped of all coin during the assassination attempt and has no intention or means of returning to his former status, in which case he is useless to me.

We stop on the first floor landing. Four doors, two on either side of the corridor. Grunting and moaning float through the nearest one. Blood rises to my cheeks. Oblivious, Tug moves along to the next and presses his ear against it.

'It is too late to withdraw your brother from the sale,' he says quietly. 'It is not how the Pit works. I cannot say I've changed my mind and leave with him.'

'So hire someone. Pay them to put in a higher offer. You advance him the gold and once the exchange is made, he will bring Kel to an arranged meeting point out of the Hybourg.'

'We are in a town of thieves and mercenaries, Mirra. If I hire a man to buy your brother, give him ten Carucan gold for the purchase, he will either vanish like the wind, or take the money and the boy and run.'

Discouraged, I puff outwards. His logic is infallible. If Tug or Brin had any reliable connections in the Hybourg, they would have asked them to help escort Kel to the Pit.

'The identity and destination of Kel's buyer,' Tug continues, 'is the best you can hope for. Cooperate and I will find out the name of the man who has bought him and where they are headed.'

This is no better than the deal I thought I could wheedle before I discovered the whereabouts of the Prince! Frustration pounds me like a kick to the stomach. I halt in the corridor, planting my feet on the wooden floor, folding my arms.

'What assurances do I have you will share the buyer's identity? You said it yourself, I cannot trust you.'

'It is the best offer you'll get.' He watches me serenely, knowing my decision before I've even made it. I should have stayed in the Pit. Close to Kel. The Gods are not helping me. The Prince is a distraction, a decoy.

I point to the furthest door where I sense the ravaged mind, and raise two fingers to show there are two people inside. Tug edges close, listens at the keyhole, then twists the handle.

'Who's there?' a voice calls.

'Tell him you've come for the sheets,' Tug whispers.

'I have your word about Kel?'

'My word is worth nothing.'

'Who's there?' the voice asks again.

If his word was worth nothing, he would not refuse to give it. 'Your word,' I insist.

The door swings open. Before either of us can react, the hilt of a sword hits Tug in the throat. He grips his windpipe, spluttering and staggering sideways.

Instinct makes me reach for his knife to defend myself, but I stop halfway. With the King's soldiers hunting the sword-wielding Prince, and an assassination attempt on his life, he is bound to be edgy.

As I do not wish to give away my combative nature, I resist the impulse. I do not want him to watch me as militantly as Tug and Brin once I'm in his hands. But I'm heartily disappointed the Prince shows skill enough with a sword to disarm Tug. A sword, which I now find myself at one end of—the tip digging into the flesh between my collar-bones just below the bloodstained rag.

'You'd better come inside,' the young Prince says, twisting a fallen lock of dark hair behind his ear.

I step into a room that, though large, is bare-boned and devoid of luxury. I cannot glean much more because I'm staring down the shaft of a sword pointed at my throat, gazing into hazel eyes.

The Prince's olive skin remains bronzed despite the sunless winter months. Gone are the bushy eyebrows and whiskery beard, though his chin is a little red from where he has pulled off his disguise. He is not plain and inconspicuous, but poised, almost handsome. If I didn't sense the distinctive shape of his blighted mind, I would think I'd made a mistake. He resembles a distant cousin to the man in the Pit. Even the way he walks and holds himself has altered.

'What is your business here?' The Prince's southern accent rolls the vowels.

I edge off my hood and lower my gaze. But not before I see uncertainty flash in his oval eyes. He must recognise us from the Pit, but it seems he did not realise I was female. Tug enters, rubbing his throat with one hand, surrendering up his knife with the other.

'We come here wishing you no harm,' he says, voice strangled from the blow, but also from kowtowing instead of fighting back. I smile to myself at his humiliation.

'Put your knife and any other weapons on the table,' the Prince orders. Tug does as he is told. 'Now sit.'

The Prince prods me with the tip of his sword until I sink into an armchair. Tug sits down opposite me. The blind man from the Prince's memories appears in the doorway of an adjacent room. He closes the door to the hall, and locks us all in together.

The Prince circles around me, studying my face. I inspect his scuffed boots, the cut and lacing typical of the north. Not only is he agile with a sword, but masterful in the art of disguise. Able to mingle with the thieves and criminals of his kingdom as though one of them. Admiration sparks in my chest, but wariness too. Is this what they teach princes in Caruca?

'You are no boy,' he says.

I pretend muteness, relieved I had the good sense not to reach for Tug's knife. The Prince's memories may be desolated, but he has a keen mind.

'Speak, Mirra,' Tug says.

I press my palms together in my lap, directing my voice at the Prince, but still looking down.

'It appears that you are familiar with disguise,' I say, trying to sound soft and feminine.

'I saw you in the Pit,' he says. 'Why have you followed me here?'

Tug pointedly takes in the half-packed bags on the bed. 'It would be a shame to leave the Hybourg without buying what you came for.'

'And what did I come for?'

'Mirra?' Tug prompts. Half of me wants to turn Beast-face into a fool by refusing to speak. He has come here knowing only the scraps I have told him. He has no idea he is face to face with the Prince of Caruca. He doesn't even know about the assassination attempt on the Prince's life. Tug, who has always been one step ahead, is for once in the dark. I revel in this for a few seconds, pretend I'm not ensnared by the hold he has on me because of Kel.

'You came,' I answer softly, 'to solve your own enigma. Why would a man raised in privilege and wealth, with freedom and power, wish to give it all up? Why would a man whose life was in extreme danger, choose a spiritual cleansing before the long-sleep that would wipe away his past and all knowledge of his enemy? You,' I say, raising my eyes and locking gazes with the Prince, 'came here looking for an Uru

Ana whose eyes have settled and who can help you discover the traitor responsible for what has happened.'

The room stills. Tug appears relaxed but there is something sharp in his tattooed face. The Prince rubs his top lip, scanning from me to Tug and back again.

'What is your relationship?' he asks.

'She is mine to sell.'

The Prince crouches beside me. His eyes take in the bruise on my face, the cut to my neck. Then he takes my hands. I am so surprised by the simplicity of the gesture, the gentleness in his touch, that I flinch. He inspects the roughness of my palms, then pushes up a sleeve, revealing the red welt around my wrist.

'How did you catch her?' he asks, eyes never leaving me.

'It is of no importance.'

'It is of the utmost importance to me. If her face is known anywhere, *I* must be aware of it. If you have purchased her from someone else, I must know from whom.'

Tug straightens. 'Her parents kept her hidden in Blackfoot Forest at the foot of the glacial mountains.'

My chest rises and falls. The fewer people who know of my family's existence, the safer my family are. Especially Kel. Silently, I beg that Beast-face will say nothing more of them.

'And where are they now?'

'Dead,' Tug says.

I feel a flush of confusion and gratitude.

'There is no one to come after her,' he continues. 'No one but myself and my associate who know her true nature.'

Well, maybe gratitude is too much. In reporting my family dead, he is only covering himself. Still, it is to my advantage that the Prince knows nothing of Kel, and believes I am alone in the world. He will assume being in the service of a Prince more favourable than wandering the dangerous outland forests with no family to return to. He will not anticipate the risks I will undertake to escape.

The Prince crosses the room to the blind man, who hunches beneath the weight of long furs, his face pale and heavily lined with age. Words are discreetly exchanged. Then the Prince nods and turns back. My eyes flash down to my feet.

'How old are you?' he asks.

'Sixteen.'

'And you have spent every one of these sixteen years in Blackfoot Forest?'

'I lived in the Sea of Trees until I was four and a half. Then we moved to Blackfoot Forest.' I omit to mention the two years we spent farming in Polek, fifty miles from here—after my eyes settled, before Kel was born.

The Prince's gaze seeks his attendant again. He says nothing, and the old man cannot return his look or even be aware of the Prince's silent consultation, but whatever the Prince sees, he seems to come to a decision. I wonder how he lost his whole escort and gained a blind septuagenarian in its stead.

'I will need to test her skills,' he says.

'Ask her what you will.'

'Under circumstances more in keeping with those she will have to perform under. There is a tavern at Bowen Hill, twelve miles south west of here on the western border road. I will wait for you there until midnight.'

Tug rises smoothly, brushing invisible flecks from his furs. 'You have not asked my price.'

A spark of amusement lights the Prince's eyes. 'You doubt my ability to pay?'

Tug's gaze roams across the sparse quarters and rests on the blind man. Not much of a servant.

The humour in the Prince's expression transforms to confusion. He glances over at me, realising Tug does not know who he is dealing with. 'And you have not asked where she is to perform her test,' he says, strolling to the mantlepiece. 'Name your price.'

'One hundred Carucan gold.'

The Prince takes up the fire poker and prods the flames. His brows wrinkle together. 'You and your associate will be in charge of bringing her with us to the fort of Lyndonia.'

'But that is a week's ride from here,' Tug objects.

'When we all arrive safely at the fort, I will pay you one hundred Carucan gold. In Lyndonia, she will be tested. If she passes her test, you will receive another hundred and be free to leave her with me.'

Tug's composure falters at the promise of two hundred Carucan gold. It is, I believe, enough to live well for the rest of his life. 'And if she fails?'

'It is a crime against the King to harbour a shadow weaver. If her true mind-reading nature is discovered during the test, she will be executed. Anyone suspected of knowing and protecting her sight will be tried and executed alongside her. I, of course, will deny all knowledge of her abilities.'

His words are like a cold stone sinking in my chest. I look to Tug, wondering if he will accept such dangerous conditions. Beast-face gives nothing away. Coin chinks as the Prince takes a purse from his tunic pocket and counts three gold coins. He places them on the ledge above the fireplace. They glimmer in the faint daylight, no mistaking they are solid.

'For considering my offer,' he says. 'If you accept, be sure to buy thoroughbred horses. I would not want you to be cheated. There will be a long ride ahead of us and it is imperative we travel fast.'

The blind man unlocks the door and steps to one side, showing it is time for us to leave.

Tug gathers up the coins in his large hands. 'I like to know who I'm dealing with,' he says.

The Prince nods. 'At present I go by the name of Ule. If my true identity is what you seek, perhaps your girl here will give it up in exchange for a proper meal.'

Avoiding the death stare Tug is undoubtedly shooting my way, I scuttle across the room.

'I will wait no later than midnight,' the Prince says as Tug follows. 'The King's soldiers are rumoured to be shutting off both roads out of the Hybourg. Once you've made your decision, I advise you leave without delay.'

He is confident Tug will say "yes", I think, as we hurry down the wooden stairs and out onto the cobbled street. And I'm scared the Prince's assessment is right. Though I'm not sure it is the promise of so much coin that will decide Beast-face. I have a feeling he will not be able to walk away from such a risky challenge.

If Tug agrees, and he and Brin accompany us to this fort, I have little hope of escaping my new owner for days, perhaps weeks. Time that will take me further and further from Kel. Time where my little brother is in danger of giving up hope, and I am in danger of losing his trail.

FOURTEEN

B ack in the lodgings where we slept the previous night, Tug ties my hands and feet to the bedpost and goes to stand by the dark slatted window. He has his knife out, flicking it back and forth in his wrist.

'This is a dangerous game,' he mutters. I do not know how to answer. He could end it now. The power is in his hands. All he'd have to do is take Kel and me back to the forest. But I know he will not. 'Who is he?'

I bite my lips together. I cannot decide whether the Prince's identity will encourage or dissuade Beast-face. Better to say nothing.

Surprisingly, he does not force my answer. 'I must return to the Pit.' He gathers a piece of cloth and comes and kneels before me. His thick fingers untie the gut string holding the bloody rag to my neck. He tears another piece of cloth from some fabric with his knife.

'The man is too unpredictable,' I say, hoping to plant a seed of doubt. Tug's steady eyes stare at me. I open my mouth to water the seed further, and his large fingers stuff the cloth against my tongue.

Once he is gone, there is no use struggling against the ropes around my feet and hands. Tug's knots are the kind you'd have difficulty cutting your way through with a knife. I watch the candle whittle down, leaving a creamy pool on the round table.

Two hours pass, perhaps longer. And with the hours, worry and hunger fester, rising in me until I am fraught and desperate. I fear Kel's reaction to his sale. I fret Tug will discover nothing about the man who buys my brother, and his and Brin's memories of the transaction, if I can find them, will be useless: a nameless face, one of millions in the Carucan Kingdom. Isn't that the whole point of the Pit? Isn't it designed to protect the identities of investors as well as sellers?

I long for anything to break the silence and darkness, even the sound of Tug's boots thumping up the stairs.

Eventually, they come.

He enters along with the mouth-watering odour of rabbit and leek stew. My stomach clenches with hunger. Tug lights a candle in the sconce by the door. I scowl at the thought of him and Brin spending the last hour or two drinking and feasting, celebrating the money they have received from trading my brother, like they would the pelts of hunted deer. Like he could ever belong to them!

The stiff leather of Tug's boots creaks as he lights candles about the room. Then he crouches beside me and unties my hands. It is unsettling how he does not meet my glare. Fear crawls through me. Did something go wrong? Has Kel been hurt?

I watch as he rises and walks towards the door. He returns with a large platter of breads and cheeses and a wooden bowl of the rabbit stew. My parched mouth salivates until I'm practically dribbling.

I should resist. Tug is clearly taking up the Prince's suggestion to bribe me. But it has been too long since a proper meal passed my cracked lips.

I raise the soup in shaky hands and slurp. It is still warm! My taste buds explode with the mix of rich meat, tangy leek, thyme and nuts. I savour this small happiness, forcing myself to eat slowly. After the bowl is half-empty, my stomach almost full, I notice Tug is gathering our packs and stacking them by the door. The soup in my stomach turns into a messy, uncomfortable slosh.

He has made his decision. We are leaving.

I nibble on bread until he comes to untie my feet.

'Sit,' he says, gesturing to the edge of the high double bed. A lump lodges in my throat. My heartbeat begins a wild dance in my chest as I push up on shaky legs. Images tumble through my mind like they're scrambling to get away. The bed, alone with Beast-face, the coupling of the man and woman we heard near the Prince's rooms.

I want to fold my shaking hands out of sight, but dare not, in case I need them to claw him off. He stands an arm's length before me, six-foot two inches, shoulders as wide as a river.

'What took so long?' I ask, hoping I sound calmer than I feel.

'You'd better tell me who he is, ' he says.

'Kel...' I croak. I need information about Kel, but his name is all I can utter.

An image bright and vivid appears in the mind-world. *A shadowy cave-like room. Four giant guards with metal bands around their necks and arms. A tall man with brown and grey-peppered hair empties a velvet pouch onto the black table. Glimmering gold coins roll out. Kel stands in a corner shaking, but he holds his head high, chin jutting out in defiance.*

Thank the Gods! I stare wide-eyed at Tug. He has pulled up a memory with total clarity and exactitude. He can dip into his own mind and reveal in the now-time whatever recollection he chooses. My father could do this, but it was something that came with practice and, I believed, because of the close bond between us.

'How did you do that?'

'I want his name, Mirra.'

'A man's face tells me nothing. It is useless if I don't know where to start looking.'

'I can tell where a man is from by the cut of his boots, his coat and his accent.'

'If that were true you would not need me to answer your question.'

'Our wealthy acquaintance has no remembered identity,' Tug says. I meet his wolfish eyes. There is something restless about him tonight. 'It makes it easier for him to mimic others,' he continues. 'His clothes are from a small town to the east, near the tundra. His native accent is from the Red City, mixed with the middle country around Lyndonia and a trace of something I have not come across.'

These are easy guesses. The Red City is the capital of Caruca. And the middle country is near the fort where the Prince wishes to take me for his test. But I wonder how Tug recognises the extent of the Prince's memory loss.

'Is it common for the Carucan cleansing to take away a man's whole past?' I ask.

'It is the first time I've seen it,' Tug says evenly.

'How do you see it?'

'One does not need the sight to observe. For example, the old man with him is a trusted tutor from his boyhood, who comes from the Deppawieden town a days ride from the Red City.'

Tug could be making it up, but I have no way of knowing. I decide to believe him. I want to believe him. His knowledge of my brother's future whereabouts depends on this skill.

If Beast-face has already decided to accept the Prince's offer, then revealing Prince Jakut's identity won't change anything. Perhaps it will even give Tug pause to reconsider.

'Our wealthy acquaintance is Prince Jakut of Caruca,' I say.

To his credit, Tug's jaw doesn't drop open. 'You are sure of this?'

I nod.

He roams the room, grabs a piece of hemp, empties the bread and cheese platter into it and thrusts it into my lap. There is a new fire in him as he tidies, gathering the last remaining furs. It scares me more than the cold impassiveness.

'Time to go,' he says. 'Brin and the horses are waiting.'

Burning flushes up through my throat. 'Please... I cannot leave Kel. I will not perform in the Prince's test.' I scramble off the bed, clinging onto the hemp parcel as though for dear life. 'If I do his test my skill will be discovered. We will all be hanged.'

Tug blocks the doorway, arms folded across his chest. 'Your brother is in the hands of one of the Lyndonian fort's inner royal guards.'

I freeze, struggling to piece together his words. 'You sold Kel to a Lyndonian?' Kel is with a Lyndonian and the Prince is going to the Lyndonian fort.

'I thought you might need an incentive.'

My limbs go soft. The bag of cheeses and bread slips from my unfurling fists. 'Kel is going to Lyndonia?' I gaze at Beast-face.

For some reason, I remember the girl with the chestnut hair and the emerald robe and how well hidden he has kept her in the fortress of his mind. I know he is not doing this for me and Kel, but I cannot help despise him a little less. He is risking his life, along with ours. Why? Not for the gold. It cannot be simply for gold.

'Lyndonia is a royal fort?' I ask.

'It is under the King's brother, Prince Roarhil's protection.'

The knowledge that Kel will travel to Lyndonia at the same time as us, that while I am there being tested, I will be able to hunt for him, makes my body pulse with hope. The tight knot in my stomach loosens and a new kind of anticipation rises through me.

For years I've been waiting for something to happen. Surviving in Blackfoot Forest is not the same as living.

I used to dream of a town built from sparkling white rock; a beautiful place filled with people connected by their sight and their deep understanding of one another. I would wake with a fleeting sense of peace and comfort. And while I knew Auran, Island of the Rushing Winds, had crumbled to the seas over a century ago, I had not accepted spending the rest of my life in a miserable hinterland village among people who despised my sight. I had not accepted that I would always have to hide my true nature, or spend my life feeling cursed and freakish until the day my heart stopped beating.

Now I will venture further from the glacial mountains than I've ever been. I will see the Carucan kingdom's wonders with my own eyes. I will enter the poisoned realm of the royal family who have turned my people into slaves, outlaws, nomads, when we helped them win the Great Carucan-Etean war.

I worry for Kel. Whatever happens, I must find him quickly. But my blood vibrates at the prospect of knowing my enemy. An enemy known is an enemy that can be fought. The tundra mine guards, mercenaries and bounty hunters are the limbs of a beast, but the royal family is the head.

Tug throws Brin's pack at me, (it is twice my size), and straps on his own. 'Brin waits for us at the edge of town. We must cross the Hybourg. It is worse here at night. And there are those who saw us in the Pit. I need you to focus.'

I nod. I am ready. It is amazing what a decent meal can do to clear one's head and boost morale.

FIFTEEN

We travel the twelve miles to the Prince's tavern in less than an hour. Riding a horse feels nothing like my father's memories. The power and rhythm of the beast makes my heart soar and fly above the ground. It is like being swept up by the wind and once I find my balance and confidence, the whoosh of exhilaration is unlike anything I've ever experienced.

By the time we arrive at the tavern, I am windswept, breathless and my shoulder burns. The strain of holding the reins has ripped the old arrow wound, and it bleeds again.

'Are you staying up there all night?' Tug asks, as a stable boy appears to tend to the horses. My hands feel locked on the reins, my aching muscles clench around the beast's belly. I lift my leg awkwardly over one side and fall. Tug catches me. I let out a yelp as one of his hands presses against my arm. Without a word, he stands me on my feet and leaves me to stagger behind him and Brin to the backdoor.

I follow them into a room lit by a large fire and lanterns on every table. The Prince sits by the hearth with a book. The blind man snoozes in an adjacent chair. As we enter, Prince Jakut rises, shoulders relaxed, expression satisfied, but I notice the tight grip on his closed book.

'Brin, Ule,' Tug says introducing the men. The Prince nods but Brin only stares, behaving one hundred percent like the loutish thug he is.

'I am pleased you have accepted my offer,' the Prince says. He searches me out beyond my captors. I let our eyes meet, allowing him to think I am relieved and grateful and enchanted—after all I have been at the whim of two brutal mercenaries and now a Prince has saved me! Then I hastily drop my gaze as though remembering my place.

He sets his book on the mantlepiece and crosses the empty dining room. I attempt a curtsey, though with one hand down my parka to staunch my reopened wound, it is clumsy.

'What's wrong with your arm?' he asks.

'It's nothing,' I say, still short of breath and buoyed up from the ride. 'Just a scratch.'

'May I?'

He reaches out, guiding my outer parka over my head. Days of sweat, grime and smoke cling to my skin but he doesn't flinch at the stink. I try to hide the way my muscles tighten. He is so conceited he believes he can help me undress! If my memories were a forest of devastation, and I relied on an old, blind man to tell me who I was, I would not be so arrogant.

Beneath my furs, my shirt and hand are bloody. The cloth around my neck is also stained with blood.

'This is an arrow wound?' the Prince asks.

Tug moves to join us. 'It is from when we caught her,' he says.

'And what is this?' he asks, touching the rag at my neck.

'A warning,' Tug says.

'We will be riding through the night. Deadran will tend to both wounds immediately.'

I frown as the blind man rouses and the Prince calls the innkeeper. Prince Jakut, or Ule as we are all supposed to call him, seems irritated over Tug's neglect of my person. Obviously he's concerned arrow-wounds and knife-wounds could lead to questions about my true identity. But some tiny part of me wonders if he finds violence towards a vulnerable girl distasteful. Even if the girl is an outlawed shadow weaver.

Maybe I have overplayed the weak feminine angle. Though it is not like I have fainted or cried. Still, I do not want him to think I am so delicate he is worrying about my health, and having me watched all the time.

The innkeeper leads the old man and me to a cellar room with one narrow bed and a washbasin. The innkeeper's wife hurries in with a pot of hot water, and a basket filled with ointment bottles, cotton gauze and wraps.

'That will be all, thank you,' the blind man says. After they leave and we are alone in the cellar room, he instructs me to take off my blouse. I glance at the closed door before slipping my injured arm out of the sleeve of my shirt.

'I am Deadran.' The old man dips a cotton pad into warm water and dabs the knife cut. It stings, forcing me to suck through my teeth. Then he cleans the arrow wound. 'We will bandage both up, and you must ride with me tonight.'

He reaches for the basket and sorts nimbly through phial bottles, identifying some by touch, others by scent. 'This is it. Let us put a little honey on to help fight any infection.' He smears sweet smelling goo over the wounds, presses wads of cotton over the paste, and wraps my arm and neck with gauze.

Once he has finished, his eyes turn towards the lantern. He seems to drift to sleep for a moment. I slip my arm back into the sleeve of my shirt. The cuts tingle. I fasten the buttons of my shirt.

'I have lived a long life without Rhag,' he says, suddenly breaking the silence, 'and now I find at the end of it I am confronted with two mysteries.'

Rhag is the name for the Carucan path to the Gods. The faithful, like my mother, walk the path through prayer, worship and once or twice in a lifetime, the spiritual cleansing.

'To be reunited with the Prince,' he continues, 'is a blessing I had not hoped for. But you...' He shakes his head. 'All those days Prince Jakut went to the Pit, searching for the impossible. And when all seemed lost, you found him.'

A true miracle! I pick up my inner parka. It will be chilly riding through the night so I will need both layers.

'I have no business with Rhag,' I tell him, annoyed he considers my capture and the "slaughter" of my family an answer to the Prince's prayers.

Though I have to admit, finding a mature shadow weaver, whose eyes have settled, is a conundrum. A mature shadow weaver means any physical proof of the mind-reading talent has gone. This is why poachers and hunters don't bother with us. I push my bandaged arm into my inner parka, grunting at the tight, painful fit.

'Stop,' Deadran says. 'I will lend you a cloak.'

'Thank you.'

'Prince Jakut,' he continues, 'is nineteen, but he has known great loss from the youngest of ages. His mother died in childbirth with a sister. He was only four. She was not in her grave when his father packed him off to his uncle in Lyndonia, accompanied by an already elderly tutor whom the boy had never met.'

'You?' So Tug was right! I try to hide the interest in my voice, but the more I know about the Prince, the better armed I am to deal with him.

'Indeed,' Deadran nods. 'He lost everything he knew in one sweep of fate. Only to lose it all again at eight years old when his father summoned him back to the Royal Court, and I was dismissed.'

'You have not seen the Prince for eleven years?'

'Eleven years,' Deadran echoes.

'And yet of all those he could choose,' I say, 'he has called on you.' If someone wanted to hide their true nature and intent from a shadow weaver, what better way than erasing their memories and surrounding themselves with people who only knew them as a child? Has the Prince so much to hide, he has risked hiding it even from himself? What does he really want from me?

'It is difficult for a young Prince, purposefully isolated by his over-bearing father, to make trustworthy friends. With the attempt on his life, he cannot put his faith in anyone from the Royal Court until King Alixter returns from fighting on the Etean front. Jakut's enemies are powerful and daring enough to have infiltrated his own escort.'

Deadran hopes to elicit my sympathy for the Prince by weaving connections between us. We have both lost beloved parents, (at least he thinks mine are dead), both been snatched from our homes and brought into strange and dangerous worlds. 'Why are you telling me all this?'

'Before we arrive at the fort in Lyndonia, if you are to blend in as part of the Prince's new escort, you will need to know much about court life, the history and traditions of Caruca, politics and hierarchy.'

How a scrawny, sixteen-year-old outlaw is expected to blend in as part of the Prince's replacement escort I have no idea. Perhaps they will pass me off as a serving boy.

'This will be the Prince's test?'

Deadran nods. 'The first part.'

'And the second?'

'Your ability to uncover useful information without being suspected.'

I turn from Deadran and, careful not to strain my wound, pull my looser outer parka over my head. If men in the court are as wary and skilled at blocking their minds as Tug, it could take days or weeks to glean useful information. Even an open mind, easy to search through, can take hours of combing to uncover anything significant. And I am not practised. I shunned entering my parents' minds for years. In the three decades since the Uru Ana were banished from Caruca, I expect the tales of what we are capable have become highly exaggerated.

'My life has been long and mostly blessed,' Deadran says. 'As a young man I had many Uru Ana friends. I am ashamed of what Caruca has done to your people. And I am sorry for the danger we are putting you in. But I will do everything I can to help you. I am sure if you serve the Prince well, he in turn, will help you.'

How honourable. And if I fail to do as he wishes, he will denounce me and see me hanged.

'I have known few men other than my father, and they have all been cruel,' I say. 'I thank you for your kindness.'

SIXTEEN

For four days we ride through the night and sleep outside deep in the shelter of fields, hills and forests, away from the roads. Sunrise to sunset lengthens, lasting almost five hours, warming the lands and the air.

We are in the habit of establishing camp before dawn and waking in the late afternoon twilight. My body adjusts to the physical exertion of riding, which puts a different strain on muscles used to snow trekking. I am energised by regular meals and the power of the sun. But every time I feel life humming through my veins, I also feel guilty. Is Kel faring as well with his Lyndonian captor? Will he remain strong, even though he does not know I'm coming for him?

After breaking fast after the fourth night of riding, Brin and Tug take care of the horses, and Deadran instructs the Prince and me on Carucan geography. Our prior lessons have all been about court politics and etiquette, a subject, which briefly fascinated me, but quickly became tedious. Geography is a welcome change.

Deadran unrolls a worn parchment, holding down the corners with stones. Jakut and I sit on the ground before him. We lean forward to see better, our shoulders brush, and awkwardness spikes through me. I pull away, but the Prince is faster to sit back, so I am free to take in the Kingdoms of Ederiss.

I used to enjoy sketching the lands of Ederiss from Ma's memories. It was what I did when she gave me ink and paper instead of practicing the Caurcan alphabet. But Deadran's map has many details and subtleties missing from Ma's map, or at least her memories of what she studied. My attention is drawn to an island southwest of the Etean Kingdom.

'What is this island?'

'Auran,' Deadran says. My head jolts back. Auran, Island of the Rushing Winds, where my people came from, and which was supposed to have drowned beneath the waves over a century ago.

'How old is this map?'

'Twenty long-sleeps, but it was copied from a map in the Ruby Palace whose date I do not know.'

The excitement in my chest flows out leaving me disappointed. This map must predate the catastrophe.

'Is this,' the Prince asks me, 'where your people came from?' I had not noticed him moving, but now his face is almost side by side with mine. He speaks softly, as though he understands how important my heritage is to me. As though he realises this is not just history, but the missing roots I feel I cannot really grow without.

'Accounts of Carucan history,' Deadean says, 'site this island as the origin of the glitter-eyed children.' Deadran's milky eyes are turned on us in his usual unfocused, but attentive manner.

'Origin?' the Prince echoes. 'Then why do they hide in the northern forests? Why doesn't the King allow them to return to their island?'

I bristle, wondering what could possibly hold Jakut's interest in Uru Ana history.

'The island drowned,' I say.

He nods. 'And so your people came searching for new lands.' He erroneously assumes my people imposed themselves on lands that did not belong to them.

'The Etean King,' Deadran interjects, as though sensing the rising tension and trying to diffuse it, 'or Alaweh as he is known to the Eteans, was responsible for Auran being swept under the sea, after he mined their crystal cliffs and coral reefs. Only four hundred or so Uru Ana children, brought by his fleet to Etea, survived.'

I feel the Prince's gaze, but when I look at him he looks down.

'I would like to know more about the Carucan cleansing,' I say. I have been wishing to ask since our first lesson, and now we have crossed the line of awkward, the moment seems ripe.

Everything I've perceived in Deadran's memories before the winter hibernation, suggests the Prince performed the cleansing as a form of escapism, like my mother. Through the old tutor, I have heard the Prince's tormented hours spent praying with a priest of Rhag, before losing his past. Nights frantically scribbling words on parchment. Letters, a confession, or an account. As I cannot read Carucan, I cannot say what exactly.

'I am no priest,' Deadran replies, 'but I will answer any questions as best as I can.'

'I did not wish the biased answers of a priest.'

The Prince snorts. I glance across, and get distracted for a moment by his lopsided smile. Frowning, I turn back to Deadran.

'How is wiping out a person's painful memories supposed to bring them closer to the Gods?'

'Why do you think it is only painful memories?'

An image of Ma a few minutes after Kel was born flashes in my mind. The midwife had wrapped Kel in warm deerskin and allowed Pa and me back into the bedroom. Ma's face was spotted red, her hair wet with sweat. An exhausted smile lit her eyes as they met my father's.

The midwife gave Kel to Pa, and he tilted the tiny bundle to Ma. My mother's expression transformed. She pushed herself up to see better, panic twisting her face.

'That's why people do it, isn't it?' I say. 'People take the mist berries before the long-sleep because they want to forget the pain of their past.'

Deadran rubs his short grey beard, and takes a moment to formulate his answer. 'From my understanding, it is not the most painful moments that are taken by the Gods, but the most potent. The memories where awareness of being alive is greatest.'

His words settle slowly through me. If what he says is true, it means Ma did not forget Kel and me because we were the most painful part of her life, but because we were the part that made her feel most alive.

My chest swells. I don't want to cry, but I suddenly want Ma so badly I can't breathe. Tears glaze my vision. Since I left my parents in Blackfoot Forest, I have barely allowed myself to think of them. But this unexpected information, slips around my defences. A tear rolls down my cheek. Deadran cannot see and the Prince is positioned behind me, so I let it run to my chin and drop away, leaving the air to dry the salty trail.

'The cleansing' Deadran continues, 'is a way of making space in a person's soul for the light of the Gods. The temporary loss of their most vivid memories is the sacrifice.'

By Deadran's interpretation, the Prince has lived in a state of heightened sentience most of his life – good or bad, or maybe both. I glance around to see how Jakut is absorbing this information. His eyes are closed and his face is still, concentrated.

I wonder if I took the mist berries before the long-sleep what pieces of my past would be buried beneath the veil. My life on the run in the Sea of Trees was punctured with intensity, but the last six years in Blackfoot Forest have been more like watching an old man dying. Before Tug and Brin turned up, time seemed to be winding down to a standstill.

'What happens if an Uru Ana takes the mist berries?' I ask.

'Traditionally,' Deadran says, 'the Uru Ana see memory as a gift, a way of understanding and uniting people. So it would not be relevant for them to remove the one thing they believe brings them towards harmony and balance. At least this is my understanding.'

'Is this why the Cacurans call us shadow weavers? They think we cannot make space for the light of their Gods because even if we could not access our own memories, we could just see the memories of those around us. We cannot make the ultimate sacrifice.'

'It is possible this is part of how you got the name. But mostly, it is because a lord who had great influence over King Rex, the Prince's grandfather, instilled deep fear in the Carucans concerning the Uru

Ana's ability. He said those slaves who escaped Etea and came across the border to Caruca, had poisoned the minds of their slave masters, and wrapped their hearts in shadows. This is why the slave masters set them free.'

For a moment we are all silent.

'Do you have any more questions on this, Mirra?'

'No.'

'Prince Jakut?' Deadran asks. The Prince opens his eyes and also says no.

Deadran continues teaching us the geography of the four remaining kingdoms: Etea, Tmà, Caruca and Rudeash.

I sit back and observe the Prince when he is not paying attention. Perhaps there is some grace in what he has done. Perhaps it is not cowardice or escapism that made him turn to the cleansing ritual, but a desire for higher guidance, a demonstration of sacrifice. The Gods didn't just take his memories. They took his whole identity.

At one moment, as I contemplate the riddle of the Prince and his choice, his eyes turn to me. He gives a small smile. I tentatively mirror it, until I register something in the distance. Tug is watching. He manages to capture both the essence of molten lava and shiny volcanic glass in his obsidian-hard stare. He does not want the Prince and I to make any kind of alliance. But for now, it can only work in my favour for the Prince to believe we are on friendly terms. It will give me an advantage Tug does not possess, and might irritate him as well.

My smile deepens.

SEVENTEEN

On the sixth day separated from Kel, I am woken by the sound of hooves. I do not sit up, but roll over in the long grass and spy the King's soldiers in their grey uniforms, riding on the distant road. Tug catches my eye. The others do not stir.

I lie still until I am sure the soldiers have passed. Then I rise quietly, stretch my legs and amble away from the men. I do not intend to run off. I only wish to be on my own for a short time, in a sunny field, with the illusion of freedom. But Tug follows, swishing through the grass behind me.

'How does the grass grow so quickly here?' I ask.

'It is like this further south. The land comes back to life more swiftly after the winter. Here.' I turn and see he has my bow and arrow. I look at him sceptically. Clearly he does not fear I will shoot him. His self-assurance on the matter makes me want to take him by surprise. Just imagine the look on his face!

But once again, he is accurate in his assessment. I had a hard enough time shooting his wolf dog. I kill beasts of the forest only for survival. Shooting a man in cold blood, when I am not under attack, goes against my nature.

'Let's hunt,' he says. 'I am tired of eating grain.'

For a moment my gaze wanders to the pack on his back. Are my knives in there? I miss them. Still, manipulating my bow and arrow again is better than nothing. I remove my cloak and drop it on the ground to collect later. Once my quiver is strapped to my back, I try pulling an arrow in its bow. I am happy to discover all the riding and Deadran's remedies have strengthened my arm.

'See if you can keep up,' Tug says. And with that he is leaping through the grass towards woodland. I run after him. It feels wonderful to be moving my stiff legs after so many days in a saddle, to have the sun on my face, to smell the warm grass, hear the birds chirping, and think of nothing. For all his size, Tug is fast. I can barely keep up.

We enter the woodland and a welcome hush fills the air. Buds sprout from slim trees. Blue and purple flowers poke up through layers of brown mushy leaves. Tug signals me to halt. I stop twenty feet from him and listen, catching the rustle of small animals foraging —a red squirrel, and birds. There are hundreds and hundreds of tiny birds with blue-tipped wings and yellow bellies.

Then I sense the mind of a larger creature. We creep forward silently. Soft white speckles appear through spindly branches. A fawn. Its tawny ears twitch as it wobbles on delicate legs. Tug raises his bow and arrow. Pa taught me never to strip the world of such young beauty.

I lower the toes of my boot across a large twig. As it snaps, Tug fires his arrow. The bow pings and the fawn scrambles away. I'm surprised he missed such a clear shot, even with my interference, until I see the rabbit lying in the undergrowth, sprawled on its side, twitching.

Tug strides through the mulch and picks it up. His wrists flick. The creature's neck cracks as it breaks. A swift, clean death. Tug holds out the rabbit for me to carry.

'Do you not like deer?' he asks.

I grab the rabbit's ears and offer up a silent thank you to the spirit world for this gift of life. 'It was too young.'

Tug's lips close in what almost resembles approval. If it were a week ago, I would have been shocked, but I have seen him changing over the last few days. Since he made his deal with the Prince, he reminds me of a sleeping volcano rumbling to life, or the earth shifting in imperceptible increments beneath one's feet.

'Let me see what kind of shot you are,' he says. He takes out his knife and carves a slash in a tree fifteen feet away. If I didn't know better, I would think he was mocking me. The target is ridiculously easy. Maybe he thinks my injury is still too much of a handicap to my aim.

I hand him the rabbit and raise my bow and arrow, flexing and testing my healed arm. I am about to shoot straight for the cross centre when I sense another mind in the woodlands. The Prince has followed us. The stealth of his pursuit and the fact he now keeps his distance, means he is spying on us.

I tilt my bow pulling my elbow a little too high and adjust my aim. The arrow skims through the air, misses the tree and lands in bushes.

Tug nods. 'Your technique needs work,' he says, retrieving the arrow, 'but your instinct is good.'

Instinct? I scrutinise his tattooed face. Does he know the Prince is watching?

'Try again.' He walks back to me and as I draw to fire, moves in to adjust my arms. My chest rises and falls erratically. He is up to something.

'He does not trust you,' Tug breathes quietly, 'And you cannot trust him.' Yes, he knows the Prince is watching. 'His whole escort was murdered, yet he, the assassination target, miraculously escapes. Be wary of him, Mirra. If you fail his test or do not help him in the way he expects, he might drop this act of kindness. Our lives are in your hands.'

He releases his grip on my arm. This time, when I fire, my arrow nips the tree, bark splinters, and a few shavings flutter into the air.

'Better!' he says loudly. 'Again!' I pull a new arrow from my quiver, placing it lopsidedly in the bow. Tug leans in to make the necessary adjustments.

'Your life need not be in my hands,' I murmur. 'You could change that now. You could let me go.'

He taps my right elbow, indicating I should lower it a little as I take aim. 'Then how would you get into the Lyndonian fort?'

'That is not your concern. You could return my knives and I'd steal my horse while you're all sleeping and you could leave me a head start.' I release the tension on the bow. My arrow shafts through the air, royally missing its target.

Tug rubs his growing stubble. 'You have some talent for a girl,' he says in a voice loud enough to carry to the Prince. 'But you could not survive out here on your own.' His double innuendo is not the height of subtlety and I grow nervous the Prince will understand.

'I knew with time you'd start to care about me,' I say dryly. His mock concern doesn't fool me. He doesn't care whether I can rescue Kel by myself, or not. He is the reason Kel is a captive in the hands of strangers in the first place. 'You're not doing this for the gold,' I hiss, drawing myself up to Tug's beast face. 'You have lived a hundred lives, but you only feel alive when you're in danger. Waiting to die is not living! Why do you wish to go to Lyndonia?'

Something waits for him there. It is the only explanation for the change that has slowly come over him.

Tug's hands whip out and he clenches both my wrists. My eyes water in pain.

'You have seen how I can obscure things from your sight,' he growls. 'Perhaps the Prince can also fool you. How thoroughly have you bothered to search the remnants of his memories?'

The leaves behind us rustle. A boot squelches in the undergrowth. Tug drops my wrists and a blank look slides over his face.

'Your Royal Highness,' he says. 'Excuse me, Ule,' he corrects. 'We thought rabbit would make a nice change for supper.'

'I will look forward to it,' he says.

I stand staring at the ground. The Prince is the first to break the awkward silence. 'It will be dark in a few minutes,' he says lightly. 'We had better return to camp.' Tug makes an irreverent bow and the three of us begin the walk back.

I am annoyed with Beast-face. He spoils my small respite from the fear and worry of what is coming. He stirs up questions I have pushed aside. What happened to all those written notes Prince Jakut made before the long-sleep? Why didn't he inform Deadran of the identity of his assassin before the ritual cleansing? What had he done that left him so tormented?

The truth is, my lessons with the Prince have been a welcome distraction. I have enjoyed learning about things my parents could not teach me. But Tug is right to sharpen my focus, to remind me of what I have pushed into the background. In two days we will be at the fort of Lyndonia, and both the Prince's test and my search for Kel will begin. I need all my wits about me.

The Prince and I are not in this together. He is courteous and feeds me, but when he doesn't get what he wants, and he cannot for I must escape, the mask may fall, revealing he is as dangerous as Tug. While I am pretending to be his friend, I had best not forget it.

EIGHTEEN

As the sky lightens, we ride into a village of thatched log cottages. Prince Jakut leads us to a dilapidated boarding house beside a pig farm. The stench of the creatures lingers unpleasantly in all the rooms. We are less than a night's ride from Lyndonia, and no one has told me why suddenly we risk stopping in a public place.

The Prince warms his hands by the blazing fire while we wait for breakfast in the small dining room. I would do the same, but I do not wish to stand so close. Throughout the night, in the intervals between our hard galloping, I avoided trotting by his side, brooding instead over how neglectful I have been in my search of his shrouded memories. The brokenness of his mind disturbs me and quickly drives me out.

'You are sure of this?' the Prince asks Deadran as the old tutor sits down by the fire.

'That will be for Mirra to answer.'

I blow on my frozen hands. 'Answer what?' I say, impatient for a warm breakfast to banish the chill of my body.

'Whether the innkeeper's wife is Delladean,' the Prince says. He walks across the room, passing the small windows and dusty, velvety curtains and takes a seat beside me. He pulls his chair close. Once again, I am conscious of how filthy I am. My dark hair is one huge tangled knot. My shirt clings to my back with sweat, despite the cold, and my face must be as grubby as my hands.

'Delladea is an isolated fort near the northern border,' he continues, gaze flickering to the door in case the woman in question returns with our meal. 'The mountain pass can only be crossed during two weeks in the summer, so few come and leave, yet it is not far from where I was healed. We will say you grew up there.'

Brin, who sits with Tug at the next table along, fiddles with the purple glass medallion beneath his furs. Tug dodges my gaze. I wonder what I've missed in the Prince's plans for me.

'If the woman is Delladean—' Jakut says.

'She's Delladean,' Tug interrupts.

'Then this afternoon,' the Prince continues, ignoring Tug, 'after you have rested, you will stay here, learning as much as you can. I have business to attend to. Tug and I will go together. Brin and Deadran will stay with you. Then we will take a late evening meal here, ride through the night and announce ourselves at the Lyndonian fort tomorrow at dawn.'

The innkeeper's wife enters with a great platter of crispy bacon, mushrooms stuffed with melted cheese, and a steaming vegetable broth. I use the entrance to move away from the Prince.

Tug's eyes track the multi-coloured bead bracelet slipping out from under the cuff of the woman's shirt. She sets the tray of food on the table, hands trembling. She has not looked at Tug or Brin once.

I have grown so used to their savage tattooed faces, I barely notice them anymore. The Prince might hope to pass me off as a Delladean serving boy, but how will he explain the company of two mercenary bounty hunters? As the woman moves to leave she nods and mutters, 'Sirs, Miss.'

'My father,' I say, addressing her, 'thinks he can tell the birth town of any person by the clothes he or she wears.'

'Which one is your father, Miss?' the woman asks, wiping oily hands on her apron. I point at Tug. His eyes narrow.

'Oh.' A little of her nervousness vanishes. 'He barely looks old enough.'

'It's the tattoos. They hide his wrinkles.' Tug's gaze locks down on me. 'My father,' I continue 'says the bracelet with the coloured beads shows you are not from these parts.'

The woman ruffles up her sleeve and her fingers hover over her bracelet. 'It's Delladean,' she reveals. 'I've not returned these fifteen years. Too much to keep me busy here.' She tilts her head in a respectful nod and returns to the kitchen.

Jakut watches me curiously.

'What was that?' Tug asks.

'You were making her nervous. She needed some assurance a human exists beneath your beast face.'

Brin snorts.

The Prince reaches forward to serve himself. 'How did you know about the bracelet?' he asks.

'Tug was staring at it,' I say. The Prince frowns. Perhaps he thinks I understand Tug too well.

We eat in silence and I am suddenly struck by something. Though I'm dressed as a boy, and my hair is a long tangle like Brin's and I am in the company of men, the Delladean woman did not hesitate in calling me Miss, even before I spoke and my voice gave me away. When Tug and Brin first saw me in Blackfoot Forest, when they took my skinny rags and bones to the Pit, people assumed I was a boy. I have fattened up in the last week. I may have to stop eating so much.

AFTERNOON SUN LEAKS through the closed shutters. I wake on the bedroom floor with tears in my eyes and the sense of Kel so close, my swollen heart feels ready to burst. While Deadran still sleeps I take off my shirt and wash using a jug of cold water, noticing my rib bones aren't sticking out so much and my breasts are fuller.

I decide to skip eating until later, and spend the next couple of hours inside the innkeeper Addy Mulburry's mind, scouring tedious memories of days that bleed into months, and months into years that all look the same.

By late-afternoon, stars twinkle in the deep night-blue sky. I stretch my legs and stare out the window at the pigs, my thoughts numb from so many hours of Addy's kitchen-hand drudge.

The sound and smells of pigs snuffling and squealing drifts up. In the stables, a horse whinnies.

'I never knew pigs could be so fascinating.'

I turn. Jakut stands in the doorway, tufts of hair falling into his eyes. Half his face glows from the candle in the wall sconce, while deep twilight gives the other half of his bronzed skin a silvery tint. He reminds me of the portrait paintings of elegant noblemen and women hanging in the boarding house dining room. His breath is ragged from riding which means he has come straight here after leaving his stallion.

I point to Deadran on the bed, then cross the room. Jakut retreats into the narrow corridor. I join him, clicking the door shut behind me and stand crushed against it to create a little space between us. At least I have washed.

'How have you been getting on?' he asks.

From his casual tone, it sounds like polite conversation, but I sense he is already testing me. 'I know the names of every cook, serving girl, butler and footman. I am familiar with the running of Lord Tersil's fort and the names of his wife and children. But my information is fifteen years out of date.'

Jakut stares as though he's listening to something other than my spoken words. The sincerity in his eyes tilts me off balance. I think of Tug's words in the forest. I should not need to be warned to distrust the Prince. A child would know this. Yet instinct betrays me.

'If that is all,' I say, fumbling for the bedroom door handle.

'Mirra, please, take a walk with me.' I grope for an excuse, but he turns before I find one and I am left to follow him through the dark hall.

Outside the moon is bright, lighting our way as we cross towards the stables. This is some consolation as I wish to check on my mare.

'Tomorrow, we will dine in Lyndonia,' he says. He ambles with his hands in his pockets, shoulders relaxed. I fleetingly wonder where he and Tug have been for the last two hours. 'Deadran has instructed us together, but I will need as much help as you can give me. I will not recognise my uncle or aunt or the guards or anyone from the fort.'

A sudden thought strikes me. 'I could sketch them for you,' I say. 'I am not practised with people, but I used to draw some of the forest animals and—' *Kel*. I stop myself before my brother's name slips from my lips. What is wrong with me? I almost said it aloud.

'Mirra,' he says in a low, gravelly voice. My stomach rolls, and I wish I had eaten earlier. I flinch as he takes hold of my shoulders and turns me so we are face to face. 'Mirra,' he says again. This time his voice sounds softer, almost wounded. 'I am sorry for putting you in this situation. If anyone suspects your true nature, I will do everything I can to help you escape.'

I stare at my boots and twist my hands together. 'My true nature?' I ask, trying to tame the anger rising from the bottomless waters inside me. 'Umbra, shadow weaver, glitter-eyed... Are these the words you search for? Is your true nature that you are a prince?'

His arms fall to his sides. 'You are right.'

The release of his touch returns me to my senses. I shake my head. 'Excuse me, Your Royal Highness. I thank you for your consideration.'

He snorts in mild amusement. 'You reveal me to myself.'

I glance up. In the shadows of his face a smile brushes his lips.

'I don't know what you mean.'

'I wanted your understanding, Mirra. I wanted you to lighten my guilt, and yet I did not realise this, until you gave me what I wanted without meaning it.'

With a sensation I have misstepped, I frown. Why would he need my understanding of his acts? The strong take from the weaker in their quest for better survival. It has always been the way of the world.

In the starry darkness it is easier than normal to meet his probing gaze.

'You do not act like a slave or a prisoner,' he muses, almost to himself. 'Because you do not believe you are one.'

A fresh wave of anxiety pulses under my skin. What is he driving at now? Does he think Tug, Brin and I are working together to trick him? Does he suspect I go with them to Lyndonia because I desire it? He saw Tug and I arguing in the forest. Perhaps captive girls aren't supposed to argue with their abusive captors. And mercenaries aren't supposed to put their lives in the hands of an untrustworthy shadow weaver after killing her parents.

'I have been free for sixteen years,' I say. 'Two weeks' captivity cannot take that from me.'

'It would most. They would know they are no longer free. They would be attempting escape, or giving up.'

'The last time I tried to escape,' I say. 'Tug left a scar across my neck.'

I walk further into the stables. A lantern hangs on the barn door, its dim candle flickering in the wind. His words have reminded me of Kel. Pain swells in my throat. The stable boy is brushing down Tug's horse. I find my mare at the other end of the shack, check her water is clean and she has plenty of hay. Will Kel have given up by now? Will he believe there is no hope?

Jakut follows me inside, stopping an arms' length away. He holds the lantern in one hand and strokes the white, splattered star on his stallion's nose with the other. I take deep breaths until the panic ebbs.

'There is something specific you wish to ask me?' I say.

'Yes. Tug and Brin murdered your parents, yet the other day Tug was teaching you to hunt.' He speaks in a low voice so the groom cannot overhear. It makes the atmosphere thrum with intensity and I regret coming in here. 'He does not act towards you the way he should. The way Brin does. He does not fear and loathe you and you do not fear and loathe him.'

'Tug is not superstitious. He pays no heed to the wild stories of the Uru Ana possessing shadow magic. But you are wrong. I would be an idiot not to fear him. And I hate him for taking me from my home, though it is true, I would hate him more if he had killed my parents.'

'He said your parents were dead.'

'Not by his hand.' I am glad it is dark so that Jakut cannot read the lie on my face. 'May I ask you something?' I say, hoping to deflect his attention from my family.

'Please,' he nods.

'If the attack was from inside your own escort and you were the target, how is it you are still alive?'

His shoulders rise and fall as he sighs. 'I have no answer for this puzzle. I only hope Rhag has spared my life because he has some higher purpose for me.'

I think of his endless praying before the long-sleep; his decision to risk the spiritual cleansing despite how vulnerable it would leave him. Tug wishes to isolate and control me through my distrust of the Prince. Yet the Prince of Caruca seeks to fill some higher Godly purpose.

'Come,' he says, raising the lantern and touching me lightly on the back. 'We must return. You are needed in your bedroom before supper. And tonight we have a seven-hour ride ahead of us before we reach the fort.'

NINETEEN

The girl standing in the hallway looks about fourteen. She wears a plain, neat dress and her long plaited hair twists down to her waist. Lined up beside her are four huge jugs of water. In her arms she carries a wicker basket and towels.

'I am here to prepare your bath,' she says with a curtsey.

Prince Jakut said I was needed in my bedroom before supper, but I had not imagined he meant for a bath. He has not been as oblivious to my stench as he pretends. I suppose even a serving boy cannot turn up stinking of sweat, rancid long-sleep oils and dirt.

'Come in,' I say. In Blackfoot Forest we bathed in streams, and even in the summer months the water was freezing. My last hot bath was six years ago. A sense of anticipation and warmth runs through me.

The girl lights the fire and I help her carry the water jugs to the washing chamber. As she empties the basket of ointments, oils and creams, I settle on a stool by the wooden tub and unplug miniature corks from the tiny bottles. Pine sap, thyme, mint. I recognise some of the scents, but many are foreign. The girl does not seem bothered by my company and I absently wonder how long she has been working. If she went to school or learnt to read and write. If she was born and raised here. The women who worked with Addy Mulberry in the

Delladean fort's kitchens talked nonstop, but the girl is quiet. I like her at once.

A perfume in a dark blue bottle fills my head with a hazy memory of running through a valley of tall purple and orange flowers.

'What is it?' I ask, holding up the bottle.

'Jasmine Summer.'

'And this?'

'Roses,' she says, smiling. 'You have never smelt a rose?' I shrug. 'This is my favourite,' she says, producing an opaque bell-shaped bottle. 'But you have to dab it on your skin to get the right effect.' She pops out the lid and reaches to take my hand. I give it to her before remembering the red welts on my wrists from Tug's ropes. As she raises my sleeve I ease my arm away.

'I can do it,' I say. I blot the liquid on the top of my wrist and notice the welts beneath have almost faded. Has the knife slit on my neck lightened to a faint scar too? Next to my skin the soft scent reminds me of the vanilla biscuits a cook in Addy's kitchen was so fond off making.

'Lovely.'

'Pink Lily of the Mountains.'

She lifts a bubbling pot from the fire and pours it into the tub. Steam hisses as hot and cold water collide. 'I was told to stay and help scrub you, but I can wait outside if you wish.'

'No, that's fine.' I kick off my boots and undress. My mother changed in front of her maid so I think little of it, until the girl's gaze runs over my body and her eyes widen. A bruise I have not remembered? Too skinny? I have never been so fleshy in my life, but compared to her I am all bones and muscle.

'Your father told me you did not like to bathe.'

I glance at the brown sheen of grime over my arms, chest and legs. Grit sits between my toes and beneath my fingernails. I laugh. Tug is getting his revenge.

'Let's give him a surprise,' I say. 'Make me so clean I'm glowing.'

I drift my hand through the silky water, then climb in, submerging myself little by little as the heat tingles against my skin.

Half an hour later, the girl, Tilda, has scrubbed me so hard my back, legs, and arms are bright red. I sit in a cotton towel on the bathroom stool and let her clip my nails and rub nut oil over my back. She combs my ponytail, slowly unknotting all the tangled lumps.

'Well,' she says when it is done. 'Where are your clothes?'

Before I can answer she heads to the bedroom. I follow, slightly anxious she'll be suspicious when she realises I have only the dirty clothes I was wearing. But a midnight blue dress lies spread across the double bed.

I stop, watching as she runs a hand appreciatively across the quality fabric. My eyes twitch to the door. Deadran's shuffle would have alerted me to his entrance, and another serving girl would have knocked. Which leaves the Prince. I imagine him arranging the dress while I sit naked in the tub chatting nonsense to Tilda, and my cheeks flame. But modesty should be the least of my concerns in light of what the dress implies.

The neck of the dress cuts high against the throat. Fabric gathers at the shoulders and extends to cover the wrists with a lacy frill. A cotton petticoat, underpants, and a corset with ribbons have been laid beside it. A pair of brown leather riding boots stand beside the rocking chair, and a matching cloak hangs above them. Jakut means to present me as a lady. Not a serving boy. Not even a serving girl. But a lady!

Tilda helps me dress and I do my best to curb my impatience at getting away from her fluttering, pruning hands. I am impatient to show the Prince what an error he is making.

'Do you not wish to look at yourself in a glass?' she asks as I head for the bedroom door.

'The mirror in the dining room is larger,' I tell her. 'I don't want to spoil the full effect!'

I leave her beaming and tramp through the hallway in tight boots and a skirt that makes me feel I've got caught up in riverbed flotsam, and I am dragging it tangled around my feet.

A clatter of plates and Tug's low voice float through the wood panelled hall. Brin, seated opposite the dining room door, sees me first. His mouth opens and he stops eating. Tug turns to stare, followed by Prince Jakut who is taking his supper with a book in his hands.

I stand in the doorway with my palms on my hips, like a peacock attempting to puff itself up and not appear intimidated.

'What is the meaning of this?' I ask.

Jakut closes his book and rises. He crosses the room, arcing around to inspect me from the sides. 'The colour and cut suit you well enough,' he says. He holds out his arm as a gentleman would for a lady to take. 'May I escort you to your table?'

'I think I can find it well enough.' I stomp past him to the table where my supper has been left covered. I yank back a chair and drop down, folding my arms. 'Eat,' he says. 'We must leave shortly.'

'I cannot ride like this.'

'It will be strange at first, but you will adapt.'

I look to Tug for help. His stony expression tells me he will not be intervening. Brin has acquired another piece of coloured quartz around his neck. He squeezes the crystal in his chunky hand. The Prince pulls up a chair at the head of the table, beside me. He leans close and speaks in a low voice.

'I will present you to the Lyndonian court as Lady Mirra Tersil from Delladea.'

My eyes slide across to Brin and Tug. It is hard to glean anything from their schooled faces, but I'm guessing they have known of this plan since their grim expressions in the dining room this morning. If they have not been able to deter Prince Jakut from this stupidity, his mind will be hard to change.

'When I was found after the attack that left me for dead, your father, Lord Tersil, took me into his home and you cared for me and brought me back to life. Your father has provided a discreet escort for my travels across Caruca to Lydnonia, where I intend to wait for news of the King under my uncle's protection.'

I rub tingling hands against the anxious squeeze in my chest.

'What sort of father,' I say, as steadily as I can, 'would allow his sixteen-year-old daughter to travel the country with a young Prince whose life is in danger?'

'My assassins left me for dead over five months ago. The King's soldiers began their search after the winter darkness, but no one believes I am alive. While I am presumed dead, my life and yours are safe.'

'People will notice me!' I hiss. 'They will ask questions. What possible reason could propel a young lady halfway across the kingdom with two of her father's kinsmen and the Prince of Caruca?'

Jakut looks perplexed. 'They will wonder whether you have captured the Prince's heart when you sat day after day by his bedside willing him back to life. They will be full of curiosity and questions, but the last thing they will ask is if you are Uru Ana.'

So I will be watched closely by everyone. The Prince will have a reason to post guards outside my door—in the name of protection. I will not be able to breathe without someone noticing. And how am I supposed to convince lords and ladies I am one of them?

'A man who has money and authority,' I say, 'would not let his young, influential daughter go without more reason than she has captured the Prince's attention.'

Jakut straightens his shoulders and touches his fur collar where the royal signet ring hangs hidden from sight. 'We are secretly engaged.'

He cannot be serious! But Tug and Brin's sombre expressions confirm that he is.

'People are not blind!'

'I will need you by my side, helping me navigate whom and what I should already know. It is the perfect excuse to keep you close.'

'Deadran,' I call, rousing the old tutor from where he half-snoozes by the fire. 'Tell him it is ridiculous.'

Jakut bites his bottom lip. 'Would it be so hard, Mirra,' he says, 'to pretend?' The sincerity in his eyes sets my nerves on edge. A sickness rises through me as I realise what Brin and Tug know. This is a lost battle.

'Perhaps,' I say, swallowing the lump threatening to strangle my voice, 'if I were travelling on some diplomatic mission for my father.'

'You are too young and too—' He cuts himself off. The unfinished sentence hangs in the air, affronting me and making me curious at the same time. I am too what?

'You are both willing to risk your lives for such a ruse?' I demand of Tug and Brin. Brin's brow dips in the slightest show of disapproval but it is the only response I get. 'So it has been decided?' I do not restrain the fury surging to the surface.

'Mirra,' Jakut says, resting a hand on my arm. I flinch and move away. Until two weeks ago, three people comprised my world. I will be lost in a royal fort, surrounded by lords and ladies, pretending I know of romance and courtship when my heart is a cold mystery even to myself. 'You won't have to do anything,' he says. 'I'll be the one that convinces them. All I ask is you stay discreetly by my side.'

I eat in silence. When I rise to gather my things for our journey, I catch sight of myself in the giant mirror above the fireplace. A cold shiver prickles down my back. It is as though a wraith from the mind-world has crept into the dining room through a forbidden doorway. I almost mistook my reflection for one of the innkeeper's ladies in Delladea fifteen years ago.

It is the first time I have seen myself in silver glass since I was ten. My face is still heart-shaped, the structure of my cheeks and snub nose bear the same neat contours as before. My skin is sandy, my brown eyes almost black they are so dark. But I do not recognise myself. I am a stranger. The eyes ageless and haunted. I look away.

Disturbed, I tell myself it is the effect of midnight-black hair pouring down my back, the uncomfortable dress, the sudden shock of seeing myself six years older. I tell myself I am not afraid of the girl in the mirror, but deep in my bowels I am all twisted up. It is as though I do not know myself. And that is almost as unnerving as what awaits me in Lyndonia.

TWENTY

After miles of vast flat forests, hamlets and villages the Lyndonian fort emerges on the horizon. It stands in the centre of a frozen lake, six towers reaching to the leaden sky. During the heart of winter the lake ice would be thick enough to walk across, but now its surface shimmers with cracks in the dawn half-light. And even if you could cross it, the smooth, damp walls would be almost impossible to climb. Besides, the guards in the towers have already spotted our arrival. Apparently, Lyndonia is not a place one enters or exits without being accounted for. I could never have made it inside without the Prince. My stomach twists. When I find Kel, how will I get him out of here?

We gallop around the shoreline towards a wooden bridge, the fort's only access. Four guards on horseback appear and head us off. Helmets shield their faces. Armour covers their breasts, and longswords hang by their thighs. As they circle us, Tug slips his hand beneath his saddle where he keeps his extra knife. Jakut's shoulders straighten. His expression at once arrogant and aloof.

'We must ask you to move on,' a guard shouts. 'There is sickness in Lyndonia. It is forbidden to enter or leave the fort at this time.'

'Whose orders do you follow?' the Prince asks.

'His Royal Highness Prince Roarhil, Duke of Rathesyde.'

'Perhaps you could tell my uncle his nephew is here.'

The guard reins his horse to a halt. He drops from his stallion and takes off his helmet. Jakut dismounts and closes the gap between them.

'Commander Fror?' he says, 'is that you?'

The commander's wide face shifts with recognition and confusion. 'Your Royal Highness,' he says bowing. 'Prince Jakut, please accept my apologies. It has been a long time.' The other guards follow his lead, dismounting and bowing.

I watch Jakut with a growing sense of disquiet. The risk he's just taken is dangerous and unnecessary. He has hazarded a guess based on Deadran's description of a man with a hoarse voice, reputed for his giant moustache being the head of the Duke's army.

'Deadran has not changed so much these ten years,' the Prince says. 'You must recognise him.'

Deadran nods in their general direction.

'Of course,' Fror answers. Confusion flutters behind his gaze again. I can almost feel the questions pouring through his mind. Not least of all, why the missing heir to the throne has arrived at his uncle's castle with his old, blind tutor, two thugs and a girl.

'Well,' the Prince says. 'I am sure we have taken you by surprise. And what is this sickness you speak of?'

'The pox, Your Royal Highness,' the commander says.

'A strange time for such a virus to spread, is it not? Usually, we are safe from such things until mid-summer. Nevertheless, I have had the pox. You must not concern yourself on my account.'

Jakut returns to his horse and mounts with graceful ease. Fror hesitates. The Prince searches about expectantly.

'Something wrong, Commander? It has been a long ride. I am hungry and I wish to speak with my uncle.'

'Your Highness.' Fror bows his head in compliance, but uncertainty shadows his movements as he returns to his horse.

The commander rides at the head of our group, a guard on each side of us and one at the rear. As our horses clatter across the pier stretching into the lake, there comes a shout from the bell tower. A drawbridge lowers connecting the pier with the fort's archway. Ahead of me, Tug tilts his head to the spiked portcullis, the armed soldiers on the walls and in the towers, and I wonder if he's thinking what I'm thinking: The Duke looks like he's anticipating an imminent attack.

Beyond the main gate lies a courtyard surrounded by high walls with fist-sized windows. Arched passages lead off in several directions. A bell tower to our left, a large brick building on our right. If an enemy made it across the bridge, they would be surrounded and immobilised at once.

Stable hands run towards us from the building. We dismount and once they have taken the horses, Fror guides us through a flagstone passageway with thick walls and arched roofs. We cross a second smaller courtyard, weave through a passage inside the wall, and come out in an open square.

Only a handful of stallholders occupy the fort's main marketplace. Soldiers parade by the water fountains and in front of the barracks. More soldiers than customers. A dozen streets wind off the plaza, arched passages constructed inside the towering walls.

Commander Fror leads us to a north-facing street. We pass narrow doorways and steep stone stairways. We wind into a small yard, walls so close together you can barely see the sky. A woman drying bed linen with a beater, orders her children inside. They gather smooth pebbles from the steps where they play, and scuttle away through a low door.

I wonder if Commander Fror's warning of the pox holds some truth. Neither Kel nor I have ever had the virus. We have never been ill with anything. An advantage, the only advantage, of growing up in isolation. My clammy skin prickles with heat and I mock myself for worrying that I could already be showing symptoms.

The commander leads us into a hall with a high wooden roof and a dining table as long as three men.

'Please make yourselves comfortable,' he says. 'I will send word to the kitchen to bring you breakfast and let the Duke know that you are here.'

'Thank you.' Jakut drapes himself on a cushioned bench while the rest of us watch Fror leave. Even Deadran listens to the commander as he strides away. Four guards remain outside the hall doors, far enough away for us to talk without being overheard.

Tug pulls at the collar of his new tunic, which looks wrong with his tattooed beast-face. He catches my eye. I look away and turn my thoughts to Kel. Has he arrived already? Could he be part of the reason they have closed the fort?

Seven days ago, my brother's eyes showed the faintest signs of settling, the golden glimmer minutely duller. Even so, it could take months for the grey-blue of his irises to swallow all evidence of his Uru Ana blood. His captors will keep him hidden until then, because if rumour got out that the Duke and Duchess had broken the law and purchased a shadow weaver, even they could be hanged for treason against the King. But if Kel is here, Commander Fror knows about it.

'Find out what you can,' the Prince says. I nod, extending my awareness in the direction the commander was headed. Minds brush into me like spider webs breaking against skin, but none match the angular shape and sawdust feel of the commander's. I continue until I find one moving faster and surer than the rest. I prod the edges, careful not to be sucked in, only wishing to flutter on the fringes where the memories form.

He marches through a long corridor posted with guards, knocks on a door, enters a round tower room. A table stands in the centre with a giant map sprawled across it. Several men discuss lands, positions of soldiers, security. They all defer to a man cloaked in white bear fur. The Duke, Prince Roarhil. He looks up at Commander Fror, blue eyes so penetrating it is as though I am there and he is looking straight at me.

'Leave us,' he instructs his advisers. Unlike Jakut, the Duke's eminence flows across the room, intimidating, unwavering. This is the difference between a man who knows he is royalty and a man who thinks he is, but who does not remember. The genuine article exposing a counterfeit.

Once the Commander and the Duke are alone, the Duke's gaze shifts to a concealed corner of the room. A woman perches in a velvet chair. Chestnut curls fall in waves around her shoulders. Her eyes match the ruddy browns of her hair and light up her face. The Commander does not seem surprised by her presence.

'What is your news?' the Duke asks.

'Prince Jakut is here, Your Royal Highness.'

A unmistakable look of fear passes between Duke and lady.

'He would not be deterred from seeing you by news of the pox.'

The Duke recovers slowly. The lady rises, swishes to where he props himself against the table, and places her hand over his in a gesture of support.

'Who travels with him?'

'Deadran, two odd looking men, and a young woman.'

'Deadran?'

'His old tutor, Your Highness.' The Duke turns to the woman. When he speaks it is as much to her as his commander. 'His timing, his sudden reappearance… The King's soldiers search for him in the north, yet he shows up here, out of nowhere, without an escort.'

'We must move the boys to the old tower,' the woman says, her voice soft but firm. 'Four men and a lady will be easy to oversee. Assign two guards to each to ensure they do not wander where they must not. It is possible the Prince comes seeking you as an ally. We must act cautiously.'

'Any word of the King's return from the Etean front?' the Duke asks Commander Fror.

'Nothing, Your Highness.'

'This is no coincidence,' the Duke says. 'It cannot be. We should get rid of the shadow-weaving boy.'

The woman's hand tightens over his. 'Husband,' she says, 'we may still need him. Let us speak with Jakut first, find out what happened to his escort. Perhaps he knows who lies behind his attempted assassination.'

The Duke nods. 'We will receive His Royal Highness in the great hall,' he tells Commander Fror. 'Bring them all.'

Extracting myself from the Commander's mind is like walking head-on into a gale of dust. My eyes blur, struggling to refocus on the dining room.

A bowl of soup now sits before me, and the Prince is by my side. Tug and Brin eat further down the table, heads lowered, eyes on the guards beyond the hall doors.

'Your hands are shaking,' Jakut says.

My thoughts reel, still spinning. *The boys in the tower… Get rid of the shadow-weaving boy.* I crush my palms in my lap, quelling my agitation. Kel is here! I can barely contain the joy, relief, and fear.

It is more necessary than ever that the Duke and Duchess believe our story, and perceive Prince Jakut as an ally. He must not give them reason to suspect he is hiding something. Kel's immediate safety depends on it.

But the Prince is as good as a counterfeit. An impostor. He might have lived eighteen years as heir to the throne, but he remembers none of it. Placed under scrutiny next to the Duke the fraud will be palpable. And they are already afraid of him. Afraid he will discover Kel's presence and know their treachery against the King.

Jakut studies me. I force my body to relax. 'I am tired from the journey,' I say.

'Did you see anything of use?'

'They question you turning up here when there has been no word of you since the rumours of your assassination. They do not understand what it means. And they fear whoever tried to assassinate you.'

He nods, muscles in his face softening. 'What of the pox?'

'They wish to deter anyone from entering or leaving the fort.'

'That much is obvious. The question is why?'

'Whoever plots against you, may also be a threat to them.' I draw up my eyes to his. 'It is crucial they believe you are here as an ally.'

He breathes in deeply, holding my gaze. Then he rises and goes to Deadran two seats away. He lays a hand on Deadran's shoulder. The old tutor is the one who convinced him to seek allies and safety here, and now I realise two things. Jakut is relieved to discover his uncle has played no part in the plot against him. And I am not the only one who might fail this test.

TWENTY-ONE

The great hall's carnelian red curtains and patterned stone floor swim in my vision. Nerves crush my ability to think. The mental abyss in my head is worse than the first time Pa left me in Blackfoot Forest to fend for Ma and Kel. Then, I barely ate for two weeks. I dreaded bounty hunters finding us, Ma's sickness worsening before Pa returned with medicine, Pa never coming back at all.

Now I'm seized with the irrational fear that the Duke of Rathesyde will take one look at me, and realise I am no lady. One conversation with Jakut, and he will sense the man before him is not Prince Jakut of Caruca, but somehow an impersonator. Because without his memories, the Prince is pretending to be himself when really he has no idea who he is.

`In less than an hour, Kel could be taken from the fort and lying in a grave.

The Prince says something. I concentrate on the sunlight dancing through the windows, warm on my face.

You've come further than you ever imagined. And you will keep going. I am not a twelve-year-old girl left in a forest to care for an infant and a bedridden mother. Be the girl in the mirror, a voice deep inside whispers. *Be strong and unfathomable.*

Beyond the grand hall's far door, eight minds swoop towards us. The Duke and his entourage approach.

I straighten my spine and hold my head high, eyes fixed ahead. Tug and Brin stand somewhere behind the Prince and I, but I barely notice their presence. The fear I once harboured for them has vanished like a cloud of warm breath on cold air. They should fear me. I am the Uru Ana girl who will soon know her enemy. The Carucans believe if you are of royal bloodline, you have been chosen by their Gods, and will be protected above all others.

But their Gods are not mine. I will carve my own destiny.

Jakut is suddenly standing too close again. Mouth, eyes, lips filling my view. I try to ignore him, guarding my attention on the mind-world and the descending threat I will somehow defy. For Kel, for myself, for all Uru Ana.

'Mirra,' he says, squeezing my arms until I look at him. 'You did not choose to be here. I meant it when I said I was sorry for that.' His stance shifts. 'I wish to confess something.'

My eyes dart between the doorway and the Prince. A confession? The Duke is seconds from arriving. What is Jakut trying to do?

'When I saw you in the forest with Tug—' He swallows, stress lines appearing on his forehead.

I narrow my eyes. Tug must be right. Jakut is trying to play with my emotions, pretend he's like the outcast who has no friends so that I'm more malleable to his needs. I'm an idiot for worrying his skills of deception would not get him through this. With the Duke to show him how, the Prince will learn to command a room within minutes. He will soak up his uncle's sense of entitlement and eminence and no one will see the difference.

Urgency ripples from the Prince as though what he wishes to say cannot wait.

'Stop,' I press my hand to his chest. 'Whatever you're doing, stop.'

His jaw twitches and twists. 'I was jealous.' He smiles unhappily. 'Tug has hurt you in unforgivable ways and yet some how it's as though you've forgiven him. You forgive him, but not me.'

Jealous of my relationship with Tug? Does he think me so gullible and needy I will fall for this? My jaw clenches and I am about to say what I think of him, when servants throw open the far doors.

'Prince Roarhil, the Duke of Rathesyde and Elise, the Duchess of Rathesyde.' The announcement carries to every corner of the immense hall. The Duke and Duchess parade in, escorted by the Commander, three soldiers and two ladies-in-waiting.

I curtsey, forcing Jakut to release his grip and face his aunt and uncle. He has done this on purpose, but I'm too flustered to figure out why. His absurd confession has stirred a longing inside me I cannot fight. I am Uru Ana, privy to men's darkest secrets, witness to the memories that haunt and the memories that comfort. It is my nature to desire a deep sense of connection with those in my company. Besides, anyone who has spent six years with only their parents would be desperate for a friend.

Eyes on the ground, I remain in a low curtsey as the Duke and Duchess approach. The Duchess curtsies and her husband bows. A fraction of a second later, the Prince returns their greeting.

'Your Royal Highness,' the Duke says. 'Your presence here is a great blessing of Rhag.' Jakut straightens and I count to three in my head as Deadran instructed, before rising. 'We are relieved to see you in good health. It has been many moons since we learnt fifteen of your escort had been found dead, and you along with five others were missing.'

Five of his escort missing, this is something I did not know. I raise my head and meet the Duchesses inquisitive gaze. Commander Fror's memories did not capture her accurately—the radiance of her skin; the auburn highlights in loose curls now pinned in a high chignon. I smile, but a new unease settles within. There is something familiar about her.

'My injuries left me much weakened before the long-sleep,' Jakut says. I stare at his right hand. The ruby-stoned signet ring he has kept hidden around his neck, now displayed on his middle finger. 'I was very fortunate to find good care and good companions to help me heal.'

His attention shifts and I blink back at him, offer a tentative smile.

'We have much to discuss,' he continues. 'But first, I wish to intro-duce you to Lady Mirra of the House of Tersil in Delladea. Her father gave me refuge in the Delladean fort over the long-sleep, provided me with excellent healers, and kept my presence a close guarded secret at my demand.'

I curtsey again.

'These,' he continues, 'are her trusted guards, Brin and Tug. And this is Deadran, my old tutor, and now my steward. We travelled under false names from Delladea for my protection.'

'We are honoured you stay with us,' the Duke responds. I risk another glance at the Duchess. She is looking over my shoulder, skin pasty with shock. 'The King's soldiers scour the north for you,' the Duke continues.

'I did not wish to be found,' Jakut answers dismissively. 'Has my father returned from the Etean front?'

'We expect news any day. We thought it would come as soon as the ice thawed, but we have heard nothing from the Ruby Court since the long-sleep.'

A memory floods the mind-world.

From a high window, the Duchess watches a lone soldier gallop towards the fort. Then she is rushing down a steep stairway. She holds the child in her belly with one hand, grips the iron rail with another. She tears through stone passages, halts hidden in the shadows of an archway. The King's soldier is greeted by a soldier from the fort. Breathless, Elise enters the courtyard.

Her mind jumps again. *She is sinking to the ground clutching a silver leaf shaped medallion and a signet ring. A gut-wrenching moan swells on the air.*

My legs tremble as I struggle to sever myself from her memories. The Duke's mouth moves but I do not hear his words. The Duchess sways. I step forwards to offer support. Her eyes flutter. She is about to lose consciousness.

'Your Royal Highness,' I hiss. Too late. She's falling. I try to catch her, but as our bodies meet, the gaps in my thinking connect and I jerk with shock. Tug! The Duchess is the girl sealed away in the fortress of his mind!

She falls sideways pulling me with her. The Duke lunges for his wife. Surprise and the force of her fall unbalance me. I'm tumbling into them, when Jakut's arms fasten around my waist. His chest crushes into my back as he holds me steady.

'Lady Mirra,' he says, breath warm against my neck. His palms skim over my ribs and settle on my stomach. Through the fabric of my dress, I can feel the tips of his fingers, the rise and fall of his chest. I should play my part, lean into him, but I'm paralysed.

A lady-in-waiting skitters across the coloured stones with smelling salts. She waves them beneath the Duchess' nose. Elise, lying on the floor in her husband's arms, opens her eyes muttering.

The Prince releases me and kneels beside his aunt. I gasp at the air as though suddenly free of a mind-numbing, body-freezing spider's venom.

Tug and the Duchess! He will betray us! Tug's loyalty has always been to the girl in his memories. Even if he doesn't tell his dear Elise what is going on here, his presence has destroyed any chance of Jakut gaining the Duke's trust.

'My wife is unwell,' the Duke says, addressing Jakut. 'There is much for us to discuss, but for now I hope you understand if I ask Chamberlain Velequez to show you to the royal guest quarters.'

One of the men in his entourage steps forwards and tilts his head in a respectful nod.

Jakut rises. 'Of course, uncle.' The five of us retreat, following Chamberlain Velequez towards the doors.

My throat closes like a fist strangling me. Tug's fist. I have guarded myself against the wrong man.

IF I HAD MY KNIVES, I would use Tug as target practice. I would take one right now and spin it deep into his ankle, snap the tendon and stop him from ever walking with his back to me again.

He strides ahead of the Prince and I, following Commander Fror and Chamberlain Velequez through the austere royal gardens. Small-leafed berry shrubs arranged in enormous pots provide the only greenery. Eight soldiers surround us, and a girl, assigned as my maid, scuttles along on the outskirts of our group.

'Is the Duchess sick?' Jakut murmurs. He observes our surroundings with mild interest, though wariness pulses behind his eyes. I shrug off the question, jaw locked, gaze riveted on Tug's head which I would gladly crush beneath my leather boot.

'What happened in there?'

'I don't know,' I snap. We are both fools. That's what happened.

'You're angry with me for touching you.'

'I almost fell and you caught me,' I say. 'Why would I be angry?' I stretch my lips, flutter my eyes, mocking our love-bird farce. We enter a dim passage, and I quicken my pace. He doesn't try to keep up, but falls back into step with Deadran. I hope my behaviour will put off his interrogations until I've decided what to do about Tug.

I see nothing of the room I'm shown to. My only thoughts are of getting rid of the girl who unpacks dresses, fine linens, and undergarments, courtesy of the Prince. I pace back and forth before three long sash windows. Tug and Brin have an adjacent room, Jakut is in the suite above us.

'Would you like me to build your fire, madam?'

'I'm not cold.'

'Then I will heat your bath water.'

'No,' I say. 'I wish to rest. You may return an hour before we are expected for dinner.' I hug my arms around my stomach and stare out the window, waiting for her to leave.

'Would you like me to draw your curtains or undress you?'

'I'll manage.'

Finally, she goes. I stretch my consciousness into the mind-world and glean the impressions of six guards stationed around the tower. Tug and Brin are in the next-door room. The Prince and Deadran are above us. Satisfied, I creep into the hall.

Tug opens his bedroom door seconds after I knock. I sense Brin concealed behind it, no doubt knife in-hand, ready to spring.

'It is Mirra,' Tug says. He steps out to join me in the corridor. Brin emerges behind him.

'What does she want?'

'I'll deal with this.' Tug closes the door in Brin's face. His eyes check left and right down the dim, stone passage.

'There is no one to hear us,' I say. 'Explain what is going on or I'm speaking to the Prince now.'

The black tattoos painted over his eyebrows arch upwards. 'What's the problem?'

'You and the Duchess are the problem. She knows you are not the man His Royal Highness Prince of Caruca claims you to be.'

My words are like the false step that sets off an avalanche. A massive shift moves over Tug. In the mind-world, it's as though the high fortress walls crumble only to reconstruct themselves into a new maze-like formation. I stare at him in amazement. In my mind, it's as though the tattoos vanish, and I am looking at the face he once had. His true face. A man ready to die protecting the woman he loves.

'You will never speak of this again. It will not affect the Prince's test for you.'

Tug's unexpected resurrection almost undid Duchess Elise in the great hall. How could this little fact not change everything? The Duchess will be in turmoil. She may concede to her husband's wishes to remove Kel from the fort. She will certainly encourage him to double or triple the soldiers assigned to watch over us. Getting to Kel will be impossible.

'I do not care about the Prince's test for me. I care about my brother. Your presence has made the Duchess nervous. And when people are nervous they are more inclined to stupidity.' I barely stop myself from spitting the last word in his face. 'Before she saw you they were talking about getting rid of Kel because of the Prince's unexpected and unsettling arrival. Now she will be even more agitated.'

A door clicks. Tug's head whips around to see Brin peering from their chambers. Brin stares at Tug pointedly, as though bringing up a conversation I have missed.

'We should get paid and leave,' he says.

'Leave with only half the gold?' Tug retorts.

'Leave while we still can.'

'You're a free man.'

'She is weaving shadows around you,' Brin growls. 'You're already different and her hold is growing on you by the day.'

I swish forwards, propelled by an inward burning to strike at Brin's unfounded prejudices. I grab the threads about his chunky neck and rip away the crystals. 'These will not protect you,' I say, dangling them in front of his flat nose. He grabs his knife and wields it at me.

'Good thinking, Brin! Try explaining to the Duke why you've stabbed me!'

'Enough!' Tug pinches my arm. I struggle to free myself, as he marches me to my bedroom. He slams the bedroom door and thrusts me down. I land sprawled on an embroidered rug, skirts creeping up my legs. I scramble to my feet, instinctively patting my hip for my knife and hissing at its absence.

'The Duchess Elise will not speak of me to the Duke or change her course of action because I am here.'

'I want my knives back!'

'She has neither heard of me, nor seen me for twelve years. Until today, she thought I was dead. It was the shock of seeing me alive that made her react so. She will show no such emotion again.'

I retreat to the fireplace, lunge for the poker. I am desperate for a weapon in my hands, desperate to feel less vulnerable. 'Why have you come back from the dead?' I ask.

'Grow up, Mirra.' Tug huffs and strides for the door.

'If you leave without answering, I'm going straight to the Prince.'

He halts and I feel victorious, until he opens his mouth. 'Five of the Prince's escort are missing,' he says without bothering to face me. 'Where do you think they are?'

'Don't change the subject.'

In an instant, he has swung around, and is barreling across the room. I recoil, until I'm squashed to the wall, clutching the useless fire poker. Knife throwing and arrow shooting are not hand-to-hand combat, and I am no match for Beast-face.

'I'll tell you where they are. Dead. By his sword.'

I shake my head. Tug has no idea what happened to those men. 'Why would the Prince kill them?'

'No witnesses.'

'Witnesses to what?' Frustration is sharper than any knife cut. Once again Tug twists my thoughts against the Prince, but I cannot ignore him. This is his world. He has survived wars, advised commanders,

fought campaigns for the King. He understands politics and the treacherous power plays that riddle the ruling nobility.

'You have nothing to gain by telling the Prince that the Duchess and
I once knew each other.'

'When you were selling Kel in the pit, and a Lyndonian officer
made an offer for him, you knew the officer was working for the Duke
or Duchess. You came here to find out why. You came here because
you thought the Duchess must be in trouble if she would risk breaking
the King's law by using the talents of a shadow weaver.'

Tug's eyes close, a beat too long to be blinking.

'I came here to get paid.' The finality in his voice says he's done.
Which is just as well because there is no fight left in me. Once he has
gone, I sink into the armchair by the empty grate. I need to start
searching the mind-world for Kel. Who knows how much time I've got
before the Duke decides to remove him from the fort? But for a while
all I can do is sit numbly digesting Tug's accusations against the Prince.
Five of the Prince's men were not found dead with the rest of his
escort. Where are they now?

TWENTY-TWO

The muscles beneath my eyes twitch with tiredness. I meant to sleep before tonight's banquet in honour of the "found" Prince of Caruca, but the last ten hours have sped by in a state of tense antici- pation. Over and over, hope swelled as I stretched my awareness through the fort. Driven by the conviction that the next mind I touched would send me tumbling into a warm cloud of feathery dandelion seeds. The next mind would be Kel's. Or the next one. Or the next.

But I have not found him. And now jittery and washed out, my taut attitude is doing nothing to appease the nervous maid. She tugs the threads of my dress too tight. She dabs garnet lip-dust on my lips and smudges dark charcoal so thickly around my eyes I look ghoulish. As she braids my hair in front of a silver-wrought mirror, I make a mental map of the fort, trying to work out what my search missed.

But doubt spreads through me. What if the Duke has ordered Kel from Lyndonia? What if there is some truth in Brin's amulet protec- tions, and they have confined my brother in a crystal-padded room where I cannot sense him. Or, worst of all, what if Kel's mind has altered beyond recognition? Experience shifts perception. The way we perceive and interpret the world alters the form and texture of a mind.

Tug's mind reshaped right in front of my inner eye! How much could Kel's have changed over the last few days?

There comes a knock on the bedroom door, splintering my thoughts. The maid jumps. Flower-headed pins scatter.

'Leave them.'

'But your hair,' she stutters, 'is half done.'

'It is fine.'

My visitor is not Tug, Brin or the Prince. I nod at the maid and when her back is turned, rush to the fireplace to stand with my hands in reach of the poker.

The door opens. The maid curtseys and shuffles aside revealing the Duchess.

'Your Grace,' I say, curtseying and bowing my head. Her guards wait out of sight. How many are with her, or where they are positioned is inconsequential. She is the threat, not them.

As the maid leaves, Duchess Elise stands by the door, watching me. I do not rise until the tilt of her head shows me I have her permission. In the soft glow of the room's torchlight, her face is a mystery. Not a single line around the mouth nor eyes reveal her thirty years. Not a hint in her expression tells of her shock and sudden illness in the royal hall. It is as Tug said. As though it never happened.

I smooth my hands over the pale-gold waist of my silk dress and take slow breaths, my chest pushing against the fitted bodice.

She sways towards me, enquiring eyes locked on my face. 'It is as I feared,' she says. 'They have exhausted you riding through the night on horseback.'

'I am well, Your Grace. Thank you for your concern. And I am happy you seem in better health now,' I add, prodding to see if there are any cracks in her mask of dignified composure.

'I am much better, thank you, Mirra. A disagreement with the dragon-fish I ate for lunch. May I sit with you before we are called for dinner?'

'Of course.' I move to the window seat, showing her my back so she cannot read the disappointment in my face. I had planned on spending a few minutes spying on the Duke and Duchess before the banquet. I wished to scan what they have done since our meeting in the great hall. The Prince will expect it. And without more information about the Duchess, I am vulnerable.

She sits close beside me. Her auburn hair has been restyled in a stunning weave of gold and silver clips. Matching gold and silver leaves embroider her ruffled cream dress.

'Your father must trust and esteem your guards very highly to have sent you and Prince Jakut all this way with a two-man escort.'

I sit up straighter, tiredness diminished by a prick of adrenaline. She is probing for information about Tug. No Tug, she won't simply forget you. She might not divulge your presence to the Duke, not yet, but that is because she wishes to understand it first.

'Tug and Brin are his best swordsmen, and Prince Jakut wished it so,' I say. 'Under the circumstances, my father accepted it would be safer for us not to draw attention with a large group. I disguised myself as a boy.' I laugh, feigning embarrassment at this confession and hoping it will win a little of her confidence.

She tilts her head and looks away, then she smiles. 'Well, I can see you are resourceful and you must hold the Prince dear to your heart.' The tiny muscle beneath one of my eyes twitches wildly. 'Tell me, what is your agreement? The Prince has asked your father for your hand?'

I do not answer, knowing she will take my silence for assent.

'Your father was not aware he is promised to another?'

'What do you mean?' I blurt, not having to fake the surprise.

'He has been promised to the Princess of Rudeash since he was fourteen. It is common knowledge in the Ruby Court and, I thought, in every court throughout Caruca.'

Rudeash. A northern kingdom separated from Caruca by a hundred miles of snow and ice.

The Duchess' scintillating gaze is like the heat of a fire. I want to turn away. Deadran and Jakut have kept this from me on purpose. Jakut's confession in the great hall was timed to turn me into an unpoised, distracted girl from the north. How better to convince the Duke and Duchess I am so naive I believe the Prince's interest in me genuine? After all, I cannot even remain composed greeting a Duke! But how will he justify such a ruse of unkindness to his aunt and uncle?

'We have not had the chance to get to know one another,' the Duchess says, adjusting a silver pendant around her neck. It is the heavy, leafed pendant she clutched in her memory of losing Tug. 'Such news from a stranger must be difficult to bear, but I can see it has not gone too far yet, and I must warn you of the Prince's reputation.'

'Reputation?' I echo. My dress grows itchy. I pull at the waist where its cutting off my breath.

'He has seduced several young women at the royal court. His recent relationship with Lady Calmi led his father to advance the wedding. Last summer, he sent Prince Jakut to the tundra, ordered to return with his bride though she is not yet thirteen.'

This explains why Jakut was in the far northern regions when his escort was attacked. I prickle at the idea of a young girl traded off to an unknown man in a kingdom thousands of miles from her home and family. Apparently, it is not better to be a princess than an outlawed Uru Ana.

'I do not understand,' I say feebly. She pats my hand, then rises and crosses to my door. I think she means to leave, but she returns with a serving boy holding a tray. She takes two shiny silver goblets and hands me one.

'It will help calm your nerves.'

I sip. The wine tastes bitter, but the warmth that blooms in my chest is pleasant. I take a longer gulp, pretending to watch the boy as he slips away, while from the corner of my eye I observe the Duchess. Does she really believe my father is Lord Tersil from Delladea, and out of ignorant good faith, he allowed me to leave home with my fiancé Prince whose life is in danger? What fear lies in this court that they risk harbouring a child shadow weaver and close the fort to visitors?

The wine unwinds my muscles. I sink back into the window seat, feeling more relaxed and confident. I will find a way of playing the naïve, wounded maiden to my advantage. Maybe Elise will take pity on me and help me escape Jakut. I could ask her for horses and secret passage from the fort. I could stow Kel in a giant chest of dresses, or a wagon, and remove him from under their noses.

The Duchess studies me. 'This is a lot to take in. But I can see you are a sensible girl.'

'Why would he do this?' I say. 'My father would have sent Tug and Brin or as many men as he wished for his escort. Why trick me like this? Am I a distraction? Something to amuse himself with before returning to the Ruby Court? And where is his bride-to-be?'

Elise frowns and twists the stem of her goblet between thumb and forefinger. 'Perhaps I am wrong.' She takes a sip of her wine. 'A year can change a young man. Perhaps to delay giving you up he has come here instead of returning directly to the Red City. He has never spoken of the Princess of Rudeash?'

'No.'

'But your father, Lord Tersil, must know the pressures on the Prince to make a formidable alliance that will strengthen the kingdom.'

'In Delladea we marry for love.'

A sudden memory overpowers my inner eye.

Sweet perfume assaults my senses. Water flows through a narrow waterway.

'He is the King's brother! The King will not permit him to marry you,' Tug snarls.

'You are wrong. He loves me. It is as good as done.'

'The heir to the throne shoulders a great responsibility,' the Duchess says, her voice snapping my attention back to the room. 'The King could never allow your match, even if the Prince wished it.'

I press a finger to my tingling forehead. I have spent too long in the mind-world today. How will I manage the banquet with all those memories swamping my thoughts?

'What good is it being a prince if you cannot marry whom you wish? No wonder he is careless in matters of the heart.'

The Duchess' eyes soften. 'I have seen the way he looks at you. He is enchanted, and you are an unusual girl. Perhaps we can help one another. Find out what happened when he went to the tundra. Perhaps the King of Rudeash changed his mind and refused to send his daughter. Whatever occurred, it may be linked to the attack on the Prince's escort. Your feelings for him now are confused, but I am sure you do not wish to see him hurt again.'

'I do not.'

The Duchess floats to her feet and sets her goblet on the

windowsill. My body is shaky, but I rise as politeness dictates. 'Let us go to dinner together,' she says, taking my arm and linking it through her own. 'We are already late.'

'I will join you in a few minutes,' I say.

The Duchess brushes her palm to my cheek like a mother would to her sick child. Her cool hand feels waxy and lifeless. 'Our conversation has upset you more than you would like to admit.'

A breath shudders through my chest. 'Perhaps I should take dinner in my room,' I say.

'You cannot run away from this. Better to tackle it straight on. Speak to the Prince tonight.'

'But I will be speechless before him.'

'You will tell him I came to see you were settled in. I asked about the Princess Aliylah. I was afraid some terrible fate met his future bride when his escort was attacked.'

'Thank you, Your Grace. I am grateful you trouble yourself to help me. Prince Jakut has deceived me as far as my own favour is concerned, but I still care for his wellbeing. I do not doubt his decision in coming here. You are honest, good people. Until his father returns from the Etean war, you are the only ones he can trust.'

'Is this why he has come? To wait until there is news of his father's return from the Etean front?'

'I believe so, Your Grace.'

She entwines her arm around mine again and leads me to the bedroom door. 'Elise,' she says. 'You must call me Elise. I am agreeably surprised to discover the young Prince's affection for you, even if it cannot come to anything. Perhaps all the rumours about him are unfounded, or he has finally grown up.'

I cannot imagine what these rumours of the Prince's conquests and lovers entail. Nor do I possess the energy or will to try. Let the Duchess ponder Jakut's uncharacteristic interest in an unsophisticated maiden from the north. He is right. Attempts to dissect our romantic relationship will distract the Lyndonian court for days.

TWENTY-THREE

High-ranking officers and royal guards display their finest uniforms. A lively fiddler's jig carries under the rowdy banter and laughter. A cluster of elegant women, silk skirts merging like petals of an exotic flower, sip from stemmed glasses. Servers deck the long tables with gravy-dripped meats, caramelised vegetables, steaming ceramic pots of beans and root plants.

The Duchess draws my halting body forwards. I am in the banquet hall of the King's only brother! A pulse of energy quickens my heartbeat and a smile flutters across my lips.

My cheeks are flushed from drinking, and from the men's glances at my bare neck and tight bodice. But another surge of heat flares in my chest when I catch sight of the Prince.

He stands with the Duke. His hair has been trimmed, lending him a military air. A moss-green doublet lightens his eyes and accentuates his muscled shoulders. For the first time, I truly understand I am looking at a warrior prince, trained from the age of eight in the King's gruelling military program. Quick enough to disarm Tug. Strong and swift enough to kill five soldiers.

My footsteps grind to a halt but the Duchess whispers encouragement and urges me forwards. At least awkwardness and distrust are not something I will need to fake. As I dip a curtsey, a servant blows a horn to hush the crowd.

'Let us celebrate Prince Jakut's arrival among us and his good health!' the Duke announces.

An approving cheer fills the hall. The Duchess watches sympathetically as I am forced to sit beside my lying suitor. At the far end of our table, Brin and Tug mingle with a group of officers. Brin slaps one on the back, chuckling loudly. Ale slops from his tankard. Tug's disapproving gaze slides to our end of the table. In response, Duchess Elise moves closer to her husband, rests her hand on his.

A server fills our glasses.

'Your beauty rivals the Duchess',' the Prince murmurs in my ear. I snort and accept the offer of wine. 'You don't drink, Mirra.' The light warning in his tone is clear. Better we keep our wits about us.

A voice in the back of my mind agrees, but tonight I want him to fear my recklessness. I have no idea what he is capable of, and I want him to feel a little of the spine-prickling uncertainty in return.

'You are not my husband, Your Royal Highness,' I say raising my glass and tilting it to his health.

He smiles unnaturally. 'So, you have been talking with the Duchess.' He enunciates his words for his aunt and uncle on the opposite side of the table to hear. 'It always amazes me what two women who are not acquainted and share nothing in common find to discuss.'

I lean closer, so only a warm breath separates my lips from his smooth neck. 'Perhaps you lack imagination,' I say. His composure slips in the slight pursing of his lips. Satisfaction worms through me. Two can play at his game. My crooked smile widens. The Duke throws an askance glance at his wife. She whispers a quick word in his ear.

'What are you doing?' Jakut says. I tilt my face close enough to detect the peppermint on his breath. His full wine glass goes untouched. He is not drinking.

'Am I making you uncomfortable?'

'Did you take wine with the Duchess?'

'Indeed,' I say.

'Then perhaps you should slow down. A lady does not get drunk.'

The Prince stabs his fork into a meat platter, takes a large slice and slaps it on my plate.

'And where is Deadran?' the Duke enquires. 'Does he not join us tonight?'

'Our journey here was not easy for him. I hope you will not be offended, but I gave him permission to take supper in his room. It is difficult for him to be around so many.'

'How considerate,' I mutter.

'It is well advised,' the Duke says. I cut my meat the way Deadran has taught me using a knife and fork.

As conversation turns to the Etean war, the wine sours on my palate. I roll my tongue over strange new flavours, chew slowly to appreciate the foreign textures and forms. But the alcohol fuzz in my head is dulling my senses. The loud table conversation and memories slipping and sliding from my inner-eye, are a constant irritation.

'Excuse me, Your Grace,' I say once the Duchess has finished asking me about the court of Delladea, 'I must get some air.' I rise from my chair. The Duke, Prince and nearest royal officers get to their feet.

'Would you like me to ask—' Jakut's voice fades as I cross the banquet hall. More than one set of eyes follow me to the open double doors. In the night's darkness, I pull at the strings of my bodice. A damp, brackish odour drifts on the breeze. It is the only hint water lies beyond the fort's endless walls. I am standing on a long veranda, which stretches the length of the building. I lay my hands on the railing and close my eyes, welcoming the slap of cold.

Footsteps clip over the wooden veranda slats. The Prince, or Tug or a guard. I do not care much whom.

'That was quite something.'

So it is the Prince.

'You were supposed to bring your betrothed Princess of Rudeash back from the north. And according to the Duchess you have a mistress.'

The Prince remains silent for so long, I turn, curious to see what he is doing. He stares at the full, speckled yellow moon. I look left and right and see a stairway twisting to a second-floor balcony. 'Perhaps we can see the lake from up there,' I say, lifting my skirt and heading for it. The steep steps wind around and around. I arrive at the top breathless from the chill in my chest and throat, the sudden exertion, and the wine.

A guard emerges below. He watches Jakut climb to join me. From here, beyond the main gates where the jetty draws a crooked line through ice-cracked water, a pale trail of moonlight shimmers on the crystallised surface.

'The Duchess wants me to discover why you did not return with the princess. She thinks it may be related to the attack on your escort.'

The Prince faces the view and leans his elbows on the balcony rail. 'My destiny is bound to a girl I have never met,' he says wistfully.

'You were promised to her when you were fourteen.'

'Deadran is no longer tied to the Ruby Court but he would hear of this. He should have told me.' He turns, spine pressed to the rail. His expression alters. A minuscule frown creases the gap between his brows. 'You think I knew?' he says, crossing his arms. 'It is my lack of memories that makes it so hard for you to trust me, isn't it?'

I do not answer. 'I suppose Deadran may not know the reason for your trip to the north. Your betrothed is too young for marriage. Your father pressed the union because of your mistress.'

'So Duchess Elise has warned you my intentions are fleeting and insincere.'

'And tonight I have behaved accordingly.'

He nods. 'Very well. We must speak with Deadran. Wait for me downstairs. I will excuse us to our host and hostess, say you are unwell and I am escorting you back to your chambers.'

TWO GUARDS WALK us through the quiet fort. Four others follow at a distance. Once we enter the circular courtyard surrounding the royal guest tower the Prince instructs our official guards to wait for him outside.

Deadran's room lies past mine at the end of the corridor. The Prince knocks on the door, but after a third try it is clear we will not receive an answer.

'He sleeps soundly.'

'You should return to the banquet,' I say. 'I will retire and we will speak with Deadran in the morning.' He nods and we return to my chamber door. I open it with a wrought silver key slipped into the miniature pocket at the waist of my dress.

'Mirra...'

'Good night, Your Royal Highness.' I start to close the door but he presses his palm to hold it.

'You think I am responsible for the disappearance of five men from my escort?'

I lower my head and nip the inner side of my cheek.

'You think I sanctioned those five men to attack my own escort, and then I personally murdered those who assisted my treachery? For what? A mistress? To avoid my duties as heir to the throne? In my bones and my blood I know I could not be such a man.'

'Why do you care what I think? I'm Uru Ana. Outlawed, captured, burned, murdered and enslaved by your grandfather. Your father, King Alixter has done nothing to change the hate and fear Carucans harbour towards my kind. Nothing to stop the mercenaries from hunting us down like wild beasts and selling us to lawless criminals for their own sadistic games. What would make you different? The only reason you insist on this misplaced notion of friendship is because I do not see inside your head. But your memories will return. With time the fog of the mist berry cleansing will rise and clear, and the truth will be shown to us both. You do not need me to tell you what sort of man you are.'

He pales. Our eyes catch like snarled hooks. A ball of saliva lodges in my throat. I have gone too far. Trembling begins as a low hum in my legs. I am unable to swallow, unable to break his gaze. He needs me. He won't do anything. He needs me too much. But I regret my words at once.

After a moment frozen in eternity, the Prince turns stiffly, and I find myself alone, blinking into darkness.

TWENTY-FOUR

I rummage through the dresser where the maid has unpacked corsets, brassieres and underpants. Then I attack the wardrobe of embroidered silk dresses, but I do not find my deerskin trousers and cotton shirt.

I take the lantern into the bathing chamber and see them lying on the tub to dry. My fur parka smells of lilac soap. Gone is the trapped snow mould rooted in the matted hair, the winter-sleep oils, the camp-fires's ashes and smoke. And though I've wished the parka clean a hundred times since waking from the long-sleep, Blackfoot Forest and my parents, have never felt so far away.

I wrestle with three buttons on the back of my silk dress, finally slip it off, and put on my hunting clothes. Happy to be dressed again in my cotton shirt and fitted trousers, I tuck the Prince's stolen room key into my empty knife belt. Lifting it from his doublet while he was distracted with my drunken flirtations was easy. In fact, it was so easy I half-suspect he allowed me to take it. But I am not about to waste an opportunity.

I crack open my bedroom door and listen. Wind wheezes around unseen nooks and gusts in from the chilly exterior. Far off a man coughs, but I do not waste precious effort stretching my senses through the tower. The six guards who followed us to the royal guest quarters all left with the Prince. Which leaves two men watching Deadran and I. Apparently, we are not dangerous.

I lock my door and carry my boots down the flagstone corridor. My hand traces bumps in the cold bricks as I climb the stairs to Jakut's suite. At his door, I smooth one palm across the keyhole and guide the key in with my other hand. The latch turns with a dull thud. I puff out a breath of satisfaction, retrieve my boots, and slink into Jakut's chambers.

With a match from the supply I've found in my guest room, I light a lantern and enter the living area. The hearth smells of smouldering ashes. In the far corner, near doors to a balcony, stands a grand writing desk. Leaves of parchment lie scattered across the leather top. I flick through scraps of indiscernible sketches and Jakut's handwriting, then check the drawers.

Once the lantern is extinguished with a little hiss from my wet fingers, I return it to the hook by the suite door, and venture onto the balcony. Keeping to the shadows of an overhead buttress, I search for signs of the guards. This side of the royal guest tower butts up against the roof of a long building. There is no escape from the closed court-yard below so patrols around the back of the tower are unnecessary.

I pull on my boots, and climb over the balcony railing. In the distance, the frosted lake glistens like a mirror. Behind it, silver-tipped pines stretch as far as the eye can see. I extend my arms so I am suspended over the edge and study the wood beamed roof. It is a small leap, and a larger drop, but the slats and beams are closely spaced and evenly constructed so I should not fall through the thatching.

I breathe in, softening my muscles, imagining I'm as graceful and soft-footed as a deer. Then I leap. In the second I am falling, I bend my legs to break the impact. My knees jar with the landing force, but the roof doesn't shake or crack beneath me, so I cannot complain. I creep to the end of the building and lower myself down a wooden door using a protruding metal knocker.

Once I am in a tunnel away from the guest chambers, I hurry towards the fort's northern quarter, hood pulled up, head lowered into the wind.

I am too exhausted to search the Duchess' mind over a long distance so I will hide somewhere near the banquet hall while I scour her memories. A detail has come back, and I intend to discover its significance, along with my brother's whereabouts. When Duchess Elise advised her husband to relocate Kel to the old tower, she suggested they move the boys. But when they referred to getting rid of the shadow weaver, they spoke of only one child. Which other boy or boys was she talking about?

On the western face of the banquet hall lies a water gate bastion where the Prince sometimes played as a child. Isolated from the rest of the fort, only the royal family's kitchen staff and maids have reason to access the water channel. It is perfect for my task.

As I approach, I sense two other minds close by, one lingering in the second access tunnel, one alone by the water channel. I creep to the edge of the archway and peer into the moonlit quadrangle. A woman stands looking down at the dark, open waterway. Loose strands of auburn hair spill out from her intricately clipped chignon. She hugs a thick cloak over her evening dress, and clutches a silver medallion. Her lips move as though in prayer and the medallion is a lucky symbol of the Gods.

For once, something has gone my way. I will not have to struggle through the mind-world to find the Duchess. She is here. Relieved at this small turn of fortune, I scan the paved yard for somewhere to hide. I do not want to be disturbed while travelling through her memories. I'm about to slip out of the tunnel and into a near alcove when she looks up. Though I'm concealed by pitch-black darkness, her gaze aims straight at me.

'Hello?' Her voice is little more than a whisper. She does not wish to alert her guard in the other tunnel who is close enough to call if needed, far enough to allow her privacy.

My hands sweat inside my fur gloves. If I run and she shouts, her guard will give chase. If I reveal myself, she will want an explanation.

As I hesitate, it strikes me she is waiting for somebody. Otherwise, a lurking figure would be cause for alarm.

The Duchess raises her skirt, steps onto the low channel wall that slices the yard into two segments, and lowers herself into the waterway. Amazed, I watch her tiptoe across a narrow beam. She performs a dangerous acrobatic tightrope walk, before climbing up the other side.

It is too late to run. I step from the tunnel and greet her. In the wash of pale moonlight, her features twist from wariness to shock. I pull off my hood so she sees who I am.

'Lady Mirra! Why are you dressed like a boy? What are you doing here? What has happened?'

'Lower your voice or your guard will hear us.'

She glances back in the direction of the soldier, then her eyes flick into the tunnel behind me.

'I come alone,' I say. 'But perhaps you were waiting for someone else, Your Grace?'

'No.' She shakes her head, dropping the leafed medallion.

'My guardsman, Tug? Or should I call him Tye?'

'What is the meaning of your question?'

'Well, Your Grace, if you were not waiting for company, why didn't you shout for your guard when you realised there was someone in the tunnel? These are treacherous times, are they not?'

Her eyes narrow. 'Explain this visit, Lady Mirra. Has Tye sent you?'

'Why would he send me?'

'You are playing games,' she snaps.

'Yet you stand here when you could leave.'

Brusquely, she gathers her skirts and turns, but something holds her in place. An invisible thread. Tug was certain she would not speak to her husband of his resurrection from the dead. Were they secret lovers before she became the Duke's wife?

If she is waiting for Beast-face, he could arrive at any moment. I must keep her on the defensive and discover what secret they share so I may use it to my advantage. Besides, I have gone too far with my challenging stance to draw back now. 'Tye has told me,' I bluff.

'Told you?' Her voice quivers. A bright room forms in the mind-world.

She wakes shivering, afraid. Grown ups crowd around her. Memories flash. Running from hunters. Getting caught. Escaping. A boy's face comes into focus. 'Calm yourself,' he says. 'You are safe now. We will look after you.'

I rear back in surprise. The boy was Tug. But that is not the reason my thoughts explode as though the skies have been set on fire. That is not the reason every hair on my arms and neck stand up as though I have grown metal spikes. Duchess Elise is Uru Ana. She is sighted, a shadow weaver, glitter-eyed.

The reason Tug does not fear me, the reason he has been able to build walls from our kind, the reason he has been so determined to hide his past with Elise, it all tumbles into place. He grew up hiding an Uru Ana, protecting her secret.

But if she has the sight, why hasn't she told the Duke the truth about me? Why did she come to my chambers and inform me of the Prince's impending marriage to a Rudeashan princess and of his mistresses, when one look into any of our memories of the last few days would have revealed I am Prince Jakut's purchased slave?

'You are Uru Ana,' I whisper. The words spill from my lips before I can stop them. The Duchess' pupils grow larger, blackness swallowing the autumn brown of her irises. She sways on her feet. If she passes out, I will get nothing from her. 'I am the only person who knows,' I say. 'Your secret is safe. Neither Tug nor I wish to betray you.'

A pained laugh escapes her. She threads her fingers, unravels and threads them again. Her shoulders slump. 'I have been careful. I never use the cursed sight. I have ignored it for so long it has faded to a faint imprint of something long removed. I thought Tye was dead and my secret buried with him.'

So she does not know we are the same! I must strike hard and fast, crush any desire she may have to trust Tug, or to turn to him after I leave tonight.

'We know you have the glitter-eyed boy,' I say. 'The Prince sent Tye on business to the Hybourg. While he was there a Lyndonian commander roused his curiosity.' The lie flows off my tongue, as though somewhere in the depths of my consciousness I was prepared for this. 'On further investigation, he discovered your commander was buying an Uru Ana boy.'

Elise shakes her head. 'I don't know what you're talking about.'

I fix her gaze. Desperation to see Kel again writhes inside me like a beast I can barely control. But I must. I wait, still and silent, face to face, until she realises her protests will not convince me of what I know to be false. She has Kel. I will make her give him back.

When I see she has abandoned all pretence of indignation, I speak.

'I'm not here tonight to harm you, Your Grace. This evening you came to my chambers and warned me about Prince Jakut. Now I must warn you if you keep the glitter-eyed boy you will gravely endanger your family.' I pause, weighing up how to present this.

'I am offering you my help,' I say, ignoring the heat crawling up my back and burning into the top of my spine. 'After what you have told me, I will not stay with Prince Jakut. I wish to leave the fort tomorrow, and I'm offering to take your captive. I do not wish to say goodbye to the Prince, so my departure will be a secret. My guardians will tell Prince Jakut I am sick and spending the day in my chambers. In order for him to believe this, Tye will remain in the fort until tomorrow evening. Then he and Brin will ride through the night and meet me in a safe location. The Prince will not be told about the boy.'

Duchess Elise smiles tightly. 'You flee in secrecy. Are you afraid of Jakut?'

I look down so she cannot examine whether my words match my expression. 'I am afraid of my heart,' I murmur. 'If I say goodbye, I might let his soft words persuade me to remain by his side.'

A cold tingling breaks across my forehead as I wait for her answer. I wish I could put a knife to her neck and demand she takes me to see Kel at once. My throat burns with the thought of him so close, yet still out of reach.

'I will need a day to make arrangements,' she says finally.

I give a quick nod of agreement. Anything more, and I fear I will give myself away. Hope and impatience pound through me—the promise of freedom, holding Kel in my arms, taking us away from all this!

'I will deal with the boy,' she adds. 'It would not be safe for you to take him with you.'

'No.'

Her eyes dart up, curiosity sparked by the vehemence in my voice.

'He was snatched from the north,' I continue, grappling to hold in check my emotions, 'and he should be returned to the northern forests near my home. You will take me to see him first thing tomorrow. I wish to ensure he is in a fit state for travel. Where are you keeping him?'

'Why so much interest in the glitter-eyed child?'

'Tye has a soft spot for rescuing shadow weaving orphans, Your Grace.' Even in the pale moonlight, I see the Duchess' deep red blush. She disgraces herself by hoping to benefit from the use of a slaved Uru Ana child, when she will not risk using her own talent, and was fortunate enough to be rescued by Tug's family from the same ill fate.

'In Delladea,' I continue, twisting the knife, hoping to injure her with my words, 'we are not as prejudiced as the south. We do not believe the Uru Ana should be slaved, or killed, or stolen from their parents as children and used for political purposes. I'm sure you can sympathise with our position.'

'I am not ashamed of the choices I have made.' She turns to face the fort's outer wall and unseen lake beyond. Auburn curls whip out around her in the night's breeze.

'Tye convinced me to keep the boy's existence from Prince Jakut,' I say. I try to sound reassuring though her lack of remorse fills me with hate. 'The Prince knows nothing of what we have discussed tonight. Nor will he ever know if the boy and I are escorted from Lyndonia at moonset tomorrow. Call for me early. You will show me the child, and you and I will spend the day together while you make arrangements.'

She nods, then looks up at the star-streaked sky. Her silver pendant is in her fingers again.

'Do you understand the terms of our agreement?'

'Yes,' she murmurs.

IN THE TUNNEL, spine pressed against the damp stone, I gasp for air. Oxygen flows into my body and the trembling abates. Elise does not leave the waterway to return to her chambers for another ten minutes. I wait. When Tug does not show, I start to believe she wasn't expecting him, after all.

Perhaps my presence in the tunnel had not scared her, because despite never willingly using her sight, the Duchess had still recognised the shape of my mind. This could be why her shock only came when she saw a small hooded figure clad in men's hunting furs, instead of the girl she was expecting.

TWENTY-FIVE

Duchess Elise calls four hours before the late-morning sunrise. The moon has not set, but I am already dressed in a cobalt grey robe, which buttons at the front. It is the only clothing the Prince has chosen that I can put on without help.

By the paleness of Elise's skin, and shadows beneath her eyes, I see I am not the only one who has slept badly. My head feels like packed snow from last night's wine. Sleep, when it finally came, was heavy and deep, and has left me groggy and exhausted.

But even with the general muffle over my senses, I have the impression we are being followed. Of course there are the two guards whom accompany the Duchess, and two more discreetly trail me, but there is someone or something else lurking in the twilight of the mind-world, plucking at my attention.

We wind through the fort, down narrow streets and enclosed courtyards, passing arches that peek through to the empty market square. A passing patrol of soldiers, bow to the Duchess. They show no surprise at the sight of her wandering before the fort has risen, and I realise she is a woman with free rein, accustomed to being among her people and going where she chooses, when she chooses.

Up ahead, two lookouts in the bell tower keep watch over the northern side of the lake. She stops before a low, freestanding structure with closed shutters. I work the frosty air in and out of my chest in an effort to remain calm, already stretching my senses to glean Kel's whereabouts.

The Duchess opens the door to a workshop. She casts a look behind as we enter, and again I have the sense of someone there, though my inner eye touches no minds other than the assigned guards.

The pottery workshop smells of wet clay and earthen minerals, mixed with a trace of the Duchess' sweet berry perfume. A pottery wheel stands on one side near a cushioned bench. Drying racks are stacked against the walls, littered with sandy, bone-hard figurines, glazed vases, and prettily painted bowls.

The Duchess closes us inside, lights a lantern and goes to a second door in a crevice at the back. Before turning the rusted key in its lock, she pauses.

'I have a daughter, Claudia.' These are the first words she has spoken since last night and her voice sounds as grey and troubled as the dark moons beneath her eyes. 'She is twelve years old. My son, Jules, is seven.' Her lips rise in an unauthentic smile.

Inside me, the uneasy bud of paranoia I have carried here, blossoms. 'Jules is third in line to the throne. When we thought Prince Jakut had been assassinated—'

'You were concerned your husband and son would be next.'

We must move the boys. She was talking about Kel and her own son.

'Jules will be eight this year and is summoned to the Ruby Court to continue his education. I have done what was needed to protect my family.'

Did the Duchess intend to send Kel with Jules to the Ruby palace as protection? Or had the Duke and Duchess bought Kel to take their son's place at the royal court once they heard Jakut was missing, presumed dead. The Duchess knows Kel's age means it will not be long before his glitter eyes settle. An Uru Ana would be able to travel through Jules' memories, learn his world, his life and be presented to the Ruby Court as the King's Lyndonian nephew. If this was her plan, she must believe the attack on her son's life is inevitable, and fatal.

The Duchess pushes open the low door, hands me her lantern and a key. 'At the end of the passage you will be met by a door. Lock it behind you. When you reach the stairs, climb to the second floor. You will see only one way in. The key fits both doors.'

The narrow handle for the lantern slips between my clammy fingers. Until last night, she intended to throw Kel into the wolfish intrigue and dangers of the Ruby Court.

'You will inspect him and come straight back. Do not get caught.'

The damp passage smells of mould and lichen, and is so narrow I have to push through sideways. Terrible images flood me. They are of my own making, as I am too afraid now to reach for Kel's mind. I can only think of getting to him, and holding him in my arms.

The passage twists and I am forced to hunch with the sloping ceiling. Half-jogging half-walking, it seems like an eternity when the crack finally opens so I can straighten up.

I am facing a rotted wooden door, bloated at the sides, damaged at the bottom. The key clatters as I turn it in the rusted lock, then the latch clicks, and I push. The door doesn't budge. I thrust against it hard, panic blanketing my logic.

What if she has tricked me? Trapped me here. Left me to die in a place no one will ever think to look. I lunge with my shoulder over and over, until the warped bottom scrapes and splinters on flagstone. When the gap is wide enough, I squeeze through, the waist of my dress snagging on crumbling brick. Powdery mortar stains the cotton, but there is nothing I can do about that now.

On the other side of the door, steps spiral up the tower. They are narrow and steep. I realise I'm inside a secret escape passage, hidden inside the tower's thick walls.

Afraid I will not be able to open the door from this side, I ignore the Duchess' instructions to lock it. A child could barely squeeze through the gap, and clearly it hasn't been used in many years.

I cannot go fast enough up the stairs. A metal rail welded into the brick steadies my ascent, so I do not trip. The lantern in my other hand offers a dim bloom of light to guide me.

I pay no attention to the two minds behind the door on the first floor. But on the second floor, when I sense Kel, I have to set the lantern down. I must appear steady and controlled, not a hyperventilating wreck. If I want him to listen to me and cooperate with the plan, I will need to win back his trust. I cannot do that if I shatter before him in a blubbering mess.

The strangling sob of emotion ebbs, as I take deep breaths. The Duchess is waiting for me. I cannot afford to delay any longer. I push down the latch and enter.

Grey shadow drapes around the two slit windows. Only the faintest traces of moonlight illuminate the circular room. I hold up the lantern, shuffling towards where I sense Kel, almost tripping on an empty mattress, and tumbling into a desk. My eye catches the faint shape of a chamber pot, and a large jug of water. The toilet must be emptied regularly because only the faintest smell of urine catches in the dusty air.

Kel hides in the darkest corner of the tower room. I peer into blackness, knowing he is there but unable to see him. And then he opens his eyes, and tiny flecks of gold sparkle.

'Kel,' I say, my voice breaking, despite my efforts to keep it steady. He doesn't move, but stares as though lost in a strange, monstrous twilight. He knows it's me. Even if he can't believe his ears, he must believe the mind he senses. He knows the feel of my mind better than my face.

I step a little closer, careful not to alarm him. Then I crouch. My eyes burn with tears as I smile. 'It's me,' I say again. 'It's Mirra. I followed you here. Tug sold me to another nobleman who was coming here on his way to the Red City. He knew it was the only way to ensure I wouldn't escape and try looking for you by myself.'

'She couldn't escape.' The flatness of his voice wrenches my gut. Flat, and dead, and hopeless. 'She wasn't strong enough.' He turns away and my composure crumbles.

'Look at me, Kel.' I edge forward. 'Look at me!' I want to touch him, I want to hold him so badly I can barely take the strain, but I can see he isn't ready. 'You promised me you wouldn't give up. And I promised I would find you, no matter how long it took. I'm here. If I could take you with me now, I would. But I can't. Not yet. Not until tonight. I'm getting us out of here.'

He shifts, unwraps from his blanket cocoon, and crawls out of the hole beneath crisscrossed beams. His legs and feet are bare and dirty. As he moves forward, squinting, the dim crack of half-light illuminates his face. It is bruised purple and blue where he has been beaten. My fist squeezes against my chest to hold in the pain. But when he drops the grey cover, I gasp. He's wearing a pair of cotton shorts, skin hanging off his bones, as though not a scrap of food has passed his lips in the last eight days. While I am fatter than ever.

I blink but the tears are too abundant to hold back. They run down my cheeks leaving itchy salt trails. His eyes find mine. I manage to hold them. Just.

He seems barely aware of the way his body shakes as he staggers forwards, reaches for my hand, pushes up the laced cuff. Though the sores of my wrists have healed, the faint blisters and redness are still visible.

There is a glimmer of realisation in his eyes and then he collapses, flopping to the wooden floor as though the strings holding him up have all been cut. I sink down with him, pull the cover around his back, and hold on as though he were dangling from a cliff edge. He doesn't sob. Doesn't move.

I smooth his hair, fingers avoiding the bruises and cuts. It is all I can do to stop my heart from shattering. I do not know how I will let him go, leave this room, leave him alone again. I speak quickly, making promises. I would promise him anything. I need him to believe freedom is possible. How could the Duchess allow this to happen?

'I'm getting you out of here,' I whisper. 'Back to Pa and Ma. They're waiting for us. Your eyes are changing, they're fading. In two months people won't even know you're Uru Ana. You'll be safe. This will never happen again. We'll be safe with Ma and Pa. I promise, Kel. You'll be safe.' I cup my hand around his chin and turn him to face me. 'Kel, can you hear me?'

There is a thin sheen on the whites of his eyes, a prick of the grief and fear pushing up through the wooden deadness. His head moves in the smallest nod. But a response nevertheless.

I rub his back while stretching my mind around the tower. The Duchess told me to inspect him and return at once. I have already been here longer than I'll be able to explain, and yet I do not know how I will ever let Kel out of my sight again.

'I'm staying in the royal guest tower on the south eastern side of the fort,' I murmur. 'Across from the market square. Tug and Brin are with me. I have arranged for us to leave here at moonrise tonight. Until then you must speak to no one about my visit. You cannot say anything.'

His arms come to life. They slip around my waist, grip growing tighter and tighter as though sensing what I am trying to tell him—I must go.

'You can find me. You can find my mind in the fort. I won't leave you, Kel. Do you hear me? I'm not going to leave you again.'

'OK,' he whispers.

'You must eat or you won't be strong enough for the journey.'

He buries his head into the soft cotton of my dress and nods. I hold him until I sense two men entering the bottom of the bell tower. Then I smother him with kisses.

'I have to go,' I say. 'You mustn't tell anyone you've seen me. I have to go.' I untangle myself from his unyielding grip, prising little fingers out of my own. I grab the crust of bread from the tray on the chair and hand it to him. 'You eat, Bud, OK?'

My legs threaten to give out as I cross to the secret door. I glance behind before pulling it closed. Kel stares at me with wide, bruised eyes. I cannot manage a smile.

The door drags across the stone. When the key is turned in the lock, and safely in my pocket, I slump against the wall, not bothering to fight the flow of hot tears.

TWENTY-SIX

There is something odd about the way the Duchess stands in the workshop alcove with her back to the passage. I expected her to be pacing, wringing her hands, anxiously checking for my return. Instead, she is as still as one of her bone-dry clay models. A deep part of me warns I should proceed with caution, but anger eclipses reason.

I slip into the alcove and bang the door shut. The Duchess' shoulders jump in fright. When she turns, neither remorse, nor shame, etch her cold expression. The sting of it, in the face of Kel's pain, fuels my blazing outrage.

'Do you even know how your guards are treating him?' I spit. 'Your son is almost the same age. You are Uru Ana. How could you let your men do this!'

'The journey here was not kind on him,' she answers.

'The journey, or your men?'

'They had to transport him in a wooden chest.'

In my mind, I see Kel trapped and crushed in a dark clothes chest, getting bashed about as the men's horses gallop south. Starved of air, and light, and hope. I stare at the Duchess with dry eyes. I have no more tears to cry. But grief can move beyond the body I discover, to furrow rifts in the soul.

'The bruises on his face were not from being bumped around,' I say, stepping closer. Before she grapples for another pitiful excuse, I slap her hard. My hand leaves a red imprint on her cheek. She gasps, and shrinks back, covering the injury.

Behind the alcove wall comes a scraping sound. We are not alone! There is another mind, dulled and hidden by mist berries.

I spin around the wall of the alcove, swiping a large ballerina statuette from one of the drying wracks to arm myself.

'Watch who you're striking, Mirra,' Tug says. He has followed us here! Or the Duchess arranged for him to come. How could I have been so naive?

I leap at him with the figurine. He blocks my aim for his head. The clay shatters across his arm. I try to punch him in the neck but he grabs me, wrapping his fist around the top of my shoulder, squeezing my healed arrow wound. The edges of my vision twinkle with white specks, but I am happy to be pitted against someone who will fight back. Someone who will make the hurt real and muffle the unbearable pain of my brother's suffering.

Kel is dying. If I do not take him from Lyndonia tonight, he will not survive another week. The Duchess will force me to break this last promise, and it will destroy him. All for Tug, and his stupid loyalty to a selfish, cowardly woman, who would willingly send another child to be assassinated in her son's place.

I spit in the direction of the Duchess and hopelessly kick at Beast-face. His grip risks pulverising my rib cage, but I don't care. Elise's eyes widen with shock at my transformation. Yes, Your Grace! Take a good look! I've grown up in the dark northern forests, hunted and hiding. I'm no more than a wild beast!

As she realises Tug's hold on me is unyielding, and I will not be escaping to strike her again, a little of her composure returns.

'This!' I sneer at him. 'This woman is who you have dedicated your life to protecting and destroyed yourself for? She is honourless! She is disloyal! She is selfish and cowardly!'

One of Tug's great, brute hands pinches my jaw to stop my insults. I spit and bite but he doesn't let go. He tilts my head, compressing a nerve. A bolt of pain zigzags up my neck. Leaning over, he growls in my ear. 'How many lives would you risk hurting to save Kel?'

'I'm nothing like her!' I hiss. But deep inside, I'm not so sure. Would I kidnap Jules and hold him prisoner, if it meant Kel could return to Ma and Pa? I would, without a second thought, betray the Prince, and leave Tug and Brin to die.

I give up struggling, exhausted, and aware it is pointless. Tug's hand loosens around my mouth.

I'm heaving and puffing and burning with indignation. 'At least I don't pretend I am noble and kind. My choices have been ripped from me. I have no other options. Unlike you. Unlike her!'

Duchess Elise swishes closer. 'You will stay in Lyndonia,' she says, 'until Prince Jakut receives word of his father and leaves for the Ruby Court. You will go with him and do what you were purchased to do. You will discover who is behind the Prince's assassination and whether my husband and son are also targets. Your brother will remain here until I am confident Jules' life is not in jeopardy.'

So haughty and sure of herself now she has Tug to protect her. She is a false and brutal beauty.

'Kel will die,' I tell Tug, 'if he remains her prisoner. He will not last until the third moon.'

'You have my word,' Elise says. 'I will do what I can to keep him alive.'

'Your word means nothing to me. Your own husband does not know who you really are.'

'You stand nothing to gain by telling the Duke the truth,' she answers. 'He would not believe you.'

Her confident bearing doesn't fool me. 'You doubt your own words. Besides, your husband might be a fool, but he would recognise the truth fast enough if I told him who Tug really was, and why you were waiting at the waterway last night.'

'I told you I was not waiting for anyone.'

'Yet Tug came,' I guess. 'And when he saw us together, he followed you back to your quarters to speak to you.' It is only an assumption, but in the mind-world a memory flits to the surface, confirming it.

She moves quickly through a dark alcove. Tug lurks in the shadows. She instructs her guard to wait for her at the end of the passage.

'You of all people,' she says, 'understand the ties between a brother and sister.'

'He is not your brother,' I snarl. 'You were waiting for him because you used to be in love with him. Because you're still in love with him.'

'Stop!' she whispers.

'And the Duke suspects your feelings, and suspects that you and Tug are not true brother and sister. How long did you put off having children, terrified one of them would be glitter-eyed? What would you have done if you'd seen Claudia's eyes sparkle in her first days of life? Would you have let her live, or strangled her in her crib to protect your secret and your own life?'

'Enough!' The violence in Tug's voice rips through my haze of contempt. 'You will go,' he says, 'with Prince Jakut to the Red City and discover who is behind his assassination attempt. You will discover whether the Duke and Elise's son are in danger. You will report back to her regularly. I will take charge of Kel. I will tell him of this bargain and return him to Blackfoot Forest myself.'

I grow quiet, weighing up why Tug would make such an offer. Is it so he'll still be paid by the Prince? Or to protect the unrequited love-of-his-life's secret? Is he trying to win her over with a show of mercy?

Away from this oppressive fort, back in the hands of Beast-face and on his way home, Kel would start eating. As always, Tug understands I will accept some hope over none. I am bound to.

Jakut cannot be informed of the situation. I have hidden too much from him for too long, and after last night, the distrust between us is unbridgeable. Besides, if the Duchess suspects I have confided in the Prince, she would be forced to get rid of Kel. She would probably send him to the tundra or kill him to save her own skin.

'If you take the boy,' she says to Tug, 'what assurances do I have she will report back?'

Oh, how I'd love to knock her down, back to the earth and grime she was born into.

Tug cracks his knuckles. 'If I hear that she has not upheld her part of the bargain, I will take a half-dozen men into the northern forest and slaughter her parents.'

I curl my lips in a contemptuous smile. Beast-face cannot hide his true nature for long. Even his efforts to show mercy and grace are steeped in violence. Good. It means I know if I stick to my end of the bargain, he will stick to his.

TWENTY-SEVEN

Tug marches me back through the fort, stars twinkling in the darkness above, the Duke's guards following us. I drown him in a torrent of insults and cutting speculation about the Duchess, and why she chose the Duke over him, dredging up the cruellest things I can think of, though I must be far off the mark because he barely reacts.

We are almost at the royal guest tower when I notice the unusual bustle of the fort. Lanterns burn in a dozen of the tower's windows. Boots stomp, swords clang, and through the myriad of stone tunnels, come echoes of orders given in raised voices.

Tug releases my arm, and we hurry towards the guest tower. A vaulted archway opens into the circular courtyard. Taking in the Prince on the steps by the entrance, panic circles through me. I cannot explain why I am wandering about Lyndonia at such an unsociable hour with Tug, or the state of my dress, or the stolen room key.

Wooden torches blaze in the curved courtyard walls, creating two arcs of light around the grand entrance. Jakut's face is lit up in a blaze of orange flames. His gaze is fixed on our approach, the hostility and warning in his eyes so sharp, I check to see if he is wearing his sword.

Gloved fingers curl and uncurl around the bejewelled hilt. He widens his stance to block our way.

Tug offers the smallest nod. 'Your Royal Highness,' he says, voice grave and cautious. I give a stiff curtsey. The Prince allows Tug past, but when I try to follow he lays a hand on my arm.

'I wish to speak with you.'

In the dimly lit corridor, Tug glances back. His look says he does not trust me alone with Jakut. Gritting my teeth, I pretend not to notice. After everything I've been through, does he really think I would do anything to divulge my brother's existence and risk Kel's freedom?

The Prince's eyes settle on my face. 'I suppose I should thank you for leaving the key where I could find it.'

A brittle wall has gone up between us. All trust and goodwill he had for me has gone. I accused him of condoning the attack on his escort and murdering those who helped him, and now he doesn't despise me. It is worse. I am nothing to him, just a nuisance. I am the dirty soil beneath his fine boots, which he must tread on to reach his destination.

An uneasy sensation wraps around me, like a thick fall of hushed snow, temporarily smothering my guilt and hurt over seeing Kel.

'Something in particular you were looking for?'

Anguish catches in my throat.

'No matter,' he says, lips twitching. 'News has come of my father. The Duke sent a messenger to wake me. We must go to him at once.'

I grow conscious of my dirty dress, which will be blindingly obvious in a lit room. 'It would seem odd if I were to go with you after last night, Your Royal Highness.'

'I do not care what they think,' he snaps. 'You have forgiven me. That is all they need to know.'

'But they would never—'

He leers in my face. 'Your dress is creased and soiled. Your eyes are puffy. You are sneaking around the fort and stealing room keys. If you think I will let you leave my sight for even a minute, you are very mistaken!'

His unmasked fury suddenly reminds me of his confession in the great hall moments before we were presented to the Duke and

Duchess. I wonder if he is jealous again, or pretending to be, because I was with Tug. What does he imagine we were doing together?

We stride through tunnels and dark courtyards, headed for the Royal Hall. I realise Jakut will continue our charade of awkward sweethearts in front of the Duchess while she will know him for a liar. I dislike giving the perfidious Duchess an upper hand over the Prince. But I don't have the luxury of picking sides.

In the royal gardens, beside an aisle of potted berry shrubs, Jakut comes to a standstill. He pulls off a leather glove and rubs a hand across the back of his neck. A small fleck of blood sits on his jaw where he has nicked himself shaving. I wait for him to say what licks like flames on the tip of his tongue.

'I will need you in the Ruby Court,' he clips, pulling his glove back on. 'Duke Roarhil sent a messenger this morning to report I am alive and well, and now news has come of my father, I will be expected to return home.'

I bow my head in understanding, then examine the cobbled stones beneath his boots.

'When you have discovered what really happened to my escort, I will have you taken wherever you wish to go. You will be free, and you will be rich.'

'Rich?' I ask, disbelief creeping into my voice. 'I care nothing for money.'

'Then what? Name it, Mirra. It will be yours.'

The question is a gouge, cutting deep into me. If I live through this, when it is over, I will either have won or lost the only thing I care for. With all his wealth and position and freedom, the Prince cannot give me what I value most.

I clear my throat. 'What will happen if I discover you were behind the attack on your escort?'

'To escape marrying a Rudeashan princess?' he retorts.

'Will you still wish my freedom, knowing I could tell someone of your crime, and you would be hanged?'

'If you discover I am responsible for the murders of my men, they will not need to hang me. I will do it myself.'

Words I cannot say thunder through my mind. They have Kel! Tug must have told the Duchess I am only with you because I am a shadow weaver!

Jakut's hand reaches for my waist. I look to the Royal Hall, certain we are being watched. Commander Fror waits outside the grand doors, but the Prince is not pretending to flirt as he lifts the torn cloth of my dress where it snagged on the crumbling passage wall.

'I have forgiven you,' I say, echoing his earlier words. 'We have made up.' Understanding flashes in his eyes. He nods.

Side by side, we stride through the grey stone gardens, two pretenders, engulfed by the secrets we carry.

Commander Fror leads us away from the Royal Hall, through a long arcade towards the royal tower. We wind up stairs to the third floor where an open door greets us. Inside the round tower room, the Duke stands by the large table where I saw him poring over a map of the land yesterday, when we arrived in Lyndonia.

He is accompanied by two advisers, Chamberlain Velequez, and a soldier. My eyes search out the darkest corner. I am relieved to see the armchair where the Duchess sat yesterday, is empty.

'Lady Mirra will wait outside with Commander Fror,' the Duke informs us. Lines of tension appear on Jakut's brow, but clearly my attendance under any circumstances would be inappropriate. As I curtsey, Jakut addresses Commander Fror.

'I would appreciate it, if you would make sure Lady Mirra waits for me until our meeting has finished.'

'Your Highness,' Fror answers with a nod, but one eyebrow arches in an unspoken question at the Prince's request.

The Commander leads me around the small landing, past two archer windows to a third with a cushioned stone ledge. I do not sit to wait, but lean forward and gaze out across the land. We are dizzyingly high. I concentrate on the horizon. The moon has set, and in the starlight, vague shadows of the wide forest touch the sky.

Fror leaves me to stand guard outside the meeting room, knowing I cannot reach the stairs without passing him. I send my awareness into the room and enter the first mind I brush against.

He holds a paper weight of a girl pirouetting. The girl's face is tilted to the heavens. The weight of the Duke's body pulls towards his feet. He stares at the

Prince. The men are of a similar height and the higher angle alters my impression of Jakut's face, softening the angles of his chin and cheekbones.

The Duke clears his throat. 'It is not good news,' he announces.

Jakut folds his arms across his doublet. The Duke's reconnaissance officer steps forward. Grime and dirt smear the edges of the man's skin trousers and grey tunic. The fabric is crushed. There is a small tear in one of the pockets, the result of hard travel and few opportunities to wash or change.

'We were staying in the town of Midlay to the south west, in the Peltik district when the news came to the Lord of Peltik.'

The officer wipes his sweating hand on his trousers. 'Word arrived in the Red City a week ago. The Carucan army was attacked while they hibernated during the long-sleep. The Eteans knew precisely where to strike. They destroyed the Watch in one swift blow, every post covering fifty miles. Soldiers sleeping in the underground barracks barely had a chance. Over half the army was wiped out.'

Jakut bends over as though he has a pain in the stomach. 'What of my father?'

'There are reports of his capture.' The officer does not meet Jakut's eyes. Duke Roarhil sucks in his breath and nods for the man to continue. 'There are other reports that he was slain and died with his men.'

The Prince pales, hands pressing into the round table.

'It is bad news for all of us,' the Duke says, reaching across the table and resting a palm on his nephew's shoulder. 'But that is not all. Other news has reached us.'

Jakut's eyes twitch. Tidings considered important enough to impart after announcing the King's capture and possible death could only mean more trouble. Tendrils of fear twine together in my chest. Could the Duke's men have discovered something we do not know about the Prince's trip to the north?

'Queen Usas is pregnant,' the Duke says. 'Her due date is close at hand. With the King's capture, an attempt on your life and now this... it raises grave suspicions against her.'

For a long moment the Prince does not speak. I imagine he is relieved evidence points to the Queen's treachery, rather than his own.

'When did your messenger leave to inform the Ruby Court I was safe in Lyndonia?' he asks.

'Just before the reconnaissance arrived. '

'Then we must catch him up. We must prepare to leave for the Red City at once and intercept the messenger. If the Queen intends to name her child successor and herself regent until the baby is of age, she will do it while the confusion over the army's defeat is at its greatest and my survival unknown. We must take her by surprise. We will arrive when she least expects it and discover the truth behind my father's death.'

'You have my utmost support and the support of my men.'

'Thank you, Uncle.'

TWENTY-EIGHT

Jakut grips my arm as we head back to the guest tower, though it is not the confident controlled hold of a master, nor the tender caress of an admirer. I am a buffer against the elements.

My own dilemma dampens my sympathy for his desperation. In two hours, I will be forced to leave the fort and abandon Kel when I have only just found him. I thought I would see him again, that I would be the one to break the news that it will be Tug, and not me, taking him home. I thought I would have time to check he is eating again, and have the comfort of witnessing his departure with Beast-face.

Even with Tug and the Duchess' threats, I hadn't given up on the possibility of finding an exit strategy—their secret could destroy any family, but its effect on the royal family, if ever known, would ripple through the whole Kingdom. There could have been a way to sway things back in my favour. But like Jakut, I have run out of time.

The Prince thrusts open the door to Tug and Brin's chamber. 'There's been a change of plan,' he announces. Brin, half-dressed in underwear with long legs, four coloured crystals hanging from his neck, is covered in shaving foam. His skin looks grey beneath the tattooed webbing—lack of sleep, excessive drinking and worry taking its toll.

'Where's Tug?'

Brin glances at me with bloodshot eyes. He opens his mouth, but at the same moment boot steps thud in the corridor. Tug appears behind us, expression neutral.

'We leave for the Red City immediately,' the Prince says. I squeeze my crossed arms into my chest, attempting to hold in the thunder-crack of tension. Say "no". Convince the Prince you cannot come.

'If Mirra has passed her test,' Tug answers, 'we are free to go.'

'Two hundred gold coins to escort Mirra and I to the Ruby Court. Then you will be free to do as you please.'

'The deal,' Brin grunts, 'was a hundred when we arrived here and a hundred when Mirra passed her test. We've still got nothing.'

'Circumstances have changed. The Carucan army was attacked during the long-sleep. Rumours claim the Eteans hold the King prisoner.'

Jakut is not admitting his father could be dead. To himself, or just to Tug? For someone who has no memories, this news affects him deeply. I study the contours of his desolate mind and notice they have subtly shifted. Does he remember something?

After my mother's cleansing, the obliterated years did not begin to come back until she woke from the following long-sleep. Like tokens buried in silt and ashes, winter eroded the sedimentary deposits to reveal fragments and shapes of the past. But Jakut wants his memories a great deal more than Ma did. Perhaps being here has jolted his memory, and I've been too preoccupied to notice.

'Half the Duke's army will be with you,' Tug reasons. 'What good are we?'

'My uncle and his men believe Mirra is a lady journeying beside me of her own free will. If she takes her horse for a stroll, they will not question it.' His gaze zeroes in on my face. 'I will need her more than ever now.'

'Where else would I go,' I say. 'You have promised me my freedom and purse, why would I run away?'

'Because there is nothing to keep you.' A simple answer, yet it carries an indiscernible undercurrent. 'But something keeps you bound to Tug.'

Brin swipes the foam from his chin with a cloth, apparently giving up on his shave. His refusal to look at either Beast-face or me, silently confirms Jakut's claim.

'There is nothing between Tug and me,' I snap, the edge in my voice not helping.

'You have broken your word once,' Brin says to the Prince. 'What is to say after we deliver Mirra to the Ruby Court you will not change your mind again and refuse to pay us?'

'Money is no object. Why would I take such a risk? Less than two weeks travel to the Red City and the gold is yours.'

'We cannot accept,' Brin says.

'But we will,' Tug finishes.

Mentally, I crash straight into a wall. I stare at Beast-face. He cannot already have forgotten his promise to deliver Kel to my parents while I become the Duchess' informant. How will he return Kel to our parents if he is with me?

I marvel at the strangeness of my own nature. Why am I constantly surprised by the myriad ways in which Beast-face manages to hurt me?

Everyone in the room is conscious of the way my eyes drive imaginary spikes into Tug, but I don't care. Jakut speaks of meeting at the fort entrance in two hours, food being packed and horses readied, our need to travel fast. His voice echoes in my thoughts, overshadowed by an image of Kel crouching naked in the tower room, watching the secret tower door as I leave, taking all my promises with me. I picture my brother following me in the mind-world as I ride forth with the Prince and the Duke, ride so far away, he cannot follow.

When the Prince leaves us, Tug is the first to speak.

'In your chambers, Mirra,' he orders.

Brin slumps into a chair and puts his head in his hands. My chest feels like it is filling with water. I'm drowning in promises I cannot keep. I clutch at my dress wanting to tear it from me. It has all been for nothing!

Kel will remain here bullied and brutalised until he realises I'm not coming back. He will wait and wait, peeking up through the tower's slit window, training his mind on the drawbridge, jumping awake every time hooves clop across the wooden pier. Days will dissolve into weeks and as he realises I'm not coming back, he will sink into himself and disappear.

'Sit down,' Tug says.

We are in my room, but it is shadow and mist as though the mind-world has materialised and the real world vanished. I hunch into a wooden chair, shivering. Tug holds a blanket. He leans forward and wraps it around my shoulders.

'He will not understand,' I say. 'He will know I have gone. He will not understand.'

Pine smoke drifts on the air. A crackle of burning wood and dead needles comes from the bathing chamber. I curl into my blankets deciding I will not go anywhere. Jakut won't kill me. I will be imprisoned until I'm sent to the tundra mines or hanged, and then at least Kel and I will be stuck here together.

Arms pick me up as though I am no more than a child. I think of Asmine's father carrying her from the tent of her abductors. Wading through smoke and blood, bodies scattered over the forest floor like autumn's broken leaves, mouths set open in death's silence. The images are blurred. A mix of my father's memories, and the way I have imagined my friend's living nightmare.

I am aware of the faintest things. Hands pulling at my dress. Steam. A fire. Hot water. Hot water on my face, permeating my body, stirring me back to the present. I bolt up. I am in my slip in the tub and Tug is pouring hot water over my head.

'Better?' he says.

'Get out!' I pick up a bar of soap and fling it at him. It smacks him hard on the forehead.

'Ow!'

'Get out!' I sweep up an arm, using the momentum to cover him with water.

He steps back scowling, tunic and face soaking wet. 'I'll take that as a "yes",' he says.

'You will take nothing from me.' Grabbing the cotton sheet that rests on the raised sink, I leap from the tub and wrap it beneath my arms searching for something with which to strike him.

'I have spoken to the Duchess,' he says, raising his hands in peace. 'Kel will be safer here in Lyndonia than travelling the country. At least until his eyes have changed and he has regained his strength. She will move him to an empty cottage outside the fort and ask Deadran to care for him. The Prince's old tutor will be told Kel is an orphan in temporary need of a guardian.'

His words land and slide across me like the droplets of water on my skin. I give up searching for a weapon, and stand hugging the sheet.

'I will come with you to the Red City,' he continues. 'You will do everything you can to discover the Queen's intentions towards the Duke and his children. When the Prince dismisses me, I will return to Lyndonia with your news. Then I will take your brother back to Blackfoot Forest.'

'Why? Why would you take him back?'

An expression skims Tug's face, as mysterious as the fortress of his mind, as his talent for hiding himself from the sighted, as his ability to bury his memories and become an enigma. He does not answer. I look down at my crinkled hands which clutch the sheet as I drip all over the wooden floor. 'How long was I in the bath?'

'Longer than there is time for if you wish to see Kel before we leave. A maid knocked five minutes ago. I told her to wait outside. Shall I tell her you are ready to dress?'

I nod. He turns to leave.

'Wait,' I say. 'What if once we arrive at the palace Queen Usas insists on the Duke's son being sent to join his father?'

'The King has been captured. It would be an odd request considering the Prince's attempted assassination and the Etean's knowledge of the Carucan army's long-sleep stations. But if a request is sent, Elise will delay her son's departure until Jakut is crowned and you have discovered the truth behind these events.'

TWENTY-NINE

Mist hangs over the new green shrubs carpeting the forest floor. My lungs fill with crisp air, as we gallop down a narrowing track, away from the high walls, cramped courtyards and lifeless maze of the fort. The rising sun glances through the trees and sparkles in my vision.

Kel could get well again living in the forest. A familiar place. Away from the countless minds of men and women with greed and fear and self-serving desire in their hearts. Now all I must do is convince him he will be safe here. Without me.

We slow our horses to navigate the undergrowth and fallen branches. The stone house lies to the east of the castle, not far from the lake, but in a thick part of woodland with few man-made paths. I spot it between the long trunks and anticipation and anxiety cut through me.

Two guards straighten at our approach. The Duchess appears from the low, simple structure. She signals to let us pass.

'You have not got long,' Tug says.

'I know.'

I dismount and pass him the reins. Strength seeps from my legs as I stride across the small clearing. The Duchess tears her eyes from Tug to step aside and allow me entrance. Once I am level with her, I pause.

'I will hold you entirely responsible for my brother's well-being until Tug returns.'

Her gaze drops to the leafed medallion in her gloved fingers. 'I was four or five,' she says, 'when Tye and his father found me.' Turmoil roils beneath her poised expression. It strikes me she has hidden her past from all who surround her almost as expertly as Tug. 'I don't remember my life before that. Only the fear. Afraid every breath I took would be my last. Afraid of living, terrified of dying.'

For a moment, I imagine the Duchess a captive like my childhood friend, Asmine. An image surfaces on my inner eye. The girl in the Pit, dressed in frills, clasping a shiny purse, immobilised with terror. I doubt she will be as fortunate as Elise.

The Duchess flinches. She may not willingly use her sight, but she cannot avoid the memories of others.

'You could use your influence with your husband to change things,' I say. 'Instead, you hide.'

She bows her head, and I push through the stone doorway, not allowing her to see the crack in my unforgiving attitude. In her position, my mother might have done the same.

The room is in a shambles. Dust covers the wooden table. A small fire burns in the hearth. Cobwebs, thicker than cloth, crisscross sloping shelves. A draught blows through the open door and whistles between tiny gaps in the walls. The one-room building hasn't been used for years.

Kel sits on a raised platform covered in brightly coloured quilts, which Elise must have sneaked from the fort. He is upright but his eyes are shut, head leaning against worn stone.

I perch on the edge of the bed and touch my hand to his face. His body tenses, but when he sees me his shoulders slump, and he gives a wan smile. His face looks tired and so serious, but life flutters in his glimmering irises. I take off my gloves and squeeze his hands.

'Hi, Bud.'

'You said you weren't coming for me till moonrise,' he murmurs. 'I didn't know if she was your friend, or if it was a trick.'

'We had to change the plan.'

He twists his arms around me and snuggles his face into my furs.

'You're OK,' I say into his hair. 'You're safe.' I wrap him close and hum one of Ma's lullabies.

He used to sit on Ma's lap while she rocked him and sang him to sleep. Nothing grated on my nerves more. Now all I want is to make him feel that safe. I wish we could pretend we've found a magic door to an enchanted wood where neither monsters nor men can come for him. He sniffles and rubs his eyes. The crying is a good sign. He is letting go of all he's kept locked inside him. Of the weight that was pulling him under.

'The lady says I'm not strong enough to leave yet,' he whispers. 'But I'm strong enough, Mirra. I promise. I ate two whole breakfasts.'

I smile while scrambling for a way to stop the little bud of hope in his heart being crushed, before it has barely formed.

'You look stronger,' I say. 'Ma and Pa will be so proud of you. I'm proud of you.'

His bottom lip trembles. 'I want to go home.'

'We both do. I want to go home too.'

'But I think the lady is right.'

My eyes narrow. What has the Duchess told him? My mind strays for a moment, wondering how she got him out of the fort, how many helped her and how trustworthy they are.

'Right about what?'

'She says if we leave now, people will see my eyes and try to capture me again. She says I can stay here until they don't glitter. Her guards will protect us.'

I look towards the open doorway. The Duchess waits outside, hugging her silver fur cape around narrow shoulders.

'What's wrong?' Kel asks. 'She is your friend, isn't she?'

'She's asked me to do something for her.'

'That's why she's helping us?'

I nod. I want Kel to believe he is safe and free, so he will regain his strength. But one day it will be Tug that comes to take him home, not me. And I cannot let him wholeheartedly trust the Duchess. Enough to believe she will take care of him until he returns to our parents, yes, but not enough to let her deceive him if I fail to discover the Prince's assassin.

'She has a little boy who's in danger. She wants me to go to a city far from here and discover who wishes him harm.'

'Will it be dangerous?'

'It will not be easy. But coming after you in Blackfoot Forest when I had been injured was not easy. Finding you in the fort and getting you out of the tower was not easy.'

A flicker of determination ignites in his sombre gaze. 'If anyone can do it, you can.'

'Yes,' I say, squeezing his fingers.

'But will she force you to go? Did she buy you?'

'Nobody can own us. We are free and there is always a choice.' He lets go of my hand and cups the lodestone necklace I gave him before he was sold in the Pit.

'I know you're coming back for me. I know now. I promise I won't doubt you again.'

Pressure crushes my head. I pretend to arrange his covers, unable to meet his dazzling gaze in case he sees my own doubts. 'You're my north,' I say, pushing the words through the slim hole of my swollen windpipe.

'How long can you stay?' he asks.

'If I accept, I must leave straight away.'

His chest shudders as he releases an anguished sigh. He rests his head back against the stone. When he opens his eyes, tears spill down his cheeks. 'I'll be OK,' he says.

I cup his face in my hands and kiss the salty trails. 'I don't want to leave you.'

'When you come back, I'll look different, and we can go home.'

I throw my arms around him and squeeze until I'm breathless. I tell him how brave and strong he is and how much I love him, and then through his hiccups and sobs he tells me to go.

Tug waits out of sight at the edge of the track. I am surprised he has not dismounted to talk with Elise. He does not speak as I mount my mare. We turn back along the overgrown path towards the fort.

I ride behind him, never more uncertain of his motives. Protecting

Duchess Elise has always been a priority. But so has staying away from her. Does he chaperone me to the Red City to make sure I do the Duchess' bidding? Or is it a way to both protect her and escape her at the same time? Yet if he was running away, he would not have suggested delivering my findings to her in person, or returning to Lyndonia to take charge of Kel.

Jakut believes finding me was the will of the Carucan Gods. He showed his devoted faith and trust through the spiritual cleansing, and I was their answer. But what does Tug believe in? It is not coin. Nor superstition. Nor unrequited love.

Reaching the pier to the drawbridge, I draw my horse to a stop. Beyond the portcullis lies the front courtyard where in minutes soldiers, the Duke and the Prince will gather, and it will be days before I might find myself alone with Tug again. Tug halts and brings his stallion round to face me.

'If I die,' I say, 'before I find out who ordered the attack on the Prince's escort, I want your word you'll take Kel back to our parents.'

He straightens in his saddle. His gaze shifts to the distant forest. He breathes deeply. Sunshine falls on the shadows of his tattoos, outshining their darkness so he appears more man than beast.

'You have my word.'

I close my eyes for an instant, and feel the warm rays on my eyelids. When I open them, I notice the mist on the lake has lifted, and the sky is a brilliant, spring blue.

THIRTY

K el's safety is a candle of hope burning in the window of a dark house—a light in my being that cannot be extinguished. Not by the hard, exhausting pace of our journey south. Not by the Duke and Commander Fror's disapproval of my presence, as though I might endanger the troop at any moment. And not by the Prince's attentive kindness in front of the men and cold dismissal when we are away from watchful eyes.

For eight days we ride through valleys and huge oak forests, branches vibrant with baby green leaves. We pass rivers and water-falls, and stop only to sleep and eat. The soldiers erect tents and establish camp within minutes. As though my presence is not awkward enough, I am further singled out by my separate sleeping quarters, which Tug and Brin take turns to guard under the star-bright sky.

On the nights Tug snores, wrapped in furs outside my tent, Jakut prowls and barely rests. He is determined to understand Tug's hold on me. I imagine he means to catch us doing something that will throw light on our little excursion in Lyndonia. But, by some mutual unspoken agreement, since the morning we left Kel, Tug and I have avoided all but the barest minimum of contact. He plays his role as protector to Lord Tersil's daughter, and I his charge, who's only interest lies in the Prince.

The days grow warmer, the nights shorter and the need for sleep leaves my body. Soon, the midnight sun will rise and hang in the sky for three moons. I try not to wonder if I will be around to see it fall beneath our world and plunge us into winter again.

For now, I am too busy tending to aches and sores from hours in a saddle, sketching maps of the Ruby Palace cobbled together from Duke Roarhil's boyhood memories; ruminating on how Jakut and I will convince the Ruby Court of our amorous charade, when he cannot stand to remain within throwing distance of me.

In front of the soldiers, our greatest challenge is pretending affection. But in the palace, Jakut will be surrounded by people he has lived alongside for years, people who cannot be bluffed as simply as the Duke and his army. He will have to face Lady Calmi, the girl he wished to marry despite his obligations to the Rudeashan princess. And Queen Usas, Tmàn born, raised as a warrior, educated as a battle strategist, will scrutinise his every move.

On the ninth day we pass through vast flat lands of fields worked by men, women and children. Jakut rides ahead with Commander Fror.

I use my time alone to mull over what I have gleaned from the Duke's memories concerning the Ruby Court. I also pick at the obscure ocean of the Prince's mind. Smudges of light and colour. Echoes of sound. Nothing I can stitch together.

We gallop for two hours, pushing the horses harder than ever. I am beginning to wonder about this shift in our habitual riding pattern when the Duke slows to a trot and confers with Jakut and Fror. The Prince and Commander step their horses to the side of the troop, wait for us to pass, and rejoin at the rear. I glance back at Jakut and see two scouts break off to scan the horizon in our wake.

Tug draws his stallion up to my mare. Brin closes in on the other side. I send out my mind, searching for the reason for this palpable electric charge in the atmosphere. Skimming across the field workers, I sense nothing unusual until I try to enter one of their minds. My spine turns to ice. I raise the hood of my cloak and fold the velvety material around my upper body. It is late afternoon and the sun warm on my side, but I am chilled through.

'Mirra?' Tug says.

'What is this place?'

'Lord Strik's castle lies twenty or thirty miles from here. These are his lands.'

'There's something wrong with the field workers,' I whisper.

'Wrong?'

'Their minds are like houses made from paper, like a mirage.' We have been riding through similar fields since lunch, and I realise I haven't once seen a worker's memory surface in the mind-world. Nor have we passed through any villages. As though their ghost minds live in ghost bodies. Where do they all sleep?

The skin beneath Tug's tattoos turns an unnatural shade of grey. He takes off his gloves, slips out the long-knife from his waistband, and tucks it beneath a leather flap at the side of his saddle. If Tug is worried, we are in trouble.

I raise my eyebrows at him. 'My knives,' I say.

'They are safe.'

'I think it's time you returned them.'

'We are fifty men strong. And Lord Strik must be an old man now.'

'And yet you and Duke Roarhil do not seem reassured.' I scan ahead, eyes falling on the Duke. He sits stiff as wood in his saddle, two guards trotting tight at his sides. I suddenly remember why Lord Strik's name sounds familiar. When the Duke and his brother, King Alixter, were boys he was their father's chief adviser. The young princes feared and despised the lord, blaming him for the death of their mother.

I lean closer to Tug. 'What do you know of this lord?'

'Enough to realise it is better if we do not cross his path.'

'Then why are we riding straight through his lands?'

On my other side, Brin grips the crystals beneath his shirt, gaze sweeping the dirt road ahead.

'Commander Fror and the Duke discussed ways around it,' Tug says. 'It seems I have been in the north a long time. Lord Strik's fiefdom has not ceased to grow. Now it is near impossible to reach the Red City from Lyndonia without travelling through his territory.'

'If King Alixter blamed this lord for his mother's death, why give him control of more land?'

Hoods draw up around Tug's wolfish eyes, concealing something monstrous. My flesh crawls. He loses no sleep over the blood, gore and horrors littering his past. And yet this lord...

'Strik takes whatever he desires,' Tug answers, venom lining his words. 'Not even King Alixter could stop him.'

Nothing throws Beast-face off balance. Who is this lord? And why did no one warn Jakut or me of the threat before we set out this morning? Or perhaps the Duke did discuss matters with his nephew, and I am the only one who was not informed, being a sensitive member of the feebler sex. They would not have wanted to throw me into a bilious panic.

We trot onwards in silence, the cavalry on high alert and uncannily quiet. And then the peasants in the field stir, as though a light in the sky draws their attention upwards.

I stretch my mind far into the distance. What I meet out there is unlike anything I thought possible. The reins slacken in my fingers. As if punched, I double over the saddle, hands shaking, breath a stabbing pain in my chest. It is just shock. Just shock, but terror sparks from the tips of my head down to my toes.

The mind of the approaching horseman is like a huge shimmering hole. A void, dragging everything into blackness.

'Mirra?'

I fight to straighten up. I must not draw attention to myself. 'Keep me away from him,' I hiss.

'Who? Mirra, what's the matter?'

'The man who comes. You will see him soon on the road.' My voice is breathless, my head spinning. Up ahead, the Duke orders our troop to a halt. The horses stop, restless, whinnying.

'Listen,' I whisper, leaning towards Tug, still hunched over. 'I don't know how you do it, but you can bury the things you value most. This protection you have on your mind, raise it as much as you can now. And do not let him talk to me.'

Tug's face sharpens. I thought the day I saw fear in those dark eyes would be cause for celebration. Instead it compounds the dread.

'Try to sit up,' he murmurs. 'Pull back your hood.'

I do as he says, tucking my hands into my mare's sweaty mane to hide the shaking.

From our position in the middle of the troop, I cannot see the road. I glance back through the men and glimpse Jakut's blue tunic, two rows from the rear. The soldiers have moved their horses closer to form a wall around him.

Hooves thunder towards us. At least five other riders accompany the dark mind, but their presence in the mind-world is smothered by the great drag of the black hole.

I set my eyes ahead. In the fields the peasants work as though their lives depend on it. A thought hits me. If Lord Strik is Uru Ana, he will sense the Prince's secret at once. I want to warn Jakut, but the cantering horses stomp closer, almost upon us. It is too late.

'Good afternoon,' a voice says, carrying across the soldiers. It sounds neither young nor old. The mind is so big it swamps the first three rows of men as though they have just blinked out and vanished. A great noise and energy floods my perceptions, making it hard to concentrate, hard to think of anything but getting away. 'Is that you, Roary?' the voice continues. 'Well, I haven't seen you since you were small enough to sit on my knee!'

The Duke's voice rumbles in reply, but the wind carries his words in the opposite direction.

'I have always said war with the Eteans was a mistake,' Strik answers. 'Your brother was too proud to listen to an old man's advice. What news from the north of Prince Jakut?'

I hear no answer from the Duke. But suddenly the dark mind is closing in. Instinct makes me want to jump to the ground, curl up small and put my hands over my ears. Lord Strik trots up the outskirts of the cavalry, beady eyes skinning the faces of the men. He stops level with Tug and me.

'You travel with a lady?' The light mockery used to address the Duke has been replaced by sinister amusement. I keep my gaze down. Tug's hands rest over the concealed hilt of his knife.

'And who is she?' Strik asks. The casualness of his question thinly disguises a twisted curiosity.

'She is my wife's niece,' the Duke says, joining us. The momentary distraction allows me to glance at the lord. Deep lines mark a handsome face. Strands of silver are woven through his thick black hair. The eyes are soulless.

'Duchess Elise's niece,' Strik echoes. 'I had been told her brother, the Baron of Keylore was dead.'

'He left behind a daughter.'

I stare at my hands, amazement warring with terror. The Duchess found safety and shelter with Tug and his father when she was a child. If Tug's father raised Elise as his daughter to hide her Uru Ana bloodline, then she is Tug's adopted sister, and Tug is the dead Baron of Keylore!

'I remember Tye and Elise,' Strik muses aloud. 'I knew their father —your grandfather Baroness,' he says, addressing me. My eyes flutter to his in a desperate effort not to show the depth of my fear. 'We have not been introduced.' His words hang in the air, waiting for me to offer my name. Any longer in his company, and I will collapse. The utter darkness of the mind-world is dizzying.

'This,' Tug says, in a voice colder than death, 'is the man who stole your father's lands.' Tug's defiance is like a blast of sunlight, allowing me to catch my breath.

Strik turns his full attention on Tug. 'I am at a disadvantage. You know who I am, but I do not know you.'

'I am the lady's guardian.'

My clammy hands grip tighter on the horse's mane.

'My men are here to give the Duke of Rathesyde escort through my lands. You and the young Baroness of Keylore will ride ahead with me. I am very interested to hear where you have been hiding her these many years.'

His words hold a strange power. I'm not sure how I will manage another second in his presence, but I am helpless to refuse. The Duke's men fan out around us. A struggle lights Tug's features as he tries to defy the order, then kicks his stallion to follow. Behind us, a horse gallops down the flank of men.

'What is going on here?' the Prince bellows.

Strik halts as Jakut rears up behind him. The force of dark energy surges.

'Your Royal Highness,' Strik says with a deep bow of his head. 'I was not aware you were with Duke Roarhil. We have had no news of you for six full moons.'

'Your services here, Sir, are unnecessary. As you can see we are well manned and the five men riding with you will not be required.'

Strik stares at the Prince until the blood in my veins congeals. If this strange power he has allows him to enter minds like the Uru Ana, we are doomed. Jakut regards him with haughty self-assurance. After a strange pause, Strik bows his head.

'If it is your wish, Your Highness.'

Tug glances at me, his expression reflecting my own relief and incomprehension. Lord Strik retreats.

Within minutes he and his men are specks on the empty skyline. The pressure in my head abates, allowing me to think again. And what I think is Lord Strik and the Prince are favourably acquainted. If Jakut aligned himself with his father's enemy before leaving for the north, the situation is deadlier and more complex than we have anticipated.

The troop slowly gathers their wits and we move on. But I cannot shake the foreboding sentiment that if Jakut was in league with Lord Strik, we are all doomed.

THIRTY-ONE

An hour later, the troop fords a river and we stop on the other side, allowing the horses and men to drink and rest.

'I did not realise you and Lord Strik were on good terms,' the Duke says, dismounting beside his nephew.

Jakut accepts a loaf of bread from one of the soldiers while another takes charge of his horse. 'I like the man no more than you do, Uncle. We will continue riding until we reach the Vales where we may set camp as agreed. The sooner we are away from these lands, the better.'

The Duke hovers, on the verge of saying more, but then bows his head and returns to Commander Fror. Once he is back in the throes of the men, Tug, Brin, and I walk our horses to the river bank.

'What did Lord Strik want with you and Mirra?' Jakut asks, joining us.

'A lady travelling with soldiers is bound to raise interest,' Brin says. 'Even the Duke and his commander do not understand why Mirra is with us when we have no idea what kind of welcome awaits us in the Red City.'

Jakut turns to me. 'What did you make of this lord?'

'He seemed to know you,' I say.

'I gathered that. What else?'

'There is something odd about his mind.'

The Prince's eyes pinch together. 'Odd?'

'It overwhelms and makes him hard to disobey.'

'He seemed willing enough to comply with my orders.'

'Yes,' I say. He also seemed to have been waiting for your return to the Red City.

The Prince swallows and pulls the collar of his tunic. Fine droplets of sweat moisten his hairline. 'Could he have known you were Uru Ana?'

'I'm not sure,' I say. 'It was more as though he smothered other minds than travelled through them.'

'Then we have nothing to worry about. We need only to get away from these lands before nightfall.' His words do not match his unease. He strides back to his stallion, takes the reins and mounts. A soldier hurries over to him with a skin water flask. Jakut sips, splashes his face, then returns it. Seeing the Prince mounted, the men prepare to leave.

I kneel down by the river's edge to fill my flask with fresh water. Brin and Tug do the same, Tug catching my eye.

Ironic that Duke Roarhil should try to pass me off as the Duchess' niece, making me Beast-face's long-lost daughter. Though of course the Duke doesn't realise the man who once went by the name of Tye Keylore, and who they all believe dead, travels with our troop.

I wonder how Tug's father, Baron Keylore, convinced the world a stray three- or four-year-old girl was his daughter. How did they hide Elise until her eyes settled? And what did Tug do when Lord Strik stole the lands he should have inherited from his father?

My anxiety over our encounter with Lord Strik stays until we enter The Vales, rolling lands that will take us to the Red City. It is late evening, the sun low on the horizon, when we stop for supper. We have travelled over fifty miles today and both men and horses are exhausted.

I watch the men set camp. I would offer to help, but from experience I know not to bother—they will refuse. There has not been time to send out hunters, which means the cook prepares leftover grain mixed with a heavy dose of herbs. He will not accept my help either. Restless,

I wander the valley collecting firewood. Tug and Brin's lasso eyes keep track of me as they hammer tent poles and drape canvases. I am returning with an armful of kindle when the Duke heads me off.

'You made a strong impression on my wife,' he says. 'I can see she is right. You are a resourceful girl. Are all the ladies of the Delladean court as willing to participate in the work of labourers?'

I glance down at the bundle of broken sticks. 'My father believes a girl should know how to take care of herself.'

'You are not tired after today's ride?'

'Of course, Your Royal Highness.' It is the first time I have stood so close to the Duke. In the sunset, his face strikes me as young. It is a strong face, with alert blue eyes that remind me of my father. He glances across the camp, and I see what he sees. Commander Fror is distracting the Prince with a map.

'Walk with me a little,' the Duke says. I curtsey and move into step beside him.

'Tomorrow we will stop in the town of Lindy and take rooms. You will be able to wash and change your clothes. Though I have not heard you complain. I've never met a woman so impartial to her own appearance.'

I smile as though he compliments me though it could as easily be an insult. The Duke stops and checks behind. My empty stomach twists a notch tighter.

'This is an awkward question Lady Mirra, so I will be direct. How certain are you of Prince Jakut's feelings?'

Oh, he detests me, no doubt about it. 'I'm not—' I falter and bow my head in embarrassment. 'I'm not experienced in matters of the heart, Your Highness.'

'My wife says he has already asked your father for your hand.' I swallow hard and nod. Did Elise tell her husband this before or after she knew it as a lie? 'And yet if my brother is still alive, such a match will be forbidden.' He holds the same hope as Jakut that the King is an Etean prisoner and not dead.

'You married Elise,' I say quietly.

'I was not next in line to the throne. And my own father had departed this life or he would not have permitted it.'

'You are wondering about the Princess of Rudeash?'

'The Prince has spoken to you about her?' I shake my head. 'What happened with the Princess is a question that needs clarification, but I will be blunt with you, my concern lies elsewhere.'

'Go on,' I say.

'Has Jakut spoken to you of Lady Calmi?'

'I did not know of her until your wife told me she had been in the Prince's favour before he left for the north.'

The Duke scratches the grey speckled stubble of his beard. The sun slips off the edge of the world, abandoning us to twilight. Soldiers gather around blazing fires. The clatter of spoons on bowls and conversation fills the valley.

If he has something to tell me, he'd better hurry up about it.

'King Alixter was particularly opposed to the Prince's relationship with Lady Calmi because she was Lord Strik's granddaughter.'

'Granddaughter...'

'You have turned pale.'

'I am fine.' My hand flutters to my bare neck in an old habit of checking for my lodestone. My north. My guarantee when I was in Blackfoot Forest of finding the way home.

'It is no secret in the Red City and many of the provinces that Lord Strik and the King Alixter are, or were, not on good terms. But as you saw for yourself today, Lord Strik commands a great deal of farming land. The Red City is in part dependent on his produce and he has much influence over the nobles of the provinces. Lord Strik will have known that Lady Calmi and the Prince were on special terms. It was said she held great influence over him, influence Lord Strik will wish to uphold. Had he learnt today of the Prince's affection for you, your life would be in danger.'

Once we arrive at the Ruby Court, I already have enough to worry about. I must help Jakut hide the state of his shredded memories from a warrior Queen and a lady he wished to marry. I must discover who lay behind the attack on his escort without revealing my outlawed talent. I do not need a tyrannical lord, whose dark-mind is like gazing into an abyss, to worry about as well!

'If Prince Jakut introduces me to the Red Court as Lady Mirra of the House of Tersil, Lord Strik will hear of it,' I say.

'Yes. Which is why I ask if you are sure of the Prince's affection?'

'What is your advice, Your Highness?'

'That you ask him to leave you and your kinsmen in Lindy. You are an intelligent girl so I will not condescend to your inexperience or youth by hiding the truth. You know of the assassination attempt against the Prince. And now it seems the Prince has aligned himself with Lord Strik. These are unsettled times. The innocent often end up suffering the most.'

'Aligned himself?' So the Duke and I have come to the same assumption.

'Lord Strik recognised Jakut. They have met before.'

'But anyone who has been to the Ruby Court would recognise the Prince.'

'King Alixter did not allow Lord Strik to set foot in the Red City. If Jakut holds you close to his heart he will grant you this request and desire to protect you. And if you are confident of his feelings, you have no need to fear the influence of the Lady Calmi.'

But Jakut will never grant such a request. He cannot.

'He needs me,' I say, though the Duke may take my refusal to listen to his advice as an insult. 'I cannot abandon him.'

Roarhil stares at me until the heat rises through my chest to my face and my hands start to prickle. I curtsey. My back foot slips on a rock. 'Excuse me,' I say, stumbling and turning. Then I stride back to the camp.

I reach the fire where Tug and Brin slurp soup from bowls.

'What was that about?' Tug asks.

I slump down near them, brushing hair from my eyes with my sleeve.

'Deadran would be disappointed. All that effort he went to to get you to behave like a lady.'

I glare at Tug, then straighten my spine and shoulders. The cook, a boy of fourteen or fifteen, and the youngest of the Duke's soldiers, arrives.

'I'm sorry, Lady Mirra,' he says, handing me a bowl. 'No time for the hunters to bring back meat today.'

'It is fine. Thank you.' He blushes and bows and hurries back to serve the Duke who passes our fire, ignoring us.

'He is not pleased with you,' Tug says.

'Where is the Prince?'

'Commander Fror has him sequestered away in the main tent, planning which way we should approach the Red City to avoid the King's army—now serving the Queen's orders.'

'I bet the food's better in there,' Brin adds, watching the Duke enter the main tent.

I take a spoon of the over-spiced grain. It burns my mouth and makes tears come to my eyes. Tug passes me a cup of water. After I've gulped it all, I put down the cup.

'Lady Calmi,' I say, 'the young woman the Prince wished to defy his father for and marry, has a grandfather, Lord Strik. Naturally, Strik desires their marriage. If he hears the Prince's favour now lies with Lord Tersil's daughter, the Duke believes he will try to get rid of me. He wants me to stay away from the Ruby Court.'

Brin splutters on his broth, flings aside his bowl, and pushes to his feet. 'If I die guarding Mirra,' he mutters, 'I'm gonna kill you, Tug.' He stomps off towards soldiers gathered at a nearby fire.

'So that's why the Duke introduced you as his niece,' Tug says. He stares at me until it is awkward, then strange, then annoying.

'What?'

'I'm sorry.'

'An apology? Well, that certainly paints a silver lining on what I rate as the second to worst day of my life. The day I met you being top of my list, of course. And what are you sorry for? Shooting my father and leaving him to die, kidnapping my brother, blinding us, beating me up, selling Kel or selling me to a Prince who's going to get us all killed?'

Tug's face doesn't shift a muscle. 'It is important you make Jakut understand just how dangerous Strik is. The King's dethronement and the Prince's return provide Strik with an opportunity for power he will not let slip through his fingers.'

I think of the deathly coldness in Tug's attitude when he introduced Lord Strik as the man who stole Baron Tye Keylore's lands. His lands. Tug's face and name have changed, but I do not imagine he was ever the sort who would accept an offence of this magnitude without declaring war.

'What happened between you two?' I ask.

He stares at me again until I want to fidget. 'You are too old for your years, Mirra. Even for an Uru Ana.'

THIRTY-TWO

The town of Lindy, nestled by a river, lies thirty miles from the Red City. Tomorrow, when we arrive at the royal court we will have made the two-week journey in eleven days.

The Duke and Commander Fror chose lodgings at the edge of the town, where there is a field for the men to camp. Through the window of my narrow room at the top of the inn, I watch Lindy men scurrying around, carrying great tubs into the field where they will be filled with hot water for the soldiers to bathe. The Duke has ordered the cook to find the town's finest caterers and bring a feast for his men with all the delicacies of Lindy. I see now how hard it must have been for Elise to lie to her husband. He is generous and well respected by the men. He tried to warn me about Lord Strik with no ulterior motive than my safety. He must think I'm ungrateful and simpleminded for ignoring his advice.

Sensing the minds at my open door, I turn. A young soldier enters with my trunk, followed by two girls barely out of childhood. They curtsey and stand back, eyes lowered, giggling and nudging each other as the Prince enters.

'These girls will help you bathe and dress for the evening meal and before we set out in the morning,' Jakut says.

I nod. Without a maid to dress and undress me, I have worn my skin trousers and men's shirts for the last ten days. This is the Prince's way of telling me that tomorrow I am expected to ride in the cumbersome dresses of a lady.

'I must speak with you a moment, Your Royal Highness,' I say. He indicates for the girls to leave and they bustle out curtseying.

Jakut's manner stiffens. He remains by the door as though he cannot wait to escape.

'We need to talk about Lord Strik.'

'I'm listening.'

'His granddaughter is Lady Calmi, the young woman in the Red Court who you wished to marry. She is the reason your father sent you to the tundra to return with the Princess of Rudeash.'

His jaw clenches, tiny muscles in the sides of his cheeks flexing as he grits his teeth. The anxiety he's struggled to conceal since our encounter with Lord Strik seems to spill across the room like an icy draught. I wonder what chills him more—that I accused him of sanctioning the slaughter of his own escort, or that he is starting to believe it?

'You have returned without the Princess, and your father no longer stands in your way. Lord Strik will want to see the two of you wed. If you present me to the Ruby Court as Lady Mirra Tersil from the north, who sat by your bedside bringing you back to health, and who has won your affection, you will position me as a direct rival to his granddaughter.'

Jakut flexes and cracks his knuckles. 'You believe Strik is dangerous and powerful enough to try to assassinate you while you are under my protection in the Ruby Palace?'

Protection? Captivity, more like.

'Your uncle certainly thinks so. He advised me not to accompany you to the Ruby Court. And Lord Strik is without a doubt the most dangerous man I have ever crossed. Something about his mind is unnatural. He could persuade a person to act against their better judgment. Against their own desire.'

'Is this some dark art I have not heard of?'

'If it is, I have not heard of it before either.'

'Lady Calmi's grandfather,' he mutters. 'This is why he knew me and gave us free passage through his lands.'

The coolness in the Prince's general manner vanishes. From his breast pocket he retrieves a leather binding. He unfastens it and holds out a leaf of well-made papyrus paper. 'Is this her?' he asks, stepping closer, hand unsteady so I have to take it to see properly.

The sketch is of a young woman with wavy hair, large slanted eyes, and a thin nose.

He remembers! The hours I've wasted combing the dark cavernous expanse of his mind and puzzled together nothing, while he has been sketching portraits of the girl he was in love with. How long has he been carrying this around?

'Lady Calmi joined the Ruby Court about a year ago,' I say, gaze fixed on the picture. 'Neither the Duke nor any of his men have met her so I do not know what she looks like.'

Jakut's talent for rendering a life-like image far exceeds my own. The girl's tormented eyes stare out of the paper, as though she is begging me to destroy the image that traps her. I look up. Jakut's gaze flits from my face, and he takes back the picture. 'Do you remember her?' I ask.

He shuffles the leaf into the leather binding before producing another. A slim faced woman with braided hair, loose cotton trousers, a fitted shirt, and a sword at her waist.

'Queen Usas,' I murmur.

'Yes, from your portrait and descriptions, I came to the same conclusion.'

'This is good news,' I say, 'your memories are returning.' But I'm not convinced it is good news, at all. The Prince's lack of memory, has allowed him to live with a clear conscience, free of any past wrongdoings, free to believe he is noble and good. He believes his destiny is guided by the Carucan Gods. But all evidence points to him once being a devious man with an unscrupulous passion to wed Lady Calmi, no matter his duty to King or Kingdom, the barriers in his way, or the dark alliances he had to form.

He returns the sketch to the binding and passes me another. My hand reaches for it, then I see what he is offering and it's as though the paper catches fire.

'Do you recognise him?'

I shake my head, heart pounding in my chest. This is not something sketched from the shambles of his shipwrecked memories.

'He does not look familiar?' he asks, watching me. I stare back, gaze scratching and chipping at the layers between his eyes and his soul. Has he been toying with me all along? Is it possible to know a man who has so many disguises? And what, if anything, lies beneath, when he takes them all off?

I can trust nothing about the Prince, assume nothing. The slap of Lady Calmi's portrait was a gentle wake-up prod, so I would not miss my torturer unravelling his instruments and sharpening the knives.

In the drawing Jakut has rendered, my brother's head is dipped, and a blindfold covers his eyes, but the mouth and chin are unmistakable.

'I presume you continue to sift the darkness of my mind for crumbs of my old life,' he says.

'Unlike you, Your Highness, darkness is all I have found.' Something flashes in his eyes. As though my barbed innuendo—that the darkness possesses more than just his memories—causes him pain.

I wish I could trust these occasional moments when the barrier drops leaving him tender and raw. If it were more than another layer of deception, if he felt some affection for me, it would be much easier to hurt him. Which is what I ache to do now he has snuffed out the candle of hope burning in that dark house. The Prince's knowledge of my brother's existence throws Kel's safety into perilous uncertainty again.

He holds the sketch of Kel closer to his face, eyes narrowing as he traces a finger around the outline. Then he returns it to the leaves of his leather binding. I want to snatch it and rip it to shreds. Tell him he may have me, use me for whatever sinister, treacherous acts he requires. But he cannot have Kel.

Instead, I am unmoving. I cannot forgo the smallest chance he does not know what he has in his possession.

'I have seen no more of my past than you, Mirra.'

'And what, then, am I to understand of these drawings?'

His gaze loses focus, thoughts travelling thousands of miles away. Gone to join his soul, perhaps, where it is trapped in the lonely glacial mountains.

'If only you and I were not quite so good at surviving,' he says.

'Then we would be dead.'

He nods, heaviness slowing his movements.

'If the sketches,' I say, 'are not from your memories, where are they from?'

'One day I expect we will both have our answers. I only hope it is not too late.'

THE BATH WATER turns cold and the girls grow tired of waiting. They knock and enter with towels. I dry myself, send one to bring supper to my room, telling her I crave only a large bone of meat, preferably the foreleg of the biggest animal she can find. The other I send to make my excuses to the Prince and Duke and then fetch needle, thread and scissors. They offer to sew or mend anything I require, but I refuse and dismiss them for the night, nodding at the guard posted outside my door before locking it from the inside.

Using a lump of sandstone from the bathroom fire, I spend the next few hours grinding and sharpening the deer bone. I don't have the tools to make a haft or balance the blade, so the result is nothing to be proud of. But it's a weapon. And I feel better when I've sewn a holder for it at the top of my riding boot where it will be hidden beneath my skirt.

When I'm done, I place the bedcovers on the wooden floor, and lie listening to the quiet. The last of the soldiers retired ages ago, their drinking and bantering replaced by the howling wind.

I can come up with only one likely explanation for Jakut's sketch of my brother. He must have seen Tug, Brin, Kel and I enter the Pit together. After days of ruminating on what possible fishhooks Tug has impaled me with to acquire my cooperation, Jakut has come to the conclusion that the glitter-eyed boy who looked nothing like me, but who was captured and sold at the same time, is more than just another bounty hunter's prize.

But why didn't he confront me directly? Why draw Kel blind folded, reveal only half his face so I am left doubting if it was really Kel, or whether paranoia has submerged my capacity to think straight?

Pa told me a man who fights monsters must be careful he does not become one. But he did not say what happens to those who fight alongside a monster without realising it. He did not say whether there is a turning point, when a man becomes a monster, or what happens when they realise they've already crossed that line.

THIRTY-THREE

I mpatience gnaws at me as the girls fuss with my dress and hair. Outside, the unit packs and prepares for the final leg of our journey, languid after a night of drinking and joviality.

We ride away from Lindy with the sun on our backs, the valley narrowing, the hills growing steeper. The river deepens and its swampy banks push us up into the sloping forest.

The forest air is close and hot, sweet with the perfume of exotic flowers. Leaves the size of plates and fans, shaped like stars, eyes, and hands, block the sun. Brightly coloured birds caw and trill.

The flora is so thick we are forced into a single line, snaking our way through a barely cut path. Tug rides behind me. Jakut is somewhere ahead with the Duke and Commander Fror.

The tangled vegetation and myriad variety of trees is so different to the pine and birch forests of the north. I can almost feel the wet soil breathing beneath me. Thousands of animals scatter and scamper at our noisy approach.

I am taking off my cloak, warm with the riding and the mid-morning heat when my attention prickles, snagging on the creatures flying overhead. I watch them in the mind-world. Their numbers are growing and their random flights back and forth seem less and less random. Almost as though they crisscross a wide circle overhead. Almost as though they are hunting in a pack.

They move too fast for me to prod their minds without falling from my horse. And I cannot see them through the thick green dome. But the shapes and textures of their minds seem too large for raptors. Some feel almost human.

I bend over my mare to retrieve the bone knife in my boot. Behind me, Tug notes the gesture and immediately unhooks his bow from the sling on his back. He squeezes his stallion alongside, pulling out an arrow.

'You've been busy,' he says, gaze roaming the dense flora, searching for what he has missed.

'If someone had returned my knives, I could have saved myself the effort.'

I roll my eyes to the treetops, showing him where I sense the danger. A memory tingles at the edge of my thoughts. I smell the stale, spicy arena of the Pit, and hear the piercing shriek of the captured velaraptor. I remember the flashes of rage as it tried to escape, thrusting itself over and over at the roof of its prison. And beneath the madness, a smoky white world of cold beauty. A winter's dream of emptiness and space.

Several of the minds circling the treetops echo that bleak arctic serenity like an answering melody.

'Do velaraptors hunt in packs?' I ask. My question dints his infamous poise.

'Velaraptors don't come this far south,' he says. He raises the cloth hanging beneath his saddle, revealing my bow and quiver looped onto the flank of his horse. He has kept them close! Happiness sparks in me at the familiar sight. He unhooks them and hands them over.

'What are you doing?' Brin demands, pushing up behind us. As Tug opens his mouth to answer, the sky fills with screaming. Not human screams, but the wild, harsh, spine chilling call of the velaraptor.

Commander Fror shouts an order. It is drowned by the deafening squalls. Chaos erupts. Panicked voices rebound up the line. Horses rear and whinny. Soldiers grasp swords and try to keep their stallions from breaking formation.

Then a crashing sound quakes the treetops, causing a second eruption of screeching forest beasts and birds. A rainbow of colour shoots into the sky, a hundred birds, accompanied by the flapping of two hundred wings deafens us.

'They're coming down the trees!' I shout.

My mare snorts, ears and legs twitching. Brin's stallion whinnies and tries to break away.

'What's coming?' Tug shouts.

'Whatever are riding the velaraptors!'

Surprise flares in his eyes. All I know about the velaraptor is the desperate creature I saw in the Pit and the stories Pa told me. Magnificent, powerful, so fast they're nearly impossible to catch. These velaraptor haven't only been caught, they've been trained and ridden. What kind of men could tame them?

A dark, human form appears overhead. He leaps swiftly from branch to lower branch.

I release my grip on the reins to take aim with my bow. Noise shakes the air. There is the sound of a loud crack. My mare jerks us sideways. My arrow shafts through the trees and misses the figure. Tug's arrow hits. The man falls hard to the forest floor, branches snapping on its way down. In the split second I have to take in our assailant, I see his face and shudder. Silvery-grey scales have been sewn into the skin.

A dozen more men are descending.

'Come on,' Tug shouts, kicking his horse ahead, navigating the twisted flora. My mare needs no urging to follow. I glance behind and see Brin and two soldiers joining our retreat.

A guttural holler splits the air. Half of the men in the trees change direction, flying forward to head us off.

We weave in and out of trees but we cannot get up the speed to outdistance them. I have never shot a bow while riding a horse and it is useless to even try. The soldiers behind Brin abandon us, rounding back towards the unit. Our six pursuers don't hesitate. Ignoring the soldiers, they close in on Tug, Brin, and I with relentless determination.

From far off in the forest comes shouting. Then an assailant is behind my horse, running faster than my mare can leap the gnarled roots, swinging a lasso. Tug swivels in his saddle and releases an arrow. It misses.

A noose of twine comes down towards my head. I duck over the side of my mare and it catches around my boot. The loop tightens and a hard yank jerks me the other way in the saddle. I cling to my mare with one hand, use the bone knife to rip the bulky skirt of my dress so I can reach the twine. I cut through the tough braided sinew, but my awkward position and the man tugging on the lasso, trying to reel me in, and drag me from the horse renders the task impossible.

He is alongside me!

I give up with the knife and kick hard at his face. His grip releases on the twine for an instant. I throw my bone knife. It spins once, balance skewed, nicking the side of his ear. Blood dribbles down the translucent grey scales.

The man's stride doesn't falter. His hands reach for the cloth of my dress. I am tugged sideways and then an arrow slams into his throat. Blood spatters my arms and skirt. He goes down with a crack, falls into the arrow so it pierces straight through to the other side.

My throat fills with scorching bile. Shocked, I look up and see Tug. He has stopped and turned his horse around so he faces me. He is already racking up another shot.

Another five men, legs covered in shimmering velaraptor skin trousers, torsos speckled with brown paint, bound through the under-growth. The giant roots and bush that slowed my horse have no impact on the speed of their advancement. One of them leaps for Brin while the others keep coming. Brin elbows his assailant in the face, but he is pulled from his horse.

Tug's eyes meet mine for a split second.

'Go!' he shouts. Another arrow twists through the air, clipping the man who is almost upon us. The man yanks the point from his shoulder, barely flinching, not even slowing.

I nock up an arrow. Tug can't handle four of them. They're all as huge as he is, and oblivious to pain. Perhaps they are anaesthetised with some herb, and this is why their minds feel odd.

My heart sticks in my throat as I take aim. The face is close enough to see that though it is human, it has been altered. Not only with the tiny scales on the forehead, cheeks and neck, but this one has also had its nose and jaw broken and crushed together to resemble a velaraptor beak.

I close my eyes, shutting out the horror, and focus on his mind. It sways with the rhythm of his body. I get the feel of his swing as he leaps in running strides.

Steady. Steady. Closer. Fire!

Lightning flashes in the mind-world. I sense him falling only a few feet from my horse. I open my eyes. Another of Tug's arrows skims the air further off. Another man falls.

Aside from the man in hand-to-hand combat with Brin, that leaves two more.

Tug zones in on the one on our left, I on the other. Neither of us make our targets. As I rack up again, the man-creature headed for Tug leaps at a tree branch, swings himself high and pivots through the air.

I watch, stunned. It's like he's flying, like his legs are made of springs. The man lands astride Tug's stallion. The horse rears up, sending them both backwards.

Suddenly, I'm falling. My mare's legs collapse beneath her and I topple off, scrambling out the way so I am not crushed.

Hooves thump the forest floor. A soldier returning to help? On my knees, I hunt for my bow. A massive weight drops down on my back, punching the air from my chest. I can't breathe. My cheek grinds into spiky seeds and my mouth sinks into mud.

The man locks down my arms with his thighs, his bulk crushing my rib bones into my lungs. The blood stops flowing through my legs, and they tingle. With each fighting effort to get control of my body, my mouth sinks further into wet soil.

I breathe through my nostrils, my chest unable to expand to let in the air. I'm fairly sure this is the end. As though to tear away any doubt, hands tighten around my neck, cutting off the minuscule airway of oxygen still serving my brain.

Searing pain shoots through me. I wrestle against the weight of the man, floundering in a sea of agony.

The agony owns me, becomes me, stretching milliseconds into minutes, until all I can hope for, is it to be over.

The next thing I'm aware of is the clash of metal. The realisation I'm not dead. The weight on my back has lifted and while pain sears through my chest, neck and head, it no longer holds the entirety of my existence.

Through blurry eyes I see a figure swing his sword at my attacker. My attacker parries with a blade half the sword's length. The men move fast, striking, leaning, ducking, grunting. My rescuer is lean and agile. I cannot make out his face, but the way he moves is as familiar as the jewels on the hilt of his sword.

What are you doing Jakut? It's me they want!

Where are the Duke's soldiers to protect the Prince of Caruca?

I try to move. Pain flares in my ribs. A cracked or broken bone. I groan, try again. My inner-eye scans the mind-world. Relief darts through me. Tug is close and he is still alive. Mind as strong and impenetrable as ever. Brin is further away, suffering, drained.

From deep in the forest, blasting over the cacophony of velaraptor cries, men's voices, and carnage, comes the gut-wrenching wail of a battle horn.

I watch the Prince's blade catch the man's arm, drawing blood. The man dives forward and head butts Jakut. Jakut staggers, twisting off-balance.

Another bellowing horn blast fills the forest. The scaly face looks up as though he's heard his name called. And then he is rushing towards me. I twist onto my knees, dragging myself through the over-growth, vines lacerating my hands, tearing at my dress. In the mind-world I sense Jakut coming after us. Then I hear the clash of his sword against the creature's blade.

Two more men sprint through the forest, avoiding Tug, heading for me and the Prince.

I crawl forwards, palms pricking on something. An arrow! I snap it in half, guard the point in my fist.

An explosion lights up the mind-world.

'Jakut!' I cry out. The Prince's mind rages with fire. I grope and scrabble back to him. He is immobile, unconscious. Not dead. Not yet. His attacker sits on top of his prostrate body, knife rising to slit his throat. I hurl myself at the man. Pain blazes in my chest as I thrust the broken arrow tip into the man's back. At the same moment a lasso comes down. It hooks around the man's throat, snaps tight, pulling him backwards.

My head whips up. Another man, broader and bigger than all the others, face and torso covered in translucent ebony scales, stands in full view. He pulls hard on the twine, choking his brother-in-combat.

Already injured, flesh bleeding with sword wounds and the arrow-head, the felled man splutters and claws at the sinew. A dozen hooves rumble through the overgrowth. Commander Fror's voice roars in the distance.

A memory ripples around the ebony-scaled man, as he chokes one of his own.

He stands before a gathering of men, with scales on their cheeks, some with scales sewn all down their torsos. Snow-capped mountains surround them. Wind tears at their furs. He speaks in a tongue of growls and foreign vowel sounds. But two words sound familiar: Preince and Streik.

The Prince and Lord Strik.

Commander Fror charges through the trees, sword raised, four soldiers in his wake. He shouts to his men to check on the Prince.

A movement catches my eye. My head whips towards the ebony-scaled man, but he has disappeared. A high-pitched screech fills the forest. And then silence comes down around us. Our attackers have vanished like mist in the sun.

THIRTY-FOUR

I lie on the gnarled forest floor, gazing at tiny ribbons of blue sky visible between high branches. My body shakes uncontrollably. I want to rise, check on the Prince. Check on Tug and Brin. But shock immobilises me.

All three of my captors are alive. This knowledge is a peculiar comfort to my shredded nerves.

My mind replays images of the attack. Scaly faces bear down with cat-like speed and dexterity. Strange guttural words echo in my head. In my mind, I hear the bellow of the war-horn, and the screaming chorus of velaraptors.

Men flock around the Prince. Others peer over me, asking questions, repeating my name. But it's as though I'm caught between the past and the present, unable to respond.

Fror barks an order. Bush and vines crunch and rustle as men scramble to comply. In the mind-world I sense the velaraptor move beyond my range of perception and I'm suddenly released from the overwhelming inertia.

I refuse the offered water. The Duke hears and rushes to my side, asking if I am able to sit up. I allow him to help me upright. The pain in my chest intensifies with movement. A rib must be cracked, but I bite down a yelp. If the Duke discovers my injury he will not allow me to ride, nor allow me to continue on to the Red City. The Prince could not reasonably argue with his uncle against the wisdom of leaving me behind. Especially, as the Duke will suspect I was the objective of the velaraptor men.

Duke Roarhil has found my tattered cloak and wraps it around my shoulders. He says something about it all being over, about the miracle of Prince Jakut and I surviving. He supports me as I stagger to the Prince, battering aside the thick vegetation with his sword.

Tug lumbers towards us from the opposite direction. Blood flows down the side of his face. He brushes off the men who hurry after him with offerings to staunch the wound.

I see the moment he spots me through the trees. The relief in his body is palpable. I could pretend it is because my safety means the Duchess' safety, but as our eyes take each other in, I understand it is more than that. I believe he regrets taking Kel and me from Blackfoot Forest, after all.

I watch him swat away soldiers, his beast-face a bruised and gory mess, and a pressure in me lightens.

The Prince groans, semiconscious. I kneel down beside him. His belt has been loosened and the top buttons of his shirt undone. A soldier dribbles water from a wet cloth into his mouth. Without a word, I make it clear I wish to tend to the Prince. I take the cloth and dab his puffed up jaw. His eyelashes flutter.

Nearby, I can hear the Duke and Commander Fror discussing the situation, options, reasons for the bird-men, as they call the men who attacked us, so far south. I glance up and see Tug headed to where Brin lies.

'How badly injured is my landsman, Brin?' I ask the nearest soldier.

'It is grave, My Lady. Duke Roarhil has already sent two scouts to fetch a healer from the nearest town.' The trembling in my hands grows worse. I lower the cloth and touch Jakut's hot cheek.

In my mind, Brin's voice rings through the snow and the wind and the northern pines. "Let's tie her to a tree and leave her to the forest." And later: "She's going to get us killed."

If Brin dies, it will be my fault.

'And what of the other men?' I ask.

'Taylor's neck was broken when a lasso yanked him from his horse as he tried to protect the Prince who broke the line to help you. No one else was hurt.'

As though hearing his name, Jakut groans again. I knew the soldier Taylor only by sight. It makes no difference to the way his loss twists my insides. A life there and then gone. It is hard to fathom. Hard to make sense of. For the first time I understand Pa's reluctance to fight back.

I sit on my haunches, shoulders shaking, which doesn't help the pain in my ribs.

'Mirra.' Jakut's eyes are open. Seeing the Prince has regained his faculties, Duke Roarhil comes to us, crouches down level with his nephew.

'You were lucky, Your Royal Highness. This time,' he adds, looking at me. 'Lucky and brave. Two qualities befitting a future King.'

'How many men did we lose?' Jakut asks. He flinches as his fingers prod an egg-sized bruise on his forehead.

'One for sure. The future of Mirra's landsman is as yet uncertain.'

'Tug?' Jakut asks. The alarm in his voice surprises me. And yet it doesn't. Our journey this far, the mistrust and necessity to trust, the disagreements and tentative deals, have bound us all in some inexplicable way.

'It is Brin,' I say.

'We have sent for healers,' the Duke continues. 'You should rest until we are sure nothing is broken.'

'Make sure no expense on the healers is spared,' Jakut answers. 'But I have no need for one. I am fine to ride.' He hauls himself up to prove the point. 'It will be safer if the unit moves on.' He glances at me. I lower my head in silent reply. The velaraptors have gone, their riders with them. Except for those who fell in battle and the one killed by his own chief for raising a knife to slit Jakut's throat.

'If the bird-men are regathering for a second assault,' the Duke says, 'whether we move now, or rest for an hour, won't change anything. They could cover the distance to the Red City and back ten times before we arrive at the palace.'

'Your arm is bleeding,' I tell the Prince.

He glances down at the slit in his tunic. He hadn't noticed the wound before.

'I will ask the cook to make a salve,' the Duke says.

'We need boiled cloth,' I add, 'and boiled water to clean it first.' The Duke nods and strides back to Commander Fror who is inspecting one of the dead bird-men. Fror sends out an order, and a soldier trots away towards where the rest of the unit is now gathered.

I try to help Jakut remove his tunic, but lifting my arm hurts. He notices me wince.

'You're injured?'

'Give me your knife,' I say. He passes it without question. I cut the sleeve where the blood has stuck his skin to the cloth. The wound is long and shallow.

'Someone must look at your injury, Mirra.'

'It is internal,' I say. 'I think a rib is cracked. Nothing can be done.' I rip some cloth from my underskirt and use the strip to staunch Jakut's blood.

'Except rest.'

'Which is why I hid it from the Duke.'

'I can do it,' he says, holding the cloth in place so I do not have to strain myself. He stares at me for a long moment. 'I release you.'

'Release me?'

'You should not ride. You will stay somewhere with Brin to recover. I will pay Tug and Brin what I owe them, and once you are fit and well enough, you will vanish from my cursed entourage.'

He wants to let me go? After all he has been through to get me this far? We are less than a half-day's ride from the Red City! I can think of nothing to say which will not make me sound as bewildered as I feel.

He takes my silence for hesitation. 'If it is Tug you're worried about...'

'Tug?'

'I will make him an offer to accompany me to the palace that he cannot refuse. My payment will release you from us both.'

Jakut is offering to cut all strings and return my freedom. A bitter-sweet mix of emotion fills me. Happiness I'm no longer considered an object for trade, confusion he doesn't despise me, shame for the way I have treated him, and regret because I cannot accept.

If I don't find out what happened to his escort and whether it was part of a plot to dethrone the King and eliminate those next in line, Duchess Elise won't allow Tug to return Kel to Blackfoot Forest. But then again, the Duke and half his army are here. It would not be difficult to ambush my brother's guards and get him away from Deadran. Would Tug let me?

If Jakut is not a threat, my brother's safety is assured. For now. But can I come this far without discovering the truth? Without unravelling the riddle of the Prince. Who is Jakut truly?

If he is the man he claims he is, if I could help him remain that man, no matter what atrocities lie entombed in his past, perhaps I can change the destiny of the Uru Ana. King Alixter may be dead. Even alive, he cannot rule from an Etean jail. Jakut is the rightful heir.

A soldier arrives with sterilised cloth and boiled water. He promises to return with the salve once it is ready. Jakut winces as I begin to clean his wound.

'You have said before that something binds me to Tug,' I begin. 'You are right. But what you do not realise is something binds me to you too. If it is your destiny to be crowned ruler of Caruca, you will have the power to change the course of my people. To stop us from living like hunted beasts in the outland forests. To stop mercenaries and bounty hunters ripping infants from their families. What went on in the Pit was only a window, a glimpse of the horrors men commit against the Uru Ana every day.'

The hurt and gravity in the Prince's expression as he listens, mirrors something deep within. Until I'd spoken the words aloud, I hadn't realised how firmly rooted my desire is to help rewrite the history of my dying people.

I pour more water onto the cloth. Jakut's fingers graze my hand and catch it in his palm so I am forced to reckon with him. 'Go back to your home. You have my word I will do everything I can for the Uru Ana. Nothing good can come from the Ruby Court.'

'Except perhaps you.'

He smiles ruefully. 'I thought I was an assassin?'

'Whatever you were is not as important as what you are now. Or what you will choose to be when we reach the Ruby Palace.'

'This is your destination, Mirra. I will go on from here alone. You warned me Lord Strik would see you as a threat to his granddaughter and today you almost died. You were the target of this attack. I know what I saw. Only those who tried to assist your escape were injured. Lord Strik must have sent them. And if he has power over men whom most of Caruca believe are a northern myth, then we can only imagine the power he will hold in the Ruby Court.'

I withdraw my hand from his. He really means to let me go. This is not some ploy to gain my trust.

The Prince's desire for me to leave him seals my determination.

'I was four,' I say, 'when mercenaries followed my family and another whom we had banded together with for survival and friendship. They had a daughter my age. She was like a sister to me. Until the night men snatched her from our bed. Our fathers searched until they found their trail. While the mercenaries slept, their throats were slit and my friend saved. But Asmine wasn't the same afterwards.' Neither was my father, I think.

'Our families separated,' I continue, meeting Jakut's attentive gaze, 'and my father moved us to Blackfoot Forest. But I made a promise to myself after we left. One day I would return to the Sea of Trees and hunt the hunters until they were all gone. Now I can do something far better. I can help a Prince rise to the throne and end the reign of terror over the Uru Ana.'

The Prince's brows crease together, perhaps with the sting of his split flesh, and maybe a little with the sting of my revelation. He remains silent as I wrap the clean cloth around his arm. When I am done he reaches into his breast pocket, takes out the leather binding with his sketches. One sketch is folded over, creased and more finger-worn than the others. He hands it to me. I open it, watching him.

A young boy in hunting clothes, bow drawn back, hair tied in a tangled knot steps out of the page. Except, the boy has my turned up nose, my high wide cheeks and narrow chin. It reminds me of the day Tug pretended to teach me how to shoot a bow and arrow.

I hold the paper, not understanding.

'I also believe we are bound by something we cannot entirely fathom,' he says. 'It was the will of the Gods I find you.'

'I do not believe in the Gods,' I answer, though my dismissive words cannot conceal the confusion and wariness pouring through me at this change in conversation.

'I know you believe in some higher power,' he says. Before I can argue that in that case, he must know me better than I know myself, he continues. 'You are Uru Ana. You see the passage of time and the paths of men. You see minds that have no physical existence in this world. Memories which can't be measured or weighed. Which appear and vanish at the will of their keeper. We could search Ederiss for a thousand years and never find where all the world's memories are hidden.'

A nervous tightening loops through my chest. 'I am not sure what you are trying to tell me.'

'I woke from the long-sleep with nothing from my past but these rings,' he says, raising the ruby signet ring on his middle finger and the hawk-headed ring dangling on his neck thread, 'an old tutor to tell me who I was, and this.' He taps the leather binder.

'So?'

'This sketch of you was already in it, along with the others.'

THIRTY-FIVE

S oldiers lift Brin from a litter to the back of the healer's cart. He whimpers, head tossing from side to side as though he's in the throes of a terrifying nightmare, despite all the medicine he's been plied with. Tug watches, arms folded, and expression neutral. But I sense war raging in the serpentine ravines of his mind.

Two soldiers mount their horses. The Duke has ordered them to escort Brin to the nearest town and see him installed at the healer's. It will be a hazardous journey through the forest, considering Brin's condition. Even when they reach the flat land beyond the river swamp, the way is not without danger. If the bird-men return, they do not stand a chance.

Only the healer who has been well paid and instructed to send regular word of Brin's progress, appears satisfied with her new charge and change of fortune.

A soldier approaches and announces my tent is ready. I thank him, and with a last glance over my shoulder at the departing cart, head for the tent so I may change my dress.

The centre of the tent is tall enough to stand in. A hemp rug lies unevenly across the hacked down bush and shrubs beneath my feet. Two small wooden chests sit open on one side of the shelter, overflowing with silk embroidered robes that look startlingly out of place.

I take my water flask and hairbrush from my saddlebag, and wash my face, wiping dirt and blood on the hem of my torn dress. Then I sift through the dresses, searching for the cobalt grey robe I wore in Lyndonia the morning Duchess Elise took me to visit Kel.

Breathing is awkward. I am not looking forward to the next five hours' riding. But at least my mare was not hurt when a bird-man tripped her with his lasso. I cannot imagine abandoning Dancer, nor seeing her suffer just so I may reach our final destination.

I struggle to rip apart the hook-and-eye closures on the back of my tattered dress. Pain flares with each sharp, tugging movement. I don't have the strength to break the top hooks. With the back of my dress gaping, I peer out from the tent, hoping to borrow a knife from a nearby soldier.

Tug is walking in my direction, away from where the troop is gathered. Unless he is going to relieve himself, he is heading to see me. Unlike the soldiers who erected the tent and promptly vanished, he is the only man around here who couldn't care less about my privacy.

I consider ducking back inside. Standing in front of Tug with my dress half falling off is not a welcome thought. But Brin has gone and the unit will want to move on. I will be stuck half-dressed with everyone wondering what is taking so long, otherwise.

'The Prince asked me to give you this,' Tug says when he is closer. He holds a slim bell-shaped phial half-full with yellow pus-like liquid. 'It's Nocturne Melody, a pain reliever.'

Pretty name for something so foul looking. I take the glass bottle, pop the cork and sip. The acrid taste makes me want to vomit.

'It is usually drunk by men dying on the battlefield. Unless you're planning on a soldier carrying you to the Red City you should slow down.' The icy shards in his voice set me on guard.

That moment in the forest, of complicity, of working together, of relief at seeing each other alive, has vanished. Perhaps he is angry with me because Brin might die.

'I need a knife,' I say. 'To get my dress off.'

He takes the short knife from his belt. The blood on it is still fresh.

He steps closer, eyes accusing, and wipes the blade on the sleeve of my dress. I flinch as though he's just spat in my face. With most of the blood now on my sleeve, he lays the knife flat in his palm like a challenge.

I slip the pain reliever into the pocket of my robe, and reach for the handle. An ink engraving on the hilt bears the same beast markings as the tattoos on his face. I take it, and with a smile I do not mean, thank him for his help.

I return inside the tent, rip the last two dress hooks with the blade and let the cloth fall to my feet. Until two minutes ago, I wanted to tell Tug I was sorry for Brin's situation. Now I want to thank him for banishing the guilt.

Brin snatched Kel. Sometimes, when I close my eyes, I hear Ma screaming as Brin tore my brother away and swatted her to the ground. If Brin dies, it is nothing to me.

I am doing up the front buttons of the grey dress, distracted by the stains on it which remind me of Kel in the tower, when Tug bursts through the flap door.

'I haven't finished!' I say annoyed. I fumble with the final buttons.

'From the lengthy discussions after the attack, I take it you and the Prince are on good terms again?' Tug says, ignoring my protest.

'He offered to let me go,' I say curtly.

Tug snorts. 'He has grown up in the Ruby Court. Survival for him depends on his ability to deceive and manipulate. He told you what you wanted to hear.'

I take out my brush and start tidying my hair. 'He risked his life to save me.'

'So did Brin, and I didn't see you hurrying to his side to check his injuries.' Tug's anger boils close to the surface. I should be careful, but it is as though we have circled around back to the beginning. Strangers. Enemies. Walls within walls.

He blames me for the outcome of today's attack. If he wants to blame someone, he should look to himself.

'Why would I care what happens to Brin? He has never considered me, or Kel, as anything close to human.'

Tug picks up a beautiful cream and lemon dress from the nearest clothes chest, and wipes his blood-encrusted face and hands all over it. I offer him water to finish the job properly. He ignores my attempt at defiance.

'So the Prince offered you freedom?' he says. 'How did he persuade you afterwards, not to take it?'

'He didn't need to persuade me. You've done that for him. I could have left Lyndonia with Kel many days ago, but you betrayed me for Elise. If I leave without fulfilling our bargain, who knows what the two of you will do to my brother.'

Tug's jaw tightens. 'Betrayal is only possible when there is trust in the first place.'

'What do you want?' I ask coldly.

'Lord Strik will hear of the bird-men's failure before we even reach the Red City.' He pauses, crouches to pick up his knife from the rug near the clothes chest. 'Perhaps you believe the Prince had nothing to do with the attack on his escort. Perhaps you believe it is coincidence that while the Prince was defying the King and refusing the Rudeashan princess in the north, the Carucan army was betrayed in the south and the King taken prisoner. Perhaps Jakut is the noble hero he pretends. It does not matter.'

He gets up, slips the knife in his pouch and stands so his face is an arm's length from my own. The rage in him has gone, or transformed into another barrier to hold out the world.

'It does not matter because the Prince is weak,' he says. 'If Lord Strik can govern the bird-men who have not been seen so far south for hundreds of years, do you think he will have any trouble bending the Prince to his will? At some point, the Prince and Lord Strik met with the same objective—to see Jakut and Lady Calmi married. We can assume the Prince was quickly brought under Strik's power. As soon as his memories return, he will be under it again.'

'If you are so sure he and Strik betrayed the Carucan army to get rid of the King and see Jakut crowned, why are we even going to the Red City? You should be telling the Duchess to prepare for war.'

'We must discover what Lord Strik has planned before taking rash actions which will set the kingdom at war with itself.'

'So the valiant Tye Keylore is back among us to save the Kingdom. Excuse me if I find that hard to swallow.'

'No one wants a war, Mirra.'

He is at the exit before I've had time to blink.

'Wait!' I say. The sketches. Until Tug arrived, distracting me, I had thought of little else. I had considered discussing Jakut's claim with him, but he hasn't exactly paved the way for an exchange of confidences.

'Where does Strik's power come from? What is it?'

Wind howls across snowy tundra. Nothing but the sting against his face, the bulk on his back, swirls of snow and emptiness stretching on and on.

For the brief moment Tug's memory absorbs the mind-world, it is as though I can breathe without the pain in my chest. A sense of aliveness, awareness, as crisp and clear as air.

'Trying to understand the origin of this power,' he says, 'will take you down a path as dark as the mind that wields it.'

I know of only two reasons to cross the infinite tundra between Caruca and the Kingdom of Rudeash. One, to access the tundra mines where hundreds of glitter-eyed children slave until they die. The other, to visit the far away, isolated Kingdom of Rudeash.

'We cannot defeat Lord Strik without understanding his power. Why were you crossing the tundra?'

'I had reason to believe he was born in Rudeash.'

'But he is a lord.'

'A title given to him when he was adviser to King Rex. But he rose to the King's side from nothing.'

'And you thought there might be others from Rudeash with similar abilities?'

'They seemed to be a simple people. Nothing I saw or heard suggested there was anyone else like him. Nothing explained it.'

I nod. Jakut's mother was from Rudeash. For a moment I thought she could have passed on a talent of foresight to her son. But if Strik is an anomaly, and the Rudeashans do not possess special powers, Jakut's claim about the sketches is highly doubtful. Unless, I grow a little faith in the Carucan Gods.

My head swims from taking too many short breaths, from the

Nocturne Melody trickling through my blood, from questions and half-truths and lies. Too many to hold straight.

But I cannot forget Jakut's attitude after the attack. The concern in his eyes when he realised I was injured was real. His offer to release me was genuine. If he is a liar and a manipulator and a coward, I have lost all instinct for survival.

'What if the Prince,' I say, 'only understood Strik's power and what he had got himself into when it was too late? What if he purposefully increased the dose of the mist berries before the long-sleep to erase everything in his past and break Lord Strik's hold over him?'

'If it were so,' Tug snarls, 'he should have informed himself of the matter. It changes nothing. As soon as Lord Strik enters the Red City or the Prince's memories return, he will fall under Strik's influence.'

I am not so certain. Yesterday, Lord Strik demonstrated a certain caution with the power in his voice, using it only on Tug and I. He did not try to control Jakut. He did not try to escort the Duke's unit to the Red City. And he deemed the Prince's long, unexplained absence and my presence, enough of a threat to his plans to try to kill me.

He must be waiting for something before he risks entering the city, a city which has kept him locked out, power or no power, for nearly three decades.

'We must learn how King Alixter has kept Strik away from the palace and ensure nothing is changed,' I say. 'In the meantime, it may take weeks for Jakut to remember pieces of his past.'

I stop. But if he has lied about the sketches, then Queen Usas and Lady Calmi are already surfacing in his consciousness.

'What is it?' Tug asks.

'Jakut showed me drawings. Portraits he said he has had in his possession since waking from the long-sleep.'

'And?'

'If he is lying, and they were done more recently, then he is beginning to remember.'

'Why would he lie?'

'I was in one of them. He says our meeting was the will of the Carucan Gods.'

A slight indent appears in Tug's bottom lip. 'If you're wondering whether there is any possible way he drew a picture of you before he met you, the answer is no.'

'He has a sketch of Kel.'

'He was in the Pit the day we bought you and Kel there.' Tug steps towards me. Up close the specks of dirt in the wide-open flesh above his eye are visible. 'There are ways to get inside a person's head. Without the sight. He's drawing his net around you. He wants to make sure you act in his interests when we're in the Ruby Palace.'

'I will act in my own interests.'

A spark flashes in his dead gaze. 'I'm counting on it.'

Once he has left the tent, I fold the bloodstained, cream and yellow dress, and return it to the chest. Something metal pokes my hand. I dig in and find a wrought iron mirror, packed by a maid for the journey and forgotten. A broken piece of looking glass would make a reasonable weapon.

Before tucking it into my saddlebag, I check I am presentable for the Duke and the Royal Court.

My pupils are large with Nocturne Melody. Perspiration gathers at my hairline, and my face has a sweaty, unhealthy glow. The evening I saw myself in the dining room at Lindy flutters into my thoughts. I had been disturbed by the strange foreignness of my appearance. By the wildness in my eyes, the semblance of a lady, the six years that had suddenly caught me up.

I am no longer disturbed. I am ready. Ready to face the Ruby Court and the truth about Jakut. Ready to end this.

THIRTY-SIX

Horse hair tickles my cheek. The smell of dust, sweat, and hay fills my nostrils. I ride half asleep, leaning into Dancer's neck. My body tingles with warmth, beams of Nocturne Melody sunlight trapped inside me. A song Ma used to sing when Kel was a baby drifts in my head. Far off in the mind-world, a dense pool of colour pulses, carrying echoes of a gigantic symphony through the mountains. The Red City is close.

A voice, irritating as a gnat, disturbs my tranquility. It occurs to me my mare has stopped. With enormous effort, I squeeze my eyelids, until they release and flutter open.

'She's fine,' I hear Tug say. 'The bird-men attack left her petrified. I gave her something to calm her nerves.' Calm her nerves! Bravo, Tug. An artful lie, in keeping with the Duke's opinion of my frailer sex.

'I am concerned her affection for the Prince will be the ruin of her,' the Duke answers. 'If her father knew what was going on, I am sure he would not approve.'

The Duke is talking of the Delladean Lord Tersil, but it is Pa's face that forms on my inner eye. My father reaches out his arms, asking me to come home. I shake my head, partly telling him "no", partly to dislodge him from my thoughts.

'As you have noticed, Mirra is a determined young woman. Lord Tersil understood preventing his daughter from following the Prince would only backfire on him.'

'I have seen it before,' the Duke answers. 'A lady with a broken heart is hard to coax back to the living.'

'Prince Jakut will not break her heart.' The abrupt finality in Tug's voice sounds false. He doubts his own words. It is as though they have both unknowingly started talking about Tug and the Duchess. 'He has agreed for Mirra to be presented to the Court as your niece.'

'For what good it will do.'

The blurry Duke in his royal tunic melts into the mass of soldiers. I strain to sit up. Tug repeats my name, but it is the view ahead that catches my attention, and rivets my gaze.

Shimmering in the fiery glow of the evening sun, a city of ochre-tinted houses climbs to the sky. And high on the top, in a misty haze, stands the palace.

White flags fly from the spires of a dozen minarets. The massive tiered structure resembles a vertical maze of arcades, walkways, and stepped gardens. It is as though the soul of the Carucan people was distilled and poured into one perfect vision.

'It's beautiful,' I murmur.

'Like all the deadliest things are,' Tug says. 'Give me the pain reliever.' I take it from the pocket of my skirt and pass it to him, wondering what my father would think if he knew tonight I would be sleeping in Caruca's infamous Ruby Palace.

An image of Pa lying in the snow snaps to the front of my mind. Dark patches staining powder-white snow as his life force ebbs away. The bewildered expression on Ma's pale face as I told her she would have to build a shelter, and fire, and heal him without my help. Pa! I cover my eyes with my hand.

Arms wrap around my waist, and I am pulled from my mare. I moan as the pressure on my rib transforms to pain. My feet touch the ground, but I am so sleepy I can barely stand. Tug kneads my sides, his oafish hands prodding and pushing. I batter him away.

'What are you doing?' My words come out in a lazy drawl.

'I am checking if it is a bruise or a fracture, and nothing is moving.'

'A bit late for that.'

My neck lolls as I tilt to look at Beast-face. Guilt slithers in his eyes.

'We are almost at the royal stables at the bottom of the city,' he says, 'where we will rest the horses and eat before the climb. It will be a slow ride up the mountain, and well after supper before we reach the palace. You will be able to go straight to your chambers and sleep. No more Nocturne Melody.'

'Have we beaten the messenger from Lyndonia?'

'It appears so. Otherwise soldiers from the royal guard would be here to greet us. Or arrest us.'

Tug holds my shoulders. I suppose I am swaying. Certainly it is a challenge to stay on my feet.

I stare at his tattooed face, but it is not what I see. The island of the Rushing Winds shines before my inner eye. White houses dazzling in a bright sun, huge waves smashing against glittering crystal cliffs.

When the Eteans arrived at the lands of my ancestors, they quarried the crystal cliffs and hillsides until their vessels were full. They left only to return with more boats, gouging out moonstone, onyx and amber, destroying the coral reef barrier, which protected the island from the great spring storms.

They finally departed, leaving the island and the Uru Ana to drown, taking four hundred glitter-eyed children with them. The children were a curiosity, an amusement, a symbol of their conquest. Of course, they did not realise, at first, the ability these strange sparkling eyes held.

I used to feel scorched with the shame of my people's weakness. What good was the power to see into your enemy's psyche, if you did not find their weaknesses and use it to defeat them? But the melody coursing through my blood and shifting the furniture of my mind has opened a doorway. I suddenly understand what my people always knew. War transforms the luminescence of the mind-world to darkness. My people hoped their compassion would be enough to change the warring spirit of the Eteans. But they refused to change themselves, to descend into the shadows of hate and violence, death and revenge.

'Mirra?' Tug's voice returns me to the foothill.

'Where's the Prince?' I scrunch my eyes at the unit of soldiers and find the answer to my question. The Prince is near the front, on his knees, praying. Before the long-sleep, Jakut spent much of his day in prayer, but since our meeting in the Hybourg, I have not once seen him turn to his Gods for guidance or help. Wariness trickles through me.

'If we're almost at the stables,' I ask, 'why have we stopped here?'

'The white flags,' Tug answers.

'They resemble birds.'

'They are a symbol of the Carucan ceremony of departing. It means someone from the royal family has just died.'

RIDING through the Red City is like moving through a dream. We wind up narrow streets, terraced houses slanting down on one side, rising on the other. The warm air smells of thyme and sage. The mind-world flows on a great ocean of melancholy. Small white flags and drapes hang from windows, doorways, and rooftops. They flutter and snap in the breeze. And beneath their flapping chorus, the clicking of thousands of insects.

The knowledge of our presence ripples through the city. More and more people gather on the steps of their homes to watch us pass. They hold candles, cling to white shawls, curtsey and bow as the Prince and Duke pass.

No fanfare of trumpets, or cheering crowds, signal our arrival at the palace. We ride alongside tall, sunburnt-orange walls until we reach gates of wrought iron and gold filigree. The gates stand open, armed foot soldiers lining an enormous entrance of symmetrical hedges, fountains and tropical plants.

I sit up in my saddle, tension as thick in the air as the sweet scent of jasmine. The Nocturne Melody is fading from my blood, the pain in my ribs taking hold, along with a needling voice, which tells me I need more of the pain-numbing poison.

We are inside the royal walls, but the ground level consists of the royal army barracks, horse stables and servant quarters. From here, there is only one way into the world of courtiers and kings—steep, wide steps to an archway taller than four men. And blocking our entrance at the top of those steps, centred between two magnificent ruby-studded doors, stands Queen Usas.

Swathes of white fall from her shoulders. Loose matching trousers hang beneath her swollen belly, and a sword sits against her thigh. Her hair is bound in a sweep of blonde curls. She is not beautiful. She is not even pretty. But her presence is arresting.

She tilts her head and murmurs something to one of her dozen guards. Three older men in long white robes step aside, and the summoned guard descends the steps, dropping to one knee in front of the Duke.

By showing her respect to Prince Roarhil before Prince Jakut, she has just slighted the rightful heir to the throne.

'Keep an eye on me,' I tell Tug.

'Welcome back,' he says, as I close my eyes and reach for the Queen's mind.

I travel an arid world, scudding and skimming over long hours of the Queen sitting beside the King's pyre, the Queen alone in her chambers, the Queen with the royal council. Her mind is organised, and disciplined. My search is as unencumbered, and swift, as sand blown across a desert. Until something interesting...

She stands before a mirror, squeezing droplets in her eyes to hide their redness. Or accentuate it. Copper brown eyes, a crooked nose, and a long, youthful face.

A knock sounds in the distant recesses of her chambers. She sails out of the marble bathing quarters, her warrior body graceful, despite the child, almost fully formed, in her belly.

A maid answers the door to her outer chambers. Queen Usas stops to light a candle. It is one of six candles standing waist-high in the latticed white arches that lead to a exterior cloister. The semi-precious stones in the arches and walls reflect soft light onto the polished marble.

An officer enters, bowing.

'Is it true?' she asks.

'He is approaching the gates with Prince Roarhil, Duke of Rathesyde.'

'And where has he been all these months? If he were in Lyndonia we would have heard of it.'

'The injuries he sustained during the attack on his escort kept him in the far north during the winter.'

'How is this possible? You said your spies knew what Lady Calmi muttered in her sleep. How could she have hidden this from us?'

'I'm convinced she was no better informed than we have been.'

'Does he wear the white mourning robe?'

'He does not.'

The Queen extinguishes the long match burning between her fingers just before it reaches her flesh. She tosses it in a fire grate and picks up a sword from the mantle-piece.

'My Queen,' the officer says, bowing. 'We must not act hastily. The child you carry is in grave danger now the Prince is alive. Circumstances stack against you. With the Prince's assassination attempt and the King's death, he could claim you have betrayed the Carucan army and tried to rid yourself of the rightful heir to throne, in a plot to continue as regent and secure the crown for your child.'

'Jakut is not the rightful heir! King Alixter would never have named the Prince his successor!'

Tug's hand touches my shoulder. I open my eyes, easing from the Queen's mind without effort. Around us, Duke Roarhil's men are dismounting their horses, dropping to their knees.

I look up. The Queen is descending the palace steps. Tug helps me from my mare. I cannot tear my eyes from the warrior Queen. She has kept her pregnancy secret from the Kingdom. She has a motive for Jakut's assassination. And she does not intend to submit the throne to King Alixter's first-born child and heir.

THIRTY-SEVEN

I kneel alongside Tug, facing the stairway and the ruby palace doors. Scattered around me the Duke's soldiers are all down on one knee, heads lowered, as stable hands weave around us, leading our horses away.

Queen Usas greets the Duke, telling him to rise. He takes her hands in his and mutters words of regret and sorrow. She nods, eyes scanning the Prince. She sways towards him, one hand resting on the hilt of her sword.

Images streak through the mind-world, so fast I only comprehend snatches and fragments, struggling to decipher one moment, while the next streams forward to submerge it.

Hands on a bloody bed sheet. A frozen face marbled with burst blood vessels. A distressed wailing.

A man's voice. 'I have lost my best assassin. And I will not lose you.' His hands in hers. 'Promise me you won't try anything.' The King's eyes. Tenderness, strength.

The Red City sprawled before her. 'You must see Lady Calmi is married.' She turns to her husband. 'See she is married and send Jakut north for the princess.'

The mind-world settles around the Queen. With my head lowered, I squint to watch her staring down at the kneeling Prince. The images were confusing, out of chronological order. But the love she felt for the King is indisputable.

'Your father is dead,' she says.

'May his spirit follow the path of Rhag,' the Prince answers, remaining bowed in the deepest sign of respect. The faintest trace of surprise alters the Queen's cold expression.

'The King's head arrived at the palace two days ago. We are preparing a body for the ceremony of departure.'

In the vast entrance gardens, from the surrounding foot soldiers, right up to the Queen's personal guard and council on the terrace, no one moves.

The Prince slowly raises his head. The moment his eyes meet her my flesh tingles. I cannot see his expression but I see the memory that has shaken loose from the darkness of his past.

Black flags with the royal crest flapping in the wind. Young men sparring. Queen Usas drawing a Bo staff. Striking. The Prince ducking. Striking back.

A tournament. Sparring with the Queen. I wish I could examine the Prince's face and see his reaction to remembering Usas. Then I would know whether he has lied about the sketches. Lie or not, there can be no doubt now, the Prince's past is emerging.

What if this is the tiny shift that causes an avalanche? How long before all the pieces rise and find their places and the Prince is under Strik's influence?

The Queen steps back and nods, signalling the Prince may rise.

I lower my gaze as she strides through the soldiers. My chest sinks when I realise she is coming towards me.

'Princess Aliylah?'

A shiver prickles up my spine. I shake my head.

'The King told Prince Jakut not to return to the Red City without the Princess. Am I to understand he has brought you instead?'

I stare at her shoes, the soft leather moulded around her feet for comfort and nimbleness. All Deadran's preparation, the Prince's test in Lyndonia, deceiving the Duke and Duchess, nothing has prepared me for this. I feel like I have shadow weaver written on my skin, crawling across my face, and she has only to look closer and she will see it.

She stands before me, silence stretching out like a promise of the silence that will meet me in my grave.

'Rise,' she orders. I push to my feet, while the mind-world flashes with a lithe female figure, swinging and ducking. Queen Usas is remembering a younger version of herself, training with a smaller, female warrior. 'Look at me.'

I breathe in deeply, the pain in my ribs vying for attention. Her eyes are as blue as the sky in the summer and behind the intelligence, the anger, the hate, swirls a storm of grief.

'You do not look Rudeashan. Your colouring and face resemble the Eteans.'

I struggle to swallow, unable to steady my rapid heart beat. If I claim to be the Duchess' niece who no one has ever heard of, turning up to find a suitor in the Ruby Court when the King has just been slain and the kingdom is in turmoil, the Queen will distrust the Duke and me as fully as she is convinced of the Prince's betrayal.

This Queen lives in a world of vipers and politicians, kingdoms, crowns and wars. Unlike the isolated Duke and Duchess she will not believe a flimsy lie.

My presence is not inappropriate. It is inexplicable.

Her gaze fixes on the scratches at the side of my face.

'Rise!' she proclaims, extending her arm across the soldiers. The Duke's men stand. Their leather boots creak, their scabbards clink against belts and buttons. They stare forward while her eyes roam across them, lingering on the fresh, honey-sealed gash above Tug's eyebrow.

'My master-at-arms will allocate your barracks,' she announces. A man with grey hair, fit for his years, steps out from the formation of royal foot soldiers and bows to the Queen. 'Prince Roarhil,' she turns to the Duke, 'your men are exhausted from the journey. I would be honoured to organise your personal guard if you wish your men to rest.'

The Duke bows in consent. Commander Fror's face hardens, but refusing the Queen's offer would be a declaration of distrust.

'And Prince Jakut,' she says turning to Jakut, 'Officer Resnit will be happy to serve as your personal guard as he has always done.'

The Duke's soldiers line-up to follow the master-at-arms. Tug moves to join them but she stops him. 'You will come with us,' she says, casting me a final look before sweeping off to the Duke.

Arm-in-arm, she and the Duke walk forward to ascend the palace steps. The Prince follows, accompanied by the man who descended and bowed before the Duke. It is the same high-ranking officer who brought her news of the Prince's arrival in the city, and beseeched his Queen not to act rashly.

Tug and I leave a respectful distance before bringing up the rear. My panic ebbs and sours at the thought of climbing so many steps while trying to hide signs of my injury.

'She is no dupe,' I murmur to Tug as he escorts me in the same manner the Duke escorts the Queen. 'She's already got rid of the Duke's men. If Roarhil tells her I am his wife's niece, she will not believe him.'

'The Queen,' Tug answers, 'will want the Duke on her side when she tries to have Prince Jakut arrested. And questioning whether he's lying about you will not be the best way to go about it.'

'You think she means to arrest the Prince?' We have only begun the climb and I'm growing short of breath. Speaking is an extra effort. The muscles in my thighs tremble. I suppose I should be grateful Tug took away the Nocturne Melody. Two hours ago I could barely stand.

'She will have to convince the council the Prince betrayed the long-sleep locations of the Carucan army, before confining him to the dungeons. You need rest,' he adds, glancing at me. 'Tomorrow we will find the Lady Calmi and you will discover whether the Prince is responsible for the King's death.'

'I am here to find who ordered the Prince's assassination, not the King's.'

Our gazes lock halfway up the steps. In my imagination, I see Tug as an officer, rising through the ranks, developing military strategy with generals. He is ambitious, and driven. Driven by the desire to avenge the theft of his father's lands. And something more. Something worth risking everything for, even Duchess Elise.

The night at the Hybourg after we met Jakut, comes rushing back. Tug had just sold Kel to a Lyndonian royal guard. He wanted me to reveal the identity of the wealthy buyer who planned to take me to the Lyndonian fort as part of a test. Even before he knew Jakut's true identity, there was something restless about him. And once I told him we were dealing with the Prince of Caruca, a fire lit him up. A fire, which if I remember correctly, had scared me more than the icy impassiveness.

After twelve years of living on the outskirts of the Kingdom, drinking, gambling, fighting, and running from his demons, Tug glimpsed a road back. Not to Elise or his old life as Baron Keylore. But back into the heart of a turbulent, volatile Kingdom.

'You are not here for the Duchess,' I whisper.

'You are not here for Kel,' he answers in a low growl. I try to stab him with my eyes. 'I would have let you go, Mirra,' he says in response to my glare. 'The Prince released you, and I would have let you go if it was what you wanted.'

Anger forks through the centre of my being. This is not the time or the place. Two of the Queen's guards remain stationed by the ruby doors. But a response flies from my tongue. 'Now who's playing games with my head?'

'I made it easy on you,' he says matter-of-factly. His manner rubs down my back, like he's peeling flesh.

'Easy on me?

'You wanted to see this through. After everything that's happened, saving Kel is no longer enough.'

I bristle. Beast-face doesn't understand my desire to help my people.

'When the Prince,' he says, 'doesn't turn out to be the man you hope, you might realise you and I are on the same side.'

'The side that hunts glitter-eyed children and sells them to low-life, power-hungry serpents?'

'If I wanted to capture Uru Ana I would not hunt in the only northern forest reputed not to have any. I was simply there for the deer season. '

'And that's why you took Kel.'

'Brin took Kel.'

'You let him.'

'Not one of my proudest moments. You shot my dog. I was angry.'

I glare ahead as we pass under a magnificent archway with matching ruby studs in the curves of sleek stone. In all our time together, I have never hated him more.

THIRTY-EIGHT

In a place between sleep and wakefulness, where dreams entwine with visions from the mind-world, I find myself in the Ruby Palace throne room. Except, I am not standing at the bottom of the dais steps behind the Prince and the Duke, as I did last night when the Queen questioned us for over an hour. I am beside the King's empty throne seat, near the three royal council members wearing billowing robes.

A strange wind gusts into the enormous hall, carrying voices. Wailing, mournful voices. Voices that scream and writhe as though a thousand minds have been trapped and crushed together.

I should not be able to hear the voices, and it is important no one discovers I can. So I pretend I'm listening to the disagreement surging between the Queen and the Duke. The Queen presses for information about the whereabouts of the men who survived the attack on the Prince's escort. The Duke wants to discuss how they will reinforce the Carucan army and drive back the Eteans who sack villages all along the western border.

The voices in the wind grow louder, spiralling around me. All the giant candles lighting the great hall blow out, and a faint voice howls my name.

I wake, heart thumping, the back of my skull prickling. Kel's cry echoes in my head beneath a chorus of insects, clicking and scratching outside my window.

I roll over and am at once reminded of my bruised rib, by a sharp pain. In my mind's eye, I recall the marbled umber and cinnamon pillars of the throne room, the elaborate floor designs, the dais with its empty throne, and the Queen calling me forward to describe the events of the bird-men attack.

Though last night she did not question the Duke's reason for my presence, it was clear she did not believe I was in the Ruby Palace to find a husband. She permitted my guardian, Tug, to stay in nearby quarters, but I was certain she'd be adding reinforcements. A sentiment already confirmed by the two unfamiliar minds lingering outside my chambers.

I kick off the bed throw and get up from the floor, avoiding abrupt movements. My loose nightshirt stops mid-way down my calves. I check my short knife is still strapped to my thigh. The familiar feel of it in my palm is reassuring. Tug has finally returned my weapons. A symbol of the fact he wants us to trust each other?

I move to the arched frame, which opens onto an ochre-tiled balcony. Heat rises through my feet as I step into the breeze. I inhale the fresh, warm air, pushing down thoughts of the strange dream-memory. Then I take in the dizzying view.

My guest room is in a high, domed tower that almost topples off the side of the palace. A vast mountain range stretches across the horizon. The east side of the mountain, unlike the west with its stepped terraces and streets winding to the summit, has a thousand-foot vertical drop. One or two houses cling to the cliff, but the terraces start so far below, the houses and people resemble children's toys.

The angle of the high sun signals it is near noon. I can't believe I have slept so long, and so well, despite the distraction of so many minds, and my own fears of this new, gossamer-threaded spider-web world.

I throw the blankets back on the bed so it looks slept in, put on a light shawl and peer into the corridor.

A maid and a soldier stand in the marble sheen. She is laughing; his hand is almost touching hers. The moment they notice me, they pull apart. Her cheeks flame. His face slackens, body rigid as his arms fall to his sides, and he stands to attention.

The maid scurries to my door, picks up a tea tray, and curtsies. 'I was told to let you rest. I hope that was right.'

A third mind moves towards us, appearing around the curved balustrade at the end of the corridor. Diaphanous blue cloth obscures all but the woman's heavy-lidded eyes. She carries a basket, and I have the sense she's been waiting for me.

The maid speaks. 'Would you like me to serve your tea and dress you now, Lady Mirra?'

The woman slips past the soldier, lowering her headscarf. From the simple shape and feel of her mind, I would never have guessed at her beauty. Contrasted with her long, black hair, her eyes are as pale as glaciers. The skin on her symmetrical face is as smooth and fine as powder snow.

'I have been sent to look at you,' the woman says. 'I am a healer.'

The maid turns, sees the young woman, blushes again and moves aside with a curtsey, gaze fixed on my legs. The sudden fear the woman has sparked in the maid, captures my interest.

'I do not need a healer,' I say. During the Queen's inquisition of the bird-men attack, neither the Prince, Tug nor I revealed my injury, and the Duke, knowing nothing of it, could not. Why would the Queen send a healer?

'I have already seen the Prince,' the woman says, stepping closer. Between slim fingers she holds a fold of paper, flicks it up so only I can see it. It bears the seal of the Prince's royal signet ring. 'It is also his wish I check on you.'

A message from the Prince? When the Queen questioned Jakut in the throne room, it was clear his every move would be scrutinised from now on. The guard allocated for his protection was one of her spies. Any attempt at contacting each other will raise suspicions about our relationship and my presence in the palace. The healer may be our best chance of arranging how and where we will exchange information.

For a brief moment, I wonder how Jakut is coping. While I am swamped by information, memories dancing in a non-stop whirling ballet, he advances through a tenebrous landscape. Every step he takes, there is a risk the ground beneath will give way.

How easy will it be to manipulate him if someone like Lady Calmi discovers he does not remember who he is? She could tell him anything about his past self. What would Lord Strik or Queen Usas do with such information?

Thoughts of the Lady Calmi and Queen Usas spur me to action. I have much to do if I am to scan both their memories of the last year. I do not even know yet where Lady Calmi lives in the vast palace, or if she has tried to speak to the Prince.

I turn to my maid and take the tea tray. 'I would very much like a pair of trousers and over-shirt like the Queen's.'

'The baggy trousers and long-shirt are Tmàn costume,' the maid says shocked.

'Perhaps you could find out for me who makes them and ask them to call on me?'

'The departing ceremony is in two hours.'

'Then you had better hurry.'

With a flustered curtsey, she hurries away, shooting one final look at the soldier. I stretch out my awareness through the tower, but do not sense Tug.

'Has my guardian passed by to see me?' I ask the soldier.

'No, My Lady.'

My eyes meet the healers. Nothing untoward stirs in the mind-world. I stand back and let her in.

The healer waits in the centre of the bedroom as I pour myself a cup of lukewarm tea. I sip my tea and take a green fruit from a bowl set on a carved wooden table that twists around like a screw. I bite into the fruit. Tangy sweetness bursts across my tongue. I savour the flavour, smiling at the woman so she does not notice my careful examination. Poised, elegant, she demonstrates the perfect balance of restraint and receptiveness Deadran tried to teach me. Her expression is open, but not curious. She is not anxious, or watchful, and her long simple dress, could not easily conceal a weapon.

'You have a message for me?' I ask.

'I know you are suffering,' she says. 'Let me examine you first. Pull up your shirt.'

'My rib is bruised. There is nothing to see.'

She sets her basket on the long table near the cream embroidered divan. The hamper overflows with pouches and medicine bottles. 'I am not in pain,' I say, stamping on that little voice in the back of my head that whines and implores for more Nocturne Melody.

'Then at least let me give you something to reduce the internal swelling and help you heal faster.' She opens a pouch and withdraws a handful of dried yellow flowers. Their appearance is similar to the star-petalled snow arnica Pa occasionally bought when he returned to Black-foot Forest with supplies. Except the petals are yellow, the seeds bigger.

The woman takes out a mortar and pestle and grinds the flowers. Then she pours a little into a miniature bowl and hands it to me. I smell, rub a pinch of powder onto my teeth. It tastes similar to snow arnica.

'I will leave you the rest,' she says. 'It is to be taken four times a day. You can stir it into the tea if you prefer.' She packs away the herbs.

'Your message for me?'

She nods, retrieves the fold of paper from her skirt. I turn it over, checking the seal is not broken. I do not open it. The Prince may have confided his note into her hands, but that does not mean we can trust her.

'Thank you,' I say, dipping my fruit into the flower grain and chewing down a little more of the clean, fragrant mix.

She stands in the centre of the room without a shimmer of movement. If the Carucan Gods existed, she would be their earthly incarnation, barely of this world with her allure and grace.

'You do not wish me to take an answer?'

I am about to decline when my heartbeat flutters. I glance at the flowers, then at the tea. Stepping back to the bed, I search the healer's face for signs of deceit. Nothing. Not in her calm expression, nor in the mind-world. I tear open the seal on the Prince's note and unfold the paper.

It is as blank as her face.

My knife is in my hand in a second. But the woman still doesn't move.

'An interesting response for a Baroness,' she says, staring.

'What have you given me?'

'I think you are probably more interested in what it will do to you. But I have given you summer arnica soaked in an undetectable snake poison. The poison is slowing your heart. In a minute it will paralyse the muscles in your arms and legs, in another twenty, your organs will shut down and your heart will stop beating.'

One fist pressed to my chest, the other clenching the knife, I jerk sideways for the door.

'Call your guard,' she says, 'and by the time he has found another healer, you will be dead. I, on the other hand, have the antidote.'

'What do you want?'

'First, I want you to answer my questions.'

My eyes dart to her basket, the herb pouches and bottles. Even if I could get my hands on them, I have no idea what to look for.

My legs and arms tingle. How long before I lose muscle control? My instinct is to leap forwards and jab her in the throat with the heel of my knife. She may be taller, but she is not lithe and agile like the Queen. I think it's safe to assume she is no Tmàn warrior, and I could have her at the point of my blade in seconds.

I shake my hands. The tingling grows stronger, creeping into my shoulders.

But she is clever. If I hold her at knifepoint, she knows in sixty— ninety—a hundred heartbeats I'll be defenceless. And even if she believed I was capable of slitting her throat in cold blood, we both know I will not, else we die together.

I lower my knife. 'Who are you?'

She does not gloat at my submission. Her mild manner conveys none of her intention.

'I am Lady Calmi.'

THIRTY-NINE

I take a step back and reach for the divan. My head spins, my legs feel as though they are being pulled down, and my fingers are so heavy the knife is slipping from my grip.

She is lying! I saw the Prince's sketches, the young woman with the wavy hair, large tormented eyes, and a thin nose.

'You are not Lady Calmi.'

'It seems you have been as little informed about me, as I about you. Has the Prince told you nothing?'

I sink into soft cushion, try to curl my yielding fingers back around the knife, but they are unresponsive. The light in her eyes alters as she realises how little I know. It is impossible to read her, but that tiny change in her flat expression does more to confirm her claim than any words she could utter.

If this is Lady Calmi, who is the young woman the Prince carries in his leather binding, along with the portraits of Kel, Queen Usas and me?

My stomach hurts. Pressure builds in my head. My limbs want to give up. I battle their desire to succumb.

'How are your arms? Have you lost feeling yet?'

'They are tingling.'

'Your body fights the poison. Still, we should not delay if you want to live through this.'

'The soldier and the maid saw you enter. If I die, you will be arrested within the hour.'

The prickling intensifies to a painful sting as though my arms and legs are buried in snow. For an instant they burn, and then numbness creeps in. My shoulders and head slump. I'm about to keel over when she catches me and lowers me onto the divan.

'Stay calm. It is unpleasant, I know. Now, tell me, why has Prince Jakut arrived with his uncle? Why did he not send news he was alive? Why has he refused to speak with me?'

I struggle to focus on the ceiling. Delicately painted birds with blue wingtips decorate a circle in the centre. I can smell her citrus perfume and coriander on her breath. The numbness spreads up my neck, but my heart feels as though it's beating double-time and my mind races.

Perhaps she is not afraid of being arrested. Or she is confident any accusations against her will be dropped. Or she is bluffing and will not let me die no matter what.

Three possibilities. But I cannot gamble without knowing the first thing about her. Eyes open, fixed on the ceiling, I dip into her mind; skim the airy, insubstantial surface. I hope to find something recent that will reveal her true nature; but quickly, so she does not guess what I have done.

She walks through an enchanting passage of crisscrossed crescent arches. Arches which start on her level and end higher up, joining to the vertical network of turrets, palace apartment and courtyards. Plants hang like long arms from overhead balconies. A buttressed glass room blocks the fading light, and a twisting stairway starts two levels up, and keeps climbing higher than the eye can see.

Footsteps patter and echo. A nearby bird takes flight.

Calmi turns.

The woman running towards her shouts, 'News of the Prince!'

She falters, lifts a trembling hand to push back her long hair. 'Is he dead?' Her voice is steady but the fear is there, hidden inside her.

'He has just arrived at the palace, My Lady. The Queen greets him as we speak.'

Enough. Calmi has chosen a fast-working poison, and I may only have minutes before it shuts down my organs. It is not much, but at least I know she fears the Prince's death as much as I fear Kel's. I move to the edge of her mind to slip back out.

She runs across the drawbridge of an austere castle, shoes clattering on the wooden slats.

Panic jumps through me. How is this possible? I have been folded further down into her past! But I was so close to the edge. There was no resistance. Getting out should have been as easy as blinking.

'Sixe! Sixe!' she shouts, spinning around the castle's small courtyard. Open doorways ten, twenty, thirty feet high spill from the sheer walls into thin air. An ill kept man, clothes ragged, face weathered, steps into the light almost twenty feet up. Like a rat in a drain tunnel who cannot escape because escape would mean falling to his death.

I test the contours of the memory, searching for an exit.

'Sixe,' she pants. 'I need my herb basket. Quickly! In the western field by the brook. The slave girl's baby has come early. And bring something to make fire. We must hurry. She's very sick.'

I sense a small gap. In my mind's eye, I move towards it, imagine myself on the other side. The outside.

She is in a field, crouched before a girl my age. The girl's bare legs are bent up at the knees, held there by another woman. Blood covers the girl's hands and dress. A baby's head pokes out from between her legs. Thick dark hair covered in a greasy white substance and blood.

'Sixe, hold the head. I have to push on her stomach.'

She moves around the girl in childbirth and the woman holding her legs. As she places her hands on the girl's belly, feeling the contours of the baby, the girl starts convulsing.

'No, no, don't hold her. Give her space. Wait!'

The seizure ends. 'We must get the child out now or they will both die!'

I change tactics to escape her mind. I push myself through the viscous, transparent film enveloping the memory. I have the sense of puncturing the seal and reaching the outside, but time folds again!

She is eight years old, running through a field of yellow wheat. In the distance, smoke billows to the sky. A small brick house is on fire. She is running so fast she trips on her long skirt and lands face down with a thump.

The fall winds her. She rises slowly, pushing hair from her face and gazing at the charred house. On her knees, she starts clawing at the ground, tearing up stems of wheat. In a frenzy, she rises, batting the crop until her arms bleed, tramping it beneath her boots, screaming in rage.

The man with the weathered face, Six, limps towards her. She claws the mud where she has pulled up the grain, draws her soiled nails across her cheeks, scratching the dirt into them. Six takes her hands. He holds them for a moment, and gives a tiny shake of his head.

I mentally kick and punch at the edges of the memory. I am too far down. Too far into her past, and each time I think I have found a way out, I am swallowed further in. The panic mounts. How much time has passed? Five minutes? Ten? If I do not get out now, if I do not answer her questions, will she let me die?

She is a child, younger than Kel. Lord Strik stands beside her in the castle entrance, four guards watching over him. She stares at the high courtyard walls with their strange arched doorways. Doorways you could step through and fall to your death on the cobbled ground below.

'This is your home now,' he tells her. 'Six will always know where you are. It is his talent.' Strik switches to a language of short, clipped sounds where sentences seem only two or three words long. And he is using the voice. She stiffens, scraggly hair falling over her lowered face, hands rough and cut, the skirt of her dress two sizes too big. Still using the voice, he says, 'You cannot leave. You will never leave the lands around my home without my permission.'

I am catapulted from Lady Calmi's mind, thrown abruptly back to the living world, without understanding how.

Blue wing-tipped birds dip and dart across the ceiling. Something sour fills my nostrils and sits on my tongue. Bile climbs my throat in waves, never quite reaching my mouth.

I cannot move. Heaviness invades my body, but somehow my chest still rises and falls, and I manage to swallow, though it's painful.

Lady Calmi peers over me. I try to adjust my eyes to focus on her face. She dabs a pungent smelling cloth on my lips and cool liquid dribbles into my mouth. When my eyes finally obey my will and meet hers, she simply looks at me, then sits back on the low table, staring.

I tell my fingers to move. Down by my side, where she cannot see, the little one twitches.

'I did not know the poison could put someone into a trance,' she says. 'I have never heard of it.'

'Have you given me the antidote?'

'I cannot question you dead. Yes, I have given it to you.' I keep ordering my fingers to respond. Twitching one, then the next, then the next. 'Why have you come to the Ruby Palace?'

'I met your grandfather,' I say, hoping to distract her as I regain movement.

Her eyes sharpen. It is the first true reaction she has given. 'Where?'

'We travelled through his lands from Lyndonia.'

She rises and goes to stand by the balcony window. She gazes out so I can only see her profile. While she is not looking, I use all my will to inch my hand down the divan. My fingers graze the bone handle of my knife. 'Grandfather saw the Prince?' she asks.

'Yes.'

'Then we haven't much time.' She turns, her forest green dress shimmering in the sunshine, reflecting in her eyes. I cannot blame the Prince for wishing to defy his father and refuse the Rudeashan princess so that he could marry Lady Calmi. Her uncanny beauty is like her grandfather's voice; there is a strange power to it.

'Much time before what?'

'Before grandfather grows tired of waiting.'

When she speaks of Lord Strik, everything about her—voice, stance, eyes—are more empty than usual. She holds no affection for the man who brought her to his castle, and used his influence and the man Sixe to keep her on a leash. Fear. Obedience. But not love.

I wrap my knife into the cup of my palm, practise squeezing it.

'I do not understand why the Prince has brought you here,' she says. When I do not answer, she walks to the table, and bends down to tuck several fallen herb packets into her wicker basket.

She has given up and is leaving. I need more time! I curl my toes, and hunch my shoulders, coaxing muscles to respond, wheedling back control of my body.

Once her basket is packed she leans over me. 'Tell Prince Jakut I must speak to him.'

'I do not imagine you have many friends, Lady Calmi, if you go around poisoning people and then asking them for services.'

'I do not,' she says.

'But it looks like you are in desperate need of one.'

'If I had come to you as a friend, and asked why the Prince has brought you here and what has happened to him, would you have told me?'

'No. But what makes you think it is the Prince and not the Duke who brought me to the Ruby Palace?'

'The Duke?' she says, as though only just considering it. 'The Duke is not a fool.'

'And the Prince?'

'The Prince is the kingdom's only hope.'

I sit up fast, head-butting her. Pain screams in my chest and my muscles moan in agony, but I have the advantage of surprise. She reels back. I grab a fist of her hair with one hand, jerk her towards me and press the tip of my knife into the vee of her throat.

'We now know you were bluffing, Lady Calmi. The question is, am I?'

No reaction. No shock. She is utterly numb to violence. For a brief instant, I wonder what happened to her in Lord Strik's home. What happened to her mother and father?

'Are you an assassin?' she says.

'I will ask the questions. What happened to the Prince's escort?'

'Five of grandfather's men went with Prince Jakut to the north. Grandfather said they would protect him, but I expect they had orders to make sure the Princess of Rudeash and the Prince did not meet. Grandfather's men must have slaughtered the rest of his escort. I expect it was so the Prince would not be suspected of betraying the Carucan army. So it would look as though he was targeted at the same time as his father.'

'Did Prince Jakut betray the Carucan army?'

She does not answer straight away, but tilts back her head so the blade no longer scratches her throat. I loosen my hand on her hair.

Adrenaline crashes through my body. Did he do it? Is Jakut a traitor after all?

'Yes,' she says. 'Indirectly. He allowed it.'

My ears ring with blood. He might not have killed his escort, but the Prince is responsible for the death of hundreds of men, including his own father.

'And how does this make him the only hope for Caruca?' I sneer.

'It was the only way.'

'For the two of you to be together,' I spit, adrenaline pumping through me.

'The only way to gain grandfather's trust and kill the old man,' she answers.

FORTY

The door to my chambers whips open. Tug sweeps in, hand on his scabbard, every muscle tensed. He takes in Lady Calmi and I, my knife still inches from her throat, my fingers wrapped around her hair. As the guard appears behind him, Tug kicks the door shut in his face.

'You're putting the knife to good use, I see,' he says. Unlike the soldier, Tug's scabbard lies on his belt at a horizontal angle. The hilt meets the blade in a small fold of metal rather than a cross. He stands steadfast, taking in the smear of blood between Calmi's eyebrows, the basket of herbs, Lady Calmi's beauty. My heart pounds, but the adrenaline rush is over. I am starting to tremble. My body is still weak with poison.

Lady Calmi and the Prince betrayed the King and his army so they could kill Lord Strik. Should I believe her? A lifetime of brutality and fear might explain Lady Calmi's decision, but what reason could the Prince have for such a treacherous endeavour?

'Lady Calmi?' Tug says. I clench my teeth. How did he know it was her, yet I missed it? Frowning, I release her hair.

'The assassin's assistant,' she says to Tug, stepping back from the divan, lowering her eyes in a greeting of respect. Tug's gaze flicks to mine, trying to catch up with what is happening. 'The Prince should not have hired you,' Calmi continues. 'It makes no difference you are a girl. You will not get near Grandfather. He has four skilled assassins guarding him at all times.'

Energy drains from my body. I sink to the divan. My forehead burns. A cold sweat breaks across me.

'It's the poison,' Calmi says. 'The antidote needs more time to neutralise the effects. You gained mobility far quicker than expected.'

Tug straightens, left hand moving for his scabbard.

'Otherwise,' Calmi continues, oblivious to his reaction, 'you would not have caught me by surprise.' She brushes a finger over the cut between her eyebrows. 'I will not underestimate you again.'

Tug sweeps the scabbard to his side, pops the guard, twists the sword away from his body and draws it without a sound. The curved blade swings high in the air and comes down as he lunges towards her.

I bite my lip to stop myself from shouting. I don't want the Queen's soldier bursting into my chambers. Tug means to scare Lady Calmi, not injure her, but the strike is startlingly close.

Calmi flinches, wide eyes fixed on the silver steel, which is now a fingernail's width from her neck. Tug's grip is steady, not a shadow of a doubt in him at the skill he wields, or how close he has come to drawing blood.

'What is the name of the poison?' he demands.

'Blue Death.'

'Show me the antidote.'

She glances at the blade, expressing her will with nothing but a look. Tug understands as well as I do. He arcs the sword away, his movements, precise, smooth, though I imagine it has been half a life-time since he last used such a weapon.

I notice now he is close-shaved. His long hair washed and trimmed. He wears black trousers and a white shirt, wide sleeves drawn in at the wrists. It is the traditional dress for Carucan mourning, reminding me we are expected to attend the King's ceremony of departure in less than an hour.

Lady Calmi hooks out a necklace from beneath her dress. A thumb sized phial dangles on the end. She unscrews the lid and hands Tug the miniature bottle. He sniffs, dabs the liquid on his tongue. Then hands back the bottle, neither of them saying a word. But he is satisfied, because he returns the sword to its scabbard. He withdraws from the centre of the room to stand before the closed bedroom door.

I wonder if he's playing his role as assassin's assistant. Calmi takes his retreat as a signal to continue talking.

'The Eteans were supposed to capture the King, not kill him,' she says. 'But Prince Jakut knew the risks. My grandfather is not a man of his word. And when he arrives, he will want to know what happened to the men he placed inside the Prince's escort. If he suspects Jakut had anything to do with their disappearance, he will be displeased.'

Tug steps forwards, not able to bite his tongue and stay out of matters for long.

'Am I to deduce that you and the Prince are such fools you have duped Lord Strik, and invited him to the Ruby Court so you may kill him?'

'Someone must try.'

'Many have tried. Strik still lives.'

'It is not a reason to give up.'

'And who will actually murder your grandfather, if you manage to get him alone?' Tug stalks towards Calmi, muscles rippling as he makes his full height and presence felt. 'You? The Prince? The Prince isn't capable, and if you were, you would have done it already.'

'Grandfather is surrounded by skilled assassins. Even in his home, even when he sleeps. I've tried other ways, spent years learning all kinds of poisons—those hardest to detect. Two food tasters died. When my grandfather realised I was behind the poisonings, I was punished.'

The corner of her eye twitches. I expect "punished" does not capture the trauma she was put through. She is telling us all this to gain our trust. She does not realise I am Uru Ana and have already seen the hate she bears for Lord Strik.

'A score of men as strong and able as yourself,' she says to Tug, 'would not be enough to stop him. Besides, Grandfather suspects everyone. It would be impossible to get close enough. And if you did, just one word from his mouth would halt you in your tracks. But the Prince is different.'

'Why?' I ask, my voice husky.

She fiddles with the handle of her medicine basket. 'Grandfather wants him,' she says after a short pause. 'He has heard of the Prince's reputation in the Ruby Court—a reputation fostered by King Alixter. Weak, frivolous, lustful, arrogant. The ideal puppet for ruling Caruca. He doesn't think Jakut is smart enough to be the enemy. And he assumes the Prince's desire for the throne is driven by greed and lust.'

I shake my head, biting the inside of my cheek. Let us hope Jakut has more than a bad reputation to protect him!

'If Prince Jakut has told you nothing of this,' Calmi says, 'nor hired you as reinforcement, why are you here?'

Tug scratches once down the side of his clean-shaven jaw. Neither of us will answer her question. She is Strik's granddaughter. She may want him dead, but she cannot know the Prince has lost his memory. Not yet. Perhaps never.

'What has kept Lord Strik from the Red City?' I ask.

'He was cast out of Rudeash as a young man. He is kept out by a power greater than his own. Perhaps it is this power, or something similar that protects the Red City.'

I glance at Tug. The tattoos replacing his brows flex. He went to Rudeash and found no one in the Rudeashan kingdom with powers similar to Lord Strik. Heard no rumours of such things. He does not believe her.

'If such a power exists,' I say, 'why did you speak of your grandfather's imminent arrival? The city is protected.'

'I lived in his house for fourteen years. I watched him grow bolder, greedier, crueller. He has been gathering forces all across the country. His lands have grown closer and closer to the Red City. The power keeping him away weakens. I am convinced he sent me here as part of a larger plan to seize the kingdom.'

'We have come from the north,' Tug says, 'travelled hundreds of miles across the kingdom and never seen or heard of any such armies.'

'Grandfather is prudent. My friendship with Prince Jakut has given him an unexpected opportunity to advance his plans. But with or without us, he will not strike in an expected manner. The Red City will be under siege before the Queen even knows what's happening. And when he attacks, it will not be unarmed soldiers that die. But men, women, children who have no means of defending themselves.'

Tug and I exchange a look.

'You think it isn't possible?' she continues. 'Thirty years ago Grandfather turned Caruca against a peaceful people using only lies, fear and rumour. He manipulated King Rex to outlaw the Uru Ana, and it was the King's soldiers and the Carucan's themselves who did the rest—burning Uru Ana, chasing them from their homes, arresting them.

What Grandfather really wanted was slave labour to harvest his lands and work in the crystal tundra mines. He will do the same again. He will use the ignorance of the people to take the throne. And we will all become his slaves.'

I shiver. The poison has depleted me and left me in a cold sweat, but it is the memory of the peasants near Strik's castle that pushes a frosty hand through my chest, turning my insides to ice. The way they'd all stirred when Strik's presence grew near. Their minds like giant paper-houses. Empty, abandoned.

'The King had his chance to stop my grandfather,' Lady Calmi says. 'He did not dare stand against him. Now it is up to the Prince.'

'The fields the peasants worked were not guarded,' I say. 'How does your grandfather stop the Uru Ana from escaping?'

'Their water supply is contaminated with mist berries. Their memories are constantly dulled and erased. They are like lost children. They can't even remember from one day to the next what has happened to them.'

Her words cut the back of my throat. Lord Strik has enslaved hundreds, perhaps thousands of Uru Ana. Stolen their memories, their identities, carved out their souls and left empty vessels working his lands.

I think of all the Uru Ana babies born into slavery, knowing nothing but emptiness, black fog, hard toil, and fear. Not even understanding the concept of freedom, which was stolen from them at birth.

Tears well in my eyes. I wipe them quickly, haul myself up, and stagger to the balcony. My whole body trembles as I gasp at the warm air.

'How many of the royal council members are under Lord Strik's influence?' I ask, my back turned to Calmi.

'One. Of the other two I do not know.'

'Wait outside,' I tell her. I listen as she collects her basket, bottles chinking. The chamber door clicks shut. When she has left, I return inside.

'You should leave the Red City,' I say to Tug. 'Take this news back to Lyndonia.'

'And what will you do?'

'I will convince Jakut he must arrest the Queen.'

'So you are buying Calmi's story?'

'I saw her memories. She does not lie. She desires Strik's death more than anything. The Prince has been trying to do what his father would not. You have been prejudiced against Jakut from the very beginning.'

Tug's jaw line hardens. 'He is guilty or he would not have performed the Carucan cleansing.'

'Guilt is not the only reason a man turns to faith.' Tug looks fixedly at me. I meet his gaze with a hard stare.

'Strik acts under the supposition the Prince wants the throne and his granddaughter's hand,' I say. 'Now the Queen carries an heir to the throne, Prince Jakut's only course of action is to convince the council to arrest her. This way he assures the crown for himself. Lord Strik will expect it. I will convince Jakut he must gain the council's consent. While he is swaying them, I will warn Queen Usas to leave the Red City.'

Tug grabs my wrist. Pain shoots through my arm. My body contorts to lessen the agony. I lose my grip on the knife. He snatches it, disarming me.

'You are barely strong enough to stand,' he says, drawing up close. 'And incapable of defending yourself. Calmi may want her grandfather dead, but we can't be sure she is not also under the influence of his power. If you get anywhere near Strik, he will destroy you.'

'Like he destroyed you?' I hiss, pushing him in the chest, furious with him, with the world. Anger barrels through me. I'm not an idiot! If something goes wrong, and Strik arrives before I make it out of the Red City, he will finish the job he started with the bird-men. I'll be defenceless. Unable to resist the power in his voice. And death would not be the worst possible fate. What if I were dragged into the black hole of his mind and never got out again?

But I will not run away. I cannot do nothing, like all those who watched the kingdom exterminate and crush my people.

'You made me a promise,' I say, pushing Tug back from where he swamps me with his great bulk. He is like a brick wall, fixed in place, penning me in. 'You made me a promise.'

'I did not promise to let you get yourself killed.' His chest rises and falls in line with my shoulders. I try to steady my breathing. I need his agreement. I need him to tell me he will go back for Kel. I struggle for something I can say to sway him, and find nothing. Frustration seethes though me.

'Why have you come to the Ruby Court?'

'I will write to Elise,' he says, ignoring my question. 'A carrier pigeon will arrive faster.'

'And who will take Kel to Blackfoot Forest?'

'You will. As soon as we have convinced Jakut to arrest the Queen, and got the Queen out of the Red City.'

He does not believe Strik can be defeated. He does not believe Jakut is strong enough for this deadly plan. So why is he agreeing to help?

'Why are you really here, Tug?' I glare at him, but I know he won't answer. He never answers! When I break his steady gaze and look away, he speaks.

'You remind me of the man I was. A man I'd forgotten.'

'And what man is that?' I say tartly.

'A man who had hope.'

I should laugh in his face, call his bluff. But I cannot. His words strike a chord deep inside me.

'You want me to trust you?' I ask.

'I want you to trust me.'

'Then why did you betray me to Duchess Elise?'

'Kel is safer now than if you two were roaming the country with his eyes unsettled. And when given the choice by the Prince, you chose to come here. As betrayals go, you did not come off too badly, Mirra.'

FORTY-ONE

The soldier assigned to guard me doesn't see it coming. I approach Calmi at the end of the hall, hear the punch, followed by a choking gurgle. Cloth swooshes across marble as Tug drags the guard into my chambers.

'Who else but my maid saw you come here?' I ask Lady Calmi.

'No one.'

'How can you be sure?'

'Right now the men assigned to guard me are following a young woman whom I have used often, and most successfully, as my double.'

I am only half-listening as I stroll past her down the hall. We have company. Someone lingers behind the curved balustrade, and either they are with Calmi, or they spy for the Queen. Queen Usas already distrusts me. If she hears of Calmi's visit, her suspicions will increase ten-fold and I will never convince her to leave the Red City.

I slip my knife from the band around my boot and skulk to the edge of the corridor wall. Then I swing around the side into a small, unarmed man. His eyes widen at the sight of me. He flinches, but doesn't reach for a weapon, or run in the opposite direction. His weathered skin is a shade darker than my own. His trousers and shirt clean but ill fitted, crumpled.

It is Six. Calmi's leash. The shadow weaver her grandfather assigned to watch over her the day she arrived at his castle.

He stares, expression transforming to fascination. A sentiment I reciprocate, though I don't understand why I should be of particular interest considering he lives on Strik's lands and is surrounded by our kind. I on the other hand, have not come close to a grown-up Uru Ana since we lived in the Sea of Trees. Unless you count the Duchess, and I do not.

An arm floats up from his curved shoulders. His cracked, rough fingers prod my cheek as though testing whether I am real. A current of recognition passes between us. Far off in the mind-world, waves crash against crystal cliffs.

'He's with me,' Calmi says. I take a step back. Six knows we are alike. If he reveals my identity and Strik learns I am Uru Ana, I shudder at what the lord would do if we met again. And it would shatter Strik's misconception of the Prince as an unmindful idiot who readily follows their plan for his own self-serving ambitions. 'Six,' she continues, 'is my eyes and ears in the palace.'

'Your eyes and ears, or your grandfather's?' I ask, allowing distrust to seep through my voice. If I'm forced to strike Six uncon-scious so he does not reveal my sight to Calmi, my distrust will be the motive.

'Grandfather caught him when he was a boy. He wishes to be free as much as I do. He has been watching over the Prince and Queen all morning for me.'

'Let's not forget he has been watching you too,' I say. He is bound by Strik's power to follow Calmi, to know her whereabouts at all times. No doubt he longs for freedom, but like Calmi, he is not governed by his own will. They are both dangerous allies.

'You have been surveying the Prince,' I say to him, 'Where is he now?'

'Six cannot speak. But if you wish to see Prince Jakut, he will take us.'

The stooped Uru Ana slave bows his head, showing he is at my service.

A distant click makes me jump. I step back to see around the balustrade. Tug stands outside my closed chamber door, brushing off a crinkle in his new white shirt. The Queen's guard is taken care of.

I turn to Calmi. 'I will speak to the Prince of what you have said, alone. Remain in my chambers until my maid returns. Keep my maid in my room by whatever means necessary. Sixe will take me to Prince Jakut.'

'How long should I detain her?'

'As long as it takes.'

'As what takes?'

Tug joins us, expression neutral, though his eyes linger on Sixe, and I imagine he wonders whom in the name of the Gods we are dealing with now.

'The less you know,' I say to Calmi, 'the safer we will all be.'

SIXE LEADS us down spiral staircases, passages hidden between walls, empty, neglected reception rooms, a ballroom and servant quarters, until we are on the first level of the palace.

We stand in a narrow corridor sandwiched between mould-infested walls. I remember how he lurked in the little rat-holes of Strik's castle. He stares at me, seeing the memory in the mind-world. An instant later, an image he is recalling swims on my inner-eye.

Queen Usas stands on a balcony, looking down over an enormous grass square. Over a hundred mourners have already gathered. They lay candles in a spiralling circle around a great stone pyre. They stand with heads bowed. A body wrapped in white cloth lies on the great pyre, and all around the square on huge poles, flags flap in the breeze.

'He said it was urgent, Your Royal Highness,' her trusted officer says. 'He will not leave the throne room until he has seen you.'

Her hands grip the balcony railing. 'What news of the council?' she asks.

'They refuse to meet without the Prince and the Duke present.'

And then:

She glides through the palace surrounded by guards. The officer who informed her of the Prince's arrival strides by her side, talking in low, urgent tones.

'I request most respectfully that you do not enter until we have secured the hall.'

'He is not courageous enough for a head-on confrontation,' she says. 'I am far more likely to be poisoned by his pretty little friend, or stabbed in my sleep. Get the Council!'

Queen Usas is on her way to meet Jakut. I have not got long.

'Stay here,' I tell Tug. The minutest flexion in his facial muscles shows his resistance to being ordered about. Particularly by me. 'Please,' I add.

'What's happening?'

'The Prince has requested to speak to the Queen in the throne room. You want me to trust you? Well trust works both ways, or not at all.' Tug's grip on his scabbard tightens. His jaw clenches. 'I need to speak to the Prince alone.'

'If the Queen finds you with Prince Jakut—'

'I know.' We will never convince her to leave the Red City and save her life and the life of her unborn child.

I slip down the passage and halt at the edge of the great hall. Sunlight streams through an enormous bay window behind the canopied thrones. Beyond the window, a vast mountain range meets a dazzling blue sky. Gold on the cornices and umber columns gleams like the hall has been set on fire.

The Prince kneels before the dais steps, crowned in a brilliant haze that shafts through a domed ceiling window. His head is lowered in prayer. A strange peacefulness fills the hall's magnificence as though he is communing with the Gods themselves.

'Your Royal Highness,' I say.

He looks up, the myriad shades of hazel in his eyes differentiated and contrasted by the sun. But the sun cannot eclipse the pain and torment written in their expression. He watches me for an instant, then he lowers his head, and closes his eyes.

I pad into the veiled stillness of this odd sanctuary. Last night, the throne room's grandeur was threatening, imposing, accusing. The unsettling memory of my dream scuds across my thoughts. But as I look around, a serene beauty stirs the lost corners of the palace room.

Why is Jakut here? Why the anguished torment? Has he remembered something? What is so pressing he has requested to speak with the Queen an hour before the departing ceremony?

'Jakut' I say, moving closer.

'Leave.'

'What has happened?'

'I said leave!' He has never raised his voice in anger. Not even when I accused him of being a traitor.

'I will not leave,' I say. 'I have risked everything to be here. To help you. You are not giving up!'

'Leave, Mirra.' His voice is imploring, begging. I kneel before him. There is such brightness around him I must squint to see his face. 'Why have you requested an audience with the Queen?'

'So she may arrest me.' He looks up, regret and disgust in his eyes. 'I am a traitor. Just as you told me that night in Lyndonia. I told you what I would do if I discovered it was the truth.'

'No.' I shake my head. 'No, no. I was wrong. You did not condone the slaughter of your escort.'

His eyes glass over, sorrow and regret consuming him. 'It is worse. I have done worse.'

In the mind-world, the Queen sweeps through an arcade of green and white diamond tiled walls. I recognise the cloister from the Duke's boyhood memories. Six shows me what he sees from inside the Queen's mind. She is close.

'Come with me,' I say. 'We will discuss this elsewhere.'

'I am sorry, Mirra. I cannot help the Uru Ana.'

I lean in to him, rest a hand on his slim shoulder, squeezing a little so he cannot drift back into his refuge of prayer and regret. 'You brought me here to see what you could not. You must give me the chance to share with you what I have seen before you throw everything away.'

'We are very, very different. You accept the darkness that wars inside a man. You accept a man's failings, hoping he may rise above them. You accepted my failings. But I... I cannot.'

So Jakut remembers betraying his father, and the Carucan army. But he cannot remember why. He doesn't know enough about Lord Strik to understand why killing him could be an act of greatness, and there isn't time to explain.

'You will accept your failings,' I say. 'You have made bad choices. We've all made bad choices! But more than one destiny lies in your hands, and if you act now out of some mistaken sense of supreme morality, we will all die.'

'I betrayed my own father!'

'Well perhaps you should take the time to find out why. Queen Usas will walk through the throne room doors any second now. If you don't come with me and let me explain what is going on, the rest of your numbered days will be in a turmoil of remorse and regret far greater than any you feel now.'

He hands me a note. It bears the seal of the emerald ring, which has been in his possession since waking from the winter long-sleep. I do not know where he has got it from, or if it proves he was in league with Lord Strik. It doesn't matter. I rip it in half.

A clunking sound reverberates from the end of the hall. The guards are opening the outer throne room doors.

I lay my hand on his cheek. His skin is warm against my cold fingers. I draw away at once, as though I have been singed. Something passed through him into me. Something as inscrutable as the diamond sparkles on an ocean bathed in sunshine.

I clear my throat. 'You have not betrayed your soul,' I say. 'Or your Gods. But if you stay and confess your crimes, you will do. You have yet to accomplish your greatest and most difficult task.'

Then I am on my feet, running to the concealed gap in the wall below the dais steps. Boots stomp across the far end of the stone hall. In the shadows, I clutch my aching rib. The whites of Sixe's eyes shine, fixed on me.

'Where is he?' Tug growls.

'He is coming,' I say, sounding more certain than I am. 'Prepare yourselves. He may not be alone.'

FORTY-TWO

The Prince's tall silhouette blots out the dull light bleeding into the passage from the throne room. He has followed me. Heart-beat thundering in my ears, I grab his arm and pull him through. Behind him, I glimpse soldiers in the great hall. They flow out in a semicircle beneath the haze of sunlight shafting through the domed window. Usas strides down the centre of them like she is parting waves.

'Where is he?' she says, her commanding voice raised to fill every inch of the hall.

I push Jakut into the passage and close the panelled door. The Prince stands so close and the passage is so narrow I cannot slip around him.

'We must go!'

I cannot make out the Prince in the blackness, but I hear his breath-ing, can almost feel the heat radiating from his body.

'I noticed in the throne room that you look unwell, Mirra,' he says.

'We may talk about my health when we are away from here,' I whisper, nudging into him to get him moving. He does not comply.

'What's going on?' Tug says. From the closeness of his voice, I realise he has moved up the tunnel to join us.

'The Prince is concerned I look unwell,' I mock.

'Sssh, not so loud,' Tug says.

I wipe a few wisps of hair sticking to my forehead with the sleeve of my dress. Of all the men in Caruca why did I get stuck with two of the most stubborn and infuriating?

'Are we going to go?' I say.

'I will speak to you of whatever I wish, Mirra, or I am returning to confess my crimes to the Queen.'

I suck in my breath and hold it when what I really want to do is scream.

A memory surfaces in the mind-world.

'He was kneeling right here, Your Royal Highness. He stood up, stepped out of the sunlight and vanished.'

The Queen's lip twitches in a sarcastic smile. 'He has not vanished. Search the hall!'

Six is still keeping me abreast of the Queen's actions, relaying what is happening inside the throne room by delving into one of the soldier's minds.

I turn to face the secret door, bumping into the Prince and elbowing him out of my space.

'Fine, we will do it your way,' I mutter, running trembling fingers across the panel. I find a thick bolt of metal at the top and fasten it across.

'Why aren't you resting?' the Prince asks.

'I was,' I say, bending to check whether there is a second bolt at the foot of the door. 'Until Lady Calmi poisoned me.'

I find another lock and struggle to wriggle it from its stuck position. I grunt with the effort. Reaching and crouching both put strain on my injury. The Prince squats down to help and together we get the bolt across.

'Lady Calmi poisoned you,' he echoes in disbelief.

'Yes, she is well versed in the art of poison.' I straighten, lean back against the door to rest a moment. He stands up beside me.

'It is my fault,' he says. 'She is as rotten as her grandfather. And I was in love with her.' I do not see him reach out, but suddenly his cool hand touches my forehead. 'You have a temperature.'

I remove his hand. 'It is imperative the Queen does not find you with me,' I say. 'Stop this and come with us.'

First, he ignores me in the throne room, and now he acts as though I'm the only living person in Ederiss. What is the matter with him?

I startle at the sound of banging on the nearby walls.

'They are searching the hall for a concealed passage,' Tug says. 'If you have finished nursing Mirra, perhaps we can go.'

In the darkness Tug cannot see how close the Prince stands, his arm brushing my side, but I flush.

'You said I am yet to accomplish my most difficult task.' Jakut speaks, ignoring Tug entirely. 'What task?'

The thump of metal on the walls grows closer. Then there is a thud on the secret panel. Beyond the door a soldier shouts they have found something.

'Jakut, please, we must go.'

'Tell me, Mirra. Tell me what kind of world I live in that such evil could ever be justified.'

'Lord Strik believes you have betrayed the Carucan army your father to marry his granddaughter and become King. He has helped you because he plans to be your puppeteer and the true ruler of Caruca.'

The door shudders against my back as men thrust against it. Tiny pieces of soil and brick crumble from the passage ceiling.

'You need him to believe in your self-serving ignorance,' I continue, 'and for him to think he has won. Then he will not suspect your true intention.'

'And what is my true intention?'

The door panel judders against my back and then the thumping abruptly stops. 'To kill him,' I whisper into the silence.

In the mind-world Queen Usas stands on the other side of the secret door. She runs a hand across an invisible seam.

'Send for the palace architect,' she says to her officer. 'I want to know where this passage leads.'

'Yes, Your Royal Highness.' He calls to another soldier and sends him to fetch the architect.

'What is the meaning of this?' she says to herself.

At the far end of the throne room there is a clamour. She turns. The soldier sent for the architect runs down the hall. He bows to her but addresses the officer as he speaks.

'The throne room doors are locked.'

The Queen pales. Her hand moves protectively over her round belly. 'How? Who has done this?' she demands.

'Guardsman Astex says he saw Councillor Lucas accompanied by a dozen foot soldiers when we were all searching for the passage.'

A hand squeezes my shoulder. 'Mirra,' the Prince says. 'Why is killing Lord Strik so important?'

I blink into the darkness, disorientated.

'The Queen and her entourage are locked in the throne room,' I murmur. We knew Strik had infiltrated the Ruby Palace, but I am shocked men from the royal army could turn against the Queen so swiftly, and without the Prince leading the uprising.

'The Queen will think I have set her a trap.'

'We must leave the palace at once.' Tug's voice startles me, rousing me back to my senses.

'We cannot leave the Queen,' I say.

'You must,' the Prince says. 'It is too late to save her. Strik has five thousand men camped at the edge of the city, waiting for my signal. The note I showed you, I received it from him this morning. He means to kill Queen Usas and my unborn half-brother or sister.'

'You must order her arrest,' I say, 'Imprison her. Delay Strik's plans.'

'What have I done?' His lamenting voice is muffled as though his face is buried in his hands.

'There is no time for regret,' I say.

'Strik has already sent men to attack Lyndonia, and kill my cousins. He will show no mercy to the Queen.'

His words are like a punch in the throat. My mind rejects what he has said, refuses to believe it, while my body struggles to breathe.

'It is in his letter,' Jakut continues. 'He thinks I brought the Duke here to clear the way for a siege against Lyndonia. He plans to wipe out all heirs to the throne so no one can raise an army against me.'

Kel! I thrust the Prince out of my way. We must leave!

The Prince sinks into the wall as I elbow past him, tripping into Tug. Tug catches me and holds on. 'Kel,' I whisper to Tug. 'What if Elise uses Kel to save her son?'

FORTY-THREE

Tug's gravelly voice is an anchor, holding my mind, preventing the waves of panic from sweeping it away.

'The Duke has not left his spouse and children,' he says, 'or his people and his fort unprotected. And Lord Strik has not prepared this attack. He may take advantage of the Duke's absence, but it is unlikely he has many men up north, if an army five thousand strong gathers on the outskirts of the city.'

His words are designed to rally me. They are no more a guarantee of Kel's safety than the paper lanterns released during the Carucan ceremony of departing will guarantee the King's safe passage among the stars to the Carucan gods. But his logic grounds me, sets my thoughts in motion. How many men could Strik have up north if the original plan was to bring them here? Pockets of hired mercenaries could hardly raise a successful assault against Lyndonia. And how long will it take the troops to muster?

'Lyndonia is one of Caruca's most impenetrable forts,' Tug continues. 'Difficult to access, difficult to scale. It could hold off an attack for weeks. We will send a carrier pigeon warning Elise, so that the Duke's army is prepared. You have kept your end of the bargain and she will keep hers. Kel will not be harmed.'

I take a deep breath and nod. I have to hope his faith in the Duchess is warranted.

A flutter of light deep in the tunnel catches my attention. Tug falls silent. A flame casts shadows through the darkness. A reedy figure approaches carrying a lantern. In the mind-world I see the passage opening into a dilapidated ballroom. Sixe has been checking our way out.

'It is Sixe,' I say. 'The passage to the ballroom is clear. Let's go.' Raising my skirt, I hurry through the damp tunnel towards Sixe. Tug jogs behind, followed by the light step of the Prince.

We advance in silence. At the end of the passage, Sixe hides the lantern from wherever he has found it, and leads us through the labyrinth of corridors, stairways and bridges to my chambers.

At one point we pass an enormous arched window. I glance out and see white flags waving from balconies and windows, tearing at their poles as though they sense the danger rumbling through the palace.

Raised voices rebound and echo through the internal corridors. A soldier stops us on a narrow stairway, but when he recognises the Prince, he steps aside, bowing.

I knock on my chamber door so as not to alarm Calmi. She opens with a collected, calm expression. But when she sees the Prince is with us, there is a shift in her cool blue eyes.

'Mirra,' Jakut says, 'please allow me to speak with you alone.'

I nod. Tug and Sixe enter my chambers. I close the door so we cannot be overheard.

'Lady Calmi,' I begin, 'does not know about your condition. She was raised by Lord Strik, but you trusted her and now we must hope that you have chosen your confidante well.'

'Who is Kel?' His voice cuts the air like shattering glass. I inhale, glance at the tawny gold ruffles of the dress I hurriedly put on before Tug and I left my chambers to find Jakut.

The time has come for the truth. 'Kel is my brother. I was not alone when Tug and Brin took me hostage in Blackfoot Forest.' I raise my eyes to meet the Prince. Has he known about Kel ever since that day in the Pit? Is this why he carries a sketch of him?

His eyes narrow slightly, then his brow lifts a little. As though something has finally fallen into place.

'I have discovered the truth about the attack on your escort and the betrayal of the Carucan army,' I continue. 'Now I must get my brother home.' He stares at me until I look away. 'I was never supposed to be part of your plan.'

'Why would I hurt so many to kill Lord Strik?'

'He is a dark force that will swallow up this kingdom if he cannot be stopped. Calmi will tell you more. Perhaps talking to her will help unbury your memories. I wish you luck.' I step back from him and turn towards my chambers.

'I will never see you again—'

A memory rears up in the mind-world halting my retreat. I see myself through the Prince's eyes. *He is crouching in front of me, inspecting a cut on my neck.* It is the day Tug and I followed him to the Hybourg inn and offered my services.

Except in the Prince's memory, the contours of my face are softer, my eyes sadder. It is not how I appear when I look at my reflection. Then the memory is replaced by another.

He is leaping from his stallion, drawing his sword, shouting as he runs towards a man with scales sewn into his skin. The bird-man sits on top of my prostrate figure, hands around my throat.

Through the Prince's eyes I see myself struggling, face sunk in mud, feel the thundering of his heart, the odd pain in his chest.

In the real world I reach for my neck, swallow down the lump in my throat.

'If I kill Strik and return the Queen to the throne,' Jakut says, 'will you come back?'

I force myself to look at him. Since the night Tug and Brin snatched Kel, I have not considered what I will do when this is over. I used to imagine when Kel's eyes settled and my parents moved to an outskirt settlement, I would find my childhood friend, Asmine. I imagined joining my people in the Sea of Trees. I saw myself exploring the world. Now my future only stretches as far as Kel in my mother's arms.

'I do not belong here,' I say.

A clamour below my little cliff turret echoes in the halls. Four soldiers appear on my inner-eye, climbing a winding staircase. Suddenly, six other soldiers, bearing long knives, swoop into them. The attack is swift and bloody. Close combat and little space impedes the use of swords. The man whose mind Sixe has entered, cries out. He raises his drawn sword, blood pouring down his fist. Silver flashes before his eyes. A knife presses against his throat.

'Where is the Prince?'

The soldier stutters and shakes his head.

Trembling, I open my chambers and push Prince Jakut inside. Tug is by the door, a sharp look in his eye that tells me he is ready for anything. Sixe stands in a corner staring at nothing. Lady Calmi watches the Prince.

'They are getting close to us in their search for you,' I say to Jakut, as I hurry to my trunk. I throw everything out until I find my skin trousers and a tunic.

'Who?'

'Those working for Strik, or for the Queen, I don't know. They all wear the same uniform.'

Calmi swoops towards the Prince as I bundle up trousers and shirt.

'We must go to the departing ceremony,' she says to him. 'Show them you are alive. You must stop the fighting before Grandfather gets here.'

Tug stands with the door cracked open to watch the corridor. I loop my bundle over my shoulder and join him.

'Ready?' he says.

I nod. The hollering and rumbles of the palace are growing closer. The Queen's most trusted entourage may be locked in the throne room, but others still fight against the orders of Councillor Lucas and Lord Strik. I glance back and the Prince catches my eye. I am sorry, I whisper in my mind. But I have done all I can.

Lady Calmi leans in and murmurs to him. I use the distraction to slip away.

I do not possess Sixe's knowledge of the Ruby Court, so finding our way down the five levels of the palace to the external walls will depend on guesswork and luck.

I lead Tug through a leafy garden to avoid four men headed in our direction. We cross a bridge, and climb over a balcony, keeping low until we reach an external stairway.

'There is a guard at the bottom,' I tell Tug, twisting my knife in my sweaty palm as we descend. I gesture for him to wait, tuck the knife up the wide sleeve of my dress, and rush down the last of the curved steps.

The guard spins round. At the sight of a sixteen-year-old girl in a pretty silk dress, he relaxes.

'What is happening?' I ask, breathlessly.

'Go back to your chambers and wait, My Lady.'

'Is the palace under attack?'

'Go back to your chambers,' he says.

I move towards him. 'But I'm afraid.'

'You are safest in your chambers.' He reaches for the hilt of his sword but makes no effort to draw it. He is trying to scare me into complying with his order. I inch closer.

'What is all the shouting?' I ask. When I am less than an arm's length away, I stamp the heel of my boot down his shin. He howls and lashes out to grab me. I dart from his grasping hands.

Tug descends, bounding through the terrace. The soldier, in his panic, struggles to remove his sword from its scabbard. He is too slow. The punch comes fast. A bone-cracking noise pops the air. The guard's head snaps to the side. He reels, tumbles to his knees, and drops forward onto a stone pot, knocking himself out.

We don't need to waste time hiding the unconscious soldier. Sounds of fighting and shouting are now coming from all directions and levels of the palace.

'Let me go ahead next time,' Tug says, stepping around him.

I am exhausted, in pain and praying to the Gods there isn't going to be a next time. At least until we are away from the Red City.

'We're going to get out of here, aren't we?' I ask.

'Of course we are,' he says.

Without thinking I reach for my lodestone necklace. Then I remember Kel has it.

I am not abandoning the Prince, I tell myself as we move on. I am leaving for my brother.

FORTY-FOUR

I thought I knew what death was. I had seen it over and over in my father's memories after he killed the mercenaries who stole Asmine. A soldier and three bird-men died during the attack yesterday, one right before my eyes. But this is different.

In the mind-world the sky has cracked and the heavens rage. A storm of memories shake like thunder. Memories so vivid, so detailed, moving faster than an arrow in flight. As though in the last moments of death, every detail of the life lived is emptied out and left behind. I stumble after Tug, half-blind and overwhelmed by so much information.

The first level of the palace is an open network of halls, libraries, galleries and reception rooms. Spaces are separated by Corinthian columns, arcades, and windows. Mirrors on the walls reflect light into the deepest recesses.

Tug stops. The clashing swords and cries and shouts of the real world trickle through my awareness. I lean against a wall as he peers around it to check the arcade ahead.

It's then I notice a soldier slumped against the opposite wall. He has dragged himself from the fighting leaving a trail of red smears across the veined marble. His eyes are open, his breathing laboured. His hand presses against his chest wound.

As I stare, his body shudders and his hand slips slowly to his side. A fork of lightning passes through me. It takes only a second, but his whole life flashes on my inner-eye. Everything he has ever experienced. Each act of selfishness, cruelty, consideration, kindness. And not only from his own perspective, but the same events from the perspectives of all the lives he has touched for better or for worse. It is over in an instant.

I come to myself, huddled on the floor. The soldier's empty eyes stare across the dim corridor. I gaze back in shock. Tug is speaking, but I cannot command my body to one place, one time, one viewpoint from which to understand the world. It is as though I have been spread across a thousand lives.

'Mirra, stay with me.' I try to look at him but my eyes are locked on the soldier. 'Mirra, can you hear me?'

'He was Uru Ana,' I whisper. From the corner of my vision I see Tug's face shift to take in the dead soldier. 'In death, he became Uru Ana.'

Tug's large, strong hand wraps around mine, and he pulls me away from the carnage. Movement drives me back to my body, my heaving chest, the cumbersome dress, the weariness of my muscles, the ache in my ribs.

A smell of burning oils and flowers wafts through the hall we have entered, replacing the scent of death. I grow more aware of our surroundings. The ceiling is vaulted, the windows pastel coloured.

'On guard!' I hiss, pulling Tug's wrist. He raises his sword. At the same moment two soldiers appear at the other end of the hall. Their uniforms are stained and tattered. Specks of blood colour their pale cheeks. They jog towards us.

'Whom do you fight for?' One of them demands.

'The Baroness of Tersil,' Tug answers. I step out from behind Tug's huge frame.

'Take her back to her chambers. The palace has been closed.'

'Closed on whose command?' Tug asks.

'Prince Jakut, heir to the throne of Caruca.'

It is a lie. When we left the Prince he was about to descend to the King's departing ceremony. He will be trying to stop the bloodshed, not trap everyone inside the palace.

Tug steps wide, pushing me back, arcing up his sword to fight.

'No,' I say, reaching for him. 'If it is the Prince's wish, we will return as we have been asked.' Tug holds the soldiers in his fixed glare. He could take both men. But I do not want their deaths on my hands.

Finally, he lowers his sword and we step back slowly across the central ruby stairway. The men quickly lose interest, hurrying off in the direction of the throne room, and the fighting.

'Come,' I say to Tug when they can no longer see us. We turn about, quickly exit the vaulted hall and continue, keeping to the darkest passages and galleries, moving more cautiously to avoid other encounters.

Minutes slip by as we search for an exit away from the throne room. I have the sense we are going in circles and getting nowhere, when we enter a corridor with peacocks painted on the walls. I recognise it from the Duke's memories. At a silver-leafed door halfway down, I stop to try the handle. After a beat, Tug realises I have stopped and pulls up a few paces ahead.

The door is locked.

'In here,' I say. He joins me, launching himself at the door with his shoulder. The wood around the lock splinters. The door swings open.

We tumble into a bright room with miniature chairs and tables, colourful wooden toys, and animal paintings on the walls. Six beds are lined up by the windows. Two cots sit in a curtained-off corner. Two young maids stand to face us, trembling but defiant. I sense seven other minds in the room but can see no one. I quickly shut the nursery door.

'We will not harm you,' I whisper to the children hidden under beds and in cupboards. Then I hurry to the arched windows on the far side and climb up onto one of the waist-high ledges.

We are on the western side of the palace. Below, lay the palace gardens surrounding the barracks. I crane out to look at the entrance gates. Beyond the tall sunburnt walls, an army winds up the adobe city, carrying emerald flags. A green snake slithering though a red desert.

There is a four-metre drop to the gardens below. I am in no state to try jumping. Tug joins me on the ledge. Then he strides back inside and begins stripping sheets from the children's beds and knotting them together. The maids stare at us as I go to join him.

'I'll do this,' he says. 'You change.' His eyes shift briefly to the thick drape cornering-off the baby cots. Two minds are crouched behind it.

'Would you help me with my dress?' I ask one of the maids.

Trembling, she ushers the children out from behind the curtains, pulls the drapes closed around us, and helps me unfasten my buttons. By the time I am wearing my trousers and tunic, Tug is tying a long strand of knotted bed linen to a window pillar.

He nods at me. I climb up on the ledge, catching the eye of a boy around Kel's age who has braved peeping from his hiding place to watch. I hesitate. What will happen if Lord Strik takes the palace? What will happen to the children?

'Mirra,' Tug says. His deep voice sends a rumbling reminder through me. Save Kel. The rest comes after.

I sit down, grip the first sheet and lower myself over the edge. My arrow injury near the shoulder burns as I dangle, taking all my weight on my arms. I move slowly. My back faces the gardens and the palace wall, so I only have my awareness of movement in the mind-world to alert me of danger.

Tug holds the sheet wrapped around the pillar in case my weight loosens the knot. Once I am halfway down, I can no longer see him. He is obscured by the wall and window ledge.

A small trickle of something runs across my arm and along my back. I focus on the gardens, and potential threats. On whether my shaking muscles can take the strain.

The sheet runs out. I glance down. My feet are suspended a metre above a grassy square of lawn, part of a patchwork of squares chopped up by stone paths. Ordinarily, I would jump without hesitation, but my bruised ribcage flares with pain at the smallest of jerky movements, and I'm worried about landing.

I hang for a moment. The muscles in my arms are turning to mush, and the moisture gathering at the waist of my tunic, making my back sticky, is growing denser. I have no choice but to let go.

My feet hit the ground. I bend my legs to buffer the impact. Pain shoots through my ribcage like a fist of knives. My legs buckle and I fall on my side. I shove my fist in my mouth to muffle the agony pouring from my throat. I want to twist and writhe but that only makes it worse.

Within seconds Tug has made a herculean descent and is crouched beside me.

'Don't hold your breath. Breathe, Mirra.' My eyes prick with tears. Tug's hands gently check my ribs. I push them away, unable to take any more pressure.

'You have to get up.'

'I can't.' He wraps an arm beneath my shoulder on my injured side. I grunt, lean into him for support, but standing plunges me into a black pit of agony.

'Give me the Nocturne Melody.'

'There is poison and the antidote coursing through your blood. The effect will be unpredictable.'

'Give it to me!' I hiss.

He takes out the phial bottle, pops off the lid, and holds it to my lips, allowing a small sip.

I clench my jaw, tears falling freely, washing my lips in salt. He helps me to stand again. We stagger forward two steps before he stops, hands me the bottle of painkiller. I drink until it's empty. Until the agony softens to a misty haze of distant pain.

Down on the ground, the palace gates and the fighting seem a long way off. We are surrounded by ferns, lush green bushes, hundreds of brightly coloured flowers, tall hedges, and little fountains. This corner of the vast mountain gardens is a haven for private walks away from the bustle of the Ruby Court. If it is possible to access the soldiers' barracks from down here, then the entrances are expertly hidden.

We head for the palace wall, stopping to let me catch my breath, or when I sense others encroaching on our whereabouts. Our search for an exit, a tunnel, a secret door, is accompanied by to the rumbling drums of Strik's army growing closer.

My mind joins my body to drift in the Nocturne Melody fog. I think of the snowy mountains in the north. The sky full of scintillating stars. The black-market town of the Hybourg stretched out in the valley below.

'What were you thinking?' I ask Tug. His arm is wrapped around my waist. I feel his breath on my cheek but I cannot open my eyes wide enough to see if he has heard my question. I am not sure I have even spoken it out loud. But then he answers.

'When?'

'After I almost threw your wolf dog over the cliff. You stood looking out over the Hybourg, not even watching to see if Brin brought Kel back.' He leans me up against a wall. Chalky, rough stone scratches my cheek. I sense him turning to face me, one arm still wrapped against my side.

'I was wondering if I'd already lost.'

'Lost?'

'This strange game we are all playing. I was wondering if I'd already lost and was too blind to see it.'

I fight the weight on my heavy eyelids. His face appears to me as a blur of beast tattoos over weathered skin, dark eyes, lean, well-cut features.

'You can win my game for me,' I say, the tears in my throat choking my words. 'Return to the barracks, steal a soldier's uniform. There is no other way out.'

'And what about you?'

'Alone you have a chance of escaping the Red City, sending word to the Duchess and going back for Kel.'

'While you stay here?'

My eyes are closing. I slump further into Tug's arms. He lowers me carefully to the ground. It is obvious to us both now. I'm not going to make it.

His rough hand sweeps back the hair from my cheek. 'I'm not good at living with regret,' he murmurs.

'Then don't regret anything. Keep Kel safe.'

'Stay alive. I will come back for you.'

I shake my head. 'Just Kel.'

'Stay alive, Mirra. You hear me?'

'Yes,' I murmur.

But his voice is far away. I am floating, riding a boat down a river, and on the riverbank, Carucan priests in flowing white robes pray to the gods. Candles burn in a spiral of light. The King lies dead on his pyre and a strong wind blows a hundred flags, their white silk bleeding blood red.

FORTY-FIVE

The aches and pains of my body burn through the fog of my mind. I grow conscious of the buzz of insects nearby, a strong scent of sweet blooms, my cheek flushed from too much sun, the thin padding of grass beneath me. I open my eyes. The sun is no longer high in the sky. Two hours must have passed since I fell into a drugged sleep.

I lie still, registering the silence. The sounds of clashing swords, shouting, and screaming are over. The drums of Strik's approaching army, gone.

I feel dazed. Every inch of me hurts, but my heart swells with gratitude. I am alone. Which means Tug has left the Ruby Palace. It is a bittersweet realisation. I will probably never see him again. If all goes to plan, Kel will be with our parents by the autumn, and Tug will be forced to spend the long-sleep in the north. By next spring, the fate of Caruca and my own fate will be already written.

Approaching footsteps cut off my thoughts. I tuck my legs into my chest and pain stabs my side, bringing tears to my eyes. Mountain laurel and bright pink azaleas block the path from view. I listen as the footsteps pass. Then a voice shouts,

'Over here!'

Others come running. I breathe deeply in and out, despite the way it hurts. Don't panic. Not yet. They may be looking for something or someone else. Curled up on my side, I focus on the rich scents of the garden. Move on, I will the men. Do not see me.

Leaves rustle. The laurel bush shudders. Then a figure leans over, blocking out the sun. He stares down. My heart flips over and lodges in my throat.

I blink rapidly, trying to rid myself of the tears smearing my vision, and adjust my eyes to his face. A young, handsome face with a prominent scar drawing a line from the side of his lip to the bottom of his chin. My muscles tighten. Terror trickles down my spine.

'It's her,' he says. The voice only confirms my fears. This man is the officer from the north. The King's officer who was looking for the Prince near the Pit, and who abandoned me in that tumbledown shed when he realised Tug and Brin were hiding nothing more than a wayward girl held against her will.

'You want me to take her, Commander?' one of the soldiers asks, stepping forward as the high-ranking officer reaches down. He ignores the man, hauls me up roughly and throws me over his shoulder. I yelp and begin moaning as he carries me, my bruised rib crushed against his shoulder, my head smacking against his back.

The mind-dulling effects of the Nocturne Melody vanish as adrenaline kicks in. I strain to look up through strands of hair at the soldiers following the commander. They scan the gardens furtively, watching for signs of trouble.

A little jolt of hope lights me up. Had the Prince sent them? I push into the commander's memories, no easy feat with the agony in my shoulder and ribcage summoning me back to the present.

The shape and texture of Commander Linx's mind is shimmering and brittle. I find my way in as easily as that day outside the Hybourg. If a castle made of glass and steel existed, rising to the sky in one sleek, smooth form, it would capture it well.

I remain close to the edge, scanning recent memories to discover who has sent him.

A torch lights his way. His footsteps and those of the man following him echo through the hollow network of tunnels. The air is close, pervaded by a smell of mould and rot.

They reach an underground chamber. It is an old wine cellar, barrels stacked in rows, packing straw strewn across the floor, soaked through, making a nasty sludge under foot. Three dishevelled men are slumped against the nearest wall, heads hung low.

'These two were carrying messages from the Queen,' the commander says, grabbing one of them by the hair at the top of his head and pulling back so that the man's bruised face is visible. 'But this one, I think will be of particular interest, my Lord.'

I shiver. The man who stands beside the commander, whose presence I sense though the commander does not look at him, must be Lord Strik.

'And why is that?' the lord asks. The captive man they are talking about slowly raises his head to look at them. I am thrown from the mind-world like I have tripped over a precipice in a dream and the shock has woken me up.

Tug! No! No, they cannot have caught Tug.

I scream, kick my legs and bite down on the commander's arm, smashing my teeth through the light cotton of his tunic. He rips back his elbow and drops me. Blinding agony tears my body. For a moment all is black. Then I am conscious again, moaning on the ground while the commander shouts at his men to get the wench up. My eyes blur again with tears while my heart fractures into a thousand glittering pieces. Kel...

'Commander Linx!' A female voice penetrates the dim hall. My senses are muffled but it sounded like Lady Calmi. The two soldiers with the commander, who have both taken one arm each by which to drag me across the wood floor, stop. The commander's boots spin around to face the woman.

'I heard screaming,' she says. 'What is the meaning of this?'

'The girl is a traitor. We are taking her to the dungeons.'

'You are going the wrong way.'

'I'm following orders, My Lady.'

'Orders from whom?'

'You should be at the departing ceremony.'

'Do you presume to tell me what I should do, Commander?'

The atmosphere ripples electrically. I strain my head to look up through the tangles that fall across my face, arms still held outstretched by the soldiers. I can only see the bottom of her silk dress, the back of the commander's legs.

'I would not presume anything of the sort, Lady Calmi,' the commander says.

'You have been misinformed.' Light shoes pad closer. Behind Calmi, I sense Sixe. 'This girl is Baroness Mirra, the Duke's niece.'

'I regret to inform you that she is no such person. She is a slave from the far north and she conspires against the Prince.'

Blackness creeps across my vision. I struggle not to let the pain overwhelm me and realise I have started moaning again.

'Put her down,' Lady Calmi orders the soldiers. They release my arms. I drop onto the polished floor, cheek smashing into the cool rosewood. 'A slave?' Calmi continues. 'By law, Caruca has no slaves, Commander Linx. Tell me how she has conspired against Prince Jakut?'

'She is an imposter. And these are times of war. Anyone suspected of treason must be questioned.'

'Treason,' she echoes. Her eyes wander briefly down to me, cold and impartial as though considering the commander's accusation. 'So your loyalties have shifted,' she says after a moment. 'The last time we met they did not lie with the Prince. What has changed your mind, Commander Linx?'

Lord Strik.

Calmi is clever. She is trying to get him to question the suggestions her grandfather has planted in the commander. I wonder if in all her years living with Strik, she has found a way around the power in his voice.

'You do not trust me,' he says.

'You claim allegiance to the Prince but you have not informed him of your return to the Red City. And now you are taking prisoners for interrogation. Whose orders are you following, Commander?'

'The King is dead. Queen Usas has tried to steal the throne. The Prince is the rightful heir.' His words are stilted and flat as though he is repeating a mantra. I strain to look at his face and see it is slack, eyes glazed over. Calmi has failed to break or bend her grandfather's authority.

I roll onto my side. 'Calmi...' my words are a puff of air, a whisper. If Lord Strik interrogates me, if he forces answers I cannot prevent myself from giving, he will discover I am Uru Ana. He will learn that I am with Jakut because the Prince does not remember his past. He will realise he is dealing with an unknown, dangerous ally. Jakut will never get close enough to take Strik's life.

Calmi moves closer but Commander Linx draws his sword to block her way.

'You cannot talk to the prisoner.'

'If your loyalties are to the Prince, then they are also to me,' she says.

'The ring on your finger shows you belong to another.'

'A marriage arranged by the King to prevent his son from marrying me.'

'You did rather well out of it, I heard.'

A hard slap rings through the hall. My eyes shoot up. Commander Linx rubs the red welt on his cheek. Lady Calmi's chest rises and falls, the hate in her eyes blazing.

'Take the prisoner!' the commander orders his men. They yank at my arms. Linx strides through the hall, the soldiers dragging me behind him.

'Free Tug,' I croak, my voice drowned by the scrape of my body across the floor, and the soldiers' boots.

Trying to understand the origin of this power, will take you down a path as dark as the mind that wields it. Tug's voice resounds in my head. My racing thoughts calm, and I suddenly remember the magnificent light that surrounded the Prince in the great hall. Everything is at once clear.

I weave together memories, showing Six the message I wish passed on to the Prince. I show him Tug being held prisoner. Tug promising me he would return Kel to my parents if I died. I show him Tug bringing me the Nocturne Melody after the bird-men attack, and finally this morning, Lady Calmi administering her poison.

Tug is fit. If he can escape the Ruby Palace, he has a chance. But not me.

Free Tug. Keep me drugged. And if that does not work, do whatever it takes to prevent Strik questioning me.

If Strik discovers I am Uru Ana, my life is over. And it will be for nothing if the Prince fails to take Strik's life in return.

FORTY-SIX

In this rat hole there is only grey light, no telling evening sun from high midday heat. I feel as though I've been down here for days, but perhaps it is the pain stretching seconds into minutes, minutes into hours, because no one has brought me food and my body does not crave it.

I am cold, shivering, which doesn't help the pain. My throat is raw and dry. My mouth bloated. I lie on the steel cage bars, unable to find any position even mildly comfortable and think of my father. He used to always tell me I could do anything I set my mind to. He used to tell me I was strong. I wonder what he would say if he saw me now.

Footsteps ring down the tunnel. Fear thumps through me. I reach towards the mind that approaches, and the wild battering of my heart softens.

The soldiers who dragged me here, and who have been left by Commander Linx to keep guard, stand to attention. I pull myself like an injured crab across the bars towards the door.

'Halt!' a soldier says. In the gloom, the white apron worn by the court maid stands out against the grey blouse and skirt. Calmi wears her hair in a handkerchief, pulled back from her face. Her head is lowered as she manages to curtsey and balance a tray. But if I recognise her, so will the soldiers.

'Who has sent you?'

Calmi's eyes rise and shift across to my prison. I watch breathless, desperate to talk to her, to find out whether Tug is still alive. Whether the Prince has a plan to free him.

'I have been sent from the kitchens with soup for the prisoner,' she says coolly, defying them to question her, even when their postures stiffen, taking in her distinct blue eyes.

'Commander Linx made it clear the prisoner was an imposter and a traitor.'

'Then why isn't she in the dungeons with the other prisoners? Why is she in a cage?'

'You'll have to put your questions to Commander Linx.'

'Were you posted in the Royal Court last summer?'

'I was, My Lady,' the second soldier says, stepping forward. He has recognised her.

'Then you know the treachery Commander Linx is capable of towards the Prince. Do you choose to question your sovereign's will now?'

'But Lord Strik—'

'What about my grandfather?'

'Five minutes,' the second soldier says. He must outrank the first because the man clenches his jaw and steps aside. The second soldier slips a key in the lock and turns. My pulse pounds against my neck, as Calmi moves into my prison and is locked in with me.

'I have been sent to look at your injuries,' she says, loud enough for the men to hear, but the urgency in her eyes says she also brings news. I lean on her and she helps me to the wooden palette at the back of the giant cage.

With our backs turned to the men she slips me a necklace. At first I do not understand, then I notice the pus-liquid in the round glass pendant: Nocturne Melody. I am so happy the tears of pain in my eyes turn to ones of joy.

'Is Tug alive?' I whisper.

She nods, helping me down on the pallet. I moan, but if Tug

lives, the pain is bearable. Lady Calmi takes a small sachet of herbs from the pocket of her apron and pours them into the steaming teapot.

'Sixe has been drawing endless towers for the carrier pigeons,' she says. 'I think he wanted you to know that when Tug sent the carrier pigeon that was shot down, he sent two others that were not. His capture was a necessary decoy to ensure two of the birds lived.'

Now I really am crying. My head spins and my chest froths with giddy bubbles. Tug got a message to the Duchess! She will be informed of the imminent attack on Lyndonia. She will realise Kel serves her no purpose. Keeping Kel safe and under her protection is more advantageous than breaking her word. Thank you, Tug!

Lady Calmi stirs the herbs in the tea and pours a cup. 'Drink this,' she says. The veil of indifference has fallen and I'm surprised to read concern in her gaze. I do not want the Prince hearing about the state I'm in and worrying when he needs all his wits about him.

'I didn't think you'd be so fast to take up the offer of poisoning me,' I say, taking the cup, trying to lighten the mood.

'You are a rival to be reckoned with,' Lady Calmi quips, playing along. 'It is arnica,' she adds. 'Now drink.'

'Will the Prince free Tug?'

'We are working on it. Grandfather thinks Tug is a mercenary who has posed as your guardian while you postured as a Lady to get close to the Prince. For now he believes the Duke and Duchess are behind the ruse.'

'When he questions me he will learn the truth.'

'After I leave you, take the Nocturne Melody. There is enough to knock you out for six or seven hours. This will give us time to get your friend out.'

My throat grows tight. Hearing her speak of Tug as a friend, I am hit by the realisation that I am no longer alone. I am imprisoned in the Ruby Palace, I may die here, I am about to face a man who plunges souls into darkness, but there are others, not only Ma, Pa and Kel, rooting for me.

I never imagined my closest friends would be a mercenary and a prince, or that my life would be in danger so often because of them, but in different ways, Tug and Jakut have bridged the enormous chasm that locked me out of the world.

One of the guards rattles on the door. 'That is enough Lady Calmi.'

'When your grandfather questions me,' I whisper, 'I will not be able to resist the power of his voice. He will discover I am Uru Ana and the Prince has lost his memories.' There is no point trying to hide anything from Lady Calmi. Anything the Prince has decided not to tell her, she would have been told by Six.

Lady Calmi retrieves an ointment and some cloth. 'I need to clean her wound,' she calls to the soldier. She rolls up the sleeve of my shirt until she reaches the arrow wound. 'The Prince's memories are coming back,' she continues in a low voice. 'When Grandfather discovers the Prince took the mist-berries, he will see it as an act of remorse and weakness. It will confirm his belief that the Prince is feeble, troubled, all the easier to manipulate. And when he understands the purpose for your presence, he will lose interest in you.'

The ointment stings my flesh. I suck in my breath. 'But if he discovers Jakut performed the cleansing, he will realise the Prince is unreliable, capable of changing his mind. Jakut will never have the opportunity to kill him. He will become your grandfather's puppet, if it has not happened already.'

'I came to the Ruby Court last spring. Before then I lived in my grandfather's house for thirteen years. I am not his puppet. And do not forget, as I told you before, the Prince is different.'

'Why?'

Calmi dabs the wound with the cloth, then pulls down my sleeve. 'It is safer for him if you do not know,' she says standing. My stomach dives to the floor and panic floods me. She is going to leave and the next person in here with me will be Lord Strik. Just the thought of the mind-world swallowed up with his black hole, sucking everything into hellish darkness, terrifies me.

'But what if Lord Strik questions whether the Prince is loyal to him? What if I do something that gives away the Prince's true intent?'

'If Grandfather harbours doubt concerning the Prince's ignoble ambitions, doubt enough to ask you such questions, then it is over for us all, and we have already lost.'

'What will your grandfather do when he discovers I am Uru Ana?'

'He assumes people are weak. Your people in particular have a reputation for passivity. He will not consider you a threat. He will assign you to the next tundra expedition to work in the mines, or as a slave in his household.'

The key turns in the prison latch. Lady Calmi steps across the metal rungs to the door. At the bars she pauses a moment, then without looking back, vanishes into the tunnel.

The cage rattles as the soldier locks it. I pop the cork from the round glass bottle on the end of the necklace, fingers shaking. My body hums, anticipating the pain relief. I think of Tug confiscating the Nocturne Melody when we reached the Red City.

If I take it, I will be oblivious to all goings on in the palace for the next seven hours. Much could happen before I wake. Much could go wrong and I will be powerless to see anything, or warn anyone. But whom am I fooling? I am already powerless.

I raise the cloudy yellow liquid to my lips. The revolting smell holds a sweet promise of oblivion. I tell myself that Tug would understand. As long as I am unconscious Strik will believe Tug is of no interest. This is his chance to escape.

I hold up the round glass as though I'm raising a champagne flute in a toast. To Tug! Then I drink until it is all gone, and sink down, welcoming the fog on my mind's horizon.

FORTY-SEVEN

I am standing in the palace throne room on the empty dais. Sunlight streams through the enormous windows behind the thrones. A hushed beauty fills the hall and for a moment I feel at peace.

I turn slowly wondering how I got here. Where is the Prince? As though my questions summon the darkness, the room turns cold and grey. Ice crystals form in the dampness I now notice trickling down the walls. Water drips from the domed ceiling and freezes. Stalactites form at an unnatural speed, their icy points resembling the teeth of a huge beast, its mouth widening, teeth extending to bite me. I stretch out my hands to fumble through the murk. Voices whisper. Wailing, crying, begging me to help them.

I wake gasping and trembling. My face is freezing. I am lying in a pool of water. Shirt, hair, trousers, every inch of me is soaked through.

'That's enough,' a voice says. A man with a scar stands over me. Fingers clenched around a jug. Huge pitchers line up across an uneven floor. I struggle to assemble the fragments of what I see into a whole picture.

Energy thunders in the mind-world, as though I am standing behind the torrential curtain of a waterfall.

The harder I try to grasp what is going on, the worse the thundering energy becomes, pulling me to the edge of the waterfall, dragging me down the crashing flow into the vortex.

Pain slices through me as the soldier with the scar drags me by one arm over metal bumps. Commander Linx. His name is Commander Linx. In an instant I regain my senses.

The commander releases me and I fall into a wet heap at his feet. He steps out of the cage.

'Leave it open,' Strik says. The agony in my ribs and arm relents and I am spinning, losing balance. Falling.

He strides into a great shimmering hall, walls of ice, floor of ice, thrones of ice. Eight thrones set in a circle, seats facing outwards. Silver carpets like the rays of an argent sun extend from each one. A middle-aged woman with long white-blonde hair sits opposite the door he has entered by.

'Every ten moons,' she says, her voice raised to travel the hall, 'the children of royal blood are tested and selected to govern the eight kingdoms of Rudeash. Every test is designed to draw out the candidate's strengths and weaknesses. When you are in the test, you will forget everything else. Your mind will believe what you see and hear is real. From this moment on, everything I tell you will become your reality without question.' The woman's face softens. 'The decision of those present here today is final. Good luck, my son.'

He gazes at her, confident, back straight, head high. My sense of my own life starts slipping away. As though her words condition my thoughts as well as his.

The ice cracks and melts, the kings and queens shimmer, growing translucent until they are a mirage of colour, until they are gone.

In the place of the ice hall is a frozen white ocean and on the horizon an army. The army wears the Carucan uniform, and bears the Carucan ruby red flags. They ride enormous horses covered in long, thick hair.

The woman, his mother, stands beside him, her shimmering silver and blue dress dancing in the wind. He hands her the looking glass that magnifies his vision. She takes it a moment, then says,

'There are too many of them. The shrouders are not strong enough.' She glances over her shoulder and he follows her gaze. Behind them, in the sun's low rays stands a magnificent ice-city, towers sculpted into spiral points,

domes *of misty blue and green swirls, enormous bridges that resemble wet glass. 'They have broken the veil. They see everything.'*

'It's not possible,' he says, shocked.

A gust of wind whips up the ice, cutting it into shards and throwing them in my face. I cry out. Blood drips where I've been cut.

I raise my hand and shudder as I regain my wits. I'm lying on my back in the cage. It is not blood oozing down my cheeks, but water. Blue eyes in a deeply lined face watch me. I am not him. This is not Rudeash. I am not Strik.

I pant gasping for air. A part of me is still trapped in his mind. On my inner-eye the Carucan army approaches, demanding my attention. I mentally wrestle against the drag of his inner-world.

'You will answer my question,' he says. The energy emanating from him surges. He is using the voice, and it strengthens his force, pushing me back towards the edge of the waterfall—the black rush. 'Why were you travelling with the Prince?' A deafening noise drowns his words.

I'm suddenly surrounded by a deep mist. A snowstorm blankets the world. And then a crack opens in the haze revealing an icy spire.

'The veil,' I murmur.

'You are in command,' the young Strik's mother says. 'The army will reach the edge of the city in less than two hours. It is up to you to decide how we will stop them and protect our home and our people.'

'Send for the shrouders. I will give them my orders as soon as I return.'

'Where are you going?'

'I will take the fastest sleigh and be back in an hour.'

'If you go out there to speak with them alone, you could be killed.'

'It is my decision. I have been elected for this. And now I will do what must be done.'

Time jumps.

He is on a sleigh, travelling at high speeds across an endless white land-scape. Wolves the colour of nuts and ashes pull him along, their bodies large and underfed. Frost forms on the lines of his cheeks. The ground rolls and bumps. The specks of black and red on the horizon take the form of figures on horseback. A wheel wolf at the back of the train starts yapping and gnashing his teeth. I lean forward to see if the harness is caught. His giant head turns and snaps at my hand. Teeth like metal skewers plunge through my flesh.

I howl in agony. Instinct makes me try to draw my injured hand to my chest, but my wrist catches on metal. I kick my legs. The chains around them rattle. My hands and feet are locked down.

'The bones of your little finger have been smashed to pieces,' Strik says. I flail around, shaking with fear, wondering where in the name of the Gods I am. 'Which leaves nine more fingers and ten toes. Enough, I hope, to hold your attention. Are you listening now?'

'Yes!' I scream. The crashing energy of his mind is muffled. He is right. Physical pain will keep my spirit clinging to my body rather than getting sucked into the black hole. I must tell him why I was travelling with Prince Jakut. I must tell him because... I pillage the corners of my muddled brain, throwing everything out as I search for the reason.

'Tell me why you travelled with the Prince and Duke Roarhil.'

'The Prince needed my sight.' The sounds from my mouth seem broken. When I stop to catch my breath, I hear myself moaning.

'Go on,' he says. A compulsion writhes in me to spill everything. Every single minutest detail from the last three weeks. I struggle to tame the desire.

'A mercenary took me from Blackfoot Forest to the Hybourg. The Prince had woken from the long-sleep without his memories. He needed an Uru Ana to find out why he was in the north and why someone tried to kill him. He paid gold for me and brought me here to discover his assassin.'

Energy gushes and swells. 'A shadow weaver,' Strik says. 'If you are a slave, why did he risk his life to save you?'

I try to sit up. The chains rattle and keep me tethered. The stabbing agony dims enough for the dark energy of Strik's mind to roar in my head again, pulling me over the edge.

From out of the blizzard rides a man dressed in heavy bear furs, sword dazzling with jewels, lumps of ice in the curls of his shoulder-length hair. His highest-ranked commanders flank his sides.

'Why have you come?' Strik says, voice booming in the emptiness.

'We come in peace to explore new lands.'

I am back inside the test the Rudeashan elders gave Strik as a young man.

'An army does not explore, it conquers. But you cannot conquer,' he continues using the voice, *'when the men riding at your side wait for the first opportunity to take your place.'*

Distrust clouds the king's expression. He looks at his second-in-command. Confusion and fear sweep over the young commander's face.

A smile pulls at Strik's mouth. His gamble has paid off.

'Brother, he lies to divide us. Why listen to a man whom you have never met before?'

An eruption of pain severs me from Strik's mind. I am screaming, thrashing, biting at the air. The agony in my foot holds me on the cusp of blackness, the twilight of consciousness. I yank against my chains. Through strands of tangled hair and watering eyes, I glimpse Commander Linx at the foot of the metal platform, a hammer in his rigid arm, shock and horror twisting his face. Strik's voice cuts through my wailing, the chains clanging, Commander Linx retching.

'It seems we've reached this young commander's threshold for violence,' he muses. He stands near the head of the platform, almost close enough for me to spit in his face. 'He could not watch the blow he administered and by the looks of it has smashed up most of your foot. So we had better move this along swiftly. Why did Prince Jakut save you during the bird-men attack?'

'I don't know.' Pain shapes my words, disfiguring them, making them barely recognisable.

'Tell me the truth.'

'He needed me,' I sob.

'And?'

The agony has me trembling and crying. The terror of more unbearable pain is overwhelming. But Strik no longer uses the voice. No longer drives deep inside me where I cannot resist.

'Arrogant!' I hiss. 'The Prince's arrogance makes him think he's invincible.'

'Is he in love with you?'

'No.' I stop straining against my chains, close my eyes, drift in the sea of agony.

'Have you won the Prince's special favour?' Strik asks, leaning over.

Waxy cold fingers caress my neck. Suddenly they pinch together, squeezing my windpipe. 'Answer me!'

'I don't know,' I sob. 'I don't know.'

'Then we will have to find out.'

FORTY-EIGHT

I rouse, struggle to open my eyes, fall back under, crushed by pain. Repeat. I have no idea how many times this has happened since Commander Linx returned me to the cage. I have been floundering in an ocean of darkness, only to regain consciousness and wish I had not.

At some point, I wake to find the commander rubbing cold cream on my toes, bandaging my foot, and crushed finger. In the light of an open torch strapped to a bar of the cage, the strain and desperation on the commander's face drives into me exactly how far Strik's power is able to corrupt a man. He forced Commander Linx to an act of violence that went against his nature.

I wanted to ask the commander whether he'd seen the Prince, but he hushed me each time I tried to speak. And it was hard to think about anything but lessening the pain and satisfying my hunger spasms, as he spooned watery soup down my throat.

The soup and cream have helped enormously. The last two times I stirred, I stayed conscious for many minutes, watched my guards dozing against the wall opposite the cage door, and wondered about the world Strik comes from.

Rudeash is a kingdom where implanting suggestions is a part of their way of life, where shrouders are capable of concealing the

Rudeashan cities from outsiders. This is why Tug saw no others like Strik when he crossed the tundra to Rudeash.

The distant sound of boot steps send my guards hurrying to their feet.

My heart pounds as I remember Strik's parting words. Calmi was wrong. Her grandfather did not lose interest because I am Uru Ana. But why this obsession with the Prince's affections? With a few words, Strik could convince the Prince he was in love with Calmi, couldn't he?

Torch light flickers down the long stretch of corridor, casting shadows on the grimy walls.

'We need the prisoner,' a soldier says.

The guard with the shaved head, who allowed Lady Calmi to visit me, blocks their path. 'Whose orders?'

'The Prince of Caruca has summoned all captured traitors to the throne room.'

My muscles tense, and my jaw locks, teeth grinding. Strik is setting a trap. He must intend to show Jakut that I have been tortured. He believes the Prince is as calculating and cold as he is, so any sign of emotion or outrage from Jakut, will be taken as proof that I have wheedled my way into the Prince's heart and must be gouged out and gotten rid of, permanently.

A key clangs in the cage door. I hope Six has been keeping an eye on me, and has found a way to warn Calmi. I hope Jakut will be prepared.

'Kneel and hold out your arms,' the soldier says. I drag myself up, taking my weight on the hand that is intact. My feet are bare. The bandaged foot protrudes from under my folded legs. I avoid putting pressure on it, but the pain flares when it touches the ground, the lightest contact is like a pulverising boulder.

Manacles slid over my wrists and lock, pinching my skin. The soldier yanks a lead of chain attached to a circle of iron. He means to pull me to my feet, but I stumble and fall smack on the side of my face. The bruise to my cheek radiates heat.

'She cannot walk,' the guard with the shaved head says.

'Then she'll have to crawl,' the soldier sneers.

A few chuckles echo in the underground passage. I push up, stare at the soldier through straggles of tangled hair. He is around Pa's forty years. The skin near his ear is ruffled where he's been burnt. I swallow hard, steeling myself against their cruelty.

When Lord Strik turned the Carucan people against the Uru Ana thirty years ago, he only had to suggest we were the enemy. Calmi said it was the King's soldiers and the Carucans who chased my people from their homes, who arrested them, and burned them. Is it really so easy to wipe away compassion by convincing a man he stands before his enemy? And yet I know the answer. If it weren't, the bloody wars that have written the history of Caruca and Etea would have been impossible.

'Move!' the soldier orders, yanking the chain. I bite hard on my lip but it isn't enough to stop a yelp from escaping. The muscles in my shoulders burn, ripped from their sockets. A few more hard pulls and I will lose the use of both my arms.

The guard with the shaved head enters the cell, pushing the soldier aside. 'She is just a child,' he mutters, scooping me up.

The soldier barricades our way. 'I will take her any way I see fit,' he says.

'I doubt the Prince of Caruca has all day to wait while you drag her up the stairs,' the guard says. 'And if he is bringing the prisoners to question them, better she is still conscious and able to talk.'

The soldier glances back at his men. Then he winds up the chain attached to my wrist, reeling himself toward us until he stands head-on to the guard. He thrusts the chain into my stomach with a hard punch. I automatically curve to take the blow and whimper at the pinch on my rib cage. I turn my head into the guard's chest, gritting my teeth.

Then we are moving. The sound of boots thumping through the tunnel, and the battering of the guard's heart against my ear, fill my senses. I am carried through dim passages, up a short flight of steps, around another tunnel, then a longer flight of stairs.

At the top of stone stairs we are bathed in sunlight. I screw up my eyes against the stinging brightness. Warm air washes across my face and into my lungs. As we continue, I squint at our surround-ings. I vaguely recognise the corridor. It is one of the many passages on the first floor that Tug and I ran through before we found the nursery.

And then the guard is setting me down before the giant umber and ebony throne room doors. It has not been two whole days since Tug and I were ushered into the throne room to stand before the Queen, yet it feels like weeks.

The throne room doors stand open, the hall beyond obscured by several rows of soldiers. Lord Strik's mind seeps out, a dark pall. I resist the rumble and drag of energy, focus on my trembling body, taking as much weight as possible on my good foot without losing my balance.

A soldier produces a key. The chain attached to my manacles is removed, and the men guarding the throne room part to create a passage. I hobble forward, the eyes of those closest boring holes in my skull. They have no idea who I am, or what I am supposed to have done yet the hatred is palpable.

Seconds pass and I have not even reached the threshold. My movements are cumbersome. There is no pain, I tell myself, but each time I put pressure on my bandaged foot, black dots bloom at the edge of my vision, and I fear I will pass out.

Dipped in stark light from the window, a dozen prisoners kneel before the dais steps. It suddenly hits me that if Calmi and Jakut did not find a way to free Tug, he will be one of them. I rub my eyes and scan the captives looking for anyone with Tug's broad back and wavy hair. I daren't glance up at the thrones. I cannot face seeing how the Prince is reacting to my pitiful entrance. And if I catch his eye, I might destabilize his efforts to remain indifferent.

'Ah,' Strik says. 'The last of the prisoners has finally arrived.' I keep my head bowed, concentrate on the next step forwards, trying to look stronger than I am. I have not reached a third of the way to the other prisoners when my legs give way and I crumble to the polished floor.

Head lowered, I silently beg Jakut will rake the very depths of his talent for deception and disguise to prove to Strik his indifference.

Light steps resound at the far end of the hall. My shoulders shake. The rush and roar of energy in the mind-world means I cannot tell who has descended. Please don't let it be the Prince.

'The only way to quell the trouble in the city,' Strik says, 'and among the courtiers, is by showing a firm hand, Your Royal Highness.'

A little sigh of relief escapes me. It is Strik moving closer, not the Prince. The irony of my line of thinking—hoping for Strik rather than the Prince—is not lost on me. I glance up. Strik stands at the foot of the dais in a striking royal blue and grey tunic, hair swept back from his face and glimmering silver in the sun.

A movement in the shadows catches my eye. A lithe man slips further up the hall to mirror Strik's position. It fleetingly crosses my thoughts that the lord's assassins are undetectable to my inner-eye, as though being around Strik for so long, their minds have been diffused and melded with his. Apart from Strik's personal entourage, no other soldiers or guards remain in the hall.

He steps closer to the line of prisoners, continuing his address to the Prince. 'The people do not need to love you. They need to respect you. You must show your authority.' His energy swells as he uses the voice. I hold my breath, anticipating the pull into his memories, but nothing happens. I wonder if it is because his words are directed at the Prince rather than me.

'I am not a coward,' Jakut says. I raise my eyes, cold tingling through my hands and feet. Jakut lounges on the throne, looking at once displeased and awkward. 'Anyone who does not respect the curfew, anyone who is caught trying to leave the city, anyone who is reported as attempting to assist the Queen, is being arrested.'

'It is not enough,' Strik answers.

My eyes shift to Calmi. She is sitting beside the Prince, staring forward, unblinking, gaze blank. My heart beats faster. Calmi was wrong when she said her grandfather would lose interest in me once he learnt why I was travelling with Prince. What if she is also wrong about the Prince? She said Jakut was different, but unless he can over-come the suggestive power in Strik's voice, he does not stand a chance against Strik.

My cheeks flare. I quickly shift my eyes from Calmi to where I sense someone watching and my stomach plunges when I meet Strik's satisfied stare. As far as I can tell, the Prince has not reacted to my presence. He is better at this than I anticipated. Or Strik has used the hours since I have been captured to convince Jakut that I am a pawn in their game, a pawn who has betrayed him and is now worthless.

Strik slowly walks the line of prisoners. Though my head is lowered, I follow him in the mind-world stopping to see if he hesitates over any prisoner in particular. I try to take in the feel of the mind's he passes, but he has this way of smothering them.

'A public hanging in front of the palace,' Strik declares.

'What about their trials?'

'Your Kingdom hangs in the balance,' the lord answers, turning towards the Prince. Hands clasped behind his back, he walks up the dais steps, feet as light and swift as a young man. 'Your uncle has not been caught, and keeping the Queen alive, while necessary for a short while, fuels the rebellion. One prisoner has already escaped. The guards responsible for this error will hang beside the prisoners as a warning.'

The Prince looks at Strik with some misgiving, but he nods, assenting.

'Greatness is shown by a man's strength,' Strik says, striding to Jakut's right-hand side. 'A man's ability to make hard decisions.'

The Prince stands. 'The prisoners will be hanged at sunset,' he says, staring forward, as though he cannot meet Strik's pressing gaze. 'I hope it will be enough to quell the bloodshed.'

Something in his voice, a sense of remorse, makes me look up. For a split-second the Prince's untrained gaze locks on me. Adrenaline surges through my body.

'I will not allow the Kingdom of Caruca to fall into tatters,' he says, ending their conversation.

I drop my head. I am trembling again, wondering if he was making that final address to me. An apology?

Downtrodden, he descends the dais and walks through the centre of the hall. Prisoners shuffle out of his way. He moves through them without glancing down, headed for the giant hall doors.

My shaking grows worse as he passes me. Now he is away from Lord Strik, I sense the shape of his mind and realise how much of his memory has returned to him. It is no longer a canvas of ash and ruin, his past buried beneath an avalanche of dust. His mind feels like an enormous, long wall. A strange, ominous wall, built to divide a kingdom from the dark creatures lurking on the other side.

Have we lost the Prince? I look up as Calmi follows in Jakut's wake, her face a numb mask.

The Prince's footsteps fade. An instant later, soldiers march in to round up the prisoners. I am left until last. Chains are locked onto the shackles of the other prisoners and they are dragged from the hall.

Has Jakut just saved my life, or condemned it? My body sways. Adrenaline fades and pain looms. Blackness swims on the edge of my vision. Thunder roars in my ears.

Strik.

He stands in the dome of light at the centre of the hall, watching me. As the four soldiers who brought me to the hall swoop in to attach my chains, he steps forwards.

'She is not to join the other prisoners until the hanging. Return her to the cage. The key comes straight back to me.'

The soldier with the ruffle of burnt skin nods. Then with a hard tug he pulls me to my feet. I cry out tripping after him. He moves too fast. Light flares on my eyes and I start to reel. We reach the throne room doors. I look up at the sun pouring in from the hall beyond, the beautiful carved ceiling with men in bloody battle, and white birds sweeping the sky.

I cannot take another step. With the force yanking on my arms I fall forwards. Faces of the guards outside the throne room blur. The guard who carried me from my cage lunges to catch me. But my gaze focuses for a moment on the soldier behind him. The tattoo markings and bruises on the man's face have been expertly concealed. He stares at me, desperation stifled by an iron-will of control.

Tug has escaped his prison, but he is not on his way to Lyndonia. He is here in the palace. And his eyes are telling me to hold on.

FORTY-NINE

My stomach is a tight knot of nerves, and despite the cool, mouldy air in my cage, I am sweating. I sit on the wooden pallet, my damaged foot raised awkwardly to lift the weight off it, but it is hard to stay still.

Picking at the thread of the bandage on my hand, I wonder what kind of dangerous plan Tug is concocting to get me out of here. He has never trusted the Prince, and after what happened in the throne room, I can't say I'm sorry for it. But he is taking an enormous risk just staying in the Ruby Palace. His presence here fills me equally with relief and dread.

And what about the Prince? What was that performance in the throne room, if it was a performance? All my previous fears about the Prince's memories coming back and transforming his personality wrestle inside me. Either way, Jakut is a long way from controlling the situation.

I force myself to stop fidgeting, breathe deeply and focus through the pain and anxiety. Eyes closed, I glide through the mind-world, move up the palace levels headed for the Prince's chambers. I want to discover if he still fighting for us, and against Strik. The only way to be sure is to root around his recent memories.

It is some minutes before I come across the mind shaped like a great wall of some ancient myth, built to keep out demons and told to scare children. Even exhausted, bones aching, pain constant, moving through the mind-world is a hundred times easier than it was when I first left Blackfoot Forest. It is like a muscle that has grown strong from weeks of practice.

I slip inside the Prince's mind without effort, skim across his recent memories until I find one where he and Calmi are alone.

Calmi stands by the door of a lavish suite with enormous wood carvings, purple pillows strewn across six low ottomans, blue hand-painted patterns on the walls. The Prince is twisting an ornament in his hands, a golden filigree egg. He watches Calmi and she stares back.

'If you want to pass Grandfather's test,' she says, 'Mirra must hang.'

'It's not an option.'

'Then he will know his voice wields no power over you. He will not hesitate to get rid of you. The Queen and the heir she carries will take your place. And Caruca will be under his rule.'

'You are asking me to make an impossible choice.'

'There is no choice. Your emotions are getting in your way.'

'Sacrifice one to save many?' Jakut says, scornfully.

'As you did with your father.'

'This is different. My father was not innocent.'

'It is not different. The only difference is the way you feel about her. Grandfather is suspicious—because of your spiritual cleansing after you massacred his men, and now the missing Duke, and the escaped prisoner. Unless she hangs with the others, you will never get close enough to kill him.'

'I cannot do it.'

'But you must.'

A shout from somewhere near my cage yanks my attention out of the Prince's mind. I blink at the murky darkness, noting the smell of burning that lingers on the air.

The torch on the wall outside my cage has been snuffed out. There comes another gruff shout, then a sound of a fist hitting flesh. A sword clangs against stone, followed by a crack. I crawl off the wooden pallet, and wriggle across the cage floor on my stomach. More grunts, gurgles, sounds of punching, kicking. I pull myself up to the bars and squint at the faint edges of shadow.

A scuffling sound, followed by an agonised cry, quickly smothered. I wait, time pounding in my ears with the beating of my heart. The darkness is like a wall, like the mountain is claiming back these subterranean passages and trying to bury us.

Don't be dead Tug. Don't you dare be dead.

A match sparks. In the light of a small flame, all I can make out are the fingers holding it. Then the flame grows as a torch is lit, illuminating the man who carries it.

I clap my hand over my mouth to stop myself from sobbing. Tug is panting, breathless, blood licking down the side of his unmarked face. A soldier moans, but I barely notice. All I see is Tug, those fierce, determined eyes, and I can't break it to him. Not straight away. He doesn't know that Strik is the only one with a key to my cage.

I prolong the moment of truth, distract both of us, if only for a few seconds. 'When you said you'd come back for me,' I say, 'I thought you meant in a few months, not hours.'

'Sorry to disappoint you.' He moves away from the cage door, props the torch in a sconce and starts hunting for the key. I watch him. For some reason I still cannot tell him he won't find what he's looking for.

I guess I'm afraid I'll see that defiance crack and if Tug cracks then I'm not sure I can keep up any semblance of bravery. His search grows more vigorous, more impatient. Eventually, once he has scoured both soldiers twice over, he turns to me from where he is crouched over one of the men.

'Where's the key?'

'Strik has it.' The truth falls down over his eyes like a pitch-black night. He looks ready to snake his arm over the soldier by his side and suffocate him. 'Tug, Tug, please. You can't get me out of here. I'm sorry.'

'You're sorry?' There's an edge to his voice that winds me.

'Please, just talk to me for a few minutes. Then go. Get away from the city. Go to Lyndonia.'

'I'm not going to let you die today. I will kill Strik if the Prince cannot.'

'You said it yourself. Many have tried. Yet Lord Strik still lives.'

'The Prince will find a way to delay. He will not sacrifice you.'

'He has no choice. Strik has used his power to order the hanging.' I do not tell him that I have discovered why Calmi puts so much faith in the Prince, because Jakut has the unique ability to resist Strik's power. I do not tell him because I know what Tug will do if he discovers the Prince could stop my death, but allows it to win Strik's trust and save the kingdom.

'You did not come here to die, Mirra.' The anger and frustration seem to bleed out from him, twisting up my insides. It is worse to be left behind. To have someone taken from right under you, and be powerless to stop it. I could not let it happen to Kel. It will be hard for Tug. He will blame himself for the fact I'm here in the first place. The Prince might be capable of sacrificing me for the greater good, but unless I persuade Tug otherwise, he will die trying to stop it.

'If the Prince cannot find a way to take Lord Strik's life before the hanging,' I say. 'then it is impossible. You cannot allow yourself to be killed. You still have a promise to keep.'

'Damn you, Mirra. Start thinking of yourself. Your brother is safe.'

'You have received word?'

'It is too soon. But the carrier pigeon will have reached Lyndonia. And an answer will arrive before nightfall.'

I look down, wondering if I will ever know that answer. Tug's hand wraps over mine where I hold the cage bars. His knuckles are bleeding. I can feel lacerations cut into his palm.

'You have to let me try, Mirra.'

He wants my permission to let him get himself killed trying to assassinate Strik. I don't want to give it. But if I make him go against his own nature, the sense of honour that he has finally won back, then am I any better than Strik? How would I have felt if my mother had emotionally blackmailed me not to go after Kel? I would never have been able to live knowing I'd done nothing.

I tilt my head in a small nod. 'But only once you've received word from Lyndonia and are certain that Kel is safe.'

'Then I will wait,' he nods, 'and whatever I do, it will be at the hanging.' I twitch my fingers to press against the bottom of his. We stay that way for a long moment, the fragile connection of touch like the delicate threads holding our lives to the world. On the edges of my inner-eye I sense someone approach.

'Someone is coming.' Tug withdraws his hand but I'm not ready to let go. I reach through the bars, and put my palm on his shoulder. The powder he has used to conceal the tattoos has smeared, revealing shadows of his beast-face. His look presses into me.

Tug the mercenary, the soldier, the diplomat, the guardian, the drunk, the hero. My feelings are as tangled and complicated as his past. Up until two days ago, I didn't think I had any, except for hate, distrust, and anger.

The lantern in the sconce on the wall flutters and dances. Tug nods at me, then steps away and silently vanishes.

I grip onto the cage door and wait for the mind that has entered this underground tomb through a forgotten passage. A passage I imagine only the rats have used for a thousand years.

Six approaches like a spectre. If I couldn't sense his mind, I would have no indication he was here. When he is close enough to see the guards, one unconscious, the other still splayed on the floor whimpering, he stops hiding and rushes to the cage.

In the mind-world he pulls up a memory.

Calmi stands in a stable, hair tied back, sweaty as though she has just returned from riding. She holds out a pendant with a glass centrepiece shaped like a crystal sword.

'This is for you, Mirra,' she says, talking to Six, but addressing me. 'It is a mix of herbs and two poisons. I have only tested it on rabbits, but it is designed to slow the heartbeat. In the long-sleep the heart rate drops to fifteen beats per minute. Two drops of this and it will drop to two or three beats per minute. When you sense the soldiers coming for you just before dusk, take two drops. No more. It is fast working. By the time the soldiers reach your cell it will look as though you are having a seizure and dying. When they check for your pulse, they will not find it.'

Calmi glances behind her, eyes wide and wary. Then she looks back at Six —at me. 'I do not know how long the coma will last. I cannot promise you will ever wake from it. But if you don't take it, there will be no stopping Jakut. He plans to surprise Grandfather at the hanging. He will try to stab him in public, in plain view of Grandfather's assassins. And while Grandfather may survive the attack, it is certain the Prince will not. I am sorry to ask you to do this, Mirra.'

She pushes the pendant into Sixe's hands. 'Go now,' she tells him.

The memory dissolves, and I am left gazing at Sixe. He slips the crystal pendant through the bars. I take it. My hand shakes as I lift the glass to the torchlight. For a moment I think Calmi has made a mistake and the glass is empty. But then I realise she has filled it up to the top so it looks as though there is nothing there.

I slip the thread off the pendant and tuck the narrow crystal into the bandage around my injured hand. Then I look at Sixe. His expression reminds me of a river pebble I once found, formed in beautiful layers. Each layer a shade of sandy brown, volcanic black, salty grey, the passage of time captured in the sedimentary strips. I showed it to Ma and she called it the silent life of a stone, a witness to the force of nature and the passing of the ages.

I reach through the bars and squeeze Sixe's arm. As he turns to leave, I see the tear glistening on his cheek. Far off in the mind-world wind howls and waves crash against the sparkling cliffs of the Island of the Rushing Winds, the home of our ancestors, drowned beneath the sea years ago, but still echoing in our people's memories.

FIFTY

I scratch up dirt from between the stones in the floor and rub the damp grain between my finger and thumb. Then I add the tiny ball to the fragments lined up on the end plank of the cage pallet. Eight pieces of stone dust and dirt. I'm uncertain how much time has passed, but for every approximate hour, I've added another piece.

What I do know is time is running out. The all-night sun may only be a couple of weeks away, but the days do not yet stretch so long that they can elude night altogether.

Soon after Sixe left, one of the guards roused and staggered off for help. The soldier with the rumpled ear-skin who wanted me to crawl to the throne room arrived. While his unit carried the unconscious guard to the army infirmary, rumpled-skin rattled the bars, spitting and cursing and promising me he would be standing in the front row at the hanging, applauding my death. Curled on the pallet with my back to him, I was thankful this time that Strik was the only one with a key to my cage.

Since then, the last few hours have been uneventful. If waiting to die could ever be considered a non-event. The cold, the pain, the hunger and exhaustion of my body are excruciating. But the real night-mare is agonising over how I will never have said goodbye to Ma and

Pa. I will never have thanked them for everything they gave up to keep me safe. I will never be able to explain to Kel why I didn't make it back with Tug.

Because Tug will make it back to Lyndonia. Neither he nor the Prince are going to get themselves killed trying to save me. When the guards come, I will take Calmi's potion. Oh, she has been clever, giving me a choice when she knows it is no choice at all.

There is every possibility the potion is Blue Death or a poison she made to kill her grandfather. But by telling me I have a chance of waking from the coma she avoids serving me the ultimate test of self-sacrifice. A test she is not convinced I would pass?

As dusk grows closer, I find myself on my knees praying to Jakut's Gods, or any Gods who will listen. Praying that by some miracle the Prince will find a way to rid Caruca of Lord Strik before the hanging. Praying I will wake from Calmi's coma. Praying Kel has grown strong in the days we have been apart. Strong enough to keep it together when he sees Beast-face coming for him, instead of me.

I should have given Tug a message, like Calmi spoke through Sixe to me. Explained that Tug is no longer our captor, but our friend. At least then Kel would have believed I had sent Tug to take him home.

I'm lying on my pallet muttering to myself and shivering when a dark cloud of energy sweeps through the mind-world. I strain to pull myself up to a seated position. Is it dusk already? Has Strik come to fetch me in person?

Pain shoots through my foot when it touches the ground. My fingers fumble over the tiny clumps of dirt. Ten. There should be at least fourteen. The sun had only just risen when I was taken to the throne room. Surely it's not time yet. It can't be.

The guards become aware of our approaching company a few seconds after I do. They stand to attention, muscles taut, backs straight.

The passage grows light. Two boys carrying torches emerge from the gloom, followed by a girl with a bowl and funnel, Strik's assassins, and Lord Strik himself, tall, dignified, changed from this morning's attire into a black tunic with dark, supple trousers.

My heart feels erratic, as though I might be having a seizure even without Calmi's poison mix. I fumble with the miniature crystal bottle, only now remembering I am holding it, and I was supposed to take it before I was collected for the hanging. Too late. With a shaky hand, I hide it in the bandage next to my wrist.

Strik steps through his entourage and opens the cage door. It swings back clanging against the wall. He is the first to enter, followed by the boys who attach metal wires to the bars to hold the torches. Then the assassins kick aside damp straw in the murky corners, pull me off the pallet, check under the boards, run their hands over my waist and down my legs for weapons.

I shiver at their touch, avoiding Strik's gaze which is riveted on me from where he stands in the centre of the cage, his strong lined face awash in orange flame.

A table and chair are set up before my pallet. The girl sprays the cage with a strange skin sac attached to a silver funnel. Misty vapour perfumed with cloves, orange, rose petals, and other scents I do not recognise, fills the air. A boy settles a silver covered bowl on the table.

My eyes whip about in confusion. Beads of sweat form on my brow and my throat tightens. What now? Some new kind of torture? Perhaps it is the fear, or the aches and pains which leave me in permanent agony, but the thunderous pull of Strik's mind has grown softer.

'King Alixter's father,' Strik says, sniffing and blowing his nose in a silk handkerchief as he sits down, 'had this cage built for his moon-snow tigress. A rare and dangerous creature. Beautiful, but deadly.'

A spindly woman hovers at the edge of the cell. He waves her in. She bows, pads across the floor, and lifts the lid off the silver bowl. Smells of cooked dough, melted cheese, meat and spinach set my mouth watering. I have not eaten since Commander Linx gave me soup, and before that, an apple yesterday morning when Calmi came to my chambers. The food taster sniffs the pastry.

'The tiger,' Strik continues, 'went crazy down in these tunnels. Couldn't be trained. Couldn't tame it. Killed eight men before the King finally agreed to have her life taken. Some creatures aren't made for cages.' I am half-listening, half-paralysed by the food taster's task, but when he speaks about creatures and cages a shudder runs down my spine. It's as though he's really talking about me. I try to break through the haze of terror and pay more attention.

The food taster chews the pastry, survives, bows again and leaves us. I glance up to see her go, noting Strik's assassins have replaced the guards on either side of the open cage door.

'It has been many years,' Strik says, 'since I've come across one of your kind that wasn't born in captivity.'

Sickness rises in my throat. A mix of hunger, and disgust, and fear. He is not here to take you to the hanging. Calm down. You still have time. Time for what? To poison myself? I struggle to clear my mind. If Strik is not here to take me to the hanging, then I must find out what he wants.

'A wild shadow weaver,' he continues. 'An outlaw. Hunted, feared, and yet you managed to convince me that you were a baroness.' He snorts. 'How is it, a young girl descended from a people who do not fight, fought off my bird-men? How is it an outlaw is taken prisoner to serve a Prince, and wins his heart?'

Heat prickles up my arms and legs, flushing across my chest and rising to my cheeks. Alertness buzzes in my head. My mind stretches wide, trying to grasp at what is happening.

'Oh the Prince has put on a good show,' Strik continues. 'I think he has almost convinced himself he is not in love with you, and because he knows himself so little, he will allow you to die trying to prove it.'

What does he mean? Has Strik realised his voice has no power over Jakut?

'He will let me die,' I say, 'because you manipulate him against his own will.'

'The Prince's mother,' Strik says, ignoring my interruption, 'was a Rudeashan princess, picked to marry Alixter because of her unusual strength. But her dedication to her ignorant, conceited husband destroyed her. She risked his hatred, his unkindness, and ultimately his neglect, all to protect him. Her power was so great that it kept me from the Red City even in her death.'

My breath heaves unevenly in and out of my chest. My mind is on the brink of piecing something together, as though I am just beginning to see a picture forming, but one essential piece is still missing.

Strik rubs his hands together, settling in, enjoying his one-sided monologue.

'Ninety-two years ago, the Carucans came across the ice with an army, intending to conquer Rudeash. All they found was a simple people. Eight tribes, governed by eight kings and queens with crowns of thorns. The shrouders hid the great wealth of Rudeash, the ice cities, the beauty and riches of their lands. But they could not hide all of their wealth. The lands were too rich in crystals and precious stone. So they gave the tundra mines to the Carucans and to deter them from ever returning for more, pledged a Rudeashan princess in marriage for each Carucan king's eldest son, as an agreement of peace and cooperation.

Forty years ago, when I became chief adviser to King Rex, the Prince's grandfather, I realised the Rudeashan princesses had been given a second, more pressing task. To protect Caruca from me.' He laughs and blows his nose again. 'Prince Jakut's mother was particularly powerful. She used the power in her voice to make me believe conquering the Red City would end in my death. I knew what she'd done, but despite all logic, I was unable to overcome the conviction she'd planted in my brain.

Then the Prince came of an age to rule and wished to sacrifice his father for the throne. I felt the power fade. You see, the King's death, and the alliance formed between the Prince and me, allowed me to crush his mother's hold over my ambitions and enter the Red City. I have not been killed yet,' he adds wryly.

Understanding plunges through me. In some way by assisting in his own father's death, the Prince has shattered the city's only wall of protection from Lord Strik.

Jakut will never win Strik's trust, because Strik is not careless enough to let his guard down around the son of a powerful enemy. And now there is nothing to stop Strik. Not even the missing Rudeashan princess Jakut was supposed to return with from the north.

Hope slithers away. I stare at Lord Strik, emotion torn from my body; numb like a ghostly witness of something I am powerless to stop.

He takes a pastry from the bowl, pops it whole into his mouth, and licks his lips. Then he holds the bowl out to me. I gaze at it, wondering what good food will do me now. He slides the bowl across the floor towards the pallet.

'What do you want from me?' I say.

He adjusts his position, crosses one leg over the other. The gesture generates a tiny electric spark, enough to snap me out of my stupor. He does want something. What could I possibly have that he wants?

'When I told you about the shrouders protecting the Rudeashans just now, you knew what I was talking about. The last time we met, you muttered something about the veil.'

'I am Uru Ana.'

'You have seen inside my memories.'

My eyes rise to his face. Is that surprise? Why would he be surprised I can see inside his mind? Isn't this the fuel he used to turn the Carucans against my kind?

'You are not like the slaves who work my land.' He rises and I sense a shift in the dark pull, as though it has glitched for a moment. He strides towards the cage door. I don't know what he's doing, but I know he has not finished with me.

In the few seconds his back is turned, I slip my fingers into my bandage and unhook the clasp from the crystal. Breath caught in my throat, face prickling with heat, I hurriedly sprinkle the poison over the remaining pastries in the dish at my feet. I cannot see where the drops land, how many, or on which pastries. My eyes flick up to the cage door as Strik indicates something to the assassins. They move further down the tunnel.

Strik closes the door and returns. I hunch my shoulders together to stop the shaking in my body. The crystal presses into my closed fist.

'I have waited a long time to return to my homeland with the Carucan army,' he says. 'I will take back what is mine. And you could help me discover something I would like to know once the kings and queens of the eight kingdoms of Rudeash are bowed at my feet.'

'The Prince will not allow you to attack Rudeash.' If I can keep him talking for long enough, perhaps luck will be on my side and he will eat one of the poisoned pastries.

'The Carucans neither respect nor fear the young Prince. He has no authority. When the Duke and the Queen are both dead there will be no one with enough influence to stop me.'

Strik has been a step ahead of Prince Jakut from the beginning. I remember our first encounter. I was right when I said he was cautious around the Prince. He already suspected the sway of his voice did not work on Jakut. But now he is in the Red City there is no need for caution.

Whether the Prince responded to his voice, or not, has never mattered. There would always be others who would. The Prince's lack of authority renders him ineffective. Even the ignoble or noble nature of Jakut's true intentions didn't matter. Strik was never going to be a partner, never going to trust the son of his enemy. His plan covered all eventualities.

Except one.

I pick up a pastry and play with it in my fingers, reminding him they are there to be eaten.

'You are considering my offer,' he says, a smile forming at the edge of his lips. If you could call the tight-lipped pull of his mouth a smile. 'I suspected when I first saw you that you had a keen instinct for survival. Heroic gestures that end in death are for those who have never struggled to stay alive from one day to the next.'

'You could use your power to make me do your bidding. Why are you bargaining with me?'

'I noticed you had a hard time paying attention when I used my influence. The journey across the tundra will not be easy. If I have to break every bone in your body just to get you to Rudeash, you will not be much use to me.'

I fiddle with the pastry, willing him to eat another. Eat it. Eat!

'Go ahead,' he says, gesturing to my hand. He thinks if I accept his offer of food I will accept the offer to work for him. If I don't eat, I'm declining. And I can't accept his offer but not his food, because he's astute enough to realise something is off. Strik is a tyrant, but he is also shrewd.

I close my eyes, and nibble at the corner. My dry mouth turns to ashes, making it hard to swallow. It feels like eating sand. In my head I count to five. Calmi said the poison acted fast. How fast?

Lord Strik watches, examining the minutest expression on my face. He is unconvinced. He will think my reticence is because I'm unde- cided. I take a larger bite. Warm cheese melts on my tongue. There is nothing I can do to stop it disintegrating. I should have waited to hear what he wanted before trying to poison him.

At least my larger bite has the desired effect. His intent look relaxes. He reaches for the bowl, and pops a mini roll in his mouth.

I freeze, waiting for some sign of poisoning, barely able to curb the anticipation. Nothing. Did I even get the potion in the dish? My hand had been shaking all over the place. I'd been too scared to look at what I was doing and take my eyes off Strik for more than a second. But there were at least twenty drops and only two would be enough to kill him. Or me.

His head tilts to the side. 'You need not die today,' he says. He reaches for another roll, now trying to encourage me. 'Eat.'

If I eat the rest of my pastry, he'll eat the second one he's holding. That's the deal. We're making a contract with food. He just doesn't know it could kill us.

I put the end of my flaky roll in my mouth, chewing slowly. Strik reflects my gesture, wiping crumbs from the corners of his lips as he eats.

We are down the road of no return. Calmi said the poison was quick but I don't know if she meant it would work in seconds or minutes. All I can do is keep Strik eating.

I am reaching for a pastry when Strik fumbles for the collar of his tunic. He undoes a button. In the dull glow of the lantern his face grows red. Sweat glistens on his upper lip.

He pushes to his feet, steadying himself with a hand on his chair. There is a moment when his eyes flame with understanding. He grasps for a small blade handle tucked beneath his tunic. Before he can remove it from his belt, a spasm jerks through him.

The pastry I'm holding falls from my fingers, hitting the ground just before Strik. His collapse sends the dish clattering across the stones. Two assassins burst into the cage. I scurry back on the pallet, tuck myself into a ball, half-expecting an assassin to take his knife and slit my throat, half-expecting the potion to start working on me at any second.

Strik flips on the ground. One of the men shouts at a guard to fetch the food taster and a healer. Mayhem erupts in the tunnel. I peek out from my ball to see Strik's eyes roll back into his head. White foam froths at the sides of his mouth. More than two drops and you are sure to die, Calmi had said.

How many seconds have passed since I ate my pastry? Is it longer than the time since Strik swallowed his first one?

In my head I am counting as the assassins lift Strik and carry him from my cell. Counting when the echo of their boot-steps falls into silence. Counting as I belly crawl towards my open cage door.

Option one, I hang. Option two, Strik takes me to Rudeash to destroy a kingdom. Option three, my personal favourite, Strik dies.

Even a brilliant tyrant can't plan for everything.

FIFTY-ONE

I'm standing at the edge of my cell, gripping the cage bar, dazed and weak and not quite sure where to go or how I will get anywhere, when I sense the Prince. Without thinking, I slip inside his mind, feel the metal of his sword hilt pressed into his palms, breathe the fetid, damp air whooshing in and out of his chest as he flies down the dim passage, feet barely touching the ground.

I try to shout his name, but my voice leaves my mouth as a broken whisper. My hand slips down the cage bar as I lower myself to the floor, unable to remain standing. Fear has kept me alert, but now the Prince is here weariness spans the breadth of me, as though my body is a piece of cloth without strings or padding to hold it in shape.

Jakut steps from the darkness, wearing a grey soldier's uniform and helmet, sword raised, ready to fight. In an instant, he takes in my open cage and the missing guards, sheaths his weapon, and drops down on his knees before me.

'Mirra,' he says, pushing off his helmet, pulling me into his chest. 'Mirra,' his voice carries the weight of anxiety and guilt. He holds me to him, stroking a hand over my head. For a moment all I can do is lean in and soak up the comfort of his arms.

'Where are the guards?' he whispers.

'They took Lord Strik.'

His body tenses. 'Strik was here? What happened?' A patter of light footsteps rebounds through a distant passage. The Prince whips around, grasping for his sword.

'It's Calmi,' I say, laying a hand over his to still him.

Torches still glimmer on the walls in and outside my cage. Enough light to note the overcast, threatening look that seeps into the Prince's eyes.

'Why was Lord Strik here?' he asks. 'What happened?'

He must have heard Strik is dying or dead or he would not have come. But he doesn't know about Calmi's potion. Before I can answer, Calmi appears at the edge of light cast from the torches. She halts abruptly, Six remaining hidden behind her in the shadows. Surprise flashes in her eyes at the sight of us. It vanishes quickly, all expression leaving her beautiful face.

'What is happening?' she asks. The Prince rises, fist tightening around his sword.

'Your grandfather came to see Mirra,' he snarls, 'and now he's in the infirmary, poisoned, dying. No doubt, just as you planned.'

Emotion smashes through her, not a fleeting change in her eyes this time, but a tremor shaking her whole body. When her features settle it's as though she's resurfaced from a violent ordeal, stepped from an ocean that tried to drown her. Six must have brought her here, but she was not aware of what has happened to her grandfather.

'I gave Mirra a potion to take before the hanging.' Her voice quivers as she steps towards us. The Prince raises a hand to stop her.

'I told you I would not risk Mirra's life, and I meant it.' He puts a protective arm around me, building a wall between himself and Lady Calmi, turning from her physically and mentally. 'We must get you out of here,' he murmurs. 'Lord Strik has many supporters and when the shock is over and people start asking questions, those who are loyal to him will begin to piece together what has happened. You will be in danger.'

'She cannot travel,' Calmi objects. 'Look at her. We must protect her until she's recovered.'

'Can you walk?' the Prince asks.

'She cannot even stand!'

Sixe slips into the light. In the mind-world I see a memory of him carrying Calmi on his back when she was injured as a girl.

'Sixe will carry me,' I say. 'He knows all the hidden passages out of the palace. No one will wonder where I am until I'm safe in the city.'

'The city is not safe,' Calmi argues. 'It is strewn with the mercenaries who were paid by my grandfather.'

'You two must return to the court,' I whisper to the Prince, 'before you are missed. You must prepare yourself for the Queen, and the council, and how you will explain all this.'

'I'm not leaving you.' He is determined, but if he vanishes while Strik is dying, he will come under suspicion from Strik's supporters for having a hand in the poisoning.

And if he does not release the imprisoned Queen now, he will never win her confidence. She will always consider him a traitor. At once I see what Strik saw. For the Prince, my safety has taken precedence over his own life, his duty, his throne and his kingdom.

A ball twists in the pit of my stomach. I care for Jakut, I will miss him, but beyond that there has only ever been room for Kel. Beyond that, my heart is a mystery. The Prince is offering to risk everything for me. What I do know is I cannot say the same for myself. So instead, I say the one thing I know will change his mind.

'Tug is in the palace.' Watching the transformation in the Prince's eyes is like squeezing a bruise in my chest. But I would be lying to both of us if I let him hope I could stay. And he would be lying to himself if he pretended he could walk out of here when he knows his duty must come first. After a silence I wish I could fill, but do not, he says,

'Sixe will hide you in the city. I will find Tug and he will take you to Lyndonia.'

Calmi sways towards us. 'You have no idea what you have managed to do,' she says. 'If Prince Jakut will not tell you, then I will. You have saved Caruca. All Carucans are indebted to you. You belong in the palace on the council, where the whole kingdom will know that the Uru Ana are respected and accepted in Caruca.'

Her words bring back my dream when I stood beside the council in the throne room. Perhaps my people will need a voice so they are not forgotten as Caruca rebuilds herself, but I will be a voice among them, not apart.

'Mirra has done enough.'

'We will need her help to smooth things with the Queen.'

'No.' Jakut rises to face Calmi, jaw clenched.

'Tell her how you feel and she will stay.'

His mouth sets in a hard line. 'She already knows.'

He helps me up. Then he leans in and kisses the edge of my mouth. A kiss goodbye. A kiss that sends heat crawling across my cheeks. I stop him from pulling away, press my lips to his. The softness of his mouth wraps around mine. I close my eyes and forget everything else for an instant. Pure emotion seems to fire back and forth between us, like a fork of lightning moving between the clouds and the earth.

Then he steps away, bows low, the way Deadran taught us a Prince bows to a King or Queen. As he turns, the heat of his gaze goes with him.

'Your mother,' I say, stopping him in his tracks. 'Did not betray your father. She protected him. It was her power that kept Strik from the Red City all these years.'

And perhaps she is the true reason he is dying now, or already dead. Perhaps her power did not fade when the King died, and as she suggested, the day Strik entered the Red City, he would pay the price with his life.

A memory shimmers in the mind-world. *The Prince is three or four years old. His mother is reading him a story about ice palaces and kings and princess. He snuggles in her arms, and when he turns to smile at her, through the haze of years long past, I see what he sees.* The woman with the slim face is the woman from the sketches he carried in his binder. The woman I had assumed was Calmi, was his mother.

Jakut does not turn back to face me. But in the soft glow of the torches, I see the tension in his shoulders shift.

'Thank you, Mirra,' he says. Then he walks away into the darkness, his strides lengthening, boot steps growing more determined.

Once he has gone, Calmi offers me another pendant. I recognise the cloudy-yellow Nocturne Melody, and shake my head. She shrugs and tucks it in her pocket.

'I sprinkled the pastries with your potion,' I say.

She nods. 'I will get rid of the evidence,' she answers, as she helps me onto Sixe's back. 'Good bye, Mirra.'

Another world, another time, and Calmi and I would have been good friends.

'Your grandfather is dead,' I say, sensing the shift of his passing in the mind-world.

She smiles, tears filling her eyes. 'Yes, I can feel it. It is like being able to breathe again.'

FIFTY-TWO

It takes Tug and me eighteen days to reach Lyndonia, a week longer than the time it took us to travel from Lyndonia to the Red City. Tug refuses to let me ride more than eight hours a day. He insists we rest in comfortable inns, until the morning he comes to my room and finds me asleep on the balcony in the bright sun. Then we only stop at taverns to eat when we grow tired of cooking, and bathe when there are no streams or rivers along our path.

The season heads swiftly towards the all-night sun. With so much rest I feel my strength returning. I am not sure my foot will ever fully heal, but as well as gold, the Prince sent Tug to find me with a pair of wooden sticks which allow me to hobble about.

Four days into our journey, Tug receives word from Lyndonia that the ragtag army gathered around the fort disbanded as soon as they learnt of Strik's death. Not a sword was raised or an arrow shot, though for his protection, Kel had been moved inside the fort when the attack seemed probable.

Word slowly ripples through Caruca that Lord Strik is dead. Stories circulate of an Uru Ana who entered the Ruby Palace and saved the Queen. A royal decree, declaring that the Uru Ana as legal citizens of Caruca, spreads throughout the kingdom. The prejudice against my people will not vanish overnight, but for now, it is enough.

Aside from the news of the kingdom, and news that Brin is alive, and recovering near the Red City, Tug and I are lost in our own worlds, and talk little.

My thoughts are caught up in many things. I am impatient to see Kel. He knows I am coming back, and that alone fills me with such warmth I sometimes don't know how to contain it. I think often of the Prince and Calmi and how they fare with the Queen. I think about whether I have the Carucan Gods, the Prince's mother, or sheer luck to thank for the fact that I was not poisoned.

On the afternoon of the eighteenth day, the fort of Lyndonia grows visible through the trees. Deep waters glisten around the tall grey walls and towers.

Nervousness cuts my breath short as we approach. I squeeze on the reins of my mare. Tug sees and smiles at me. Heart battering in my chest, we trot the horses across the jetty to the drawbridge. Soldiers greet us and Tug produces a letter from the Duchess stating we are her honoured guests. The guards let us pass.

As the clop of hooves over the wooden bridge clatters in my ears I send out my mind through the fort, anxious to touch Kel, to tell him I am here. The fort is abuzz with people. I search the old bell tower and the palace but do not find him.

We give our horses to the stable boy, and on the Prince's crutches, I hobble through the courtyards towards the royal quarters. The sound of children laughing rings in my ears, increasing my impatience.

I wonder how Kel will look when I see him. Will he still be pale, fragile, and bruised? Will the Duchess really have taken proper care of him?

My crutches are too slow, but Tug puts a hand over mine, telling me without words to take my time, Kel's not going anywhere.

We pass through a stone arch, reaching the large courtyard where the laughter came from. Children in cotton shirts, smelling of sweet melon, play blind man's bluff. I hurry through them, desperation to hold Kel in my arms more than I can bear.

As we pass three tier steps at one of the houses, I stop. Deadran, the

Prince's old tutor, sits on the middle step, smiling to himself. I am about to accost him, pull him up by the collar and demand to know what he's done with Kel, why he isn't looking after him, when a child squeals and Deadran grins.

I turn slowly. A girl dives past me giggling as the boy in the blindfold, arms outstretched moves towards her. The boy's step falters. He reaches for the cloth around his eyes. My left crutch slips from my grip. I fall to one knee, tears welling up over my vision.

The blindfold comes off. The girl running away shouts he's cheating. But Kel doesn't hear her. He walks towards me carefully, as though I might be a dream, might vanish if he moves too fast. I am rooted to the spot, choking on the sight of him. His eyes have almost settled, his face glows coppery from days spent outdoors, his sleeveless arms are strong and muscular.

He doesn't say a word as he stops right before me. Tears roll down my cheeks. I brush them aside but they keep flowing. As though still uncertain I am really there he reaches for the lodestone pendant I gave him and squeezes tightly. The other children with him are growing curious.

'Who is it? Is it her Kel?' they ask, circling around us. I am sobbing as I hold out my arms. He throws himself into them and I muffle my face against his shoulder, breathing in the scent of flowers in his hair.

I hold him close, knowing when I let go, neither of us will be the same people we were that day I lay on a boulder soaking up the first rays of the spring sun, and he speared frozen fish from the river. That disillusioned girl and innocent boy have been left behind in the hushed quiet of winter. In my mind, I say goodbye to them.

Eventually, I let go of my brother, and unwrap the wooden carving I have made for him on our journey from the Red City.

'Happy birthday, Bud,' I say. 'I'm sorry I missed it.'

He rips off the twine around the leaves and holds up the wooden figurine. The lizard like creature's huge wings are spread wide in flight, a rider on its back. Kel turns it in his small fingers. Then he kisses me on the cheek and links his fingers through mine. 'Thank you.'

He looks down, noticing my twisted little finger. Then he notices Tug, and his sunny face darkens.

'Why is he with you?' he asks.

'I have things to do,' Tug says. He takes his leave with a small nod.

'It's going to be hard,' I say, 'for you to understand, but Tug is my friend now. He saved my life. Because of him, I came back.'

Kel's eyes narrow. 'It's because of him you were in danger in the first place. And why are you hobbling? What happened to your foot? What happened to your finger?'

I push away the memories. I don't want Kel to ever find out what happened in the Red City. What I had to do to win both our freedoms and make it back here.

I envision those memories sinking down to the bottom of a great deep well, submerged beneath beautiful visions of the Ruby Palace. I think of the palace's sunburnt walls, toppling towers, and winding passages. I remember the lavish interiors, luxurious baths, four-poster beds, ottomans, and rich foods. If I have learned anything from Tug, it is that even the Uru Ana cannot easily penetrate what a person wishes to hide.

As I am doing this, I remember the way Ma always called up memories from her youth to echo whatever age I was. It suddenly strikes me that maybe Ma was doing what I'm doing now. Maybe her reminiscing wasn't wishful thinking, but a gift to Kel and I. An antidote to all my bad memories.

A child who's been playing with Kel steps closer to see the wooden toy he holds.

'It's a velaraptor!' she says. 'I've seen pictures. But they don't really exist.'

'Yes they do,' a smaller boy pipes up.

'You're five. You believe in monsters and fairies.'

Kel looks at me and I wink. This is our secret.

'Are we still playing?'

He looks at me again. 'Go on,' I say. 'I have to speak with the lady who's been taking care of you.' His hand tightens around mine. 'I won't be long.' He shakes his head. 'OK, let's go together.' He nods as though his words have dried up.

He runs to Deadran. Deadran fastens a blindfold over Kel's eyes, and though he is blind himself, his milky white irises are turned on me as he ties the fabric knot with his frail fingers. He has recognised my voice. He knows I am the captured shadow weaver the Prince took to the Red City to discover who assassinated his escort. And now, if Kel has not let it slip before, the Prince's old tutor must realise that the boy entrusted to his care is my glitter-eyed brother.

Kel waves goodbye to the other children. As he cannot take my hand, he takes Deadran's. I hobble alongside them through the dim archway.

'Lady Mirra,' a soldier says, approaching me and bowing. 'The Duke welcomes you back to Lyndonia and requests your presence in the great hall.'

The last time I saw the Duke before the Ruby palace came under attack was the evening we arrived in the Red City and the Queen summoned us to the throne room. Unless the Duchess has told her husband the truth, he still believes I am Lady Mirra Tersil of Delladea, the Prince's secret fiancé.

Kel is asked to wait outside with Deadran. I enter the enormous stone hall, draped in carnelian curtains. Tug waits before a wide oval in the centre of the room. He watches as I hobble up to his side. Then he turns to face the giant doors where the Duke and Duchess will arrive with their entourage, except they are already there. I sense their minds on the other side of the doors and slip into the Duke's.

He stares at Duchess Elise. She stands before him face turned down, eyes red and puffy.

'You have made a fool of me. Hidden information that could have got me killed. Could have got our children killed.'

'I did it for our son.' The Duchess looks up, defiance burning in her gaze, but her hands are trembling. He takes hold of her hand.

'What else haven't you told me?'

'Nothing.'

'What else!'

'Tug.'

The Duke releases her suddenly. 'What about him?'

'He is my brother, Tye Keylore.'

I withdraw from the Duke's mind, open my eyes and swallow hard. 'What?' Tug asks.

'Elise has told the Duke who you are.'

Tug flexes his shoulders and glares at the doors. They open a moment later. But only the Duke enters. His face is as stony and impenetrable as Tug's. I lower my gaze and bend my injured leg to curtsey, supporting myself with the crutches.

From the tension in the air I'm convinced deep down the Duke has known all along who broke the Duchess' heart before she became his wife. Which means he must have suspected for years that Elise was not Tug's flesh and blood, but adopted by their father. Not even a lady.

His guards fan out around him as he comes to stand before us. He looks warily from Tug to me, and back again. Tug clears his throat and raises his eyes to meet the Duke. A storm of recognition swirls across the Duke's face. He sees it now. The man he had known twelve years ago, Baron Tye Keylore, transformed into a beast-face with his tattoos, his long tangled hair, his broad frame, and scars from combat and drinking.

The Duke's expression grows icy. 'My brother, the King, is dead,' he says. 'The Carucan army is weak and the Etean army pushes back our borders daily. These are times of distrust, when friends are hard to distinguish from enemies. Until I hear word from the Ruby Court, I will not decide whether we accept your presence in Lyndonia. For now, you are my wife's guests. She is responsible for you and will be held accountable for your actions. During your stay here, I do not wish to see either of you again.'

He turns his back on us, and strides towards the doors followed by his entourage. A minute later, the giant doors close. Tug and I are alone in the grand hall's silence.

'Well,' Tug says. 'There's nothing like a hero's welcome.'

I smile and jog my arm against his. 'Lets not forget, everything we did was just to save our own skins. Oh, and Kel.'

'Course it was,' he says, cocking an eyebrow at me. Then he looks back at the doors where we last saw the Duke and shakes his head. Perhaps, at last, he realises that Duchess Elise doesn't deserve his undying devotion. Perhaps, at last, his heart can move on.

FIFTY-THREE

Several days later, news comes from the Ruby Court that Prince Jakut is engaged to the Etean King's eldest daughter. They are to be married the following spring. The wedding is part of a negotiated truce, though it is Queen Usas who remains on the throne and Jakut will not be crowned. War on the Etean border has come to an end.

I try to avoid thinking about the Prince. When I am not resting, I spend all my time with Kel and his friends, basking in my brother's happiness. Sometimes, I catch myself remembering times the Prince and I were together, and wondering how different things would have been if I had known all along I could trust him. But it is foolish to ruminate about what cannot be changed. No matter what, I was always going to leave the Red City, and he would still have been obligated to marry the Etean Princess to end the war.

On our tenth day in Lyndonia, Kel wakes with eyes like any other six-year-old child. The last flecks of gold have faded. It is time for us to find our parents.

THE SUN IS a low disk on the horizon as we clop under the arched entrance and across the drawbridge, the fort of Lydnonia receding behind us. Kel's friends come to wave us off. The Duke and the Duchess do not.

We camp in forests, remaining hidden from the roads, hiding our horses behind shelters of pine leaves, and lighting few fires. News of the King's death has spread and the north is more restless than ever. We are safest avoiding people.

Tug suggests leaving Kel with a friend at a place he calls the meadow, while we search the far north for my parents. He says Kel will be safer there from looters and mercenaries. He has even suggested I stay with my brother, and he journeys alone. I am tempted to accept his offer. I am tired and cannot imagine leaving Kel again. But assuming Pa is in good health, he will be looking for us. If somehow he recognises Tug before Tug sees him, there is a chance the outcome will be ugly.

Despite my unwillingness to commit to a decision, one afternoon I find us all sitting on our horses facing down a hillside. The valley is a wide stretch of grassland, uncultivated, wild. Part of it is scattered with flowers, another part appears to be bog.

A memory flutters to the surface of the mind-world.

She holds a purse of leather heavy with coin. Behind her the scraggly, undulating grassland still covered in snow. Long curls of hair drape around her slim face. Her skin is pale in the blue winter half-light. When she looks up there is pain in her eyes.

'You're not coming back.'

'It is just for safe keeping,' Tug replies.

I gaze at the wilderness, trying to give Tug the privacy of his own thoughts, when it suddenly comes back to me. I remember the day in Blackfoot Forest when I shot Tug's dog and he and Brin snatched Kel. Kel and I were by the frozen river, looking at the fish he'd dug up, when a memory grazed the mind-world, like a whisper on the wind. The first sign that we were not alone.

Ruffled blankets. Wreaths of curly brown hair. Twilight glowing on wooden tumbledown walls.

It was the same woman as the woman in Tug's thoughts now.

'This is your meadow,' I say, the realisation dawning on me.

Tug gives a short nod, and gets down from his horse. Kel

dismounts and comes to help me down, as I mentally piece together these fragmented memories of Tug's complex world.

The last time Tug was here, he had given the woman with auburn hair a purse with five times more coin than he could have earned in a season hunting with Brin. She had believed he would not come back. What unknown path had he designed for himself before he crossed Kel and I in Blackfoot Forest, and why had it meant not returning?

In the open valley there doesn't seem to be anywhere you could conceal living quarters. A few scraggly, wind bent trees, and in the far, far distance, forest. There is no sign of human life. I turn to Tug, perplexed, and for a brief instant catch a look in his eye I've never seen before. Doubt.

'I see it!' Kel whispers, voice full of awe and wonder. A soft cloud has blown across the sun, throwing shadow on the great patch of wilderness. I squint in the direction Kel is gazing, study a mound, longer, and perhaps more regular than others. There is a dip in the ground on the far side, hidden by another sharp rise in the earth. The dip is possibly large enough to hide a river or path.

The wind carries a dog bark.

Tug grabs his bow and arrows, and I fumble for my knives. Far off, a shape waggles through the long grass. The hound grows closer, shaggy grey and white fur disappears and reappears.

I frown. The dog's movements are restricted.

You stay here, while I take care of the dog.

The wolf dog reaches Tug and jumps up as best it can to lick him. Tug lowers to one knee and strokes her.

'How did you get back here, Trix?' he murmurs.

Two children appear in the grassland, heads bobbing up from the hidden dip. Then they are running at full speed, their shouts over their shoulders, lost on the wind.

Tug sets down his bow and arrow, lifts the dog easily in his broad arms and watches the children. They're older than Kel, and if they were Tug's children I imagine he'd be throwing himself down the hill to meet them, but you never know with Tug.

Suddenly, Kel grips my arm. His face turns pale. I look out to where he's staring. A blonde head of hair has appeared. A man limps slowly towards us, one arm raised against his head to block the sun so he can see in our direction.

Kel pulls away and bounds down the hill at full speed. It is Pa's mind, as clear as a boulder in a steam of pure crystal waters. Pa's mind, as deep and silent as the endless tundra in the spring.

I collapse onto my knees, the taut strings of tension that have kept me going for weeks, vanishing and leaving me weak, exhausted.

Pa is alive! He's found us. Tears roll down my cheeks, dropping into the sleeves of my worn shirt.

A hand squeezes the back of my neck. I twist around and look up through blurry eyes. Tug looks back, fully understanding. I let out a choked sob. The emotion is a broken dam rushing over me. It knocks me down. I am relieved Pa is alive, relieved I have finally achieved what once seemed impossible, returned my brother to the safety of my parents. My shoulders shake as I cry.

Tug crouches beside me. I lean into him. Like the time in the palace gardens before I was captured by Captain Linx and became Lord Strik's pet prisoner, Tug's strength bleeds into me, seems to mould to my soul, so that I don't feel quite so alone.

The shaking stops but I can't move. This is it. When Tug lets me go, our journey will have ended. I will be free.

'Someone still has to save the Rudeashan princess,' I whisper, sobbing, and sniffling, and only half-joking.

'Your body and mind need rest, Mirra. You have been through an ordeal. It hasn't caught up with you yet, but when it does—'

'I wasn't talking about me,' I say, nudging his shoulder.

He snorts and shakes his head. I allow him to help me to my feet. Pa and Kel are coming up the hill.

Tug passes me my crutches. I assemble them under my arms, avoiding Pa's eyes, avoiding Tug's. We both seem to still at my father's approach.

The children reach Tug and throw arms around his waist.

'I knew you'd come back!' the girl says. She's ten or eleven.

'I caught a hundred rabbits!' the boy says. 'I made four new snares just like you showed me.'

'Not a hundred.'

'Almost a hundred.'

Their chatting vanishes into the background. I finally force myself to raise my eyes, and find Pa's blue gaze leveled at me from a few feet away.

I hobble forward to meet him. At first it is awkward. I can tell by the way he's looking at me that I seem as much a stranger to him, as he seems to me. Then he steps forward. His arms rise and he pulls me into a tight hug. At the same time, I am enveloped by his beautiful, desolate mind, and a feeling of security and safety rouse within, not gone forever, after all.

'Mirra,' he murmurs.

He draws back and we stare at each other. My eyes burn with tears, reflecting his own.

'Where's Ma? Is she OK?'

'She's fine. She's fine.' Pa's gaze flicks over to Tug, questioning, guarded.

Tug takes up the reins of his horse. 'Let's go and find Sarah,' he says to the children. He strides past us down the hill, the boy and girl running ahead calling for their mother.

Pa's confusion is even greater than Kel's at seeing me with Tug. He came here hunting the man who destroyed his family, only to find Kel and I both safe and under the mercenary's protection.

'How bad is your foot?' he asks.

A healer in Lyndonia had helped set the bones, and the pain, while not all together gone, is bearable.

'It's getting better. How did you get here? How did you find us?'

'Once my injury had healed enough to let me move around, I went straight to the Hybourg. Just as well your mother wasn't with me. After what I saw there, I imagined the worst.'

I could imagine the glacial fear Pa must have experienced entering the dark Pit where glitter-eyed children were put into cages and sold like farm animals. Not knowing if Kel had been held in those cages. Not knowing what terrible things had become of his children.

'Then you found Tug's wolf dog.'

'Not the first time. But I kept searching. And eventually, I found a woman who had been paid to care for Trix.' His eyes dig into me like fishhooks. 'I will not ask for explanations now, Mirra. I have no idea how you have managed to bring your brother back to us against all odds. But when you are ready to talk, I am here.'

I nod. Pa takes my face in his hands and kisses my forehead.

'Thank you,' he says. 'Thank you, my brave girl.' The he helps me back onto my mare, and we walk downhill to the longhouse.

I cry tears of joy, tears of heartache, tears of exhaustion. Tears for the suffering that the greed of a few can cause to so many others.

But in the deep caverns of my heart, I'm standing on the crystal cliffs of my people's islands. I feel the strength of those rushing winds, and know, unlike the mind, which can be shaped and distorted by pain, the light inside each of us can never be dulled. Our memories sculpt the story we tell about our lives, but they do not decide who we are.

THE END

COMING SOON

A SHADOW WEAVER PREQUEL

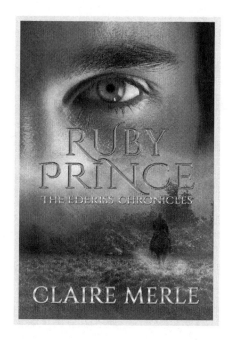

ACKNOWLEDGMENTS

Thanks to all my wattpad readers and friends whose enthusiasm and support for Shadow Weaver encouraged me to complete this. You guys rock.

Thanks to my editor Lynda Floyd.

Snow Horse Press icon made by Freepik from www.flaticon.com

ABOUT THE AUTHOR

Claire Merle grew up in London and moved to the outskirts of Paris in her twenties. Her first two books for young adults, *The Glimpse* and the *The Fall*, were published by Faber & Faber in 2012 & 2013. Two years later, uncertain of whether her new fantasy book would find an audience, Claire began posting Shadow Weaver on wattpad. Enthusiasm from the wattpad community inspired Claire to finish the book. Shadow Weaver became a wattpad phenomenon, reaching #1 on the fantasy charts and now has over 2 million views.

For more information
clairemerlebooks.com

Made in the USA
San Bernardino, CA
28 February 2018